Also by Karen Millie-James

The Shadows Behind Her Smile

In memory of my grandparents,
Erich and Freda,
Sybil and Laurence.

Always in my heart.

ACKNOWLEDGEMENTS

Welcome to Where In The Dark, the second in the thriller series featuring Cydney Granger, first introduced in The Shadows Behind Her Smile, in which I continue her story.

I owe huge thanks to so many people for their help and guidance, without whom I would never have reached this point. First, my wonderful editor and dear friend, Elaine Denning. I have no doubt exasperated her on quite a few occasions, giving her impossible deadlines at the last moment, but she always smiles through it. She understands my characters and, I believe, loves and cares for them all as much as I do. A glass of Prosecco or two always helps. Thank you for all your encouragement.

Once again, I have sought the advice of a friend of mine regarding the world of the Special Forces in the British Army, which has been invaluable. I thank him for answering so many of my questions, and with patience.

I met with two amazing men, holocaust survivors, Zigy Shipper and Ivor Perl. I listened to their stories with awe at how they managed to remain alive despite suffering the most horrendous and unimaginable hardships. I thank them for their time and appreciate all the questions they answered with such honesty.

I would also like to thank my staff, and the marketing team at King of the Road Publishing for all their support - Mark, Paula, Lucy, Chloe, Sear, Vagma and Malcolm - Mark Iles for his proof-reading skills, Steve West for his design work, Arnie Harris for reading the first draft for me and making some extremely helpful comments, Deena Niren for all her suggestions in the final read-through, my dear friends, Alex and Anne, for their continued support, Jim Sheehan from Signature Books, and Tony Mulliken, Fiona Marsh, Tracey Jennings and Rachel Kennedy, plus all the staff at Midas PR Agency.

My daughter, Rosanna, has always known of my desire to write and fulfil my lifetime dream of having my book published and seeing it on the shelves at all the well-known book stores. She has stood proudly by my side during my signings and words can never express how much that means to me. She is my world. I love her and am so proud of everything she does and all she has achieved through hard work and determination to become a professional performer. She should always reach for the stars.

Last, my husband, Peter, for everything he does and all his support, for giving me time to shut myself away and write for hours on end, although it helps if football is on the television, for being my rock, my protector and for simply loving me for who I am. It is appreciated more than words can say.

Karen Millie-James
London, September 2017

PROLOGUE
2005

It was the shock. As he fell, the pain ripped across his heart and he felt the familiar vice-like tightening of his chest as the muscles attempted to respond to the restricted blood flow, his arteries already hardened and narrowed. An overwhelming sense of anxiety enveloped him. Harold reached into his inside jacket pocket and grabbed the pump spray he kept with him at all times containing the medicine he now urgently needed to relieve his symptoms. He opened his mouth and pressed the bottom of the pump firmly and placed a couple of squirts under his tongue; he had always hated the taste. The relief was immediate and as the pain eased he felt the onset of the pounding headache the spray always gave him. Slowly, he managed to pull himself up into a sitting position so he could examine the cause of his attack.

The knowledge that in his hands he held a bearer bond certificate for one million dollars made Harold's hand tremble to such an extent that he dropped the bond and the envelope in which it had arrived and saw it flutter and disappear under one of the Queen Anne chairs in his living room. It was with some considerable effort that he stretched out his arm and rescued the document with the tip of his middle finger, despite the arthritis that also beleaguered him. He straightened up and mopped his brow with the back of his hand to remove the sweat that had accumulated, unsure if it was the shock that had brought it on, or the strain at his age that it had taken to retrieve it.

Still sitting on the floor, nervous to stand in case the pain returned, he examined the document in more detail, turned it over to check both sides and wiped away the film of dust from its fall. It was printed on thick cream quarto size parchment with a picture of Abraham Lincoln on the front in dark grey, and a red inscribed serial number to the right-hand side. The words 'Bearer Bond to the Value of One Million Dollars' were centred in large black letters. An utter sense of dread filled his entire being. It made no sense, unless ...

Eventually, Harold got to his feet and waited for his world to stop spiralling down in front of him. He felt nothing but doom. The eyes of his parents and sisters framed within the sepia photo on his desk, taken before everything had overturned their lives, stared back at him, almost willing him to remember. As if he were capable of ever forgetting.

His fingers shook as he ran them long the gold trim edges of the bond and stroked the red seal and ribbon at the bottom. Further review of the envelope, including peering inside it in case there was a letter, revealed nothing further to assist him, not even after he had turned it upside down and shaken it to double check. It bore an airmail sticker and US postage stamp, and his name and address were typed on it, however, there were no clues as to who had sent it or why it had been sent to him. It certainly appeared genuine but the question that came to mind was whether someone was playing a joke on him. The bond was drawn on an American bank, the name of which meant nothing.

Not only did he feel completely bewildered, but absolutely frightened. He really needed to sit again before he passed out. He had no idea what to do so he called the person he always turned to when he had a problem. The phone was answered immediately.

"Alfie, it's me. Harold. I have to see you."

"I have to see you, too."

"What?"

"You got the same envelope." It wasn't a question, simply a statement, spoken in the same quiet tone that Harold was accustomed to hearing.

"That's impossible. How could you have got a million dollars, too? Where did it come from?"

"You'd better come over to me. Is the notebook in a safe place?"

"Of course it is. It's not something I would ever lose, though heaven knows I've thought about destroying it so many times."

"It's all we have, Harold. It's our security."

"Do you think it could be …?" He paused for a moment, gathering his thoughts. "Has he found us, despite all we've done?"

"I don't know. I've phoned Rupert. We need his advice now."

"We never told him, you know that. We've held this secret for so long. Can we trust him?"

"What choice do we have, my friend?"

CHAPTER ONE

A VERY well dressed and beautifully coiffed lady, probably no more than in her mid-thirties, greeted Cydney Granger when she strode into her office on Monday morning, her mind set on the work ahead of her that day. Sat in front of Cydney's desk, she tapped her foot impatiently.

"I was expecting you earlier. Where have you been? I'm anxious to talk to you. You have kept me waiting." The woman spoke in English but with a distinctive German accent. *"You're meeting my son, Hans, soon. You must help him. I am beside myself with worry."*

That familiar feeling of cold rushed through Cydney and along her right arm as she surveyed the woman in spirit in front of her. She was dressed in a stylish, mid-calf black dress, reminiscent of the 1930s. There was an air of authority about her that made Cydney believe the woman demanded, even expected attention and would no doubt receive it.

"I have a meeting this morning with Harold Franks. Is that who you mean?"

"Yes, my son. Hans Frankelman. Why do you not know?"

"He's not due here yet for another half an hour. How can I help you?"

"He's in trouble. He was always a problem, ever since he was a child. Always getting into mischief and worrying me and my dear husband, Mordecai."

Cydney had not been completely briefed about the forthcoming meeting with Mr Franks. All she had received was a phone call from her client and close friend, Rupert Van der Hausen, in

South Africa, who had asked her to meet with two men he'd known for many years and help them out. He'd offered to foot the bill. When Rupert requested something of her it was not in her thinking to refuse him or question him; after all, he had done so much for her and her family in the past.

"Do you want to tell me why you think he's in difficulty?"

"Ach, do you not do your research first? So, I have to do your job for you."

"Mrs Frankelman, may I suggest we start from the beginning? Tell me about yourself and your family, which will help me to understand. We have time." Cydney watched the woman compose herself and take a breath before she began.

"You have to appreciate, this is not easy for me. The memories … well, there are so many. My poor husband, and my two daughters. Our families. All gone and so young. So terrible."

"You've come through to me for a reason. I realise this may be difficult for you, especially if this is the first time you've reached out. If your son's in trouble, I'll do my utmost to help you both. Please believe you can trust me."

The words were sufficient. Cydney closed her eyes and allowed her mind to be taken to a magnificent and richly decorated drawing room where many people were celebrating. The sweet and melodious music, hauntingly reminiscent of centuries-old lively Russian folk tunes came from a small trio of fiddlers set up in the corner of the room. Everyone held their hands up in the air together and danced around fast in a circle. The music was loud and, clearly, the guests were enjoying themselves as there were smiles on faces and laughter rang out. Mrs Frankelman and a tall, dark-haired man held hands and smiled at each other in the centre of the circle with three children. The tallest was a boy and with him were two smaller girls.

"It was Hans' Barmitzvah party. It was 1940 so the war had been going on for some time and we were in the midst of a world of change. He was thirteen and such a good-looking boy, so tall and strong, like his father.

Who would have known? And our two daughters, Gerthe and Mathilde; they were eight and five at the time. They couldn't wait for the party we had planned, despite everything going on around us. I had the same blue dresses made for them by our local dressmaker. My darling husband gave them both little gold necklaces with a Star of David on them as a present so they wouldn't feel left out when Hans got all his presents."

"Where is this?"

"In Charlottenberg. Berlin. We had a beautiful house on the best street in town. My husband was a banker, you know, in the family business, and doing so well for someone his age. He worked hard every day of his life to give us everything he possibly could. I loved the home we made together. We had it decorated exactly as we wanted it soon after we got married in 1926. Our parents helped, of course, which was the natural thing to do. I didn't mind at all. I was young and so in love with Mordecai. He was like a prince to me, my own special prince, and I would have gone to the ends of the earth for him."

"How did you meet?" Cydney felt the air around her become calmer as Mrs Frankelman started to talk about her life.

"I was at school and only fourteen. Every day I would pass some older boys on their bicycles going to the local gymnasium. One of them would always smile and wink at me as he cycled past. He was a bit older than me and I felt so happy he noticed me and not one of my friends, who always giggled when I went red in the face at his attention. On the way home from school, he started to wait for me and we would stop in the local public garden to chat about our days and our studies. He would help me with the mathematics I could never work out. He was tall and so handsome with dark hair that, even then, I wanted to run my fingers through. He called me 'his little Sybie'. My given name is Sybill.

"I let him kiss me when I was fifteen and it felt so wicked. We talked about what we would do when we grew up. He was two years older than me and when he was eighteen he was going to join his father's bank as a junior clerk. He was very excited about it as he would have money and we would be able to marry. It was always discussed, along with how many children we would have. He wanted ten, five of each. I knew he was teasing me. He liked to make me laugh, you see. He said I had the sweetest smile."

3

"And were your parents happy about the match?"

"Oh yes. Very happy. My father was a doctor. We lived well, although we did not have as much money as the Frankelmans, who had the best house in town. To think I was marrying into a wealthy banking family was very good for all of us. I still remember my father walking me down the aisle in our synagogue towards Mordecai, who was standing and waiting under the chuppah for me. I circled around my husband-to-be seven times, as was our custom. At each turn he would beam at me in that way he had that melted my heart. He lifted my veil to give me the wine the Rabbi had blessed and we drank from the same cup. As he smashed the glass under his foot to seal our marriage, I knew we were destined to be together forever."

"And then you had Hans?"

"Yes. He was born a year after our marriage. I loved my son the moment he came into the world and I stared down into his deep, sapphire-blue eyes. His life held such promise and we were determined to give him the world."

"Yes, I understand. Please continue."

"He walked and talked very early. He was so inquisitive about everything. He would ask questions non-stop of his father, who would sit him down and patiently explain everything to him about how plants grow, why we have night and day, how cars work and airplanes fly. Every possible question was answered. How could you possibly ignore such inquisitiveness? As he grew older he became impatient with everything because he couldn't find out things quick enough. At school he was naughty because the teachers didn't answer him properly and they always reported how disruptive he was in class. I used to laugh at this with Mordecai when we were alone. Nobody knew Hans like we did, even when he got into trouble."

"And there were also your two daughters?"

"Yes, my beautiful, dark-haired gorgeous girls. They were our princesses. Of course, I married my prince so we had to have the little princesses." Her eyes lit up as she smiled at the memory and Cydney imagined what a perfect family they must have made.

"We were so happy until the Nazis came with their murderous black boots, marching through and thundering down on us, breaking our lives into thousands of pieces that could never be put together again."

"Can you tell me about it?" The question was posed gently as Cydney was entering unmarked territory. Naturally, she had read stories of the holocaust but it had never crept into her life, as it was doing now. She hoped fervently she was brave and ready enough to withstand the inevitable pictures that would come to her. However, working with spirit was never about her. So, shaking any selfish thoughts from her mind, she concentrated on the woman before her.

"It was slow at first, starting in the mid-1930s when Hans and Gerthe were so young and before Mathilde was born. We hardly knew it was happening until we heard of Jewish people being beaten up on the streets of Berlin. It didn't affect us on a daily basis and we kept ourselves to ourselves. By 1938 everything was so much worse. We heard of our friends' shops and factories being burned to the ground and their losing everything - their homes, their livelihoods, their families, and even their lives as the Nazis confiscated everything. We had no say in anything. It was horrific. We were terrified to leave the house so I stayed at home as much as possible. Mordecai still went to the bank every day and the children went to school. One day I went to pick Gerthe up from school and she came out with her lip swollen and bleeding and her dress torn. She was only six at the time but she cried that some older children had pushed her to the ground and hit her. She couldn't understand why they hurt her or tore up her favourite story book and stole her favourite doll. Even at eleven, Hans was furious, wanting to rush out and beat up everybody in sight. He was so protective of his sisters. I calmed him, and told him it was the way of the world and that two wrongs didn't make a right."

"Did he do anything?"

"Of course he did. I expected it and so did his father. We couldn't stop him retaliating against what had been done to his little sister. I never knew exactly what he did and, thankfully, he didn't get into trouble as nobody found out. He sported a black eye and several bruises proudly for a week or two for his efforts. I'm sure the other person came out worse, though. He risked a lot but he was always brave. My courageous boy."

Cydney watched as tears coursed down Mrs Frankelman's face. "Are you okay to continue?"

5

"Yes. I need to explain so you will realise what my Hans was like. We began to feel a discernible change in the air as the months wore on. Hitler's power over everyone was unchallengeable and food was becoming more and more difficult to obtain. I spent hours waiting in queues just to get a simple loaf of bread, which was stale anyway and cost a fortune. Then there were notices put up everywhere ordering all Jewish people to report to the local town hall for registration purposes. We were all given a garish yellow cloth star to wear on our coats and jackets with the word 'Jude' written on it. We needed to be identified, apparently, to show us up, and we couldn't avoid being recognised wherever we went. It was another humiliation. Failure to wear them meant we would be arrested. The children never understood why we were all singled out in this way and asked what we had done wrong to make Hitler so angry. How could we possibly answer?"

"You had done nothing wrong," Cydney offered, feeling the anger emanating from this lady before her.

"Exactly. So life carried on, though the children were now prevented from attending their schools. Imagine how bored they became. I was too afraid to let them out of the house, although Hans still rebelled against this. Until, one day, Mordecai came home from work. He was in pieces. I had never seen him so upset. He had been ordered out of the premises and told never to return. The Nazis were taking over his family bank and expelled everyone from there, including my father-in-law and all the people who had worked for him for so long. You have to understand we were helpless in the face of such aggression. With nothing remaining of their home, which was also confiscated, Mordecai's parents joined us, leaving everything behind, apart from some valuables and a few clothes, things they could carry. My parents also moved in. We felt together we would be safer and protect each other. Hans was the one who went out to hunt for food for all of us. He would sneak out at night without wearing his yellow star and return a few hours later with bits of bread, the occasional vegetable, anything he could find or steal to sustain us all."

"I can't imagine how you all coped."

"We had to. We had no choice. One day the Rabbi came to see us. He had managed to obtain papers to leave Germany and go to his cousins in

New York. He told us he could help us, that we could all go together. It sounded wonderful but Mordecai refused to leave, believing everything would calm down eventually. I believed in my husband but we had no idea of what was ahead of us. I wanted to get Hans and the girls out of Berlin on the kindertransport and went to get the papers for them without even telling my husband. I was desperate but I returned home disappointed, in pieces. You see, by now it was too late and the officials were letting nobody leave. So we were stuck in the house, though at least we were together.

Soon rumours were spreading that all Jewish people were being rounded up and moved to other areas by train. To ghettos where we would all live together. We didn't believe this at all. Why on earth would they do this? We wanted to live our lives in peace and quiet and we were doing no harm to anybody at all. Nevertheless, we started to make some plans and gather our valuables together so if we did have to leave, at least we would have some money to help us buy food, more than anything else. All of us women spent hours sewing diamonds and jewellery into the hems of our clothes, in case, and my husband buried a lot of our other personal possessions in the garden for when we would return from wherever we were being sent. We did expect to return."

"Where was Hans all this time?"

"He was now thirteen and a man, in the eyes of our religion. He was always out of the house with his best friend, Ari. We had little control over him. As long as he came home in one piece, I didn't ask him what he got up to. I had an inkling, of course, that he and his friends were retaliating against the Nazis and if they managed to hurt one or two, well, there were less to hurt us. The worry was killing me though, and every day I wondered whether I would see him again."

"How long did this go on for?"

"We only had another week together. One evening we were having dinner, what we had managed to find to cook, when we heard this thunderous banging at the door. It was one of the most frightening moments. My husband told us all to remain seated while he went to see who was there. But we knew. Suddenly, all these soldiers with rifles barged into our house, pushing Mordecai aside as if he were nothing. The senior one, a lieutenant, told us

7

we had thirty minutes to pack our belongings and get out to the waiting trucks outside. We were only allowed one small suitcase each. Thankfully, we had them ready, with the money and jewellery sewn into our clothes."

"And was Hans with you?"

"Yes he was, for once. When the soldiers left he shouted and screamed at us to run away and hide. He told us not to take orders from these men. Mordecai was very calm and patient with him, explaining it would be better to do what they commanded and, as long as we stayed together, no harm would come to us. Hans gave in eventually. We knew he would fight all the way though. My two girls were crying and Hans went and cuddled them until they stopped. He would protect them always, come what may. My parents and Mordecai's parents were old people and could not cope with all the stress of the move so we helped them. Thirty minutes later, we all left the house wearing as many clothes as we could to ward off the inevitable cold, and each of us carrying a single suitcase, and went to the street where the trucks were waiting for us. We clambered up with all our neighbours and all the time the soldiers were yelling orders at us and hitting out at people with their rifle butts if they weren't quick enough. It was utter chaos. There was nowhere to sit, not even for the elderly. We had no idea where we were going or what would be in store for us when we got there."

The story unfolding before Cydney made her impatient to hear more and she was irritated at the interruption when Jenny Vere-Nicholson, her personal assistant, knocked at the door.

"Are you ready for your meeting? I've shown Mr Franks and Mr Goodman into the boardroom."

CHAPTER TWO

C YDNEY was loath to break off her conversation with Sybill
Frankelman but was eager to discover the reason the two
men had come to see her. She was in no doubt that Harold's, or
rather Hans' mother would join her in the boardroom and she
was right. As she entered the room to greet the two gentlemen,
Mrs Frankelman was already there and had taken her seat at the
head of the table as if she owned it. It caused her to stop in her
tracks but then she regained her composure, not wanting to give
anything away of what she alone was able to see.

The two men stood to attention as she entered and shook her
hand in turn. Both were dressed very smartly in suits and crisp
white shirts and ties, as if they had decided beforehand they
wanted to create the right impression. Cydney reckoned they
were in their late seventies, which would have made them very
young when war broke out. From what she had been told by
Sybill they were in trouble and their demeanour made it clear
they were certainly quite apprehensive. Harold Franks fiddled
with his hands and kept looking at his friend, Alfie Goodman,
who was perched on the edge of his seat.

"I believe you're friends of Rupert Van der Hausen. I've
known him for many years."

"Yes, so he told us, along with a lot of information about your
background. All good, by the way. I'll get right down to this. Mrs
Granger, we have a problem. Some would think a nice problem
to have. Rupert advised you were very good at your job and
would be the one person who could help us."

"Please, call me Cydney."

"Harold, shall I start, or will you?" Alfie asked.

"If we want to get out of here by tomorrow morning, I'll speak. You can interrupt as you normally do if I miss anything."

"Is it so terrible if I do?"

"Let me start already. Not a word."

Alfie shrugged his shoulders on the order from his friend, and raised both hands in resignation. Cydney was slightly bemused by their interaction. Clearly, they were extremely comfortable with each other and she easily warmed to them.

"Mrs Granger, forgive me, Cydney. Last week, my good friend and I each received a bearer bond for one million dollars and we have no idea where they came from. We were hoping you could investigate this for us. Look, we brought them with us." Harold handed over two identical white envelopes. On opening each one, Cydney found exactly what had been described to her. She examined the wording closely and placed her finger over the flowery signature on the bottom right-hand side by the red seal.

"These look genuine. I don't understand. This is an awful lot of money. Why would anyone send you bearer bonds?"

"That's why we're here. We weren't expecting anything at all, were we Alfie?" His friend shook his head. "That's the thing, Cydney. We want you to find out where they came from and why. We are old men now and we don't have the time or the energy to go out and search."

"This may be a funny question to ask, but do you want to keep the money if I do find out? You know they can be encashed at any time, if they are genuine?"

Cydney's eyes locked with Mrs Frankelman.

"No good will come of this."

"Why do you say that?" Cydney asked, communicating telepathically as she usually did when talking to spirit.

"It is raking up the past, which is best buried along with my Mordecai

10

and my beloved daughters. However, be warned that the past needs to be pacified before the present can continue."

"Mr Franks, Mr Goodman, to ask again. Do you want the money even if it means bringing up things from the past you would sooner forget?" Cydney chose her words carefully, trying not to give away anything she had learned from Sybill.

"You think this is something from our past?"

"It may well be. Are you prepared for this?"

"Alfie, do you think we are?"

"Harold, we need to know. What if the money is rightfully ours? Think what we could do with it, for our families. This money is something we've never had before. Suppose we deserve it?"

"How can we deserve money? We've done nothing to earn it."

"It may be theirs by right, for what they suffered, but it will be a very tough road to travel."

Both men turned to each other and nodded, and then faced Cydney.

"We want you to help us."

Cydney focused back on the men. "Good. You know I'll need to interview both of you further, find out some background. I can't go forward until I know what's gone before."

"It's going to be so difficult for them."

"We appreciate that. What can be worse than what we've been through and lived with every day of our lives?" Harold gave a sigh of resignation.

"What do you mean?"

He looked down at his hands and glanced at his friend for encouragement. "I'm sorry but now is not the right time for me, for us." Cydney realised they were not prepared to give her anything more.

"I suggest you give me a while to investigate these bonds a bit more. Why don't you both come in next week so you can tell me your stories in more detail?

"Thank you for this. I will be with you to assist you. You must be strong for my Hans and his friend. They are determined to discover the truth, so what can I do?"

"And Sybill, I want to hear the rest of your story, too, because that's going to make it easier for me," Cydney said.

* * *

Almost four thousand miles away, the Governor of the State of West Virginia sat in his sumptuous book-lined library behind a large mahogany desk, which easily could have belonged to any US president, and watched his father, who seemed oblivious to the untenable situation in which he had placed him. The governor's anger was palpable. The lines on his forehead were creased and his face turned a brilliant red as he slammed his fist down hard on the desk, ignoring the glass of water that toppled over onto his various papers.

"You could lose me the election. Why in God's name didn't you tell me this before? You knew I was going to be running in the primaries and this sort of scandal could break me. All these years we've been living a lie. You've been living a lie. Did Mom know? Though, God knows, there was no love lost between the two of you."

"No she didn't. There was no need."

"My God! I can't believe this. Now, of all times, you come at me with this. Why now? Christ, the press would have a field day."

"I was worried people would find out. I'm nearly ninety now. I thought everything would die with me."

"I wish it damn well had. So what do you suggest we do? I was on course for the White House, for God's sake."

"I really should have explained, many years ago. I've dealt with it, though."

"Well, whatever you've done, it had better be good, that's all

I can say. And good enough to keep it out the papers or we all might as well be dead with Mom. I want to be told everything, every detail, so don't you dare lie to me."

"Ted, this is not the right time. Anyway there's nothing else for you to know."

"You mean, nothing you're prepared to tell me. Always the damn same, ever since I was a kid. You have to control everyone and everything, don't you? Why can't you be honest for a change?"

"Enough! The conversation is closed. I've said all I'm going to say on the subject." He turned on his heels and strode out without a backward glance, leaving his son shouting behind him.

"This is never going to be finished. I want the truth and I'll damn well get it, you can count on that."

CHAPTER THREE

THE rendezvous had been arranged for seven o'clock in the evening in a small pub off the Kings Road in the heart of London's Chelsea district. To say Sean O'Connell was looking forward to this was an understatement. Ever since he had returned from Israel without Captain Steve Granger several months ago, he had been calling in every favour he could to find out what had happened to the captain and had drawn a complete blank. To him, this made no sense at all. Not long after arriving back in the UK, General Ian Bowles-Smith, his commanding officer in the Special Forces, had informed him that Steve's body had been found just beyond a small settlement in the Golan Heights and, consequently, they had buried him in Israel. It was all for the best, he had been told. In other words, let the matter drop.

Sean didn't believe a single word of it. Everything was that little bit too cut and dried for his liking. First of all, he had no proof of Steve's death, apart from the CO's explanation, and that wasn't good enough for him. Now he was meeting with one of his pals from his unit who had been there when the captain had allegedly been killed during the mission in Syria some five years previously.

Mark Hemmings, also known by his army nickname of Mo, was extremely easy to spot because of his mop of ginger hair that had now grown to almost shoulder level.

"Christ, what on earth have you done to yourself? Gone hippy all of a sudden?"

"Good to see you too, Cono," Mo greeted in his thick, Geordie accent. "I decided to rebel and see how long I could grow it. Saves a fortune in haircuts." He got up to shake Sean's hand and the two of them hugged. "It really is great to see you. Lost a bit more hair, I see, and put on a bit of weight." He patted Sean's stomach and pretended to punch him. Sean ducked to miss the clenched fist and they both laughed.

"Nothing I can't get off. Thanks for coming to meet me. I'll go get us a couple of pints and then we can talk. By the way, I presume your shoulder is now in good working order?"

"It's working fine. No bullet's going to stop me." Mo moved his arm around in a circular motion to prove the point.

Sean flicked his eyes up and down the man who had been under his command. He was certainly in good shape, all six foot three of him, and still stood out with his shocking flame of hair that surrounded an extremely pleasant and freckled face. Renowned in the unit for his practical jokes, a scar now ran across his right cheek, the spoils of war, giving him a lopsided grin.

Returning with the drinks, Sean sat down. After taking a huge glug of his beer, he wiped his hand across his mouth and launched into the reason for the meeting.

"Whatever I tell you now, you must never repeat. This goes against everything we signed up to under the Official Secrets Act. Mo, I need your help and you're the only one I could think of I can trust."

"Sounds serious. Go on then. I'm intrigued."

Sean took a pack of cigarettes from his jacket, offered one to Mo who refused, then lit up and took a long draw. "I couldn't approach you before as I knew you were still in the army but now you're out, well here goes. I got a call from the general a couple of years ago because he was contacted by Dragonfly, requesting to be pulled out."

"Dragonfly? Captain Granger's codename? But he's dead."

"Yes, so we were led to believe. Anyway, I got ordered into HQ. You can imagine the shock I had when Dragonfly made contact, and I realised who it was, and that he was very much alive. He didn't die in Syria. Apparently, he had lost his memory and had been recovering in a small village outside Damascus for three years. He wanted out but the general was having none of it. He decided to keep him in the field for another year, despite my protestations it was the wrong thing to do. He needed to be home and back with his wife and kids."

"Too bloody right. And they never told Mrs Granger he'd been found?"

"No."

Mo sat back in his chair. "I can't take this in. You're telling me he's alive? You mean, we just left him there?"

"Yes. He survived somehow."

Mo shook his head in bewilderment. "We went to his memorial service, all of us that were left. He was buried with full honours, for God's sake. This makes no sense. How?"

"Believe me, If I'd known back then ..." Sean's voice trailed off for a moment. "I saw him take the full blast from the grenade. I saw him get killed. Or at least I thought I did."

"You weren't to blame. If we had any idea, we would've gone back for him. We never leave a man when he's down, you know that more than anyone. That night we had no choice. Those helicopters were attacking us from all sides. Our position was compromised. We had to save ourselves and all the men we could, or nobody would've got out alive, including us."

"I do feel guilty, though. I've lived with this ever since, which is why I resigned and went to work for Mrs Granger. Still there."

"Ah, so, that's where you are now. I was wondering about that. How is she? What does she think about all this?"

"She still doesn't know. And that makes me feel even worse. I haven't told her."

Mo raised his brows and leant his elbows on the table.

"Don't look at me like that. I couldn't tell her when I found out at HQ. How could I? And what good would it have done? Anyway, that's not the end. Captain Granger remained working for another year in the field, reporting back further activity in the area. We discovered he was in real danger and I persuaded the general to let me go out to Israel to bring him in. I couldn't tell anyone. Also, Mrs Granger had been hurt in an accident - I won't go into all the details. Suffice it to say, someone wanted her dead."

"Jesus. Is she okay now?"

"Yes, but this whole thing with her husband could, well, you know … and especially now she's moved on and met someone else."

"So what happened in Israel? Where is he now?"

"That's the thing. He knew the reconnaissance point and we arranged to meet there five days after his call. I would wait the allotted ten minutes and if he hadn't arrived for whatever reason, I would leave and return the next day. You know the drill. Day five, there I was, and we spotted a body from the chopper. We landed and the guys ran out to retrieve it. Christ," he said, remembering the day as if it were yesterday. "It wasn't the captain."

"Did you go back the next day, to the reconnaissance point?"

"No. I was ordered home."

"Why? That's not the procedure. Didn't you think to stay behind and take up the search?"

"No. I know that, you know that, but I was under orders. Easier said than done. The general reported we'd found a body and thought it was a warning to us."

"So, you returned to the UK?" Sean nodded in response. "I don't believe it. That's not like you at all."

"Look, man. I had no choice. Not long after, the CO got in touch and told me they'd found the captain's body. They buried him in Israel. They thought it was the best thing to do, to let sleeping dogs lie."

"So that's the end of it. Why did you want to meet me? What can I do now?"

"Well, in my mind it's not the end. I think he's still alive. And I'll tell you why. He never gives up and would have done his utmost to reach our reconnaissance point."

"Unless he was dead."

"Or unless he was taken," Sean said, his brows drawn together in a frown. He lit up another cigarette. "Sorry, needs must. I'm actually down to ten a day, most days."

"I'll be glad when they're banned. Anyway, taken by whom?"

"I have a couple of theories. If he was taken by the Syrians they would no doubt have paraded him in front of all of us and either demanded a ransom or an exchange with their soldiers imprisoned by the Israelis. Or, they would have killed him immediately and paraded his body. With his rank in the Special Forces, the captain was too important for them to miss an opportunity."

"And they haven't?"

"Not that I'm aware of. However, the general liked having someone in the field of the captain's calibre. It made him look good, brought him kudos from the powers that be because he was the one filtering through all the information to the top."

"Top meaning someone in government. So, what do you think's gone on?"

"I've been giving this a lot of thought. We all know how tough it is getting across the Golan Heights. The conditions are terrible and it's either bloody freezing, or the temperatures are at boiling point, and with little water it's hard to sustain. If the captain wasn't in good shape, and we have no reason to believe he was or wasn't to be honest, looking back on things, I doubt he was ever going to make it. The CO must have known this and I think he got him picked up and he's holed up somewhere being used again."

"The body you found. Who was it?"

"No idea. Probably a decoy for my benefit to prove a point to me and to warn me nobody can survive out there. I really don't know."

"It's a good theory but you have nothing to back it up. Only your thoughts. No proof."

"Nothing. That's where you come in."

"You want me out there?" Mo asked, his mouth tense.

"I want all our boys out there. I want to ensure the captain comes home, or we find out for definite that he's dead."

Mo scowled. "What, you think we can just go blazing into Israel like some renegade army?"

"Course not. No, we need to plan this carefully. We need Sparks, Baz, Dixie and Davo. We'll go in from different points and meet up quietly somewhere."

"Even that's not going to be easy," Mo pointed out.

"Agreed. We'll come up with something, though. But Mo, I need to know if you're with me, and if you are, you need to do something."

"What?"

"Go and get your bloody hair cut."

CHAPTER FOUR

"You look done in. Had a bad day, darling?"

Cydney accepted gratefully the glass of chilled white wine from George and took a long sip, letting out a huge sigh of relief to be home.

"You could say that. How come you're still here? I thought you were off back to South Africa tonight. I could have sworn you gave me a rather special goodbye this morning." She watched as a broad grin spread across his face.

"It was just an excuse to have your body." He wrapped his arms around her waist and pulled her towards him. Cydney peered up into the eyes of the man she loved, despite everything, and put her lips to his as she felt his hand slide down her back. Every time guilt washed over her. She couldn't help herself. For all intents and purposes she was a widow and had every right to be in a relationship with a man. Quite a few months had passed since Steve had come through to her finally and she'd been hit with the thunderbolt that maybe he wasn't dead after all; maybe he was still alive somewhere, but hovering between life and death. His image had kept coming through and fading away as if he was on the verge of leaving for the spirit world and the shock had knocked her sideways. Ever since, she had felt nothing from him at all. Now she asked herself if it was all a dream. The world he was inhabiting, wherever that was, was silent, and Cydney had no choice but to get on with her life and that's exactly what she was doing.

"For God's sake, Mum, get a room," Jake said as he strode into the kitchen. At fifteen he was already more than six feet tall and towering over Cydney. She reached up to him and playfully clipped him around the ear. "Behave. Not so much of the cheek, please."

"I thought you were leaving today," Jake muttered, glancing at George.

"What is this? Does everyone want me gone for some reason?"

"Hi Mum, hi George. Are you still here?"

"Thanks, Lauren. Yes, as you can see, I have not gone to South Africa. My plans changed. Rupert wants me to go over some new contracts here for the Battersea development. I'm meeting the architects this week. It's very exciting. They're pulling down the old tenement blocks there and building new apartments aimed at up-and-coming professionals."

"You're excited? Who could possibly be orgasmic over a building?"

"Lauren, watch your language!"

"Sorry, Mum. Are we eating in or out tonight, now George has decided to grace us with his company for a bit longer?"

"Lauren! Behave yourself."

"Sorry, George." She sidled up to him and gave him a hug. "I love having you here, really."

"Just as well because I'm here to stay, as long as your mum will have me, anyway." George glanced enquiringly over at Cydney, who nodded in return with a look of amusement.

"I'm sure she'll have you."

"Jake, enough please. You two are as bad as each other."

"Actually, I am off a few days after the meetings, to Germany, so you'll have me out of your lives again, for a while."

Cydney gave George a brief, questioning look. She was aware of how quickly plans could change but he hadn't told her before. "Anyway," she said, changing the subject, "Sophie's cooked something for us all so we're in tonight. I want an early night. I'm beat. Has anyone seen Sean? He had the day off. I thought he'd be back by now."

21

"He called," George said. "Meeting some ex-army pals so will be back late. We're not to keep anything for him."

Cydney went cold as a shiver ran through her. She immediately turned to Lauren and caught a glimpse of a shudder. Lauren shrugged her shoulders as if it was unimportant, and carried on laying the table for dinner. However, she had this really strange feeling, which continued to haunt her all through dinner and even while she was getting ready for bed.

"Are you okay? Your mind seems to be elsewhere," George said, as Cydney got undressed. "Are you thinking about your mum? I know it's only been a few months since you lost her."

"Oh, I'm fine. It's been one of those days." It wasn't a complete lie. The meeting with Harold and Alfie had left her feeling terrible, however, now it was thoughts of Steve that were troubling her.

"Do you want to talk about it, sweetheart? You can always bend my ear."

"No thanks. Honestly, I'm fine. Just tired. I reckon I'll be asleep before my head touches the pillow."

Pulling the duvet over to his side and stretching his arm out, George beckoned her into bed. Her relationship with George was different to the one she'd had with her husband, who was and always would be her first great love. Cydney recognised that, but after five years she couldn't help herself and she loved George as much as anyone could love their partner. She felt so lucky to have been blessed with two great loves in her life when some people never succeeded in finding even one.

Settling into the crook of his arm, Cydney closed her eyes and willed sleep to come, but it evaded her. After an hour of listening to George's soft breathing she was still awake. So many thoughts were running through her mind that sleep was impossible. She turned onto her side and desperately tried to summon one of her spirit guides through to help her. The shiver she'd experienced earlier in the kitchen was playing on her mind. She needed her husband. Needed answers. Needed him to come through to her. For nearly four years after his 'alleged' death she had been trying to contact him. However, all her powers of mediumship had evaded her, right up until that single moment when he'd made contact in the hallway just before Jake's concert the previous year. There'd been nothing since. If he was dead she knew he would do everything to make himself appear to her again. If he was alive she was going to find him, wherever he was.

She had never discussed that night with Sean and instead had tried to investigate the circumstances on her own. Countless calls over the months to the Special Forces' headquarters had proved useless and she was simply given the brush-off. Calling General Ian Bowles-Smith also proved to be a complete waste of time as she was told he was either away or busy, neither of which she believed for a second. Nobody would assist her and in the end she had given up, sensing she was almost becoming deranged from the torment.

However, during all of this she kept her counsel, not giving anything away to her family, hiding the secret within her, waiting to see if Steve would make contact again with her or Lauren, hoping against hope he was still alive. The worst was living with George and not letting on something was wrong. At times she forgot about Steve and carried on with her everyday life but then something would happen to bring it all back to her with a resounding crash. This time it was the shiver. She knew Lauren had experienced it, too.

If George knew she was doing everything in her power to contact Steve he wouldn't be happy, and who could blame him? However, that wasn't her issue now because nothing else was as important. If she was unfaithful, even in her mind, so be it.

After only a couple of minutes Cydney felt the presence of a man. She couldn't quite make out who it was at first and did everything not to become too excited, praying it would be Steve again. However, it was never her choice as her spirit guides didn't necessarily bring through whomever she wanted but, instead, those who wanted to contact her, which was not the same. Focusing her mind fully, the person before her started to take shape and she felt the familiar cold rushing down her right arm and across her shoulders as he came nearer.

"Oh, Ray. It's you." Ray Gordon had been her spirit guide since he'd passed away the year before. In his desperate attempt to prevent his errant brother defrauding his estate, he had sought Cydney's assistance and thankfully his brother had been brought to justice. Now he was always close to hand whenever she needed him.

"Sorry to disappoint you."

"No, you haven't. It's just ... Is it Steve? Please tell me it's him." Even to herself she sounded desperate. "Or Mum?"

"Not Steve, not this time. He's not with me, and it's too early for your mother. She's recovering. That's not what you want to speak to me about, is it? I'll bring her to you when she's better."

"Yes. I know it's too early. I was thinking of my husband. You brought him to me before, so …"

"And now you want him again. I realise that, but first I need to explain."

"Where is he? I really don't believe he's in spirit."

"He was very ill."

"What does that mean exactly? Was? What are you keeping from me?"

George stirred in his sleep and turned over, away from Cydney, almost as if he knew subconsciously he needed to give her space. Tears began to form and she shook her head, willing them not to fall, knowing she had to somehow keep emotion out of this. It was important to keep her wits about her and listen carefully to what Ray was going to tell her.

Images of high mountain ranges surrounded by rough and deserted land with the sun blazing mercilessly down came into her mind and she was reminded of the premonition she'd had a couple of months before Steve had allegedly been killed. Now she saw him laying seemingly unconscious at the bottom of a small hill, blood pouring from an open leg wound. His lips were cracked and dry and his face was burnt red and peeling from the sun. He had a beard and his hair was longer than usual and slightly greying. Suddenly, he opened his eyes and searched around. His hand stretched out towards her. There was no doubt it was him. Those eyes were the same piercing blue she saw every time she looked at their son.

"I can see him, Ray. He's hardly breathing. I can hear a helicopter approaching." The sound of the rotor arms reverberated around her. It was like watching a film playing out in her mind, but so real. "They've lifted him up."

"I know. He was taken to hospital. That's when I brought him to you before, six months ago"

"I don't understand."

"Your husband was in Syria working for the British government. He was severely injured but saved by a local doctor who was part of an organisation that wanted to change the face of national politics."

"That's when I first saw him injured in the chest, just before the army told me he'd been killed by a landmine in Afghanistan. He wasn't there? They lied to me." Her face drained of colour as she remembered.

"Don't be too hard on the army. They didn't know. For nearly three years Steve had a loss of memory. He was on the verge of death so many times and nobody knew if he would live. After that he slowly began to regain his memory and when he was ready he asked to be returned home to you."

"So why didn't he?" Her eyes welled with unshed tears that threatened to escape. She turned to George sleeping next to her. How could she possibly love two men?

"He was told to remain in Syria, or rather ordered to. His job was to report back his findings on the build-up of troops in the area. Everyone thought war was about to break out and they needed to ascertain the target."

"They kept him there and stopped him coming back to me and the twins? This is crazy."

"I told you it was going to be difficult to hear about this."

"And then what? Why can I see him lying in a hospital?"

"After the year was up it seems his presence was compromised and they agreed to get him out. He had to make his way from Syria and into Israel, across the Golan Heights."

"Ah, I see it now. The mountains. They seem so treacherous."

"Yes. They found him and took him over the border."

"So you're saying he's alive? I need to go to him. I'll find him. I'll talk to Sean. He'll help me."

"That's not what I said. You're not listening to me. He was hanging on to life, but now …"

"Now what? Ray, please, you must know. You've got to tell me."

"There's nothing more I can tell you. Speak to Sean. He knows."

"What? What does he know?"

Ray faded away from her side. "Come back! You can't leave yet!" Cydney's bottom lip trembled at the realisation he was gone, leaving her sitting up in bed, speechless, and without the confirmation she needed. Without the closure she so desperately desired. Sleep was off the agenda.

* * *

It was instantaneous. As soon as Sean stepped into the kitchen Cydney felt an enormous shift in her mind. She had no idea what he'd been up to recently, but he was evading her, not looking her straight in the eye, and there was something wrong about his whole demeanour. Cydney sat at the wooden table, fully dressed and ready for work, watching him carefully, gauging for any reaction. It was before seven in the morning, not a time she was normally awake and raring to go. A mug of coffee was in front of her plus one she had poured for him. She was ready to interrogate him and could see how completely unnerved he was behaving.

"Come in and have a seat, please."

"Christ," he murmured under his breath, pulling the wooden chair out from underneath the table and sitting down with a sigh of resignation.

"I know." The enormity of her two words drifted into the air and hung there between them.

"Know what?"

"Everything."

Sean slumped further into his chair. "I don't know what you mean."

"Don't take me for a complete fool. All that disappearing to your ailing aunt in Ireland last year. You didn't go there, did you? There was no aunt."

He picked up his coffee and took a long noisy slurp. "I've been outwitted, or rather cornered. You seem so calm about this."

"I am far from calm. I want to know your involvement, and I want the truth this time, exactly what happened and why." Cydney was doing everything within her power to keep her wits about her, especially after what Ray had reported. The man in spirit was someone she had confidence in unquestionably and what he'd told her must be the truth because she knew he had her best interests at heart with no ulterior motive. Added to the fact she was mourning her mother, it certainly wouldn't take much for her to break down in pieces.

It was as if she had been waiting for this moment to confront Sean ever since Steve had come through to her those months ago. How stupid of her not to have recognised his involvement and question him. She knew she was chancing things, calling the man's bluff, checking him out to see if he revealed anything. He was not a man to play with and if he was lying she knew he'd never look her straight in the eye and his actions now spoke volumes as he was doing anything but look at her.

It had been hard, initially, to accept the fact her husband could be alive and that's why she had called the Ministry of Defence to obtain some clarification from his commanding officer, General Bowles-Smith, some peace of mind, as she couldn't bear to live with the thought that she may have abandoned him. The answer from them was always the same; her husband had died five years ago. They gave her short shrift and who could blame them? They probably thought she was going out of her mind, the crazy widow, and that's exactly how she felt. However, at the back of her mind, this little doubt crept in - either that or she really was going mad.

"So Sean, the truth please. Lauren and I both know you were up to something yesterday."

"Lauren? How can you …? Are you sure you two don't have Irish gypsy blood in you?"

"I'm not laughing. Stop delaying matters. Steve may be alive and I want you to tell me everything."

"Listen, please don't be angry with me. I didn't know myself until a year and a half ago and I'm not so sure now, to be honest."

"Over a year! During which time you lied to me. Me, and the twins you profess to love like your own."

"I do. You're my family, along with Sophie. I didn't lie, just didn't tell the truth - entirely."

"So, what's the difference? I can't believe this. Everything you've done since then, well, I'm almost speechless at your disloyalty."

"You were an army wife. You know the score. We have no choice when it comes to keeping things secret. I couldn't tell you even if I wanted to."

He sank further down into his chair. Cydney got up from the table and walked around to the other side of the kitchen. She wanted to get as far away from him as possible and this time she was not playing. She turned to face him.

"I was hoping you would open up and tell me, and I kept giving you opportunities. I am so hurt."

"Christ, Cydney, it was impossible to do that. How long have you known?" Sean glanced up at her as she tried so hard to stem her unshed tears.

"Several months. About your involvement, only recently."

"I won't ask how. Why didn't you say anything?"

"What good would it have done? I'm just the little army wife, right? I was trying to dig around myself for information. I spent so much time calling the army HQ, the general himself. They kept repeating the same thing. That he was dead."

"I've been digging around, too, and I've come up with nothing."

"What do you mean? Nothing? What a waste of time, when we could have pooled our resources."

"Please don't look so sad. I'm so sorry for all you've been through. I'm only working on a hunch. I was told he'd been found dead and they buried him in Israel. Listen, promise me this will go no further than this room. I didn't believe what I heard and I've a plan now. I met with one of my guys. He's going to join me and some of the other lads. We're planning to go out to Israel to find your husband."

"Dead or alive?"

"Whichever. If he is alive, we'll do everything to make sure he comes back to you and the twins, if we can."

"And if he's dead?"

"At least we'll know the truth at last." He glanced at Cydney's face. "You have to be prepared for the worst. It's not going to be easy. We're up against the British Army here and they won't like what we're doing, especially the CO. Do I have your backing on this?"

"Only if you promise never to lie to me again, no matter what I have to hear, good or bad."

"It's a deal." Sean reached out across the table and placed his hand over hers. "I promise on everything that's sacred."

"Then you have my full support. No hiding anything from me, or don't bother to come back."

"And what about George?"

"What about him? That's something I'll have to deal with when we know about Steve. You never liked him anyway, so why the concern?"

"Well, I didn't at first, but I can see he makes you happy and the kids have become very fond of him. We've also reached some level of understanding."

"And you like him now?" asked Cydney, realising she was on risky ground with that question.

"Ah, well, yes. I think he's redeemed himself."

"And tell me one more thing, Sean. Do you believe Steve is alive?"

"That's the one question I can't answer. Yet."

CHAPTER FIVE

WHEN Richard Barrett had sauntered, fit and healthy, into her office a few months ago, it was pure delight for Cydney, as she'd never envisaged she would see the day when he would be back at work, albeit not quite full-time yet. The accident they had been in the year before had taken its toll on both of them, more so for him as he was now in his mid-fifties, and they still had the scars to prove it. Being run off the road and shot at was not something one could easily forget. Richard's memory was not quite as it had been before his head injury and the coma in which he had lain for nearly three months, and her knee still gave her problems occasionally, however, they had both survived.

Every so often she was reminded of what they had gone through after investigating insider dealing in the U.S.A. by two brothers-in-law, Craig Benton and Robert Crossley. They were both dead now, Crossley from cancer, and Benton from suicide. Cydney would never forget Benton had been responsible for kidnapping her son, and when they had discovered his deceit he had taken the coward's way out and shot himself in front of her before anyone could stop him. The vision of that bullet blasting through his skull would stay with her until the day she died.

"Have a seat, Richard. We've taken on some new clients, Harold Franks and Alfie Goodman. Rupert's introduction. Apparently he's known them for years. They were originally from Berlin but survived the Holocaust and came to England after the war. Then naturalised."

"Survivors? Very strong people to have done that."

"Absolutely. They're coming in again next Thursday. In the meantime I need you to investigate these two documents." Cydney handed over both bearer bonds which she had removed from the office safe.

"Where did these come from?"

"My question exactly. Both men received them in the post last week on the same day and they have absolutely no idea who sent them or why."

"Weird. That's an awful lot of money to come from a stranger. One million dollars. I wish."

"I agree, but there has to be a connection from somewhere."

'I'll get Ash to speak to his mates and see whether we can get any information about this bank that issued the bonds. Have you ever heard of Prime Global Trust Corporation?"

"No, I haven't. It could be one of those small provincial banks in America with only one branch. I'd also like you to look into the backgrounds of the two men. We know their names, though nothing else about them. See what you can come up with and ask Tom to get involved. That's what he joined the team to do and I don't want you over-doing things."

Cydney was pleased Richard's former colleague from his Metropolitan Police CID days had joined her company as his assistant. Tom Patterson was in his late thirties and had been brought up in the East End of London. He had been called in to help her when Richard was laid up in hospital when she was working on the Benton and Crossley case. His services had proved invaluable. Prior to his appointment he had been working within his own security company but the offer of buying it out was not one to be turned down, and Granger Associates was certainly busy enough to warrant having two such men on the payroll.

"I'll get straight on to that. Might be worth having a chat to Rupert. Perhaps he can fill us in. Does he have any connection to Germany?"

"He has some investments there. Steel industry, nothing else as far as I know. Why?"

"Might help us."

"I'll call him later but whenever I ask him about his past he changes the subject. Anyway, let's meet up tomorrow."

"I'll see what information I can get. Ash is a wizard on the computer so he's bound to come up with something."

"Thanks, Richard. On your way out, can you send Jenny in? I have a job for her."

"Sure." He got to his feet. "How are the twins doing now?"

"Studying for their exams at the moment, although I doubt Jake is doing more than five minutes at a time. He's always at his keyboard, writing songs. Since he won that competition last year, there's no stopping him. He wants to become professional though I'd rather he passed his exams first. Anyway, we'll see."

"Is he still having counselling?"

"No, that stopped after a few months. He seems to be coping after the kidnapping, as far as I'm aware. He's quite a strong young man. I did worry at first, you know, but he's getting on with things, which is the best way."

"And Lauren? I haven't seen her for a while. I bet she's growing up to be as beautiful as her mother."

"Stop it! You'll make me blush." Cydney gave a small laugh. "She's a bright girl. Very interested in law, so I'm hoping she'll join the practice after university. At least one of my children should."

"Absolutely. A few years to go still, though. And what about you? It's been a tough year and you went through so much. Don't hold back, especially with us. We're all here for you. If you need me you only have to ask."

"Thanks. I do appreciate it, but I'm fine. Honestly."

"Um, I do know you, maybe better than you think." He gathered up his papers. "Right, I'm outta here. Will report back later."

Harold Franks and Alfie Goodman were huddled together in a corner of a small coffee shop in Hampstead, a few miles north of central London, so they couldn't be overhead. In front of them sat their normal lunch of bagels and smoked salmon but neither of the men were in the mood to eat.

"She seemed very nice," Harold said, breaking the silence.

"Yes. Highly recommended. What do you think? Should we tell her?"

Harold left the question unanswered. "Should we tell the kids?"

"I'm not so sure. They have their lives to lead and I don't want them to be worried about this. You know what Matt and Sarah are like, always busy, always rushing around taking their children here and there. No, I don't think we should."

"True. Though with my Mikey being a lawyer, he understands about these things." Harold heaved a sigh and lent back in his chair.

"Maybe. Let's wait and see what this Cydney comes up with," said Alfie.

"I wish my Rose was with me still. She would know what to do."

"And my Libby. Oosh." Alfie sighed and waited a few seconds, lost in his thoughts, before coming back to practicalities. "We need to get all our papers together. This isn't going to be easy for us. It will bring back a lot of bad memories. We may have to tell her things we never wanted to bring up again in our lives, especially ..."

Harold nodded and breathed in deeply as if the whole weight of the world was on his shoulders, remembering the angina pain he had felt before, which was worrying him. He needed to sort this business out in case something happened to him. He pulled up the sleeve of his jacket to reveal the series of six numbers tattooed on his left arm. "Look. This is what they did to us in Auschwitz. How can we ever forget? She should know the truth."

"Remember his passing words? Remember his look when you showed him what you had found? If looks could have killed ..."

"I'll never forget as long as I live. It pierced my heart. The evil in that man. He must have discovered where we are now and after all these years he still wants to buy our silence."

"Now is the time to get everything out in the open. No secrets. For the memories of our families. We have to tell all before we die, or everything will be lost."

* * *

Dachau 1945

"I want to die. Hans, I can't go on like this any longer. Just leave me here when they come for us."

"If you think we've come this far and I'm going anywhere without you, you have another thing coming."

"I need food, water ..."

"We all do. You have to hang on. It may not be for too much longer. We've heard the Allies aren't far away now. I'll try and steal an extra piece of bread for you when I can but, for God's sake, you're going to have to work. We have no choice. We have to get out of here alive. It won't be long."

"Keep your voices down, you two. The guards will come in if they hear you talking."

"Okay, Marcus. You don't have to tell me. God, Ari, can't you move your elbow? It's digging right into my ribs."

Hans Frankelman thought he was about seventeen years old though really wasn't too sure. Time was not relevant to him as every day was like the one before. Regardless, he felt one hundred and fifteen. His teeth were rotting, the little hair he had was almost gone and his hip bones were protruding. It hurt to lay on the straw pallets covering the wooden planks, an excuse for a bed, and he had to share this with his three friends so there was little room to move.

The barracks in which they were attempting to exist housed over one thousand men and boys on bunk beds three levels high, though in reality it was only fit for two hundred. There was no heating, which hurt as winter approached early. In the middle of the walk-through there was a stove which never worked and there was no ventilation so disease moved quickly around with no thought for whom it attacked next. People huddled together to share body heat but, despite that, every morning saw another death at least. You could always tell because of the multitude of flies hovering around the body and then Hans had to be quick and grab the dead person's clothes or shoes, and any food hidden, before anyone else did; he was a boy in waiting for someone to die. The nights were the worst imaginable, not knowing who would not wake from their sleep, and he hated hearing all the younger ones crying out for their mothers, and from hunger and pain, because that's exactly what he wanted to do himself.

The guards were rigid in their mission to get everyone up and working by five o'clock in the morning, and thus commenced their minimum fourteen hour days. Roll call in the square started the nightmare, no matter the weather or the condition of the people. Many times they were forced to stand out in the courtyard for hours on end, their hands on their heads, or in a crouching position, for seemingly no reason whatsoever except to amuse the guards, dressed only in thin pyjamas and normally with no protection on their feet if their wooden clogs had somehow gone missing. Anyone falling was shot immediately and dragged off, their body never to be seen again. Sometimes they were forced to witness the person flogged or, worse still, hung from the nearest tree or pole, their body left to rot for days on end as a warning.

The enclosure was heavily guarded to ensure nobody escaped

and soldiers were ready to fire from one of the seven watch towers that rose menacingly around them. Hans considered trying to escape, putting his idea forward and discussing with Ari his plan of action. Ultimately, they knew it would be an impossibility because of the ten-foot wide no-man's land which they would have to cross, plus the barbed wire fence which surrounded the enclosure. They would surely be killed and the intention was to survive at all costs, although occasionally suicide crossed their minds and would have been so easy; all they had to do was cross the line, and many of their comrades did that very thing. Their conversations, however, merely served to pass the time. Nobody talked of their lives before their incarceration as it was far too painful and without purpose.

Breakfast consisted of hickory coffee, a slice of bread and nothing else until lunch, which normally was no more than some type of indefinable watery soup - the ingredients of which were anybody's guess, all poured as one into a tin dish. They tried to eat slowly but hunger got the better of them and the food was gobbled up in seconds, the dish cleaned out thoroughly with their tongues, not one scrap missed. The noise of everybody licking their bowls was one that would stay with him for the rest of his life.

That was it for the entire day so Hans and his friends were constantly thinking of food, and how and where to get it. They sometimes located an old potato peel which they shared. They even resorted to eating grass, which simply gave them stomach cramps. Their camp was in Allach, one of the almost one hundred satellite camps of Dachau, right in the middle of the forest, so occasionally they were lucky enough to find and eat some edible vegetation, as long as they managed to hide it from the guards.

It was as if they had been there for years though it was probably only months. He recalled their march through the iron gate and into their current hell. There was a motto above the gate, *'Arbeit macht frei'*, 'Work Will Make You Free'. Free! As if that was the case. It was simply Nazi propaganda to trivialise their labour when in fact every day was torture.

During the day, their work was hard, digging for an underground munitions factory, dragging huge bags of cement their poor shoulders were too young to bear, and there was no respite even for the much younger boys who were beaten if they could not perform even the lowliest task. Hans and Ari had formed a close bond with two other boys, Marcus and Leo. They looked out for one another and ensured they were always together in the same work group, helping each other through the long march to the hell of work that was their everyday existence. Then, back again through the Bavarian villages, where people would point and stare at them trudging past, swearing and spitting, although one time some kind person pushed a lump of stale bread into his hands. Hans marched past with his head held high no matter how he felt, ignoring the pain coursing through every muscle, bone and joint, and insisted his friends do the same. He was never going to let them know that inside he was broken and he doubted he would ever mend.

CHAPTER SIX

"I T'S an interesting one, this," Richard said when he was in the boardroom a couple of days later with Cydney, Tom Patterson and Ash Khattak, their computer expert.

"Explain."

"We made enquiries into Prime. It has a couple of branches still in Richmond, Virginia and near Charleston. Now it's owned by Whiteman Trust and Mutual Bank with its HQ in Charleston itself. It was set up by Cedric and Philip Ross, originally in Richmond in 1870. West Virginia was quite a new state after its dismemberment from Virginia in 1863 and the branch's main purpose was to lend to farmers. They expanded quite quickly, underwriting government bonds and securities and becoming involved in stock issues for steel related industries. Cedric died suddenly at a young age and Philip's son, Jolyon, joined and carried on working with his father."

"Good history, and still in the family. Interesting," said Cydney.

"Well yes, but there's a couple of strange facts I've discovered. First, they survived the panic of 1907 which spread through the nation, and secondly, they managed to sustain the Great Depression in 1933 when so many state and national banks fell."

"How did they manage to keep the doors open?" Cydney asked. "Why them?"

"Well, that's where it gets even more unusual, especially where Europe's concerned. You all know about the 1929 crash? Well, about that time, American banks who had previously made loans to Germany started to recall them because of the uncertainty there. Following the Depression, banks recovered and that continued throughout the war. Prime grew in strength, especially because of the demand for the state's resources - coal and natural gas, timber of course, glass and steel, and for its chemicals and manufactured goods."

"That's not unusual," Cydney said, lifting her head up from the notes she was taking.

"That bit, I agree. However, what is a little strange is that Prime had established branches in parts of Europe, specifically Germany."

"Do you know why?" asked Tom.

"I believe so. Investors there wanted the opportunity to buy US government and railway bonds. Philip's wife was German and through her connections, presumably, they became involved with a large German industrial family who wanted to have a US presence."

"And Prime were the only bank doing this?" asked Cydney.

"I don't know. I haven't looked at that. Anyway, Prime went on to become one of the largest private investment banks in the southern states but came under scrutiny in the 1930s when Edward, Philip's grandson, was chairman. I managed to find archives of old newspapers and it was alleged they were buying and shipping millions of dollars of gold and treasury bonds to Germany, helping Hitler in his build-up to the war by financing his rise to power. The U.S. was shipping fuel, steel and coal to Germany during this time so probably nobody went into this too much. Here, have a look." He passed around a series of photocopied pages.

"And were they doing this, or was it merely speculation?" asked Cydney.

"It was never discovered. The case was closed."

"Closed? Why though? That makes no sense. They must've had evidence to even investigate in the first place," Tom said. "No smoke without fire and all that."

"I agree. For now I can't find any more facts. My thinking is nobody wanted to rock the boat. A US bank helping Germany? That could have put into question the whole system and I presume it was put to sleep."

"So, do we have a German connection and, secondly, is this what we're looking for with regard to the bearer bonds received by our new clients?" Cydney glanced at her colleague.

"Possibly. Let me carry on, though, as I want to tell you what was going on in Germany before war broke out, and a lot of this was only discovered afterwards. Sorry if I sound like a history teacher but it is important for you all to know the background."

"You going to test us afterwards?"

"Yes, I might well do that, Tom. Anyway ..." Richard cleared his throat before continuing. "In the early 1930s, nobody expected a second world war. The loss following the first world war had a draining effect on the country and Germany was forced to make huge reparations to France and Great Britain. They started spending, creating transportation projects, modernising power plants and gas works, but the spending was at an unbelievable rate. In 1930, the municipal finance collapsed and revenue from taxes fell. Foreign countries placed tariffs on German goods which depressed the German economy even further and caused a state of super inflation where millions of marks were virtually useless. So what did Germany do? They printed huge amounts of money. You remember the famous cartoon of the people with wheelbarrows of money who couldn't even afford a loaf of bread?"

"Yes, of course." Cydney said.

"As the crisis worsened, and specifically unemployment, foreign lenders withdraw capital from Germany, as I mentioned before. That's when Hitler took his opportunity to seize power and convinced the country the Jews were responsible for the poor economic state."

"I always wondered why they were singled out," Tom said. "I could never believe it was only a religion thing."

"Well that's why, but the history of hatred and conflict against Jewish people is centuries old. They had everything and he wanted it and now he had someone to blame and make a scapegoat for all the country's problems. He convinced Germany the Jews had too much economic power. He hatched a four-year plan to eradicate the unemployment situation and enrich the people but he did this through military strength and bullying, and particularly towards this one group of people. Yes, Hitler was a thug who rose to power by force. Did you know Germany was still trading with other countries? In particular, Switzerland."

"I thought that was a neutral country," said Cydney.

"Yes it was, but the currency of that time was gold. It was normal for a national bank to buy and sell gold because it was at the base of the international currency system. The Swiss National Bank was buying much more gold from the U.S. in the same period, and millions, possibly billions, from the German Reichsbank which was the central bank until 1945. The SNB had granted generous credits under the terms of the clearing agreements and offered them financial privileges. However, and this is the most important aspect of all, the gold they were buying from Germany was stolen."

"From the Jewish people?" Cydney asked.

"Absolutely, and this started even before war broke out. The Nazis began plundering their assets or forced their victims to sign everything over. The Nazis seized everything they could of value, from works of art, to properties, to the contents of banks and treasuries and they were ruthless in their organisational theft, which is basically what it was. They stripped billions of pounds' worth of assets. Even their Swiss bank accounts which they thought were safe, they were forced to sign over, possibly to protect themselves, but who knows."

"The Swiss never doubted these orders or questioned them?" Cydney asked. "They were colluding?"

"Yes, but actually they had no choice, as I'm about to explain.

A lot of the high ranked SS officers, bureaucrats and other corrupt officials took the wealth personally and in secret without declaring anything even to Hitler's administration, all of this done to eradicate the influence of the Jews in Germany. Then they started rounding the people up and sending them off to concentration camps, which made the thefts easier. Many of the victims who died in the camps had been robbed of all their valuable property, which was sold on to the Reichsbank, and the Nazis particularly wanted gold because that was how they could trade with Switzerland."

"Still trade? How? Why would Switzerland want to trade? I'm puzzled," said Cydney.

"The Swiss were allegedly neutral but, obviously, they needed to keep their economy going, even in the face of terror from their neighbours. They depended on German coal, which it imported in the millions of tons and it made up nearly half of their energy supplies. It was their decision to have dealings with Hitler to prevent him invading their country. They laundered much of the gold received into cash and sold war materials and arms to Germany. They had arms' factories and, because of their neutrality, they couldn't be bombed by the Allies."

"You're saying the factories churned out weapons and supplied Hitler? This is incredible. Weren't the victims able to claim back their assets after the war?" Cydney asked.

"Originally, all confiscated property was catalogued. Everyone had to fill in forms giving an inventory of their assets and lodge it with the government. The owners were given receipts. However, when the Jews were sent off to concentration camps, it was impossible as all the assets were mixed up so nothing could be identified, although the Nazis still kept lists; they were good at that. Have you heard of the 'Gold Trains'? Everything from jewellery to gold teeth were packed into crates and sent by rail from all over occupied Europe back to Germany. It was also discovered in 1944 that other countries' central banks were purchasing Nazi gold from the SNB. A lot of this didn't come to light until 1945, of course."

"So it was business as usual. Did they think they were immune?"

"They played both sides," Richard said, shaking his head. "You know, they allowed trains carrying victims from Italy and other places through its borders, taking them to the death camps."

"They were complicit in these crimes?"

"Well, so it would seem, and they persuaded Hitler not to invade them, which he was agreeable to do in exchange for handing over Jewish refugees escaping into their country."

"A question. How did the Nazis force them to hand over their assets?"

"Well, Ash, once they were sent off to the camps, they had no say in the matter. Also, don't forget they counted as some of the wealthiest in Germany. They were either kicked out of their homes or businesses were simply confiscated and the deeds to the properties handed over. Those with bank accounts in Germany or, in fact, in Switzerland, were forced to sign over orders to transfer all their monies to the Reichsbank. It was all so easy."

"The Swiss turned a blind eye. My God." Cydney shuddered. "What happened to the rest of the gold bought by the Swiss Banks?"

"It was exchanged for Swiss francs and other currency so the Nazis could buy important raw materials like tungsten and oil from so-called neutral countries. The Allies warned Switzerland in 1942 that they knew of their involvements, and in fact Swiss assets in the U.S. were frozen."

"Were there other neutral countries?"

"Yes. Romania was one of the biggest suppliers to Germany. Portugal received the largest amount of gold from Switzerland as they were the main centre for the production of tungsten. However, allegedly they sold to both sides."

"Why tungsten? What's it used for?" asked Tom.

"Bullets and shells," Richard replied. "Also, Turkey, at least until a few months before the end of the war, mainly because they wanted to avoid a conflict with Russia. They were producers of huge amounts of chromite, which the Germans needed for their stainless-steel industry. You know, the Germans couldn't function without these. They had limited oil reserves and even other commodities such as wheat, maize, tobacco, meat, which they needed."

"And countries were willing to supply them, obviously." Cydney shook her head. "Was Russia a big threat to those particular countries?"

"Oh yes. That's one of the reasons. Hitler knew that and used it for his own means."

"Anything else?" asked Tom.

"Only that the U.S. was implicated, although this is speculation. They possibly, unwittingly, supplied copper, tin and industrial diamonds to Germany via Dutch traders."

"So this was going on not just in Europe? I feel ashamed I knew nothing of this."

"Well, it's new to me, too," said Richard. "You aren't alone in this. I doubt many people knew."

"And what about our new clients? Have you managed to find out any information there?"

"Actually, I've searched Harold's background. His grandfather owned their family bank in Berlin, which was taken over by the Nazis around 1940 when they were confiscating all assets."

"This is incredible. They certainly don't teach you all this in school. Anything about Alfie's family?"

"His father was a tailor. They weren't a rich family it seems, not like Harold's, but comfortable. Anyway, I've nearly finished my report." Richard continued. "The German Jews were subjected to a range of pressures to force them to surrender their property or sell to non-Jews, and this started as early as 1933.

45

The Nazis also imposed restrictions whereby people had to boycott the businesses, which meant sales were lost and revenue decreased so many went into liquidation. By 1938, any enterprises remaining were forcibly given to Nazi party members who sold them on to make money."

"What happened to Frankelman's bank?"

"From what I've discovered, they managed to carry on a bit longer until the family were literally kicked out. Although property was thought to belong to the state, a lot of people believed it should be distributed to loyal party members and many of these breached government regulations. The SS were a law unto themselves and would do whatever they wanted."

"And?" Cydney said.

"Well, that's when our research comes to a slight halt, unfortunately. Prime is no longer operating in Germany. I have a feeling someone related to the Ross family took it over and somehow managed to move the assets back to the U.S., maybe through Switzerland. This is pure speculation. It would have been easy for them through their branch."

"Do you know who owns Prime now?"

"Yes, it's someone called Albert Whiteman who's the majority shareholder. Even though he's about ninety now and seemingly retired, he chairs the board which is made up of about fifteen people. No other family members."

"Is he related to the original Ross family?"

"I'm not sure. However, it does seem highly possible through Philip's wife, Elise, back in the 1870s. I'll get back to you on this, though. I've found out this chairman's son is the Governor of West Virginia."

"Really? That's a huge deal. Obviously they're an extremely wealthy family."

"Yes. I'm still searching for information."

"Okay, so are you saying you need more time?"

"Yes, I am, though I think we may be opening a can of worms, which could affect the whole banking world. Are we prepared for this?"

"Well, Richard, who knows? Our mission is to help Harold and Alfie as our clients. They're paying us, or rather Rupert is, on their behalf."

"Do we know their connection yet?"

"No, we don't. I'll ask our clients, though, and see if that sheds any light. Okay, gentlemen, back to work. I need more on this. Very interesting so far, though. And thanks for the history lesson. Tom, I've a feeling you might be going to the States next week."

CHAPTER SEVEN

ALBERT Whiteman had led his life for the last fifty-eight years feeling confident he had left his past behind. Now, through his own fault, it was about to come back and bite him extremely hard and harm everything he had set in motion for his son to become president of the United States of America. How his fellow officers would have laughed to even think that the son of a Nazi officer, his own child, might one day hold that position.

He had not thought about his past until recently. It was almost as if it hadn't happened, an episode in a book he'd read, as if he was so detached from his previous existence, repressing any memories and never haunted by images. Now, he questioned whether in fact he should feel any guilt for his actions. He'd never considered this or any consequences of the actual mass murders he had committed and the exterminations, but the thought alone and the questioning in his mind was eating away at him on a daily, almost hourly basis. He couldn't sleep, couldn't eat, and was unable to function. It was essential to his existence and to his life to have answers, especially now he didn't have long left on this earth and would have to face his Maker. He felt no remorse; how could he when everything he had done had been on the orders of his senior officers?

Never a religious man at all or God fearing, he had started to attend a catholic church in the last year, initially chosen purely because the architecture and the statue outside of the Madonna and Child attracted him more than any others. The church dated back to the 1830s and was built in a pseudo-gothic style, and somehow it had managed to escape destruction in the civil war. With its sweeping vista across the gorge of the Shenandoah River, it gave the man a sense of peace which he didn't receive where he lived one hundred and fifty miles away, and he was struck by the richness of everything about it.

When Albert sauntered into the church it enraptured him, which came as a shock. The first time he had simply entered through the open door and stood inside the vestibule before going through into the nave where he gazed wonderingly around him, admiring the stained-glass windows and statues that honoured religious figures and illustrated the Bible's words. Around the walls were plaques of the story of Christ's crucifixion. He felt drawn by the sense and smell of it all and the fullness of an all-consuming silence, and the cold, instead of repelling him, was somehow comforting. From childhood, religion to him was cold. The few times he was forced to attend church with his parents as a young boy, he'd found it unemotional and uncaring. He had never understood the draw or why you had to pray to God or anyone you couldn't see or hear. Was the lack of heat to give you a sense of Hell in comparison? The preacher always drummed into him that was where everyone would end up if they didn't abide by the rules set out in an ancient text. Now he may be thinking differently because that's all he had left.

Ahead of him were rows of wooden pews which he approached tentatively, almost in embarrassment, and sat down. He watched with curiosity as a young priest in his every day vestments knelt in front of the font to pray before a massive statue of Christ. Albert received no admission of his presence but the priest must have heard him, for as soon as he rose he headed down the aisle towards him and stopped by his side.

"Good morning. Welcome to St Peters. Can I help you in any way?"

"May I sit here, Father?"

49

"Of course, my son. If you wish to speak to me I'll be in the vestry."

Two hours later, after he had been totally lost in his internal fighting, and when he realised the cold was starting to penetrate into his bones, Albert had felt a desperate need to speak to the priest and wandered towards the back of the church in search of the so-called vestry. He didn't have to wait long as the younger man stepped out of a side door, almost as if he had heard him. This time he was wearing black trousers with a white shirt and the sleeves rolled up.

"I was clearing out the robing room, so please excuse my appearance. I'm sure it hasn't been done since the last century." He smiled slightly and then gave a small laugh as he ran his hand through his blond hair, pushing the fringe away from his face to remove the cobwebs and dust that had accumulated. He brushed his trousers. "Can I offer you a cup of tea or coffee? I'm about to have one myself. This is thirsty work." As Albert shook his head, refusing his offer, the priest pressed him further. "It really is no bother, honestly, and you look frozen. Do come through to my office."

Albert followed the priest into a large and untidy room surrounded by hundreds of books that spilled from the dark mahogany shelves built into each wall. There was a threadbare rug on the floor in faded shades of beige and pale blue, and in front of the window was a dark red leather chesterfield on which he was invited to sit. The priest brought a tray complete with a small flower-patterned coffee pot, two matching cups and saucers and a plate of biscuits, and set it down on the small table in front of Albert before seating himself in the adjacent armchair.

"I don't believe I've ever seen you here before. Are you new to the area?"

"No. I've never been here. Or, in fact, inside a Catholic church before."

"Can I ask you why? You seem to be so lost." He picked up the coffee pot, ready to pour. "Strong? I mean, do you like milk?"

"Thank you. Two sugars, please."

Albert took the proffered cup and sipped from it. The hot liquid ran down his throat and he felt the warmth beginning to circulate around his bloodstream.

"You have a slight accent. Were you born here?"

"No. I'm from Switzerland, originally. I arrived in about 1946." The lie, spoken so many times over the years, slipped out easily. "After the war. My father died when I was very young. We had relatives here. They helped, of course."

"And you live near here?"

"No. I'm sorry, Father. I don't wish to talk. I can't. I have to go now." He placed the cup back on the tray and rose from his seat.

"I understand," he said. "You seem troubled and I'd like to help. It will save me finishing the clearing up I started." He grinned and Albert felt the rush of trust with this priest he had never met before and who seemed so young and inexperienced in comparison to what he had encountered in Germany at the same age when the whole world had changed. "I'm here if you want to visit again. At any time."

That was his first contact with the man with whom he had since built up some sort of relationship. Now, so many months later, Albert had taken to having long and meaningful chats with the priest, aptly called Christopher Goodheart, on matters concerning life and death, punishment and retribution, heaven and hell. Albert was desperate to fathom what would await him, frantic almost in his quest for information, as time was running away from him. Suddenly a way forward presented itself. "Father, would you hear my confession?"

"But you're not a Catholic."

"No. I'm not anything." He observed the younger man, not

51

taking his eyes away, willing him to feel his distress and hoping he would believe he was telling the truth.

"So why now, my son?"

"I have to get so much off my chest. I need to speak to you, to God, your God, and you're the nearest I can think of. I have not been good in my life, I have done such terrible things, so many dreadful things. My heart is heavy and I can't live with my thoughts anymore. Please, I beg you. Hear me, Father, because without you, I am truly lost."

"I knew you had something to tell me when we first met. However, before I can do that, I need to be sure you are truly repentant for your sins, and you intend to make amends. Then I can obtain from God through absolution that your sins can be forgiven and that you are reconciled with the Church you have wounded by sinning. Is this something you are ready to do? Can you accept me as your priest and that I am able to forgive your sins, and do you accept God as your one and only God who has entrusted our Church to fulfil His word and His word alone?"

"I do, Father. Oh yes… I do." Tears came to Albert's eyes as he stammered the words.

"Then, my son, I will hear your confession."

CHAPTER EIGHT

THE moment Steve woke up and saw his commanding officer perched by the side of his hospital bed was when he knew he had to escape the man's clutches somehow, or at least convince him he was of no further use to the army.

"Ah, so you're awake, Captain. I was wondering if we would ever see the day."

Groaning, Steve attempted to sit up but the tubes attached to various parts of his anatomy prevented him from doing so. He had excruciating pain in his leg beneath the plaster cast, which made every movement agony and sent flames flying up through his nerve ends. Beads of sweat appeared on his forehead.

"Shall I call a doctor?"

He ignored the question posed to him as there was no way he was going to admit to anything but being okay. "Where am I?" His voice came out barely more than a whisper.

"Safe," the general answered, equally as evasive. "As you wish. How are you feeling?"

"Oh, absolutely brilliant. I could easily run a marathon."

"I don't care for sarcasm."

"Well, I don't care to be stuck here," said Steve, his mouth set tight, wincing as a shaft of pain ripped through his leg again.

"Are you sure you don't need a doctor? No? Okay. Well, we had no choice in the matter. The Syrians knew you were out there, our sources told us, and we couldn't allow you to be taken. It wasn't easy to find you, though we did, and thankfully first."

"How long have I been here? No-one's telling me." He

decided it was more beneficial to behave in a more acquiescent fashion towards his commanding officer. It was no good getting the man's back up.

"You've been very ill, Captain. We nearly lost you, and you nearly lost your leg."

"I'd like to go home to my family."

"All in good time."

"What does that mean exactly?" Steve could sense his anger rising, which was going to do him absolutely no good whatsoever. "I would like to speak to my wife please, sir."

"Yes, your wife. A remarkable lady. Very persistent."

"She knows I'm alive?"

"On that point I'm not exactly sure. She's been phoning rather a lot recently to get information on your whereabouts for some reason, even though you're dead."

The word 'dead' felt so final when said aloud. So what did Cydney know?

"Sorry, I don't understand. You've spoken to her? When?"

"No, not personally. She has called HQ several times and we very calmly and politely explained the situation to her, again, that you were killed nearly five years ago. I fear she may be slightly off balance. Unwell."

Steve observed the man who now was playing with him and his emotions. The general sat back in his chair and crossed his rather long legs, smoothing his hand down his trouser leg to ensure the crease in his uniform was centred. Such attention to detail irked him, along with the habit his superior had of pulling at his left earlobe every so often.

"Christ almighty! What on earth are you doing? Is this some sort of game you like to play with people's lives? I have a wife and two children. They need me! I need them!"

"Please, calm down, Captain. You'll pull your stitches, and they're healing quite nicely, I'm told. You knew the score when we kept you in the field a year ago and, I have to say, your work

54

has been invaluable to us, also to the Americans and Israelis. It earned us a lot of respect from them, and quite a bit of kudos, and the powers that be are very grateful for everything you did."

"I'm sure. And your point is?" The realisation hit him that the general had a completely different agenda and was never going to let him go.

"I am simply stating the facts. You will need to remain here a bit longer whilst recovering. I would say another couple of months at least before you can be up and about properly. I suggest you try and keep yourself occupied during this recuperation time, and now you're fully *compus mentus* you can write your report of the last few months. If you're not up to writing, we'll get one of the secretaries in to take your dictation."

"And after that? What then?"

"Well, we shall review the situation and see how your recovery goes. I don't want to lose you again. I think you can be of further use to us."

At last – now the truth was coming out.

"I don't believe I'm up to this anymore, sir. You've had the best of me and I need to get back to England." He felt like a tiger straining at the leash to return.

"There is more than one way to skin a cat, Captain. Maybe the field job is not quite the way forward. There are other ways you can help." He rose from the chair and patted Steve on the arm in what was presumably supposed to be a fatherly manner, but which felt rather patronising. "Let's not make any decision now. I suggest we both think about this and I'll come and visit you again. Remember, for all intents and purposes, you are dead. How would your family react to your standing on the doorstep, shouting out, 'I'm home'? I can't see how that would work in reality."

Steve realised how right his CO was in his assumptions and this put immediate doubt into his mind. Cydney was a strong woman but would she and the kids ever forgive him? Five years was a bloody long time in anyone's book, especially for young children. It would certainly take something for them to be able to take him back into their lives again, without feelings of anger and resentment. How would they all cope? And how would he cope with his integration into their lives? From all sides it seemed so wrong. Christ, what a mess.

"Let's concentrate now on getting you better before we discuss your next assignment."

"I don't want another bloody assignment." Steve was struggling to keep the tone of his voice on an even keel. He took a breath. "Am I no longer missing in action?"

"You never were, Captain. MIA that is. You were *killed* in action, if you recall."

"There is a protocol here which you seem to be forgetting. You have a moral obligation to report my being alive to my wife. You can't hide me forever."

"It's not forever, as you put it. I think you can be of more service to the British Government if you are assumed dead, to help your country. Do you realise how much time and effort has been put into getting you here? Not to mention the high level medical intervention you required, and the cost."

"Ah, money! And for how long do you propose I remain 'dead'? If I agree to do one more assignment, will I be returned home?"

The general ignored the two questions totally. "I'll be back. Oh, one thing I forgot. You've been awarded the Military Cross for gallantry above and beyond, etcetera."

"What? You've got to be kidding. So am I supposed to turn up at the palace now?"

"No. We're taking you to receive it somewhere else. Try and rest now." The CO turned his back, marched towards the door and left without another word.

"And I didn't ask for that, either," he said, his voice a mumble, more to himself, as the man was out of earshot already.

The fact was, he knew he was never going to be released. The army had him exactly where they wanted him, not that he could move anyway, especially now. Nobody would be given the MC if they were going home. It was tantamount to a promotion and the CO knew exactly what he was going to be doing next. Detaining him in such a secure environment, wherever it was, it was impossible to escape. Even if he could, where would he go? Who would be there to help him? Where the fuck was Sean when he needed him?

He recalled a helicopter picking him up and being vaguely aware of his surroundings, although he didn't let on but kept his counsel, to his advantage. When he landed, he was taken by ambulance. The journey took a couple of hours at least, during which time he listened out for recognisable sounds and monitored the shift in the sun through the gaps in the doors, the distance calculated by counting in his head as he tried to put a virtual map together, things learnt as part of his professional training. When the ambulance finally stopped, a gurney was brought to meet him and he was moved into a lift and went down many floors, though how many he couldn't tell. None of the staff accompanying him spoke in English. He could understand more or less and he gauged he was not in a simple installation as he was wheeled directly into theatre. The next thing he knew he was waking up in a windowless room with the door locked, where he now found himself.

He had to think outside the box. He would give his CO the impression he was going along with his game, for now anyway, and take the opportunity to get himself up to maximum strength. He had no choice but to wait until he was given his next assignment. His objective would be to try and contact Sean, as he could think of no-one else who could help him out of his situation. Even if he could get away, Israel was the most difficult place to escape from; the country was always on critical level and they would be watching out for him. Simply said, he was a displaced person. Dead to the world.

CHAPTER NINE

HAROLD and Alfie were once again shown into the board-room and this time Cydney, Richard and Tom were waiting for them.

"Please come in and take a seat. What can I offer you - tea, coffee?"

"A nice cup of tea would be wonderful, thank you," Harold said.

"Coffee for me, please. I need to be alert."

"You'll be awake all night, more like it."

"Coffee, please," Alfie insisted, glaring at his friend.

Cydney recognised again the easy and rather amusing exchange between the two elderly men. "Let me introduce Richard Barrett to you, who's my head of forensics here, and his assistant, Tom Patterson. I hope you don't mind them joining us. They'll be working on your case with me."

"That's fine. Pleasure to meet you both." Harold reached into his inside jacket pocket and pulled out an envelope. "I thought you might like to see this. We had nothing when we arrived in England apart from a few photos. This is one of my parents and sisters." He passed Cydney an aged black and white photograph, the corners of which were slightly bent and torn. "I always carry it with me, so please excuse the state it's in. It dates back to 1938. I was only eleven at the time so it was a few years before we were sent away from our home."

As if on cue, the image of Sybill Frankelman appeared before Cydney.

"Ach, so he still has it. We were so happy in our lives. More importantly, we were all together. Soon everything would get so much worse."

"What a beautiful family picture, Harold. It's lovely you still have this. I've recently been doing some research into Germany during the war. I admit with some shame I didn't know too much about what went on, apart from the normal history we all learnt. I've now spent some time reading up on it in quite some detail."

"Thank you," he uttered, his eyes beginning to tear. "You mentioned before that we may have received the bearer bonds because they could be connected to our past."

"That's right. I apologise if it's bringing back horrible memories."

"You aren't the only one," added Alfie. "It was a period most would like to forget, including us."

"Now we have to remember everything again," Harold said. "It's not something we talk about, even to each other. Nobody does. It's enough it's there in our minds."

"I assume you do want to find out about those bonds and who sent them to you? We decided on that, if you recall."

"Yes, of course. That's why we're here. I think it best if you hear everything about us from the beginning. We've decided you need to know the truth from us."

"Oh, my poor son!"

"Don't worry. I'll look after him. Let me hear his story."

"Mr Franks ... Harold, I promise we will do the best we can, for both of you. I appreciate this is going to be difficult, but we're on your side," Richard assured him.

"Okay. Let me take you back to the beginning."

* * *

Berlin 1941

The twenty-ninth day of October 1941 was the last time Hans saw Berlin. It was the date the Nazis gave everyone the orders to leave. He and his family were bundled with urgency and extreme force into one of the many lorries waiting to expel all Jewish people from their city, and together with thousands of others they left their home not knowing where they were headed. The sense of bewilderment for Hans and everyone around him was palpable. There was standing room only as they were taken to the western outskirts of the city to the *S-Bahnhof Grunewald* and the adjacent goods station. On the immediate order to get down from the lorry, they were deposited on the sidings by the loading tracks with everybody else, where they found themselves surrounded by troops with rifles, who were shouting at everyone to be quiet. As if families with young children and the elderly could pose a threat! Hans and his family stood closely together in a circle, protecting their only possessions - one suitcase each. It was starting to get very cold and in the next month it would be freezing and snow would start to fall.

"Why are we here, Papa?" said Gerthe, beginning to shiver. "I don't want to go on a train. It makes me feel sick."

"Don't worry, my darling. You'll be fine. It's an exciting adventure because we don't know where we're going."

"I don't want to go either." Mathilde started to sob, which started her sister crying.

Searching around, Hans saw other platforms running parallel to the one on which they were standing from where the long distance trains left to travel to other cities. Why were they here, where cargo arrived and was loaded up and transported? After several hours of waiting around with no food or water, he found out. The arrival of a train was signalled by lots of whistling by the guards and they soon discovered when the doors were opened that, instead of normal carriages, they were a series of cattle trucks.

"Surely we aren't going to get into those," Hans' mother, Sybill, said.

"I doubt it, darling," her husband replied, trying to keep an overwhelming sense of anxiety from his voice. "That's probably for our cases. They'll be sending another train for all of us here."

"I hope they don't get lost. I have all my valuables in there. Good job I put our names on everything."

"Very wise. Just make sure we keep everyone together, and Hans, don't run off for once. I need you here with us."

Further along the platform there was a commotion. Many people were shouting and there were sounds of the troops yelling orders to everyone to climb into the trucks. The words filtered down to the Frankelmans.

"I'm not getting in there. There must be some mistake. Ask the officer over there, Mordecai. Tell him we have money and want to go on the proper train," Sybill said.

Mordecai turned to speak to the officer but stopped in his tracks as a shot rang out. He watched in horror as one of his neighbours fell to the ground with blood pouring from his head. It was the local pharmacist, someone he had known from his childhood. He pulled his daughters towards him and buried their heads so they couldn't see anything. From the chaos and noise surrounding them previously, the whole platform lapsed into silence.

"Listen to me, everyone." The officer knew he had everyone's attention. "You are all to get into the nearest truck. And in silence, or you will suffer the same fate.

The officer signalled to his troops to start moving people forward, ignoring the dead man on the platform, whose now widow and children were being dragged away from him, their screams of grief echoing around the station.

"Move, all of you. Now!" ordered the soldier nearest to Hans, pushing his shoulder roughly with the side of his rifle. If it wasn't for his father grabbing hold of him he would have fallen and probably have been trampled on.

"We'd better do as they say. Hans, you go first and I'll pass up your sisters, mama and grandparents. Try and get as near to the wall as possible. There doesn't seem to be any seats so it would be best if we can lean against something. Come on, girls. The quicker we get in the quicker we can get to our new home."

"Papa, I'm going to escape. I've got to get out of here." Hans spoke quietly so his sisters wouldn't hear, rubbing his shoulder which was already starting to bruise.

"I'm telling you now, and make sure you listen. We are staying as a family. Is that clear? We will all be fine if we keep together. We were told we would be going to a place with everyone else to work, and that's what we will do."

"Do you really believe that?"

His father ignored the question. "And anyway, where would you go? It's too dangerous. No. I need you to take care of your little sisters. I can't do this on my own. I believe what I've been told. What else would they do with so many of us? When we get to the work place, we'll have another home where we'll all live. Together. It won't be like we had in Charlottenberg. We'll manage until the war ends and then go back to our home."

Gerthe grabbed her brother's hand and stared up at him, her eyes brimming with tears.

"Please don't leave us. Are you really going to go?"

Hans really had no choice, faced with such emotional blackmail, as he saw it, so he did as he was told and jumped up into the truck and helped the women of his family before taking the cases from his father who handed them to him. The last one to join them was his father, followed by almost seventy men, women and children. Each person was crammed tight against the next and was unable to move without knocking their neighbour.

"I can't breathe, Mordecai. You need to pick up the children and hold them or they will have no air," Sybill told him.

"Hans, you take Mathilde and I'll hold Gerthe," his father ordered. He turned to his wife and grabbed hold of her hand. "Don't worry. All will be fine. Just hold on to me."

The trucks stood on the platform for another hour or so with five soldiers standing in front of each one, their rifles at the ready, ensuring nobody got out. A whistle sounded and the troops stepped forward, threw in one bucket for the disposal of human waste, closed the doors and locked them. Thus the nightmare began. The windowless trucks were plunged into complete and utter darkness. Hans had never experienced such silence. Then the yells and screams began. He imagined that, to the soldiers, the people on the train were not worthy of their consideration, were no better than animals, so the sounds of the people incarcerated fell on deaf ears. Many of the women and children were weeping and Hans wanted to join them, but he had to be a man. Feeling to the left, he managed to take hold of his father's hand and squeezed it tightly.

"I know, son. Be brave for your sisters," he said in a whisper.

The train started to move slowly out of the station and the movement caused everyone to lose their balance and fall backwards as one. There was not an inch of space available and most were forced to hold their hands above their heads as they were so penned in.

For days on end Hans stood in the cramped and freezing conditions next to his father, keeping guard over his sisters, who were sat now between their feet. The cold was beyond anything imaginable and every one of his limbs was so numb he had lost all feeling. There was no night, no day, and he couldn't adjust to the utter blackness of everything. The occasional light from slits in the flooring simply created shadows and it was impossible not to feel absolute and intense fear with every fibre of his being. It was the stench that overwhelmed him. With hardly any air except from the small slits, no food or water, and no toilet facilities, he had no idea how he or his family would survive. He already knew the more elderly were dying; the smell was unmistakable. The guards were impervious to anybody's needs. If anyone was sick or needed the toilet, they were forced to do whatever they had to do in the truck, so the floor became awash with vomit, urine and faeces, which added to everyone's humiliation and suffering.

Thoughts of food kept jumping through his mind as the family had soon exhausted the small supply of bread and cheese brought with them. Hans had never experienced hunger or even imagined what it could be like. His house was filled with food, every night was a feast and on the Sabbath and high holy days, theirs was a gathering of close family and friends, where everybody would enjoy the rituals and eat until they were full to bursting. Now, there was an orchestra playing out in Hans' stomach and everybody else's in the truck through lack of food, an unwanted tune for all to hear. He was more worried about his two little sisters, who remained silent for the most part. All he wanted was to protect them, shield them from the horror of their current circumstances, from the death and the smell, but he was incapable and totally useless in his own mind. If only they had listened to the Rabbi. The anger at what he perceived to be his father's indecision engulfed him and left him with a complete and utter sense of helplessness. It was not what he would have done; he would have left, not wait for things to calm down as in his view it was never going to happen, not for a long time.

Throughout the tens of hours, the train travelled slowly on its journey to its unknown destination, seemingly shunted from one railway siding to another. Occasionally it stopped and everyone thought they had reached their destination at last. They waited expectantly for the doors to open but after a few hours, on it would go. These were the bleakest moments for Hans, when all he wanted was to close his eyes and die. People at the front would pound on the doors to be let out, however, there was no point tiring themselves with the effort and eventually even that stopped. The silence was worse. In between times, everyone tried their best to sleep standing up against their fellow passengers but it was hardly possible.

Hans tried desperately to be the man he was expected to be.

Inside he wrestled between wanting to be a boy and the fury he felt towards the Nazis for placing him and his family in this horror, away from the life they loved. He vowed to kill them all once he got out, if he survived.

"My mother isn't breathing! Please do something!" Sybill shouted out in blind panic. "Papa, save her! You're a doctor!"

Hans moved his head in closer to look at his grandparents and tried to make out their shapes in the darkness. They appeared to be asleep but he knew, without asking, without his parents telling him, that they had both passed away, his grandfather probably the day before, as he had heard no sound from him, and now his grandmother was gone. He heard his mama scream out as if she was incapable of taking this in, knowing it was probably the lack of sustenance causing her to act so out of character. This normally elegant and attractive woman, so fashionable and well-dressed, bejewelled and coiffed, so calm and patient, so in control of any situation, the person they all sought for guidance, was now a broken woman standing in human excrement and vomit, and he knew this revised image of her would never disappear for as long as he lived.

"I know, darling," his papa responded. "We will stop soon and we'll be able to bury them and you can sit *shiva*. In the meantime, there's nothing I can do."

"God has deserted us," she whimpered.

To the sounds of her crying, Hans heard one of the men at the other side of the truck chanting the prayer for the dead. The familiar words chanted in Hebrew echoed around the confined space and rose up to surround them until everyone joined in, apart from Hans, with what breath they had left in their bodies. *"Yitgadal v'yitkadash sh'mei raba ..."* He considered the words - May His great name be exalted and sanctified - and was astounded that, despite the circumstances in which they found themselves, people could still praise God.

Sybill's parents were not the only ones. Many of the elderly were dying on the journey from asphyxiation, lack of food, or dehydration but the bodies stood next to those who remained living, unable to be laid down or covered. Hans knew this would continue until the train stopped and he questioned the God he had believed in all his short life, the God whom he had been taught to love and who in return would protect him. How could He allow such things to happen to His people?

On the fourth day, the train came to a halt once again. This time the doors were flung open, to everyone's relief and elation, and fresh air like nectar entered their enforced prison. Hans watched as the guards fell back and covered their faces at the stench that greeted them. He listened to their words of disgust, their calling out, calling them no better than pigs in a sty. That's what he felt. However, what he viewed outside were beautiful fields and forests that went on for miles and miles, slightly sprinkled in white from a recent fall of snow. The irony of it all, again, that God could show this contrast, good against evil.

"Do not get down from the trains. Stay exactly where you are. Pass out your dead. Quickly."

"When can we bury them?" someone shouted out.

"Do as you're told immediately and nobody will get hurt." The words were intended to pacify but they had the opposite effect.

"I don't believe them, Papa."

"Shush, Hans. Don't let your mama hear."

Shouts and hurried orders could be heard up and down the train. Mordecai and Hans carefully passed Sybill's parents to the waiting soldiers. Other people did the same with their relatives. The truck now carried just over half of the people who had started the journey, but at least there was room to sit properly. The guards had thrown in some water and replaced the bucket, nothing else. The look on Sybill's face bore into Hans' very soul. He had never seen her like this. It was as if she was dazed and had disappeared into a world of her own. Worst of all, she was not even crying now at the loss of her parents. Hans felt even more frightened.

Two days later it was exactly the same. The train stopped and more dead were handed out - now they included Mordecai's parents. Hans considered they were probably lucky to have escaped the future that was awaiting everyone. He was too numb to grieve properly and his time was taken up looking after his sisters, who wept silent tears, too scared to do anything else.

Finally, on the eighth day, the train came to a grinding halt and the doors were flung open. Orders were shouted for everyone to get out and stand with their families and their cases. Hans peered around him. Of the seventy starting out on the journey in their truck, more than half were dead. What on earth was the point? He clambered down with his sister and helped his parents, and took Mathilde from his father, who was the last. They were all that remained of his family now. He wished Ari was with him and wondered what had happened to him, whether he was still alive and if so would he ever see him again. A whistle blew and everyone quietened; they knew by now how dangerous it was to disobey orders.

"You have reached your destination. Line up. No talking. Anyone."

"I still don't believe it, Papa," Hans whispered. "They are lying again."

"Let's see, shall we? We need to do as they say for now."

"Mordecai, please stay close to me with the girls. I don't want to lose them," his mother said, her voice quiet and void of emotion after the trauma she'd been through. "Can you ask about our parents?"

"I don't think I should at the moment. I will, once we reach our new home."

They were standing on a station platform but who knew where. Snow was falling around them, slowly descending in frozen particles and settling on their inadequate clothing.

Another freight train had arrived on a platform opposite and Hans watched the people ordered out and told the same thing: to line up with their families. They began to do that but it wasn't quick enough for the guards, who were shoving everyone with their rifles, even the elderly, not waiting for anyone to stand up if they fell over, or caring, dragging them away from the throng to the cries of their families. Nobody had the strength to move, including Hans. The entire situation was bewildering and noisy and so many people together in one place after enduring the worst conditions added to the confusion. It was impossible to know what to do.

Suddenly, a series of shots were fired and everyone stopped in their tracks.

"I ordered everyone to be quiet."

One man had the audacity to shout out, "Where are we, sir?"

"There is to be no speaking." Without giving him a second thought, the officer turned to the man who had spoken out of turn and shot him through the heart. That was enough warning. The platform became instantly quiet. "You are in Lodz in Poland. Do as you are told and you will be taken to your new homes and found work to do."

Hans and his family each picked up their suitcases and got into line with everyone else.

"Move! Now! Quickly!" the orders were shouted, and everyone who was physically able to walk or be carried by their families or friends were herded out of the station, practically at running pace, and taken to the ghetto.

They never found out what happened to the rest of their family or their friends who didn't make it through the journey.

* * *

Present Day
"And you were the only survivors of your families? At fourteen

68

you lost everyone? I can't imagine what you went through. To see your friends and family dying in front of you, and helpless to do anything. It defies belief." Cydney shook her head as thoughts of her own children soared across her mind. Lauren and Jake were the same age, almost, as Harold and Alfie had been, and what an absolute contrast to their young lives. Her kids had known tragedy when they had lost their father, but they had never experienced hunger such as Harold had described, never seen death at close quarters, never been treated like animals and never encountered hatred on such a massive scale. No child or anyone should have to go through what these men had suffered. "How on earth did you cope?"

"We still have nightmares. However, we are thankful to have lived through this. Not so many were as lucky as we were," Alfie said.

"I'm glad you can see it this way. I'm not sure I would be so forgiving, and I've seen some sights in the Police Force," said Richard.

"We never forgive or forget. What's the point of dwelling on the past? What does it possibly achieve?" He smiled sadly.

"Except now it has come up to confront us again," Harold said, and then realised what he had said out loud, almost by mistake, when he saw the warning glance from Alfie.

"So you do think this has something to do with your past?" Richard asked, seizing on his client's words.

"Who knows? I can only surmise."

"Do you have any idea where the money could have come from? Any idea at all? It would help if we had some sort of clue."

"No. We don't. At all," Harold said quickly. "If we did, we would tell you, wouldn't we Alf?"

"Well, yes, of course we would."

Cydney sat and studied them. She had a feeling they knew exactly, but for some reason, whatever it was, they weren't prepared to give anything up.

"Okay, let's adjourn now. Richard and Tom will carry on with their research and we'll try and meet up with you again next week, if possible. If you think of anything at all, please call me."

She noticed how relieved they appeared and recognised the signs that their discomfort revealed; they were clearly hiding some information from her. At this stage she would not pursue it directly with them. There was time, and Sybill was on her side, which would help.

"Thank you," Harold said. "We appreciate your looking into this for us."

"That's okay. Think things through. Let me reiterate. Anything you tell us will go no further than this room. We are on your side."

"Of that, we know," said Alfie as they left the room. "Just give us time."

CHAPTER TEN

CYDNEY felt drained. The meeting had revealed so much more than she had expected to hear and she needed time to assimilate all the information from Richard and what she had learned from Harold and Alfie about their journey. She couldn't ignore the sudden nasty taste in her mouth, which seemed to emerge from nowhere, and she reached for her water. She knew it wasn't going to disappear in a hurry.

"Tom. I think you should go out as soon as possible to Charleston. We need to investigate Whiteman Trust, and its subsidiary, Prime Global, plus the owners. If we're there it will give us a better sense of how they operate. I want to find out who sent these bearer bonds."

"Okay, boss. How much time do I have?"

"As long as it takes. This has come out of the blue. I doubt the two gentlemen have any intention of encashing the bonds. We need to do a bit more research."

"Can I make a suggestion? We have to be a bit clever here," Richard said. "I have a mate at one of the daily newspapers here. He owes me. I think we might be able to get Tom a press card."

"Great idea. That will get him into places. He will need access to the bank itself, though. How do you propose doing that?"

"We would need to set it up first. Jenny could do that. However, I think you should go, too. Harold and Alfie are relying on you, and who better to get to the bottom of this? Also, don't forget, Rupert's footing the bill."

"Well, I'm not sure I can go." Cydney hesitated. "I've got so much on now."

"What exactly is there? We can manage here."

Cydney pondered for a moment through all her commitments. She would need to explain to George she was going away just when things were settling down between them, which wouldn't be easy. The main issue was Steve and the conversation she'd had with Sean. If he was heading off to Israel, she didn't want to be running around on the other side of the ocean. She needed to be within easy contact, and her mind wasn't ready for interviewing bank presidents.

"No, sorry. I can't go. I'll brief Jenny. She can go with Tom."

"This isn't like you. I really think *you* need to take the lead on this one. If you're worried about being out of the office for a week, I'll be here. Sean's around still for the kids and I'm sure Jenny can chip in, too. The States isn't far these days, what with computers and skype."

"Richard, I don't want to go. I can't."

"Why? What's so important? What's going on here?"

"Nothing's going on," she said, weighing up the options. "Okay, I'll go, just to stop your questions. I'll condense it to no more than five days. Right, we have a plan. Tom, you are now our official reporter. I'll brief Jenny on everything else. However, I don't think I should use my real name. Anyone can find out about me and I'm quite well known internationally."

"I've always thought of you as a sort of Demi Moore," Richard said.

"That's very flattering of you."

"You should use your own name. Security is going to be tight getting into the bank and they'll ask for proof of ID, I'm sure."

"On what basis? Why would I be going out there, and with a reporter?"

"Simple. You've been commissioned to do a report, something aimed at comparing US and British systems in small states. Tom is assisting you and taking photographs."

"Can we get things in place in a couple of days, do you think?"

"Don't see why not. Just got to hope someone in Whiteman's likes the idea," Richard replied. "I'll make a few calls now." He stepped towards the office door, but made a passing shot, turning back to Cydney. "By the way, a question came to mind. How does Rupert know our clients? Do you know where or when they met?"

"No. I'll ask, if only to assuage your curiosity."

"Thank you, kind lady." He made a mock bow at her. "It interests me. I've always wondered about him and how he made his money. Oh well, I'll leave you in peace now."

Typical of Richard to leave on that note. It wasn't something she had ever enquired of Rupert outright; she assumed it was from his many corporations and investments. She knew him from her days in the bank when she'd first met Steve. A seed of doubt entered her mind momentarily and passed, and then she returned to the job in hand.

"Tom, you wait here and we'll get Jenny in. You'll need to go out and buy a professional camera and video recorder. You've got to look the part, at least."

* * *

After her team had been briefed, Cydney was finally able to sit back in her chair and take a few moments to gather herself. However, left alone with her thoughts was something she hated; it was her daily intention to keep herself as occupied as possible. Time and again, all she could think about was her mum's death. She was reeling from her loss, which was still uppermost in her mind, although she tried to hide it and immerse herself in work. When her mum was first diagnosed, the consultant had given her only a few months to live and Cydney felt entirely grateful they'd had her with them for an extra eight.

Her thoughts turned to George. He'd been such a support to her since her mum had died. It was a strange relationship, as they were hardly ever in the same country at the same time, but that was the business world they both inhabited, so when they were together they made the most of it.

There was a lot going on around her now, thankfully, what with the investigation for Harold and Alfie, which was the type of work she enjoyed, and also with Sean and what they had discussed. The voices in her head shouted out to her that she was having an affair and being unfaithful to her husband, and what's more, openly in front of Lauren and Jake. It wasn't a label she cared to use but how could she be blamed when she had been told he was dead? Even now, she didn't know the truth, only that he had definitely been alive, or hanging on to life, last year. There were so many questions with no answers and everything plagued her mind.

Perhaps she needed a holiday and should take up Rupert's offer to visit him in South Africa for a few weeks. Maybe that's exactly what she should do, when she returned from West Virginia. The question was whether that should include George. The summer holidays were coming up soon and the kids would love an adventure. Perhaps Richard and Jenny would hold the fort again, as long as she was back well before her sister, Claire's, due date. Claire had told her she was pregnant moments before their mother's funeral, three months ago. The news had shocked her, maybe shaken was the correct description. Her sister was the last person she imagined as the mothering type. Admittedly, Claire had changed somewhat since their mother had been diagnosed with terminal cancer but there was still a part of her that Cydney believed would always remain selfish. Was she being unkind? The thought of her sister with a baby to care for, who would have to come first in her life, was quite an amusing one. Certainly, the shopping trips and spa days would have to be put on hold for many years to come.

As if to invade her thoughts, the phone rang. Ever since the funeral, every little sound made her jump. It was impossible to get out of her head the thud of the earth as it resounded on her mum's so small coffin, so it was with a start that she picked up the receiver, her heart pounding.

"Hi, darling, it's me. How are you doing?"

"Oh hi. I'm fine, George. I was going to ring you."

"To tell me you love me?"

Cydney laughed, despite herself, willing the previous thoughts to disappear from her mind. "You know I do. I don't have to call to tell you that." She felt it was wrong, speaking the words out loud, although she did love him, if it was possible to love two men simultaneously. "No, it's work, I'm afraid. I have to go out to the States. Charleston, in fact. It's part of this case I'm investigating. You remember I told you?"

"The one involving Rupert's friends?"

"Yes. I'm trying to organise it for next week. I hope it won't take more than five days. When are you leaving for Germany?"

"Not for a few days, so we can spend some time together before we both head off. I will miss you, Cyd. Especially that gorgeous tush of yours, and your fabulous breasts. Am I making you blush yet?"

Cydney threw back her head and laughed again, playing subconsciously with the strands of her hair. "Yes you are!"

"And stop playing with your hair. You always do that when I start to talk about your glorious body I can't wait to run my hands over."

"George!"

"Oh, nobody can hear us. And I love it when you start to make those little noises, almost whimpering, just before you…"

"Enough. Now I won't be able to work for the afternoon."

"Okay, I'll see you when you get home. I do love you, Cyd, every little bit of you from the top of your head to the tips of your toes."

"I know you do. See you later. And George?"

"Yes ..."

"I love you, too."

She put the receiver down before he could say any more and make things even more difficult for her. Standing up to collect a file, Ray's voice suddenly came resounding through to her, deep in her reverie.

"Did I startle you?"

"Have you been listening in on my conversation?"

"No."

"Hmmm. Some things are private." She paused for a moment. "I've been thinking about Steve. You left rather abruptly last time. Do you have anything to tell me yet?"

"I've brought someone for you."

"Steve? Oh my God!" Her eyes flitted around the room, searching for her husband.

"No. Not him. That's not why I'm here. I have nothing else on that - I gave you everything last time. And please don't be so disappointed. I hate to see you sad. No, I have Sybill here and her husband, Mordecai. They wanted me to bring them through. You see, what they have to tell you is harrowing and they didn't want you to hear this alone."

"Yes, of course, sorry. It's just ... well, you know," she replied, remembering it wasn't always about her and she had a role to play in helping Harold and Alfie.

Cydney felt the beginnings of a coldness around her. However, this time it seemed to penetrate deep into her bones unlike anything she had ever felt before. This wasn't only Harold's parents coming through; the haunting faces of so many men, women and children, distressed and wailing, calling out, their arms beseeching her, flashed through her. The walls were closing in on her as the room filled. All these people needing her help, unable to move on because there was nobody to aid their transition to another world for them to find peace.

The pain of their suffering pierced her soul and she stumbled back against the wall, grabbing her chair to prevent herself falling. Why her? What could she do that others before her had failed to do? This was too much of a responsibility and she wasn't prepared. With her eyes closed, she begged for the images to disappear but they kept on coming. Now there were thousands of these visions coming and going, people all in a long line, stretching out as far as her mind could see, dressed in various attire, some well turned out in suits and overcoats, others in rags, blue-striped pyjamas, Rabbis with their long beards and black hats, children emaciated without the energy to cry out. She could see fire before her, smoke rising from tall chimneys, ashes blowing across a cold grey sky. Images of naked men, women and children, piled on top of each other, pushed into mass graves. So many sounds of screaming, all melding together.

"I can't … I can't help you all. Ray …?"

"You can do this."

"Who are these people?"

"These are my friends and family and those who were killed in the camps," Sybill said. "They need to be able to move on, as we do; me, Mordecai and our princesses."

"I can't help," she repeated. "It's too much. I'm not capable of this. I wish I could. How can I when there are so many?"

"I want you to realise what went on. I'm sorry for bringing everyone through and for what you have seen. It's important. What you are doing for Hans and Ari, it may well change their lives, but by doing what you are, you will bring solace to all of us. We must have peace."

"I need time. Sybill, you have to give me some time," she begged.

"We didn't have that luxury. This is how it is. We are their voices."

Slowly, the people and images receded and Cydney's heartbeat slowed but she would never forget what she'd seen and knew that was just the start.

CHAPTER ELEVEN

TEN and a half hours after boarding, the American Airlines 747 touched down at Yeager Airport, Charleston, West Virginia. Coming into land, Cydney enjoyed the view of the city centre and the rolling hills three hundred feet above the valleys of the Elk and Kanawha Rivers, as the sun was setting.

"Do you know, the airport's named after Brigadier General Chuck Yeager who flew the world's first supersonic flight?" Tom said.

"Um - that would be a no! Where on earth did you pick up that vital piece of information?"

"And, the local Air National Guard are here, right next to the airport. They've got nine Hercules planes."

"Is that so?"

"Do I sense some sarcasm, boss? I like to learn different stuff about where I'm going. Anyway, Polly's sorted a car to pick us up. The airport's got a bit of a reputation for getting people out sharpish. It's only a short trip into town."

"You're like a guide book."

"Cheers."

Making their way out of the airport in the predicted short time, they easily located the limousine waiting for them and sat back for the seven-mile journey into downtown Charleston. They had reservations in a small boutique hotel located about ten blocks from the State Capitol Complex, home of the state archives and within a short ride of the city centre. As they pulled up outside, Cydney was impressed with the pale brown painted exterior and the beautiful ornamental shrubs in geometric shapes like sculptures, all sitting along the front wall in enormous blue ceramic planters illuminated by antique lights.

The interior of the hotel also didn't disappoint. The spacious entrance exuded charm as they ambled along the dark polished parquet flooring towards the mahogany reception desk. The whole place was inviting, from the pink flecked wallpaper surrounded by gold marbled pillars, to the red velvet guest chairs positioned on sumptuous rugs. Cydney gazed upwards to the white balustrade on the first floor, which opened onto the reception area, and wished she was wearing totally different attire to fit in with the southern American atmosphere.

One of the bellboys accompanied them to their adjoining rooms.

"Shall we meet in the lobby in half an hour? I could do with a beer and something to eat."

"Yes, sure. I only want a small bite and then I'm ready to hit the sack. I can never sleep on planes at the best of times," Cydney said, now yawning at the wonderful thought of climbing into a bed and drifting off to sleep.

"Nor me. Okay. I want to phone the wife first so she knows I'm alive. See you shortly."

Entering her room on the sixth floor, Cydney was captivated by the beautiful swags and tails in heavy floral brocade dressed across the window, which stretched the width of the room. The view beyond was truly amazing and she was itching to explore the town, despite all her misgivings the previous week. However, she and Tom were not here on a jolly, they had work to do. Tomorrow they intended to search the historical archives and check out the bank, and its owners, and in the afternoon they had an 'interview' set up, courtesy of Richard and his friend at The Times, with the President and Chief Executive Officer of Whiteman Trust, a certain Mr Jackson Dwyer III. How he had managed to swing that one was anyone's guess. The pretext was they were comparing banking laws between the different states, and would be writing a special piece on the varying rules and how they weighed against the UK. It was important Tom played his part as a photographer and got to snoop around and talk to a few people whilst she was engaged with the president. Sounded so easy on the surface, of course.

Cydney turned away from the view and plonked herself down heavily on the queen-sized bed, testing its comfort. Out of the corner of her eye she caught a flashing red button on the phone indicating she had a message. Perhaps it was the children checking she had arrived safely, or Sean with some news. She was eagerly awaiting the outcome of his meeting with his army guys about getting back into Israel. Lifting the receiver and pressing the required button, she listened to the message spoken in a wonderfully clipped drawl.

"Hi, Mrs Granger. This is Isabella Grant from Mr Dwyer's office. I'm phoning to confirm your appointment tomorrow on Capitol Street. Mr Dwyer is very much looking forward to meeting y'all and he has no problem with having his photo taken for your newspaper in England." If only they knew, she thought. "See you at two-thirty. Mr Dwyer does love people to be punctual."

Does he indeed? Well, this was one meeting she was looking forward to, so being late was never going to be an issue. It could prove very informative and there was no way she was going to compromise the situation.

* * *

It was about a half hour walk to the State Capitol Centre and, specifically, the Division of Culture and History, where the archives and records for the mountain state were held. Walking along the tree-lined route of Capitol Street with the quite unique turquoise streetlights, which made the whole area visually picturesque and reminiscent of 1960s charm, Cydney and Tom passed various small eateries displaying colourful canopies, which protected the morning diners from the sun that was already beating down, and a rather inviting bookshop she promised herself she would visit during her trip. The smell of freshly brewed coffee, baked bread and sweet cinnamon wafted across the street. The day was just beginning, and entering into the main Kanawha Boulevard the noise became louder from the sound of cars hooting impatiently in their bid to get their occupants to work on time. Everywhere was the normal bustling of people; no different to London but on a smaller scale.

The need to discover information for Harold and Alfie preyed on her mind, which made her anxious to reach their destination and begin their search for whatever they could find. The building they required was adjacent to the State Capitol, dubbed as West Virginia's most recognisable and notable edifice, standing tall and fronting the Kanawha River. It was made of buff limestone and capped with a majestic dome almost three hundred feet in height, showing strong Greek and Roman architectural influences with both east and west wings.

"I'd like to go in there, Tom, if we have a chance."

"Did you know the dome has a Czech crystal chandelier weighing almost two tons? It's almost two hundred feet off the floor, and it's lowered whenever they get a new governor, to give it a clean."

"Funnily enough, no, I didn't. You've been reading a lot of tourist guidebooks, I think."

"Yep, boss. One of my hobbies. History, architecture ..."

"You're a surprise to me every day."

As they entered the building, the silence was heavy.

"Blimey, have you seen the rules here? We have to sign in, request any file we want to view, and there's a long list of stuff we can't take in."

"I hope that includes your chewing gum," Cydney said.

"Matter of fact, it does. Not sure I can manage without it, though."

"Well I can!" She joined in with his laughter. "Let's get a locker and put all your photographic equipment, my bag and our phones in there. Can you get directions for the files we want?"

"All seems a bit daft to me, but right you are."

Three hours later they were still sifting their way wearily and painstakingly through the records and collating information on the background of the original bank, Prime Global, which basically confirmed all Richard had discovered. Now it was in black and white in front of them. They had gone through microfiche and newspaper records that stretched back to the middle of the last century.

"Philip Ross, followed by his son, Jolyon, and his grandson, Edward, were quite the entrepreneurs, growing the bank steadily over the years it seems. This reflected the growth of the West Virginia coalfields and they increased its assets, surviving the Depression. Edward definitely saw the war as an advantage," Cydney said.

"Obviously it says nothing about their possible nefarious activities."

"No. I did read it had branches in Europe but they were closed in the early 1950s."

"Ah, after the war. So there was no need to have a presence there? They got out everything they could beforehand."

"Maybe you're right. That's the detective in you speaking. However, I tend to agree. So the question is, were they guilty of misappropriating monies through Switzerland?"

"How would we find out? And if we did, how could we prove it?"

"Don't forget, also, there's a big chance the Ross family were connected to Germany via Elise, as Richard told us. We should try and put together some sort of family tree. Can you go through those files again?"

"Okay, boss. Probably need to go back to early 1800s and see when this Elise's family came to the States. I'll give Rich a buzz when we've finished here. Get him to find records for Prime in Europe. What they were up to, how they operated, who ran them. We might get some answers. What else does it say about the brothers?"

Cydney continued reading from the old files. "There was another economic crisis in the mid-1950s, which again the bank managed to survive. They seem to be quite good at that," she noted as an aside. "I think we need to look at the online records also. Everything about births, marriages and deaths can be accessed via the Division of Culture and History records."

"Okay. We can use the computers over in the corner there."

"The bad news ... I've discovered we can't access the 1940 census until 2012."

"We'll have to come back in seven years then."

"Smart remark," Cydney said. "There must be something else though. Theodore Whiteman is the governor so there's going to be tons of family information about him."

Another exhausting and painstaking hour later, Cydney finally found some relevant facts. "Well, look here, the first mention of the family name. Edward and his wife Prudence had a daughter, Carolynn, who went on to marry Albert Whiteman in 1947. He's the one who eventually took over the bank and changed its name from Prime, relocating its offices from Richmond to Charleston. Albert was quite a bit older than his wife, it appears, but they went on to have Philip, who died quite young, and Theodore, now governor."

"And what's this Albert's story?"

At the mention of the man's name, Cydney felt as if a streak of pure ice had been shot through her body. It put her totally off kilter and as she attempted to shake it off, the sound of shrieks and cries surrounded her.

"Are you okay? You've gone a bit pale," Tom said, glancing across at her.

"I'm fine. Just felt a bit cold. Must be the air conditioning. What did you say?"

"I asked about Albert. You're shivering. You sure you're alright?"

The same feeling returned and the image of a distressed Sybill appeared. The woman moved behind her and peered over Cydney's shoulder at that name written before her. No words were uttered, there was only silence, which was unusual in itself. "Sorry, no. Oh … what, Tom? I've no idea." She tried to concentrate on Tom and what he was asking, whilst acknowledging the presence of Sybill and the sense of extreme rage and hatred that was emanating from her, which she felt with every fibre of her being. "For now I can't find anything about him at all, which is quite strange."

"Just the name written in front of me makes me feel sick."

"What do you mean? What has this man got to do with Harold and Alfie?"

"Everything. He is the devil incarnate. What he did - it defies God and everything we hold dear."

"Please tell me."

"He threatened Hans and his friend. He got away with the murder of so many innocent people. He was responsible for putting them to death, for leading them to the gas chamber, for killing my friends, all my family, my … my beautiful daughters." The grief and absolute wretchedness radiating from this poor woman made Cydney's senses reel.

"Are you sure you're okay?" Tom asked again. "You look as if you're going to pass out. Shall I get you some water?"

"Yes. Please. Would you mind? I think it must be the jetlag. It always affects me."

"I'll try and find some downstairs. Be as quick as I can." Cydney hardly noticed he had left her.

"Sybill, this pain … this agony … I don't know how you bear it."

"You cannot imagine. I have held this in my heart for so long. The man - ach, he was no man, not of this earth. No-one could be like that, and yet he still lives whilst almost every one of mine was murdered in the most awful way. Listen to me, and do not forget what I tell you. His name is not Albert Whiteman. It is Adolf Weissmuller. A name I detest. A name I can hardly bear to utter. A name that conjures up death and destruction. That's what you need to look for. He escaped from Germany. You have to get retribution for all he did. Please, I beg of you …"

"Here you are, drink some of this. We aren't allowed drinks here but I managed to persuade the old dear on the desk."

"Thanks. Yes, that feels so much better." She felt the water flowing down and revitalising her energy and watched as the image of Sybill faded from her side. "Shall we get back to work?"

"Yeah, if you're sure you're alright. Anyway, I've found this article in the Charleston Gazette. A local rag. You remember what Richard told us? That Prime kept a few outposts in the smaller counties under different guises for the farmers and miners, to protect them from the bigger boys?"

"More like to have the monopoly and charge whatever they wanted."

"That's what it's all about, isn't it?" Tom said. "Anyway, have a look at these." He slid a huge file across the desk and pointed to two articles on the same page.

Cydney read through them but her eyes were drawn to a photograph of the chairman standing outside one of these small branches, and shaking hands with one of the locals. "Albert Whiteman?" She could barely speak his name now, knowing what she did.

"No, it's not him. Says it's some guy called Liam Ross. Probably another relative. I can't find a picture of Albert anywhere and I've searched through years of stuff. My bloody eyes are hurting with the strain."

"Wonder why that is? The chairman of the state's largest bank with no presence anywhere. Doesn't sit right with me. What about his son? Ted, isn't it?" Cydney asked.

"Yep. Theodore Gerald Whiteman. He's in his second term as a Republican Governor. Married to Alice with two kids."

"So he obviously didn't want to go into the family business."

"He was an attorney in the DA's office for a few years, it says here."

"So he had huge ambitions it would seem, or his father did for him."

"And look, here's another article from a few months back, saying he's about to run in the primaries."

"With what objective? To run for president? Of the United States?"

"That's what it says."

"I'd like to know much more about this Albert Whiteman. He seems to have appeared out of nowhere, married the boss's daughter, and by all accounts his son is one of the wealthiest in the state." She was loath to mention the name she now knew him as, and would have to introduce this into their findings at a later date, but with Richard.

"Yeah, I've checked through everything. All I found was the marriage record, and the birth certificates of his two boys. It does say against his nationality, 'Swiss' and he was naturalised in 1949."

"What's his name on the original papers?"

"It says here, Dieter Scholler. Born 1914 in Zurich."

Cydney knew this was wrong and it was entirely possible he had stolen someone else's identity before arriving in the U.S. How had he managed that?

"I'll mention it when I call Rich. But Swiss? Does that sound a bit odd to you? Here we are investigating stolen German monies and then this guy appears from nowhere from a neutral country right after the war. Sounds a bit fishy to me. I think we need to check him out, and his background."

"I agree. I'll speak to Richard though, if that's okay. He can check out records in Germany and Switzerland. What I don't understand is that the bonds Harold and Alfie received were blatantly from Prime - no disguise, nothing at all - and it must have come from one of their old branches, not Whiteman's. So whoever sent the money must be known to the bank and also have quite a bit of ready cash available."

"And want to hide the fact, which would fit this Albert Whiteman down to a tee," Tom surmised. "He has easy access to do what he wants, as chairman, and obviously has the funds, but what's he got to hide?"

"Well, that's something we need to find out. If he is behind this, whatever he's trying to hide is going to come out. This seems far too easy."

"Do you think he wants Harold and Alfie to know he's involved?"

"I'm not sure. My instinct says yes. They did seem very nervous when we met them both times in the office. I don't think they're telling us everything."

"Let's grab some lunch and head off. I'm itching to meet this Dwyer guy."

"You're all about your stomach, Tom. I'm surprised you don't weigh ten stone more."

"Someone's got to keep their strength up."

Cydney laughed and looked him over, noticing that he didn't have an ounce of fat on him. "Okay, let's go eat. I'm hoping we're going to learn much more today. We have to play it cool - be the nice interviewer and her helpful photographer."

"I am *quate* the consummate actor, you know," Tom quipped in the poshest voice she'd ever heard slip from his lips.

"Please try not to speak like that, though. It's enough trying to get rid of your cockney accent."

CHAPTER TWELVE

P ACING his room was becoming so much easier now the plaster cast had been removed from his leg. However, it hurt like hell. He had to do any additional exercise in secret, pretending he was barely able to put weight down. The daily visits from the physiotherapist were helping considerably and, despite the fact he was told to rest up afterwards, he put in the extra hours. Steve could feel his body getting stronger but he was constantly worried about his leg, which he was unsure was ever going to be right as the pain was incessant. It would certainly hinder any action he wanted to take. He couldn't ask for higher dosage painkillers in case the doctors or nurses became suspicious, though he had managed to store up extra supplies when the pain had been manageable, to be used as and when. He currently had quite a large stockpile that was secreted in a plastic bag inside a place where no-one would wish to go.

Getting himself up to full strength in order to get out of this facility occupied Steve's mind constantly, although he couldn't work out how it was going to be possible. He was contained in one windowless room, with a separate bathroom. The whole place was guarded like the Crown Jewels and his door was unlocked and locked again every time someone entered and left. No sounds permeated the walls from outside, so he was obviously still in the underground hospital facility. They really did want him kept a secret.

He had started to get friendly with one of the nurses, an American who was very talkative, unlike the others who entered his room and did what they had to do in silence - take his temperature, check his blood pressure - and then left. However, this particular nurse, Charlie, took the time to chat to him, maybe not obeying her orders. All his questions were thought out in advance to try and get her to reveal some clue as to his whereabouts. So far, nothing, but with a little patience and a bit of his old English charm, there was a possibility she might reveal a snippet.

Every day his thoughts were running riot. The question that puzzled him the most was why on earth they wanted *him* so badly. What could he offer? He had a gammy leg, was now in his forties and had no thirst for the game his CO and others wanted to play. There was something somebody wasn't telling him, for sure. The general had a plan for him in mind. For now he would bide his time. It wasn't as if he had a choice in the matter.

His dreams were filled with Cydney and the twins, now teenagers. He had missed their coming out of childhood with such regret. And what about his wife? What was she doing now? Perhaps she had remarried. Thinking he was dead she certainly had every right, although if that was the case she wouldn't be calling up HQ repeatedly, making herself a nuisance. He knew his wife and when she was onto something she was never going to let it go, no matter what obstacles were thrown at her. No, she was definitely not with someone else, he knew that now. Would Claire still be giving her a hard time, her selfish younger sister? Cydney did so much for her and their mum - was she still alive or had she gone to join their dad? And then there was Sean. Had he and Cydney discussed him? Were they working together to try and find him and get him back? If he ever did get back, the twins would never forgive him, although perhaps his sweet Lauren would, as she was always a daddy's girl. Jake must be so tall now, at almost fifteen. Steve recalled his own growth spurt at that age. What were their interests? His little girl was always very arty but so bright, whereas his son was constantly playing on the piano and drumming his fingers to some tune in his head that used to get on everybody's nerves. Now he would do anything to hear that constant beat.

All those years missed. So much to catch up on, if that was ever going to happen. Such dangerous thoughts, in a way, as the battle within him to find a way out could lead to him making a serious mistake. What were the chances of escape? He pondered the question and realised the impossibility. It was obvious General Bowles-Smith needed him for some operation, and to go through all this to save one man, well, they had serious plans for him. He had to work out why and what, and do something about it. Play them at their own game.

* * *

"I'm not sure, Cono. You really think we can pull this off? And where is the captain, exactly? We don't even know."

Sean searched the faces of the guys from his old unit, who were sitting around the scratched and beer-stained table in The Cock and Hoop in Tooting, South London, trying to look as normal as possible. Mo had already agreed to be on side, he knew that much, but what about the others? All were now retired from the army and had retained their unique tags and that's how they addressed each other. Working as a tight-knit team for so long and especially if in a hostile situation, it was important to identify one another instantaneously and also to maintain anonymity. There had to be no mistakes in radio communications or when shouting out orders as it could cost them their lives. It was all part of team building, adhesion, and obviously added to the banter. He was pleased everyone appeared fit and healthy, and moreover in good shape and had certainly not let themselves run to fat. Although a little older, it was what Sean required of them.

Their voices remained low. Every so often they laughed, as if someone had told a joke. Beneath their pretence, however, their conversation was focused.

"You know something? I agree with you, Sparks, but in the pit of my stomach I believe he's still in Israel, held somewhere. What we need to do is work out where."

"Oh, well, in that case, no problem," Dixie said sarcastically. "Israel may be a small country and if the powers that be want someone hidden, they have enough secret facilities and underground bases to do that. Where would you start?"

"I thought of that," Sean said. "He was lifted, probably not far from where I was in the Golan Heights. At the Mount Avital Base. I doubt he was taken back there as that would've been too obvious and they would've wanted to keep him secure."

"Unless he's dead and we're all wasting our time."

"Thanks, Baz, for stating the obvious. I'm trying to stay positive so help me out here. The other way round and Captain Granger would be sitting here trying to work out where you were." Baz was suitably chastised as Sean continued. "Anyway. Let's try and think. The captain would not have been in a good state. Probably dehydrated. Definitely exhausted. We have no idea, either, of any injuries he may have sustained."

"He was definitely hit by that grenade in Damascus," Mo recalled. "That may have done some lasting damage."

"True. So that means he may not be fit to be brought out on foot."

"This is going to be a major operation." Davo stared at his mates and shook his head. "Can we manage this, the six of us?"

"I have no idea. But we're damned well going to try. So, where do you think he could be? Let's go through some of the bases."

"There would need to be a hospital there," Mo continued. "Good recovery facilities for war wounded."

"Secure. Intelligence based," Baz pointed out. "He was working for the Special Forces in the field for a few years so they would need to debrief him. We need somewhere allied with the British army."

"Good. Keep going, lads."

"Mossad?"

"No. They're not part of the army and in any case no-one would know where they were, anyway," Sean pointed out.

"Near an airfield? His debrief would involve the CO, so he would need to get in and out fairly quickly and un-noticed."

"What about the Americans? Do you think they might have any involvement?" Baz asked.

"I can't rule anyone out. I think it's just us at the moment, although I'm sure information is shared if required. However, we only share if it's in our best interests."

"British government?"

"Has to be, doesn't it?" Mo said. "But why are they keeping him?"

"I reckon they want to use him again. I told you that when we met up. He's 'dead' so nobody would expect him to be anywhere."

"What if he really is dead?" Davo said, silent until then. "I'm not sure about this at all. I don't want to put myself in a dangerous position any more. I have my wife and kids to think about, and a job. I can't just up sticks and go off on a wild goose chase."

"Look, if this isn't for you, I understand. I'm asking for volunteers. This is not an order."

Davo stood up to go. "I'm sorry. I can't do this. Not to Emma. I'll support you and I won't speak a word of this, but I can't." The others watched as he nodded his goodbye and walked out.

"Anyone else want to go? Mo? Sparks? Dixie? Baz? Are you with me or not?"

"You know I am," Mo said. "We've spoken - we're all in."

"Great, so let's carry on. Have we eliminated any sites apart from Mount Avital?"

"What about in other parts of Northern Israel? There's that

unit by the airfield. I thought that was where they disseminate intelligence."

"Yep, that's certainly a possible."

"I would have thought underground would be better. Little chance of getting out, but nobody could get in either," added Sparks, "which doesn't help us."

"There are so many bases. Where would you start?"

"Imagine a map of the area. Avital is situated in the north and I told you where the reconnaissance point is, where I was supposed to meet with the captain."

"The area is treacherous, as we know," Mo reminded everyone. "Let's assume he's in really bad shape."

"The nearest hospital would be there," Dixie replied. "Maybe too obvious?"

"Let's think south."

"Where's the best army hospital?"

"Tel Aviv, for sure," said Sean.

"Hold on a minute. What about the central one near that shopping centre they built around it? What's it called?"

"Azrielli. Oh yes." Sean felt a flutter of excitement in his gut. "Why didn't I think of that? It has a hospital facility and military security is there - logistics and intelligence."

"Okay, Cono, so if he is detained there, how the bloody hell are we supposed to get him out with such tight security?"

"Thanks, Dixie, for that. Helpful."

"Also, isn't that an underground installation?"

"Yes, which makes our life so much more difficult. Tel Aviv has all the amenities. It's by the coast, so we could get him out via Jordan. Near an airfield, if we need it, but I doubt that's the best solution."

"And there's the train station from the shopping centre to anywhere in Israel."

"If we could get him to Jerusalem and out through the West Bank ..."

"No, guys. It has to be via boat. All we have to do now is try and find out if he's there."

"How do we do that?" Sparks asked.

"Well, we go there and …"

"Knock at the door. Can we come in? Can we have our captain back, please?"

"No, Sparks. I think I should go there, and Mo too, first, on separate flights. You and Baz go to Jordan and establish the get-out route. Be ready to come into Israel. Dixie, you fly into Jerusalem. We'll investigate in Tel Aviv and see what we can find out."

"What will we need?"

"Everything. I've set up an account for this. I've got someone sorting out equipment for us and I'll arrange for you to have cash. Be ready to move immediately on my command and remember - nobody is to know about this. And I mean no-one at all. Is that clear, guys?"

Out of the corner of Sean's eye he sensed a movement, a slight something out of the ordinary that didn't resonate properly with him, almost imperceptible but, to him, always on the alert, it was wrong. Something was burning into his back. It was a sixth sense which had got him out of trouble many times. Now the warmth centralised and it was as if he were a target, though not like there was a rifle trained on him. This was quite different. His impulse was to turn around. Instead he nodded at Mo and raised his eyebrows, indicating there was a problem to the back of the pub, and carried on talking as if nothing had changed. Acknowledging this, Mo rose and sauntered to the men's toilets, his eyes taking in everybody and everything around him. He was not a man to be lost in a crowd due to his size and the colour of his hair and he also felt eyes on him as he pushed open the door to the men's. He missed nothing and saw exactly what Sean had felt.

Returning to the table with a few more pints, which he sloshed carelessly on the table, some of the beer spilling onto Sean's lap, he gave an almost imperceptible acknowledgment to his sergeant.

"Watch it, you drunken idjit. Christ almighty, man."

"Want to do something about it?" Mo stood over him, his giant of a frame menacing.

"Come on lads," the landlord shouted over. "Call it a night. I don't want no trouble in 'ere."

"Yeah, let's go. I've had enough to drink anyway." Sean stood up. "It's late. Drink up, Mo. You can take me on another time."

They all piled out, hanging on to each other, Sparks starting to sing, 'We are the Champions' at the top of his voice. Once outside, they dropped the pretence.

"Someone's on to us, for sure. That means we have to be even more careful how we go about this."

* * *

Inside the pub, a young man and his girlfriend finished their drinks and placed their glasses on the table, stood up, signalled goodbye to the landlord and strode out the door, all the while talking animatedly to each other, stopping for a quick kiss, as lovers do. The scene they had witnessed had been most interesting and they were impatient to report back to their CO. The man had been ordered to keep an eye on the Irishman and had been doing just that for the last month. He reckoned the sergeant had no idea he'd been followed, and why would he? He was rather enjoying this assignment; the girl with him was another officer in his unit, a rather attractive decoy, if the truth be told.

CHAPTER THIRTEEN

"DO come in please, Mrs Granger."

The man stood from behind his desk, which encircled the floor to ceiling windows behind him, giving a spectacular view from ten storeys up over the Kanawha River. The building in which the bank was situated was modern and glass-fronted, constructed about nineteen years ago, and dwarfed by the much higher, but older, Chase Tower sitting adjacent.

"And this must be Mr Patterson. Have a seat. Can I get you anything? Some coffee? Maybe an iced mint tea? That's our speciality here. Very cooling on such a hot day as this."

"That would be great. Thank you so much. And thank you for agreeing to see us. It's most appreciated."

"Well, little lady, that's my absolute pleasure." He smiled condescendingly at Cydney. She tried so hard not to baulk at his words and returned his smile as he moved back behind his desk. She studied him, wondering at his derisive behaviour. The slightly pretentious name said it all; Jackson Dwyer III. The man she had visualised beforehand, as president, was in his sixties, thinning hair and a little overweight with a slightly red bulbous nose, indicating high blood pressure. Her pre-conceived thoughts could not have been more wrong. The man before her was relatively young, probably in his mid-forties, dressed extremely well in a grey bespoke suit, a matching grey tie with pink stripes and a crisp white shirt. At well over six feet, he was undeniably fit, judging by his trim physique. Centred in the hefty gold wedding ring on his left hand was a rather large and ostentatious princess cut diamond, which Elizabeth Taylor would have been proud to wear, and peeking out from his shirt cuffs was a gold Rolex. The man had money, evidently, and liked to spend it.

Searching around the spectacularly designed office, she was impressed to spot various certificates lining one side of the wall, including one from the Harvard Business School where he graduated *Summa Cum Laude*, naturally. On the wall behind was a grand oil painting, slightly out of character with the rest of the room as its thick gold-leaf frame surrounded a picture of a rather distinguished looking gentleman in a dark dress suit and tall hat, reminiscent of a previous age, his large white moustache curled at the edges. The fact his eyes seemed to be following her caused the hairs on the back of her neck to prickle and a cold feeling flew through her. She shivered.

"I understand from my secretary you're doing a little piece on our bank for a good old English newspaper. That's not normally your type of work."

Cydney attempted to hide her surprise at his statement but why wouldn't he have checked up on her?

"Yes, true. My normal work is in the corporate field. Sometimes I receive different assignments, mainly because of my background with one of the London city banks. I'm sure you know all of this." Dwyer's expression remained in place. "This is for one of the Sunday supplements, though we may syndicate it. We're meeting with various corporations whilst here."

"Starting with us."

"Then going north, Mr Dwyer."

"So, how can I help you?"

Cydney glanced across at Tom, who was setting up his camera and video on a tripod, and he winked over at her. Behind Dwyer, in the distance, a colourful steamboat was making its way along the Kanawha, its huge paddlewheels churning the water, leaving its spray behind. She could just about make out the name emblazoned on the side: 'The Spirit of Charleston'. She turned her attention back to the man in front of her.

"Well, Mr Dwyer. I …"

"Oh please, call me Jackson - all my friends do."

"Jackson then. I see you studied at Harvard. Can you give me a bit of information about your background and when you became president?"

"My father and his father before him all went to Harvard. A family tradition. It was always the intention I would join Whiteman's, which I did after graduation in 1984."

"And at the time, Albert Whiteman was the chairman, and still is?"

"Yes. He had been for quite a few years. In my capacity as president and CEO, I report to the Board, essentially him as chairman. Even at his age. I doubt he will ever resign. He married my daddy's cousin, Carolynn, in 1947 and replaced Carolynn's brother, Liam Ross, I believe about twenty-three years after that."

"Do you know why?"

"I wasn't privy to any of that information, Mrs Granger. I assume it was a business decision after Liam's wife and children were killed in a tragic car accident."

"What a terrible thing to have happened."

"Yes, it was an awful time for him, for all the family."

"I'm sure." She paused before continuing. "Please, call me Cydney. Maybe we can come back to that later. Perhaps you could explain how the banking system works in West Virginia. I know the state is one of the smallest in the U.S. and primarily caters for certain industries - coal, mining, farming. Oh, and I hope you don't mind, Tom is going to take some pictures and record this interview." Flattery normally would work but she wasn't quite sure with this character, so she kept her explanation short.

"That's correct. We pride ourselves on our history of helping the little man. We started off back in the late 1860s under the name of Prime Global Trust Corporation, after the War of Independence."

Tom moved around, taking lots of pictures, and every time the camera flashed, Jackson Dwyer III turned and gave a big white beam. It was obvious he was enjoying the attention and he certainly knew how to pour out that southern state charm; it was oozing out of every one of his pores.

"Yes, so I read. And the Ross brothers?"

"Philip Ross was my great, great-grandfather. He is quite legendary. In fact, that's his picture behind me. Funny how the eyes follow you around. It's disconcerting, even to me."

"I noticed." Cydney smiled properly for the first time. It was really uncanny that a picture could evoke such feelings. She wondered if the man really was smiling down at her from afar, and knew why she was there. Another blast of cold air ran along her arm. "Quite handsome. How old was he when that was painted?"

"Oh, he must have been about seventy-five. It was painted by a local artist and commissioned by his wife. You know, she had originally come to the States from Germany with her family back in 1858. She was such a beauty, and old Philip obviously liked what he saw as he married her within a month of their meeting, so the story goes. I'm a bit of a romantic and I choose to believe what I read."

So, that's where the original German connection came from, Cydney thought.

"Seems like a lovely story, indeed. The name, Dwyer?"

"Philip's granddaughter, Elizabeth, who was my grandmother, married Jackson Dwyer back in 1917. His family were also in banking, so it made perfect sense. Two dynasties coming together. We follow the family tradition of the eldest born always taking the name Jackson. My father was the second, and I'm the third."

"What a lovely custom. You must be so proud to be able to

99

trace back your family and heritage so many years. I wish I could say the same."

"I sure am. All the records are kept here in the vaults."

"Is there any chance we could see them?" Cydney said, expecting a negative response.

"I'll see what I can do. All in the name of journalism."

"That would be great. We're here for a few days. And what about the other brother, Cedric?"

"Well, that was a real tragedy. He died in April 1865 at only twenty-two. He was in the army and a stray bullet got him days before the surrender of Robert E Lee to General Ulysses S Grant in Petersburg, Virginia."

"Didn't Virginia split in 1861?"

"Yes. The population was divided on the secession from the Union, so West Virginia was formalised by admittance into the Union in 1863 and Virginia carried on, despite this being right at the time of the civil war, which ended in 1865."

"How awful for the family."

"We all have tragedies in our lives." She nodded in agreement, wondering what that meant in relation to his family or life. "Anyway. You know Prime was the original name, and we retain a few local branches in outlying areas, which report to us still. We didn't want to let the local farmers with small holdings think they were being taken over by a huge corporation, so we still service the mortgages, but to be honest there aren't many left. Once the farms have passed down a generation, the young folk either come out of the dark ages or change their mortgages to us, or they up and leave after selling off the land."

"Can you look over here Mr Dwyer, while I take a shot with Mr Ross in the background?" Tom said. Cydney was impressed with his professionalism.

"Why certainly." Again that super flash of white.

"I thought branch banking wasn't allowed in West Virginia."

"Yes, that's true, until 1986, and it's something that divided our state for many years before that. Our branches were purely for lending and deposit taking."

"When did it change to Whiteman Trust?"

"Let me think. Just before I joined, I reckon."

"What about Albert Whiteman? He joined the bank after his marriage?"

"He was a distant relative, I was told, though I don't know for sure. Only rumours, as he came from Switzerland after the war. He must have had experience because he was on the Board by the time I was born in 1961. I remember hearing some talk that he ousted cousin Liam, Carolynn's brother, from the position around 1970 but I was too young to remember and, like all families, nobody talks about it."

Cydney continued, pressing the points she wanted to make. "Here in West Virginia, I understand you have dual banking systems. That's what really interests me, as it's unlike anything in the UK."

"A bank can choose whether to operate under a national or state charter. All this goes back to Philip and Cedric Ross in 1863 and 1864. There were no state banking laws until 1872 and a lot of banks either transformed or closed."

"And you chose …"

"National, and that hasn't changed. All the big banks here in the U.S., such as Citibank and JP Morgan, are regulated under the same charter, to this day."

"Why is that?"

"It was all about the bank's powers, reserve requirements and lending limits."

"And what about acquisitions?"

"We acquired some smaller banks and also merged with Dwyers Mutual, which was set up by my grandfather. That was always the intention. We also needed to increase our reserves so we expanded into insurance and brokerage services."

"I find it really impressive Prime grew to such an extent and, what's more, managed to survive through quite a few periods when others were forced to close their doors, for example the Great Panic of 1907 and the stock market crash of 1929 and the few years after. Can you explain a bit about that? I'd like to know why your bank, in particular, and not others."

"Sometimes it's about looking into the future, sometimes maybe a bit of luck."

"Luck?"

"Why, sure. The Panic of 1907 only lasted a few weeks, although the repercussions were felt over the next couple of years. There was no central bank to regulate the system at that time, or to inject liquidity back into the market. Trust companies such as ours were booming and our assets were increasing, so we managed to see things through."

"And what about the crash, though?"

"Back in the 1920s, many Americans were borrowing money to buy stocks and shares. We lent money the same as all other institutions of our kind. However, the difference with us was the chairman at the time, who would be Philip's son, Jolyon, had the foresight to predict the bubble would burst. He saw that people were in too much debt and he told all our customers to sell. In that way we protected them and our reserves, and we were prepared. We and our customers survived the fall-out."

"How could you have known? Bigger banks than you failed."

"Dollars during that period were backed by gold held by the U.S. Government. In 1931, speculators began selling dollars for gold at elevated rates, and the central banks here, and private investors started to convert their assets, which reduced the federal reserves. This created a sort of panic with many foreign and domestic depositors withdrawing their funds to convert to gold. Everyone thought they would fail again. So the Fed decided they had to stabilise the dollar and protect it by stopping the loss of gold and increasing the interest rates so people would keep their money with the banks. This was done quietly and cleverly as if nobody would notice and thus retain the gold standard."

"What is the gold standard? I've heard a lot about it."

"It's a system under which all countries fix the value of their currencies in terms of gold. Domestic currencies could easily convert into gold and there was no restriction on import or export of gold."

"From any countries?" asked Cydney. "Even between the U.S. and Europe?"

"Yes, especially. The central banks all cooperated and received assistance from others. You see, the banks were responsible for all of the movement of monies. They could manipulate gold points and increase or decrease the profitability of the flow of gold according to what they wanted to achieve - profit, or cause the downfall of another's currency."

"I read Prime had several branches in Europe, primarily Germany and also in Paris."

"They were closed after the war." She detected a slight shift in his attitude, defensive almost. Was he sensitive to the 'German' question?

"As you are aware, Philip's wife was German. She had many relatives there still and they wanted to invest in the U.S."

"Gold?"

"Maybe. I don't know. I was too young. Why the interest?"

"Nothing in particular. However, I heard Prime was investigated for buying and shipping millions of dollars of gold to Germany to help Hitler."

"Pure speculation. The whole of the U.S. was shipping goods to Germany."

At that moment, Tom chose to take a further shot of Jackson Dwyer III, in all his discomfort.

"Does he have to do that?"

"Tom, why don't you go and take a few shots of the building and interior whilst we have a chat?" She turned to Dwyer. "Would that be okay with you?"

"Sure. I'll ask my secretary to show him around. We have strict security here."

"I'm sure you do," she responded.

Once Tom had gone, Cydney was not prepared to let the comment go.

"Please continue."

"Not much else to say. We had no idea a war was heading to Europe again. After the First World War there was a fall in the value of currencies in Europe, especially Germany, after they lost. Germany printed a load of paper money in order to buy foreign currency, and gold offered the most protection."

"Ah, back to gold."

"The gold standard was determined again."

"Surely, having branches of Prime in Germany itself, helped."

"They were established purely to aid the U.S. economy. The railways were the thing, and also government bonds. The branches helped investors there to buy bonds here. It was a very simple process."

"I'm sure it was, and helped you to sustain through the Depression also."

"That may have been one of the factors."

"And during the build up to the war?" Cydney added, trying to get to the point. "If gold was the stabilising factor in a country's economy, surely Hitler knew this and increased his power and wealth by holding gold reserves?"

"The bank *may* have shipped gold to Germany prior to 1939, but so were other banks and industries all over the U.S. I have no idea why we were investigated specifically."

"Maybe because of your family's German connection."

"I don't like the way this is going. Is there something you want to ask? If so, go right ahead and say it."

"No, I'm simply commenting. The Nazis used gold as countless countries had done beforehand. It was like a weapon."

"If you say so." Jackson Dwyer was becoming tired of the

questioning, Cydney could see that, but she wasn't finished by any means and wanted to probe further.

"Can I ask if Prime was involved in the purchase of Reichsmarks from Germany with dollars at discounted rates, and went on to receive possibly millions in commissions?"

"No. Where are you getting this from, Mrs Granger? I don't know what you are trying to say. To what purpose would we have purchased these?"

"As Nazi sympathisers. The Marks were below face value because they were stolen from people fleeing the Nazi regime."

"I've never heard anything so ridiculous. Because we opened branches there? We had branches in France, too. This interview is getting way out of hand."

"You agreed to meet with me. I have a few more questions still. It would be better if you could answer them, of course, or I would have to surmise you were trying to hide something."

"We have nothing to hide. Please continue, if you have to."

"So you mentioned France. Your branch stayed open throughout the occupation, as did the ones in Germany all through the war. How did you manage this?"

"It was before my time. I have no idea. I wasn't even born."

"You seem to know so much already of the bank's background. Surely, you heard about looted gold, this being the means of trading at the time, it would seem?"

She had wondered how far she could push him, but that point had obviously been reached as the man before her slammed his fist on the desk and threw back his chair as he got to his feet.

"I don't know who the hell you are or what the hell you think you're doing. This interview is closed. Now get out and take your little sonofabitch with you."

"I *will* be back, Mr Dwyer, and I *will* have answers to these questions. You can guarantee it."

* * *

Jackson Dwyer III leaned back in his chair after Cydney had left, waiting for some sort of calm to wash over him and wondering what had just happened. He had heard rumours of the investigation but he didn't like being questioned or accused of something he knew nothing about before his time. Now he needed to discover what had really gone on before this woman did. He was damn sure if there was anything untoward, she would have no qualms about putting it out into the media, and there was no way he would allow that. No way she was going to rock the boat.

The person to ask was Liam Ross, who had been the chairman of Prime before Albert had arrived. Yes, and that was another unanswerable - how come he had resigned and a stranger to the family, almost, this Albert Whiteman, had been appointed? A man he tried to avoid. There was something about him he couldn't put his finger on. The family would have to start talking, they had no choice. Liam was now in his late seventies and somewhat of a recluse. Jackson decided to go and see him before he upped and died. There was no smoke without fire, that was for sure, and Cydney Granger obviously knew something he didn't. It wasn't a position he liked by any means, or one he was going to ignore. Damn her, and damn Albert Whiteman, as surely he was involved. Perhaps he should also speak to cousin Ted, and before he ran in the primaries, just in case.

CHAPTER FOURTEEN

"I THINK that went well."

"You're kidding me, right?" said Tom.

"Yes, of course. I think I was onto something but I don't think he knows too much about Albert Whiteman. Don't get me wrong, he's extremely knowledgeable about the history and the system here, almost as if he's learnt it off pat, however, when it comes to this man ... well."

"His curiosity's peaked?"

"He'll get to the bottom of this. As soon as I mentioned looted gold from Germany, that's when he flew off the handle."

"So he does know something. Why would he act like that if he was innocent?"

"I think he's more worried about his position than anything else."

"You can't blame him. He stands to lose everything if the truth about Prime's funding comes out."

"It could have so many repercussions, I can't even let my mind go there. We would need to inform the FBI."

"Why them?"

"They are the bureau if you have evidence of any fraud in the banking world. This, of course, is slightly more than fraud if the bank was founded, or even funded, by stolen assets."

"That's a huge presumption. Isn't it beyond the statute of limitations?"

"No. Where crimes are considered heinous by society there is no maximum time legal proceedings can be initiated or when the FBI can investigate and take appropriate action."

"And if this is, it certainly fits the bill."

"Indeed. We need to find out more first, so I have a good case to present to Washington where the FBI are based. Did you manage to find anything out?"

"I took a few snaps of the building and got chatting to the porter on the front desk. Name of Joe Carpenter. He's been with Prime for decades, and his father before him."

"And?"

"He doesn't like Albert Whiteman, not one bit. Not a popular man, it seems. Quite ruthless in his treatment of his employees but he did make the bank even more successful, which is why they're now in this building here. He started back when Liam Ross was chairman. Now, he was a good man, according to Joe. A real gent. Always a greeting no matter the time of day, always asking after his family, sending gifts when his kids were born. Then Joe came to work and suddenly Ross was gone. Apparently resigned overnight and Whiteman was in his place."

"And no reason? No rumours?"

"Certainly rumours. One that he was sacked after *borrowing* bank funds. Staff heard shouting in the boardroom and then Liam stormed out the building before anyone could speak to him."

"Hmmm. So I wonder what went on. We should go and see Liam Ross, maybe."

"He lives somewhere up in the mountains now. Recluse. Sees no-one. Spends his days shooting and fishing, so I'm told."

"No family?"

"Nope. He had a wife and two kids - twins. They were killed in a car accident after he left Whiteman's."

"So he told me. No wonder he lives where he does. Poor man. And he never leaves to come into town?"

"Apparently not. Joe's son delivers food and supplies to him at a central place, drops them off but never sees the man."

"What a lonely existence. Do you think you could speak to your new friend and ask if he can set up a meeting for us?"

"I'll give it a go. What now, boss? Where do you want to go?"

"I'm not entirely sure. I think I'll walk back to the hotel and call Richard. See if he's got anything more for us."

"Okay. I'll go talk to Joe some more. See you later."

It was only a fifteen-minute walk back to the hotel. Cydney was not in a hurry and wanted to ponder on the events of the previous few hours. None of it made sense to her and she was not a woman to let things pass her by. If there was a possibility of a story, she would get to the bottom of it.

As she sauntered through the park, enjoying some thinking time, it felt good to feel the warmth on her back from the sun still blazing down, such a change to the weather back home. With such a lovely view of the mountains, she decided to take a moment to sit and admire the beautiful scenery, until her mobile rang, interrupting her thoughts.

"Mummy, it's me. You're probably going to say no, but I had to ask, and if you say yes, I'll be the best daughter in the world and I promise to make my bed and clear up for the next week, no for the next month, and wash up the dishes."

"What? Slow down, my darling."

"You have to say yes. It's something I simply *have* to do. And with Mellie, who you know is my bestest friend in the world. And I promise it will be fine. I'm fifteen now, and her parents are going to be there, so we will all be fine. And it won't cost much, in fact I can use my own money from my birthday."

"Lauren, will you please slow down. I can't hear what on earth you're saying. Take a deep breath and start again."

"I'm so excited. Please say yes! There'll be horses there and everything."

"To what? You haven't even told me."

"Oh. Well, okay. They've invited me out to their villa in the south of France. And it's in the Camargue so we can go riding every day, and they have this amazing pool and we'll have our own bedroom to share."

"Who is 'they'?"

"For goodness sake, Mum, you're not listening. Mellie's parents. You've met them. Jonathan and Suzanne."

"Yes, I know who they are."

"So why are you asking? You're so annoying."

"Because you haven't explained properly. So now I understand. And when is this trip supposed to take place?"

"Well, it's at the weekend, only for a week. Please say I can go. I can, can't I?"

"What about school?"

"It's half term. We have a week off."

"I'm away. I'm not back for a few days." Cydney realised she was going to have to give in on this one and she hated the thought of not seeing her daughter for another week after her return.

"So? Sophie's here and so is Sean. They can help me pack and Sean will drive me over there."

"You seem to have all this very organised, darling."

"So it's a yes?".

"Yes, Lauren. And Jake? What about him?"

"He's alright. He's planning to write his number one hit, apparently."

"Lauren! That's not fair. Is Sean there? Can I speak to him, please?"

"Okay. If you have to but I've already asked him. Hold on …"

Cydney waited a few seconds until the soft Irish voice of her chauffeur and sometime investigator picked up the receiver.

"Hi. How's it going over there?"

"All well, thanks. We've discovered quite a bit of information. I may have to stay a few extra days here as not everything is as clear cut as I expected. Are you okay, by the way, taking Lauren over to Mellie's parents? She seems to have twisted me around her little finger again."

"She has this habit, does it to all of us." He chuckled. "Of course."

"Can you make sure she has some money to take with her? I've left some in the usual place in the kitchen cupboard. One hundred pounds for the week should be enough, and she can change it into Euros at the airport. Can you get Sophie to make sure she has everything she needs, and maybe take her out shopping for some new bikinis and toiletries. Tell her to use the household credit card."

"Yes, ma'am."

"I'll offer to pay for her flight. I'll phone Suzanne and you can take the money round to them at the same time. How's Jake?"

"He's fine. Busy with his music after school. He'll be well looked after next week. I'll probably be going away myself for a few days, once you're back."

"Yes, I was getting to that. Is this your ailing aunt again?" This was their pre-arranged code. She stopped for a second, having nearly forgotten about it all in the aftermath of her meeting.

"Indeed. I think I have to visit her. She needs me quite urgently."

"News?"

"Not especially, but we have a plan for her treatment. I'll explain when I see you. When do you think you'll be back?"

"I should be another four days, I expect. Not sure. I'll keep you posted. Please look after the kids for me, and try not to let Lauren go too overboard in her excitement, especially when Jake isn't going anywhere."

"Ah, he'll be as good as gold."

He couldn't have chosen a more apt phrase, considering what she was currently investigating. Everything on the world monetary scale always went back to gold, the rise and fall of Man's destiny based on some bright piece of yellow metal, precious to many in their quest to gain wealth and prestige, wars lost and won, countries brought to their knees by this most desirable commodity that could cause so much economic disruption. She had never thought of gold in this way before, but if what they were finding out was true, Whiteman Trust's assets were built purely on stolen gold from all those millions of people killed at the hands of the most evil people of all time, the Nazis, including Albert Whiteman himself, or Adolf Weissmuller, as he was then known. Gold had a lot to answer for and it was possible theirs was not the only bank involved. Suppose this went deeper than anyone had thought? Who knows where Hitler may have sent his looted gold so many years ago and the reserves of many central banks throughout the world may have been sitting on this since before the end of World War II. And suppose it was one of those well-kept secrets everybody knew about within the machinations of the banking world? The whole thing was totally unimaginable.

* * *

Back at the hotel, Cydney started to feel the effects of the jetlag she knew was about to hit her. First she had to speak to Richard, even though it was so late.

"Hi. How's it going?"

"You sound tired. I wasn't sure you'd be up. You're not doing too much, I hope? You remember what the doctors said. Don't push yourself over the limit."

"Christ, I only uttered five words. You're just like Christine. She's always nagging me. Anyway, I'm fine. So tell me, what's been going on?"

After a brief explanation of the day's events, Cydney turned to the investigatory work in which Richard excelled and was the reason she employed the ex-Detective Chief Superintendent in her team.

"I want you to check the records in Germany for a Nazi called Adolf Weissmuller. I reckon he was born around 1915, which would make him about ninety now, give or take."

"Who was he, or is he?"

"I believe he's Albert Whiteman."

"Really? The chairman? You sure? How did you discover that?"

Cydney didn't answer. "I want you to check out someone called Dieter Scholler from Zurich, born around the same year, possibly. Weissmuller may have stolen this man's identity."

"The name now is certainly quite similar to the German. Why would he do that?"

"I don't know. Trying to be clever. May be a coincidence, but I don't necessarily believe in them."

"What makes you so sure about this? Have you received some 'inside' knowledge?" Richard knew his boss had this ability to communicate with people who had passed into spirit.

"Yes. That's what's so disturbing. I can't get the picture of what he did out of my mind."

"If he's an escaped Nazi, plus heads one of the biggest banks in the southern states, and his son is governor, the implications are so widespread - it could easily bring down the entire system."

"I realise that, Richard, which is why we have to get this right. Call me as soon as you get anything, and heaven help us all if we're proved right."

CHAPTER FIFTEEN

"LIAM, let me in or I swear I'll kick through this door."

No sound came from the log cabin, despite Jackson Dwyer thumping continuously. He felt positive his cousin was playing with him so he searched around the sides, peering through the darkened windows.

"Liam, I'm not joking here. You let me in, you old sonofa-bitch. I've not spent the last four hours driving up this damn mountain for you not to speak to me. Open the goddamn door!"

Still nothing. Where the hell was the man? Jackson surveyed the expanse that stretched for hundreds of miles around him. The entire vista was enough to take anyone's breath away. Against the rugged Allegheny Mountains dominating the land-scape that had stood there for time immemorial, he was one small human and he felt it keenly as he followed the contours of the land, the wild sprawling Monongahela National Forest and the flowing river beds and bubbling streams below him. Memories of trout fishing in the spring with his father and sometimes with Liam so many years ago sprung to mind when, as a young boy, he was taken camping in the area. Since his father had died, he hadn't bothered to come up here, not even to bring his own children. It was too painful. The man he had worshipped was his hero in so many ways and had taught him everything about life and surviving the family bank, especially about dealing with the usurper, Albert Whiteman, whom his father had detested for what he had done to his cousin, Liam, so many years ago.

"You looking for me?"

Jackson spun around on hearing a voice from behind. The man standing before him, now in his seventy-seventh year, was dressed in a blue checked shirt and light beige chinos and carrying a hunting rifle under his arm. The thing that struck him most was the change in the person he used to know. His white hair was worn long and held back in a ponytail and his face was tanned leather and creased from the mountain sun. His eyes, their soft brown gentleness, despite his now abrasive manner, however, were unchanged and Jackson recognised them with a shock and realised he missed this man in his life.

"Hi, Liam. I've brought you some things." He pointed to a few bags of supplies, which he had left by the front door. "Things you might need."

"That's mighty kind of you, Jackson."

"So, you remember me."

"It's been a long time. You were only a fledgling when we last saw each other, but I'd remember you anywhere. You're like your daddy. Just the same interfering busybody as him, I'd say."

"I need to speak to you."

"Well, I guessed you weren't up here for the fishing, boy. You'd better come in. Bring those bags with you, too. My back's playing up and I can't lift the way I used to."

The interior of the cabin was a complete surprise. Everything was neat and tidy with beautiful rugs bedecking the floor, colourful native Indian throws over two large settees, and multitudinous paintings of splendid forest scenes and wildlife mounted on every wall. On the dark wood sideboard were various framed family photos, smiling faces of a younger Liam with a rather pretty dark-haired woman, and two young boys, both laughing into the camera.

"I can almost hear what you're thinking. How did you expect me to live? I wanted seclusion, not to live like a hobo."

"Sorry," said Jackson.

"I'll go brew some coffee. I can guess why you're here. I knew someone would be at some stage. Can't escape forever, eh?"

Jackson followed his older cousin into the small and well-equipped kitchen and watched whilst he set up the coffee machine.

"I never could stand instant coffee. Only like this pure Brazilian blend. Joe's son brings it up to me every month."

"Joe?"

"Yes. Who works for you? The porter. Do you even know the names of your employees?"

"Yes, of course I do. I wasn't sure who you meant. I had no idea." He raised his hands in resignation and looked his cousin straight in the eye.

"I'm sure you didn't. How things have changed. How is the bank these days? I believe Whiteman's alive still, more's the pity. And they say God looks down on the merciful."

"I imagine there is, or rather was, no love lost between the two of you."

"You can say that again. Here, take the coffee and let's go sit." Liam trudged over to one of the couches and plonked himself down. An old golden retriever wandered out of one of the bedrooms and wearily climbed up next to him, flopping across his lap. "He's old, like me. We'll live our lives out together up here."

"What's his name?"

"King. He always seemed like an old English royal to me."

"He must be a good companion to you," Jackson said, patting the old dog on his back.

"He sure is. Now let's get to the real reason for your visit. I've not seen anyone for years."

"Joe's son?"

"Nah. He brings supplies up and leaves them. I have no real need for anyone, apart from King. I have the animals and birds around me, the mountains are my friends, and I have my music."

He pointed to a modern system with two large speakers either side. "I have a generator, in case you wanted to know."

"So, all the mod cons, but no-one to talk to."

"I had enough of talking. Didn't get me anywhere."

"You've been up here for how many years now? What do you do?"

"I guess coming up to thirty-five years. I worked as a volunteer ranger at first. Now I can't get around too much. I spend most of my days cataloguing rare species of plants for the university. I don't need the money - not much to spend it on around here. Give a lot to Joe's family ever since his daddy was hurt in the mining incident and before he went to work at the bank."

"I guess I should have known that, too," Jackson said with regret.

"Yes, you should." Jackson felt firmly put in his place.

"You moved here after Margaret and your boys were in the accident?" He watched his cousin carefully as his expression changed and his eyes glistened with unshed tears. The fact he had hit a nerve wasn't intentional; he was not completely without heart, no matter what people said, or thought about him, come to that.

"Tell me why you're here. Stop procrastinating. It's about time this came out in the open." The subject of his wife and children was passed over.

"I had a visit from someone called Cydney Granger. From London."

"Never heard of him."

"No, it's a woman. Me neither. Apparently, her assignment was to look at our dual banking system here in West Virginia. She was asking a lot of questions about the investigations back in the 1930s. Also about Albert. I checked her out. This isn't her normal line of work. I think there's more to her than meets the eye."

"I was only a boy. My daddy, Edward, was chairman and I

only heard rumours. I went onto the Board when he died suddenly, and was chairman from 1963."

"Albert arrived here when? 1946?"

"Yes. He was a distant cousin from Switzerland but I hated him at first sight. There was something about the man, as if he had a secret to hide, and he managed to con himself into our lives, or rather my sister, Carolynn's life, very quickly. Too quickly for my mind. My daddy welcomed him into the family, especially as he had untold wealth, which he was prepared to put into Prime."

"As capital? Did they need it at the time?"

"Banks always need capital. Don't forget, we'd come out of a very expensive war and people were loath to borrow during that period. We expanded back in the late 1980s when your grand-daddy's bank, Dwyers Mutual, merged with Prime, but all our resources were being used. In the late 1940s and early 50s, there was a national boom due to consumer borrowing and that's when things changed."

"We couldn't say no to his money?"

"No, who would? It was always our intention to expand."

"Didn't anyone check into him, this distant cousin?"

"Apparently not. It was enough receiving the money, I presume, and by that time he was engaged to Carolynn. Our daddy would do anything she wanted."

"What was Albert like, from what you remember?"

"Oh, I remember alright. He had this haughtiness about him. A superiority. He saw himself as better than anybody, especially once he had bought his way onto the Board."

"Your sister fell in love with him?"

"His money, maybe. She was quite a southern belle, you know. So pretty, and she knew it. The boys in the area were like bees around a honey pot but she swatted them away, even at twenty, when most of her friends were getting wed. Albert was at least fifteen years older than her, and she succumbed to his European charm. His English was almost perfect, apart from a very slight accent. He was like none of the other boys - tall, handsome, a man, though not much younger than our daddy. I don't think he would have taken no for an answer anyway. He was not a man to reckon with."

"Was she happy with him? How did he treat her? Sorry for all the questions. I'll get to the point, I promise."

"I know you will. It's important for you to be aware of these things first. And I have time. I never get visitors, nor wanted them, so what else am I gonna do? I'll make some more coffee, unless you want something stronger. I have a very good malt whisky Joe brought me, and there's no way you're driving back tonight, so you might as well."

"Yeah, sure. Thanks. I'll join you."

With two rather large whiskeys to hand, Liam continued. "I believe she fell in love with him. I can't say about him. I don't know if he was even capable of love but she was under his spell. They had problems having kids at first and it took them almost nine years before Philip was born, and Ted came along three years later."

"Albert helped the bank grow. I know that."

"Yes, he did indeed, but he was ruthless. He was in charge of loans and mortgages, primarily, and if anyone couldn't pay he called in the loan and repossessed the property."

"Which I would do now. It's business. We aren't a charity," Jackson pointed out.

"Maybe I was too soft. You know some of these farmers were people who'd been our customers for years. I would've helped out a bit."

"So what happened? Why the falling out?"

"Whiteman was always goading me in the boardroom, trying to score points and make me look foolish in front of the other members. He used to get my back up all the time, arguing with every plan I had. It was inevitable we would come to blows."

"It can't be only that. Tell me what really went on."

"He got talking to the other directors and getting them on side. He was set for a take-over and by then I'd had enough anyway. Banking was never really for me. Too cutthroat. I loved being with Margaret, especially when the boys came along. Anyway, one day my senior clerk came to me. He'd noticed there was a regular payment going out from every customer's account to an unknown account."

"How regular?" Jackson asked.

"Weekly. Daily, sometimes. Only a few cents and never more than a couple of dollars, so not a lot in the scheme of things. The amounts were so small nobody would notice and certainly no customers questioned it. We checked back and it had been going on over many years."

"How much in total?"

"It was into the millions of dollars. Plus, we delved into the mortgage accounts and checked the interest paid against the actual interest which should have been taken and every account was paying over and above. Someone was syphoning off those amounts, too."

"That's impossible. How the hell could that happen?"

"It was ingenious. It had to be someone at the highest level and the amounts so small it passed inspection. Remember, we had no computers in those days, at least not until the early 1960s. Yes, we had a structure in place. The account master file had every customer's account details and balances showing all transactions over ninety days. We had the ledgers to track cash and other assets as they worked through the system, and the journals to hold the transactions received from the many teller stations."

"And the audit trail?"

"It was there, sort of, but overseen by Whiteman. It had to be him. He'd been very clever, and it wasn't only the false charges he was taking. This is what I think happened in very simplistic terms. Suppose a customer paid one hundred dollars into his account. The teller would record that credit against the person's account ledger for the same amount, and debit the same amount to the bank's cash ledger. All the ledgers should add up to zero - same amount coming in, same going out. If these were ever out of balance, an alarm would sound and searches would be made. However, if someone wanted to add an amount to his own account balance he would have to take the money from the master file and somehow tweak the ledgers to balance the books so no alarms would go off. Also, we had a system of suspense accounts which could be used temporarily if we couldn't easily clarify a transaction - if an account number was entered incorrectly for instance."

"Basically, human error."

"Yes. It happens. Anyway, these accounts would be investigated after three days but if someone posted a debit to the suspense account and credited another account within that timeframe, and then raise another debit a few days later to clear the first one, no-one would know."

"And you had no dual controls?"

"No. That didn't come until later. Take the case of bank guarantees. If we were to issue a loan, we sometimes got other banks to give a guarantee to carry the losses should it go wrong."

"Why would that be?"

"Basically, to spread the risk, and it helped to have another entity vetting what the bank was issuing. Also, they took a percentage of the money we were making when it went right. Easy money for them. However, it would be simple for someone to plunder the loan account and no-one would discover it for months so it would be unlikely they would even raise the alarm."

"Why didn't you introduce dual controls? That would have made sense."

"We did, eventually. We were quite a small town bank compared to JP Morgan and others. Sometimes, things fall down the middle and get lost. Human factors are neglected and nobody likes change, so we had opposition to this control, at Board level. And in any case, it was possible to create a bogus dual logon and to send money wherever. This was possibly all my fault. We had lax internal controls. I was chairman, after all."

"And let me think, you thought all this was due to Albert Whiteman. No doubt in your mind at all?"

"It had to be. Who else? He had the means at his disposal, plus he had the ability to give bogus guarantees," Liam said.

"I thought he was wealthy? Why would he do it?"

"A rich man can never have enough money. Power corrupts, isn't that what Orwell wrote? And it's true."

"Where did the money go and what did he do with it?"

"I can only imagine he had an account somewhere, away from Charleston, or even West Virginia. What the money was utilised for is anybody's guess but he did live a very lavish lifestyle, as you know."

"So you confronted him?"

"Oh yes, indeed I did. We'd had the monthly board meeting and when everyone left it was just the two of us. I told him what I'd discovered and threatened to make it known."

"Brave."

"You betcha. This was my reputation at stake. My daddy had entrusted the bank to me and this guy comes out of nowhere and tries to push me aside as if I was nobody, plus he was heavily defrauding us. Damn sure I confronted him."

"Did he admit to anything?"

"Well he didn't *not* admit. He shouted it was all a load of nonsense, and in any case I couldn't prove it. Then he turned the tables on me. Accused me of embezzlement, that I had never liked the fact he'd brought money into Prime to save it, and married my sister. Voices were raised and I was nervous everyone would hear us."

"My God. I can't believe this."

"Neither could I at the time, although now I've had plenty of years to think about it."

"Why did you walk away? How come he took over your position?"

"I was a coward. I hated the thought of the bank being called into disrepute. After all, it was our great-granddaddy who had built it up. If it came out I'd accused a fellow director… well, you can imagine the uproar and the press. They would have had a field day and we would've been investigated by the banking regulators and, no doubt, the FBI. Our doors would've been closed, which would have been disastrous."

"So you left."

"I did. He won, but I've no doubt he's used to winning. That's why Ted is the State Governor, and why he'll be running for president."

"What about the money that was taken?"

"As I left I told him that if this continued, I'd have no hesitation in reporting him. I would walk away but he should always watch his back."

"Then what?"

"He killed my wife and children." It was said so quietly, as a statement, almost matter of fact and void of emotion, as if he had repeated the words over and over in his head so many times it almost failed to have impact when spoken.

"He did what?" Jackson jumped to his feet. "He killed them? I thought it was a road traffic accident."

"Sit down, sit down. So the report went. The whole thing was hushed up. The brakes had been cut. I knew one of the guys who checked over the car. The evidence was there but I couldn't prove it, and Whiteman must have paid someone off. The man is a murdering sonofabitch who will do whatever he can to protect himself."

"Oh my God, Liam. This is incredible. I can't believe what you've told me."

"I had to leave town and get away. This is my sanctuary."

"So all this time …"

"Yes, son, for so many years."

"What if this comes out, this fraud? And now this woman is investigating us."

"Do you think she knows anything?"

"I can only imagine she does," Jackson said with a sigh of resignation at the thought. "I have no choice but to see her again, and speak to Ted."

"Well, maybe it's about time."

"And the ramifications?"

"Let's have another whisky. I fear it's going to be a long night."

CHAPTER SIXTEEN

GENERAL Ian Bowles-Smith marched unceremoniously into the hospital room without knocking and caught Steve totally unaware during his hourly exercise around the confines of his compact area in an effort to strengthen his leg.

"I see you're quite fit now."

"Okay, I know when I've been caught."

"At least you have the decency not to deny this. I'm delighted you're up and about."

"So now what? What are your plans for me, seeing as I have no say in the matter anymore?"

"We're moving you."

"Where? And when?"

"Now. Here, take these and get dressed."

"Just like that? With no preamble. That's unlike you. Sorry, I forgot - sir."

"I'm not sure I like this attitude of yours, especially after saving you. Can you please remember who you are and that you are still a member of the Special Forces, whether you like it or not."

The general made himself comfortable whilst Steve got dressed in the bathroom into the army fatigues and boots he'd been given, taking his time to think. Where was he going? They obviously had something in mind for him and this could be the awaited opportunity, his chance to escape and somehow return to England, or any country on the entire planet, as far as he was concerned, and be reunited with the family he desperately yearned to see, and touch, and be able to love again. He felt he had let his family down. His thoughts were full of Cydney and the twins, every night and every day, but he had no game-plan and he needed one, and quick. Sean was his only hope and he knew that sergeant of his would not give up the trail, if only to prove he was dead, and that was one thing he wasn't, and didn't intend to be, for a very long time.

Begrudgingly, he returned to the general who stood up and studied him.

"You're looking good, I'm pleased to say. Still limping, though. Come on. We're going to get you up to fighting strength."

Leaving the room that had been his home for quite some months, Steve felt somewhat disorientated, as if he didn't quite believe he was moving away, although to where he had no idea. The steel-grey painted corridor they strode along was endlessly long, empty and silent. There were no nurses or doctors walking around, no stations where they would all congregate, just endless doors behind which anybody could be laying, sick or drugged, even. Eventually, they arrived at a lift where two Israeli uniformed soldiers were standing to attention, obviously waiting for them. The lift doors opened and Steve and his CO entered with the two soldiers, one of whom pressed the up button. So, he had been kept in an underground facility after all, as he had surmised. Not long after, the doors opened to reveal another similarly empty corridor.

"After you, and don't try to get away. It will be impossible anyway, and these two men will be with us - and watching you."

Steve thought back to his recent conversation with Charlie, the nurse with whom he was now on extremely good terms. He empathised with her and the pain she was going through. Her Israeli husband had been killed six months previously by a landmine when he was on reconnaissance with some other soldiers in the desert on the border with Syria. The land-rover he had been driving had been blown to smithereens, but she'd decided to stay on, working in the hospital to help as much as she was able, to try and save the young soldiers who came in with such dreadful injuries. It was to salve her conscience, she'd said, not that she should have one to salve, he'd told her.

It was easy to speak to her and he'd told her something of his life back in England with Cydney and the twins, and the predicament in which he now found himself, with not being able to return. He was also concerned about his elderly father and how he would be coping with the loss of his son, if he was even alive. It hurt him so much to think of his family and that he wasn't there to protect them. He'd wondered whether she could possibly call him and tell him secretly he was alive, and he was fine. Nothing else. Not his whereabouts, as that would be giving away official secrets. Not tell his wife, as that would really upset her, which he wouldn't do for the world. Maybe just call and say a couple of words, mention something that only he and his father would understand. That would really help, he'd told her. Steve almost felt guilty that he was using her. She'd agreed so readily and afterwards she confirmed she loved his dad's Irish accent and he was so pleased when she'd talked about the beautiful walnut tree they'd had in their garden when he was a young boy. He vowed to make it up to Charlie at some point, when he was free of his military chains.

His aching leg shook him out of his reverie and he realised he was struggling to keep up with the CO, who was striding yards ahead of him. His recent exercise had consisted of jogging back and forth around his bed and doing multi push-ups and, although he felt stronger, he clearly wasn't as prepared as he'd thought.

"Through here. A car's waiting for us."

Suddenly he was in sunlight. The unexpectedness of it hit him and he swayed, only to be caught by one of his escorts. It must have been the middle of the day, with the sun at its highest. It felt so good to feel the heat on his face but his immediate reaction was to shut his eyes against the rays.

"I should have prepared you. It can be a shock to the system. Keep your eyes closed and slowly open them. We'll get you seen by one of our own medics shortly. This way." Steve was led with one arm on his elbow to the awaiting army vehicle, which was heading to goodness knows where this time. He was well and truly cornered and he knew it.

* * *

Cydney woke with a shock. A sensation of light beaming onto her face jolted her from a heavy dream-filled sleep, almost as if someone had shone a bright spotlight directly at her. It took her a minute to get her bearings and realise where she was - in a hotel in Charleston, West Virginia. The clock next to her indicated it was only four-thirty in the morning and the room was in complete darkness with everything quiet outside, as the world this side of the pond waited for the sun to rise and the day to begin. For some inexplicable reason things didn't seem right to her, as if something was brewing under the surface and waiting. But for what? As the hairs on her arm began to bristle and cold air washed over her, she realised exactly why she was experiencing those feelings and, precisely at that moment, Ray Gordon appeared by her side.

"I have brought Sybill and Mordecai through to you again."

The outlines of the tragic couple came into view and painfully slowly became more defined, almost as if they were reluctant to show themselves.

"This must be so difficult for you," Sybill said. *"Please believe me - we are so frightened for our Hans and his friend, Ari. Adolf Weissmuller has found them."*

"What? I don't understand. Please explain."

"The money. It is from him."

"Why didn't you tell me before? Why would he do this? Pay them money - for what? To silence them?"

"*He is not paying for their silence,*" Sybill told her, shaking her head in dismay. Her husband remained quiet and moved his arm around her shoulders protectively. She patted his hand in response. "*He is a coward. He requires redemption for his sins.*"

"Does Hans know this? That the money came from Weiss-muller? I always thought nobody told me the full facts."

"*He believes he does, yes. I can't shield him, though, only you can do that. You need to speak to him and he will tell you everything. There is no alternative.*"

"I realise this will hurt, but you have to tell me more about what happened to you. Please, if you can. I need to know why this Adolf Weissmuller is doing what he is."

* * *

Lodz 1941

"How are we supposed to live like this?" Sybill turned to her husband with despair as they stood in the twelve by fourteen-foot room in which there was one single iron framed bed, with a couple of threadbare blankets bundled on top, where all of them had to sleep. On the dust covered floor, two straw mattresses had been thrown without a care. There were a few odd items of clothing scattered about, discarded from previous occupants, possibly in their rush to leave, for whatever reason. Spying something on the floor in the corner, Mordecai walked over and picked up a child's hand-drawn picture of a man, woman and three children, almost a parody of their own situation. He stared at it for several moments and placed it on the top of what once would have been a beautifully crafted mahogany chest of drawers by the window, scared to throw it away in case it was a premonition of the outcome to his family's plight. A steel bucket sat to the side of the door, its intended use and the lack of privacy apparent.

"We should make the best of it, liebchen. Let me give you a hand with the cases. Hans, help Mama, please. Girls, go and see if you can find us some water from the kitchen downstairs."

"I don't want to go by myself. The horrible men may come and take us away," Gerthe cried.

"I'll take them, Papa," Hans said. "I'll show them where everything is so they won't be frightened. Come, girls." He grabbed hold of Gerthe and Mathilde's hands, first wiping his little sister's tears. "I'll be straight back and then will help you."

"Oh, Mordecai," Sybill sobbed when they were alone. "What shall we do? How shall we manage?"

"We will. We're all together and that's the most important thing. Come and rest here." He pulled her next to him and onto the mattress, his arm protectively around her shoulders with her head rested on him.

There was a knock at the door and two men entered, one carrying a sheaf of papers in his hand. They appeared to be in their sixties as their faces were weathered and lined, with their sparse hair greying. They were probably much younger but the resignation behind their eyes of their fate, due to being stuck in their everyday hell, was sufficient to age them. The dark suits they were wearing, to create an air of officialdom, were aged and creased and covered with a light grey dust. Mordecai stood up immediately when they entered.

"Good afternoon. Mr and Mrs Frankelman, I believe. We represent the Council of Elders. You have both your parents and three children with you, I see," one muttered, turning over several pages of his list and passing his finger down the alphabetical order to find them.

"No. This is all we are. Our parents died on route." Mordecai turned at the sound of his wife's crying. "Is it possible we can have another room, please, something bigger? There are five of us, including two young children. Maybe with a toilet."

"Mr Frankelman, Mordecai if I may, let me introduce myself. Mikael Schwitz. I oversee housing and welfare. This is Piotr Lederman, my assistant. I would like to welcome you here but ... well, you can see what we have." He cast his hand around to demonstrate. "We are nearly one hundred and sixty thousand people living all together in one and a half square miles of very cramped and poor, unhealthy conditions. Mostly Jews from all over Europe, not only Germany and Poland. Rooms are scarce and the only way you can move is if someone dies - and disease is rife here, especially tuberculosis - or is sent off to work in the factories and labour camps outside. I'm sorry to say, this is all we have. Piotr will arrange more bedding and some food for you, as much as we are able. We rely solely on the Germans for our sustenance and we are severely rationed, and each week this is reduced. How we survive? Ach, God only knows. I'll be back in the morning with Klaus Osterlitz who will find you suitable work. We all do our bit here, and we will arrange for you to see one of the doctors, if you wish."

"Please can you find out about our parents?" Sybill asked. "They were taken off the train a while back. I was told they would be buried on arrival and I would like to see where."

Both men shook their heads and Mordecai knew they were about to impart some extremely difficult news to his wife. "I'm so sorry, Sybill isn't it? I suggest you get on with things now. Look to the future. Your parents are with God now and that's what's important. Sit *shiva* if you wish. The main criteria here is to survive. We work, we eat what we can find, we sleep, and tomorrow is the next day and hopefully we will wake to better things, God willing. I will ask Rabbi Rabinovitz to come and see you later for prayers."

The next day, after a very difficult and troublesome sleep, the Frankelman family were all allotted work. The schools in the area had been abolished the year before and Sybill was assigned to the hospital as a cleaner, where there was an 'illegal' day-care centre for the smaller children so she could also be with her daughters who were going to help in the laundry. No-one was spared work. Mordecai and Hans were sent to one of the industrial bases which was manufacturing war supplies for the

Germans and assigned to produce uniforms and other garments, nothing with which they had any familiarity.

Hans was equally amazed and astounded at how organised everything was in their new home. The entire area was run by Elders and everyone was obligated to work; no work, no ration card, no food. Very simple. The ration card enabled them to obtain a small amount of food, the essentials such as rice, bread, flour and sugar, but the quantities seemed to get smaller each day.

The ghetto had its own police force, mainly to ensure nobody escaped, a hospital with hardly any medicine, doctors who had barely any medical instruments, a school with no pupils, books or writing materials, bakers but no flour - the list was endless. There were no Nazis within the walls, only outside where the place was surrounded by armed German guards. Lodz was situated, he learnt, in what was originally the poorest part of the city. When the German forces occupied the city in 1939, all businesses owned by Jews were appropriated and the Jewish population was centred by force around certain streets until, in 1940, the area was fenced off to contain nearly one hundred and fifty thousand people. The figures were higher now and conditions were more cramped, as he knew to his cost, as more and more people flooded in daily from other parts of Poland and most of the European cities.

* * *

Present Day
"And that's our story. We arrived, we survived the horrendous journey, but didn't know how long we would be there," explained Mordecai. Cydney studied him as if for the first time. He was much taller than his wife, dark haired and extremely handsome with piercing almost cobalt-blue eyes, as Sybill had described. His manner was quietly charming, a gentleman with a calm demeanour. They suited each other.

"How did you cope, each of you losing both your parents? I can't imagine, and in such circumstances." Cydney shook her head to remove the image. Having lost her own mother so recently, the pain was still raw.

"We were both numb with shock but we had to keep going for our children. Where there's life, there's hope, and that was our mantra each day. We had no choice."

"What about after those first few days? I presume you didn't discover the whereabouts of your parents."

"No. It was clear we would never see them again. God alone knew what happened to them and certainly it is doubtful they were buried. Of course, now they are with us."

"And did you sit, what did you call it, *shiva?"*

"We did, yes, only for one day. This is a time when everyone would have gathered at our home to help us during the seven days of mourning. Shiva means seven, but we were not allowed to mourn for longer. We had to work. Also, we knew nobody there. All our friends had been sent to who knows where. Our new neighbours helped as much as they could, and the Rabbi came to say prayers. We had to finish before curfew and then the next day we worked and carried on as best we could, as if nothing had happened."

"How long were you there?"

"Everything changed in September 1942."

"Why?"

"They took our girls, our two beautiful girls, and we never saw them again."

At those words, Gerthe and Mathilde came forward to stand at their parents' side, their movements slow and cautious, wary of appearing in front of Cydney and reluctant to show themselves, it seemed. Their father picked them up and cradled them in his arms where they remained, their faces buried in his shoulders, their long dark hair falling in cascades down their backs.

"They took our precious girls. We were helpless to do anything to prevent this. A father's role is to protect. I couldn't. I blame myself and did so every day of my life."

Words failed Cydney. Her thoughts turned to Lauren, at aged eight, skipping and playing with her dolls without a care in the world, and back to the daughters of this couple before her, who were relying on her to help them so they could move on in peace.

"How?" she asked in a thin whisper, her voice tremulous, as she waited for Sybill to speak.

They announced it. Twenty thousand children were to be sacrificed so the people of the ghetto could survive. Then it happened without warning. The soldiers charged in and rounded up all our children at gunpoint, tearing into the hospital and every household. I tried to hide Gerthe and Mathilde but there was nowhere and Mordecai and Hans were at the factory. My daughters pulled at my skirt whilst these men from hell dragged them off. I can still hear their screams. One man amongst them stood there watching, his hands folded against his chest, his eyes impassive. I ran to him, got down on my knees before him and pleaded with him to spare my girls, no matter what it took. He simply kicked me away and laughed as I lay on the ground bleeding, watching my beautiful kinder leave through the gate never to return."

"This man, Sybill …?"

"I would recognise him anywhere. Adolf Weissmuller!"

With those desolate words echoing in Cydney's ears, the family faded away leaving her alone with Ray and her tears cascading as she sobbed into her hands.

"I'm not up to this. I can't … the thought … oh my God, this man!"

"You are. Why do you think you have been shown all of this? You are only given things you can cope with, you know that."

"Please help me. What should I do?"

"You will find a way, and I am here to guide you."

Completely alone, Cydney had never experienced such feelings of desolation, but more importantly, pure inadequacy. This Albert Whiteman, or Adolf Weissmuller, had to be made accountable for everything he had done, no matter how many years had passed, and she vowed with every bone in her body and with whatever it took, that she would make this come about.

There was more information to be gathered and Harold and Alfie were going to be her first ports of call. They had to tell her all the truth now; she couldn't rely totally on what Sybill and Mordecai showed her. There was also the matter of a certain Jackson Dwyer III; although everything had occurred before he'd entered the bank, it was possible he was in possession of certain invaluable information.

Despite the hour, Cydney telephoned through to Tom's room. Evidently, he was equally as awake as the phone was picked up immediately. In the background, she could hear the television.

"Morning boss. You up early, too?"

"It's the blasted jetlag. Anyway, I want you to use your influence and get us a meeting with Liam Ross."

"Through Joe, you mean?"

"Yes. You obviously got on his side. Take him a bottle of whisky or something to whet his appetite. I think we need some more background information."

"And Liam's the one to give it to us?"

"Well, he's a start. I doubt we can get to see the governor - not yet anyway, but that may well happen."

"Okay. I'll get out there again. What about you? Where are you going?"

"I've got some things to do here and I'm waiting for Richard to call me back. If we can get out to Liam today, that would be really good. I don't want to waste time on this."

"Especially as these guys are nearly pushing up daisies."

"Well, that's not quite how I would put it myself. I would suggest we act sooner rather than later."

"What about our friendly president, Jackson Dwyer III? Do you want to see him again?"

"Yes. Definitely. But not yet. This is like a giant puzzle and I'm still putting together the corners and outside pieces. Once that's done, we can fill in the middle."

"Sounds like a plan. You meeting me for breakfast?"

"No, Tom, you carry on. I'm going to take a short walk first so let's meet around midday. That will give us time to go and see Liam, hopefully this afternoon, if you can use your charm."

CHAPTER SEVENTEEN

R ICHARD was in shock. He'd had a rather long telephone conversation with one of the directors of the Holocaust Survivors Centre in London and was now staring at his computer screen with the eyes of a certain Sturmbannführer Adolf Weissmuller, in a black and white photograph, staring back at him. It was the darkness of those eyes that unnerved him in a way he had never experienced before; it was as if they had no soul, like looking into pure evil. A shiver went through him as he read about this man who had worked himself up the Nazi ranks from such a young age, culminating with him being responsible for the deportation of many thousands of elderly and sick people from the ghetto to the extermination camps of Chelmno but, more particularly, with the taking of twenty thousand children from their families to their deaths. It seemed his work at Lodz had been recognised to such an extent that he had been sent as second in command to Auschwitz, where his main responsibility had been to supervise the gas chambers, and finally on to Dachau. Richard was sickened to his stomach reading the stories from survivors of this man who had never been captured after the war and had, for all intents and purposes, completely disappeared off the face of the earth.

The other name Cydney had given him, Dieter Scholler, gave him less chills. He was able to check the Swiss registry of births and deaths and he discovered the man had indeed been born in 1914, a year before Weissmuller, in Zurich. His life had been fairly mediocre. He'd been a clerk at the Swiss National Bank, single with no family, until he died, suddenly, in an accident in 1945. Richard studied the picture of the man in closer detail. Strangely, both he and Weissmuller bore an uncanny resemblance; same height and build and with equally blond hair. The only difference were the eyes, which in Scholler showed a gentleness that Weissmuller's lacked.

Richard read the details again and the fact that Scholler had worked at SNB jumped out at him, especially after his current research into the part that the bank had played during the war. He sat back in his chair and stretched his arms above his head, pondering everything he had discovered over the last few days. It all seemed so coincidental, but in his trade and with his experience, he knew that coincidences rarely occurred. Now he had to report his findings back to Cydney and, judging by the time difference, he hoped she would be awake and that she would enlighten him more as to her thinking and what she had discovered to date.

"Good morning. Glad you're up."

"I've been up for ages."

"Are you okay? You sound a bit snuffly." It sounded as if she'd been crying but he knew she was never going to tell him, even if that was the case.

"I'm fine, thanks. Must be the air conditioning in the hotel room. How are things going? What have you got for me?"

"Everything you wanted and I have to say, for a change, that it was relatively easy. Adolf Weissmuller was quite a high ranking Nazi officer considering his age. He escaped after the war and nobody has ever been able to trace him. There were a lot of people who tried, specifically from the Simon Wiesenthal Center, who are renowned for capturing escaped Nazis. However, this one eluded even them and he is still on their records as having evaded capture. I'm sure if they knew we may have discovered him, they would be more than delighted."

"What about the other guy, Dieter Scholler?"

"It would be nice if you could give me a bit of background on why him. It would seem he was a normal guy, working at the Swiss National Bank. However, Switzerland had a small number of members of the Nazi party so maybe he was involved and helped Weissmuller as a sympathiser. It would make sense as nothing else in particular in his life stands out, except for the fact he died suddenly in 1945. A car accident, apparently."

"Why do you say 'apparently'?" Cydney said, but already from her voice Richard knew she was having the same thought about there never being coincidences.

"Come on, tell me. There's more to this, especially as we're investigating the money received by Harold and Alfie coming out of nowhere."

"I believe Albert Whiteman is, or was, Adolf Weissmuller. In fact, I have little doubt in my mind. When he escaped from Germany, I think he went to Switzerland where all his money was secreted."

"The gold he had looted?"

"Yes. However, he couldn't use his own name so who better than someone who worked at SNB."

"And by all accounts was the spitting image of him," added Richard. "I've seen the photos."

"Well, even better."

"Scholler dying like he did was probably no accident."

"Absolutely. Weissmuller was no innocent to murder and probably planned the whole thing."

"Do you think they knew each other?"

"I would guess they must have done in some way. Weissmuller was obviously using someone there to help him, possibly unwittingly, but not sure, and to account for all the monies coming in. He probably chose Scholler for the very reason he was a loner, unmarried from what you've told me, and wouldn't be missed too much."

"And he took his identity? That must have been quite easy in

139

some ways, especially after the war when the banking system was in disarray and Switzerland was in the firing line so nobody would have been too busy looking at passports and checking up."

"This made it easy for him to leave the country," Cydney said. "I have little doubt in my mind."

"So what now? Can you get me a recent picture of him? I obtained one from the Holocaust Center, though it's from his early days."

"Well, that's what's strange, although knowing what we do, maybe not so much, considering the circumstances. We can't find any pictures of him in the media. At all."

"He's still hiding, although at ninety it would be difficult to check if he's one and the same man. I have to add I've seen this guy's eyes and those would never change. Can you try again?"

"I'm going to. I want to show the picture to Harry and Alfie and see if they recognise the man. If they do, I think you need to get them out here."

"What? To Charleston?"

"Yes. Who else can do it?"

"I agree, but they're elderly and may not want to travel, or to look this man in the face again. It could be too traumatic for them."

"Perhaps ask them, in your inimitable way. I suggest you arrange another meeting in the office. Tell them what you've found out, gauge their reactions. Adolf Weissmuller was a wicked, evil man and if it were me, I would want to see him brought to justice during my lifetime, no matter what."

"Okay. I'll call them and get them in. You and Tom could be in danger. If Whiteman is our man, do you not think he'll take every measure imaginable to stop you discovering him and getting this out into the open? He has a lot to lose, especially with his son as governor and about to run in the primaries. West Virginia is a small state in comparison to others, which is probably why he chose to hide there. Don't forget he was chairman of one of the biggest banks in that state."

"I know, Rich. I met up with Jackson Dwyer, the third no less."

"And?"

"Well, he threw me out of his office." Richard laughed at the thought of his boss being chucked out of anywhere. "And it wasn't funny. I was trying to obtain information from him about the investigation into Prime's affairs in 1939, their possibly aiding Hitler's cause. He wanted nothing to do with us. However, I think it was because he was protecting the bank's position, not because he knew anything. This was way before his time."

"Are you going to see him again?"

"Too right I am, but I want to be armed with more information first. Also, I have a feeling Weissmuller wants to be found."

"Why do you say that?"

"Because this is too easy. He's making it easy for us. Yes, we're doing our normal due diligence and investigations. He must realise this information can't be difficult to find. Anyone could, once they had all the facts."

"What are your next steps?"

"Tom and I want to go and meet up with his predecessor, Liam Ross, and see what he can tell us. I'm also going to speak to my friend, Anthea Grunewald. You remember her, don't you? She's the psychologist I've known for years. Specialises in psychopathic behaviour. I'd like to understand this Weissmuller. Anyway, I'll call you later. Let me know how you get on with our clients."

* * *

To take her mind off things, Cydney spent the next couple of hours meandering around the little boutiques and book shops of Charleston, buying a few presents to take home for Lauren and Jake, a lovely new-born set for Claire, which she would put away for a few months until the baby was born, and stopping to have brunch outside one of the lively coffee shops she had spotted the previous day. Sipping her Americano and biting into the succulent cinnamon Danish she had craved, she attempted to take stock of all the events since her arrival in Charleston only two days ago, although it seemed so much longer. Her brain was in overdrive with the thoughts running through it. So much to absorb, so much pain she had taken from Sybill and Mordecai that it was hard for her to cope and she still had to deal with her own situation, never mind anyone else's.

She called Sean from her mobile and in those few seconds before he answered, some sort of clarity entered her mind. Until Steve was found, her life had to be put on hold. More importantly, her relationship with George, whom she had come to love without a doubt, would not be able to go any further. Explaining that was going to be one of the hardest things, and one he couldn't possibly understand. The husband who had been declared dead over five years ago was perhaps still alive somewhere and she was receiving messages about him from someone in spirit. When spoken aloud, it was definitely not something someone like George, with his logical, legal brain, would find easy to accept.

"Hi, Sean."

"I wasn't expecting to hear from you today. Don't worry about little Lauren. She's all packed up and raring to go."

"No, I'm not calling about her. It's about your aunt."

"Is anything wrong?"

"We talked about this before and I had my doubts about her welfare but now I think it's really important you go to see her. I think she needs you as soon as possible."

"My poor ailing aunt. Yes, it's a constant concern for me."

"Glad you understand. Once Lauren goes off, you should fly out. Jake will be fine, he's busy anyway. Tell him your aunt is ill again, that you need to be there."

"And the rest of my family?"

"Definitely. They should go with you as planned. I'll leave it up to you how you go about this."

"And George?"

"I can deal with him. For now he's away and so am I, and might be for longer than I expected. Do what you need to do. However long it takes."

"Yes, ma'am."

Disconnecting the call, Cydney wondered, not for the first time, where on earth her life was leading. If there was a plan, she wished to God it would reveal itself to her because this not knowing, this uncertainty, was breaking her apart.

CHAPTER EIGHTEEN

BACK in the hotel room, Cydney was waiting for Tom to report back when there was a knock at the door. She opened it, expecting her associate to be there.

"I apologise for disturbing you. May I come in?"

"I recognise you. Liam Ross, isn't it?"

"You don't seem surprised."

"You know, nothing surprises me anymore. I have to admit you weren't the first person I would have put here. You've pre-empted my visit to you. Do come in, though. Take a seat." She directed him into the suite. "Can I get you anything?"

"Coffee, please. You know, I haven't been in town for nearly forty years."

"That must be a shock to the system. How did you find out about me?"

"My cousin, Jackson. He visited me yesterday. I hadn't seen him since he was a boy. Told me you were looking into the affairs of the bank, and Albert Whiteman."

"Interesting that whatever I said must have got to him so quickly."

"He's worked hard to get where he is, no thanks to Albert."

"I'm sure, but whatever he said to you, it must have taken something for you to leave your home."

"It certainly did, ma'am. I've been a recluse for many years. After my wife and kids died, well I disappeared."

Cydney viewed the man sitting opposite her. His hands were visibly shaking but he was doing his utmost to hide the fact by holding them together in his lap, wringing them occasionally. She immediately took to him. His eyes held a gentleness that belied his anxiety, plus a deep sorrow that seemed to emanate from his soul. In spite of his discomfort, he was not afraid to look directly at her.

"I'm not sure why you're in Charleston, to be honest, or what brought you here, but you sure enough wrangled my cousin."

"Enough for you to come to see me?"

"Yep."

"You're right. I've come to check out the bank's activities."

"Not for a newspaper article?"

"No. I'm going to be honest with you because I can see what this means to you."

"I appreciate that, ma'am."

"Cydney. You're correct, there is no article. I am what they call a corporate forensics expert. My firm is brought in to look at particular cases, or events ..."

"Such as Whiteman Trust," said Liam.

"Exactly. More particularly, Albert Whiteman."

"It's about time."

"Why do you say that? Here, have some more coffee," she offered, pouring some into his cup. She noticed his hands were still shaking. "Please be assured anything you say to me is in the strictest confidence. I am not the police and I'll keep your name out of anything I learn. I have clients who have an interest in him and they are my priority. Do you mind if I ask you a few questions? I understand you were the chairman before Albert Whiteman. Can you tell me about that and why you gave up your position and place on the Board?"

"It's very simple. I'd been chairman for only a few years when I discovered he was embezzling funds, and over a long period of time. He'd been extremely clever and assumed nobody would notice as the quantities were so small."

"How did he get away with it?"

"Probably my fault, or my daddy's. We didn't have the right internal audit controls in place. He must have been laughing at us for so long."

"How much are we talking about here?"

"Millions of dollars, all taken over what must have been a twenty-five year period or more, pretty much since he joined the bank, and he could have been doing this for long after I left also."

"How come it wasn't noticed? I don't get it. You were a leading bank."

"In some ways it was quite easy, as long as you knew how. It was all done through suspense accounts, changing ledgers, hiding transactions. Whiteman oversaw the everyday workings and there was nobody to verify his work. Then it was brought to my attention by one of the clerks and I quietly investigated everything over a few months and realised what he was doing."

"And you confronted him?"

"I sure did. He threatened me. Said he would bring it to the Board's attention that I was the defrauder."

"Why would anyone believe that when you were the chairman?"

"He'd covered his tracks. Somehow he'd got hold of my control passwords and a lot of the movement of monies were done under those controls, so, for all intents and purposes, it would appear I'd been the one. We argued. He said I couldn't prove anything. Hell, I had no choice but to walk away."

"Which left him with everything, and he took over as chairman. So easy."

"You don't seem too surprised here, ma'am. What's your interest?"

The image of a car driven by a beautiful brunette and two young children came into her vision. They were singing and the children were clapping their hands in time to the music when suddenly the car catapulted off a mountain road and down the side, turning over and over until finally coming to a crashing halt and bursting into flames. Their screams filled the air and echoed in her ears. She sensed acutely their connection to the man sitting opposite her.

"Before I tell you, Liam, is there anything else you've forgotten? Your wife and children?" Cydney spoke tenderly, now aware of the circumstances surrounding their deaths.

"He killed them."

"The car accident?"

"You know? How could ...?" She watched as his eyes teared up, the pain raw still and so brutally apparent.

"Suffice it to say, I do. I'm going to tell you everything I've found out about Albert Whiteman. Some of it will come as a surprise in many ways. However, I have to get you to promise you will keep this to yourself, for the moment anyway. I have to be able to deal with it my way, and only my way, is that clear? The consequences of what I'm going to tell you will be far reaching and could bring about the collapse of the bank, although I'm sure if Jackson finds out he will do everything in his power to keep this quiet."

"I promise. You realise he needs to protect it, whatever it costs."

"Yes, though I doubt the bank can be saved. This is too significant and the FBI will need to be involved. However, my interest is purely to protect my clients and to expose Whiteman for the mass murderer and fraudster he is. Anything else is up to you. Originally, I had no intention of making this public but I can't in all honesty let this pass."

"Mass murderer? Is that what you said?"

"Yes indeed. You heard it right. Let me explain and you can make up your own mind."

"I would believe Whiteman capable of anything. I hated him with a vengeance, from the beginning. What could be worse than murdering my family?"

"I have to rely on your promise though, to keep this quiet for the moment."

"You have my word."

The next words were crucial but she wasn't sure how he was going to take the news of what she had to impart. "I have reason to believe Albert Whiteman is in fact an escaped Nazi called Adolf Weissmuller."

"He's what? What the hell …"

"This is the story we've uncovered."

"But that's absolutely …"

"Hard to believe, after all this time. We discovered this as part of our investigations. Two of my clients, both survivors of the concentration camps, received bearer bonds for one million dollars each, drawn on one of the subsidiary banks, Prime. They first encountered Weissmuller when they were in the ghetto of Lodz, and again in the camps at Auschwitz and Dachau. When I say encountered, I mean they were witness to the many crimes he committed against the Jewish people, but not only them. He was responsible for thousands upon thousands of deaths, sending people to the gas chambers, and when Dachau was liberated, he disappeared from view, completely off the radar."

"I can believe this. So murdering my wife and children meant nothing to him? At all?" The sorrow on Liam's face was difficult for Cydney to witness but she had no choice but to continue. It was important he realised the full capabilities of this man.

"It was a means to an end, hard as that may sound. Everything he does, or did, was to cover his tracks."

"When he came here, we were told he was a relative from Switzerland, very wealthy, and in fact he injected huge amounts of cash into the bank to capitalise its assets."

"And where do you think that money came from?"

"Nobody asked. Do you think my daddy knew?"

"We're still investigating the money side but from our investigations, it's probable the funds were looted. He must have had some help here."

"Oh my God - he married my sister! What if she had found out?"

"I think he was good at hiding everything, basically, but I have no idea."

"And Ted, my cousin, the governor. If this were to come out ..."

"Yes, I know," Cydney said. "He couldn't continue - and it will come out." She had gone through all the ramifications so many times in her own mind.

"How in God's name did he get the money out of Germany?"

"Let me explain how I think he managed this. I can only surmise for the moment, and forgive me if I'm preaching to the converted. You were a banker for many years so I may be telling you things you're already familiar with."

"Don't you worry. I've been out of it for many years. Banking was never in my blood, not like the rest of my family."

"Okay. It's a bit long-winded but bear with me. As you're aware, gold is universally treated like money, but the fact it can be touched means it can disappear. Germany was plagued with inflation and had stopped backing its currency with gold during World War I. However, when Hitler came to power he exploited the economic meltdown and drained Germany's gold holdings, including assets he seized from the Jewish population, to fund World War II. He desperately needed money for the army, navy and air force.

"In 1939, Hitler issued a decree placing the Reichsbank under his control and extended its role to store the loot taken from the victims of the war, such as gold, jewellery, money and other valuables. As Hitler's hold strengthened, the Reichsbank seized the gold deposits of all the occupied countries, had it re-smelted by the bank and stamped RB, with the German eagle, and dated

1938; in other words before the war, so it would look as if it belonged to them.

"As the war progressed, more assets were seized, including money, and these were credited to the SS accounts held at the bank. A lot of the money, according to a theory, ended up in Switzerland in an account to help the Nazis escape should the war not end in their favour."

"Wasn't there a Bank for International Settlements set up purely for central banks to work together before the war?" asked Liam.

"Yes, exactly. The BIS was a joint creation in 1930 and it included the Federal Reserve Bank in New York as well as the Reichsbank and the Banks of England, Italy and France, amongst others. Its inspiration came from the president of the Reichsbank who was partly raised in Brooklyn and had powerful Wall Street connections."

"So, the assets couldn't be confiscated, even in war?"

"Well, yes. Gold was central to this as it could be easily transferred between the nations, which was essential to Germany. Also, they needed Switzerland as much as Switzerland needed Germany, because that's where they held their gold reserves. Switzerland had its doors open to all nations and traded with all governments, despite its neutrality. If Germany wanted to sell gold for fuel or grain, for example, the SNB moved the gold accordingly.

"However, Germany didn't keep to their word. When they invaded a country, they looted the gold reserves which had been placed in a BIS account and transferred it to an account at Reichsbank in central depositaries so it couldn't be traced, and finally into Switzerland. By 1939, millions had been invested into Germany by the BIS."

"And what about Whiteman?" asked Liam. "Or should I say Adolf Weissmuller."

"He was in a very good position at the various camps to steal, or re-locate monies and gold from the people he had sent to their deaths, for himself. It would have been easy for him to put them into his own account and nobody would check it out as it was going on all the time, and in large quantities. Don't forget your family had branches in Germany and France themselves, which would have aided this."

"My grandfather, Jolyon, was chairman at the time," said Liam. "He must have been in his early sixties before my father, Edward, took over the reins. This is unbelievable. They must have known about this. How could they have not been involved?"

"I've no idea, but just to finish off, and this is the most important part, the gold that was taken - jewellery, dental fillings - would have been re-cast by Weissmuller's associates at the bank and laundered into currency so it would come out the other end in Switzerland looking legitimate and untainted. No gold would have changed hands as it was purely a paper transfer between the banks in different countries, simply a matter of transferring ownership of assets held in vaults. Monies could then be transferred to America. A sort of money laundering at the basest level."

"Which is why he had monies to capitalise Prime after the war."

"Well, that's the theory. Yes. Also, he would have had the means to move monies within Germany to Ross' branch from accounts he had seized."

"My God. And then to Prime here? So our bank was capitalised by looted gold? And my daddy had no idea all this was going on behind our backs?"

"I can't say."

"It sure seems so easy on the face of it. How did he escape from Germany after the war?"

"We believe he made his way into Switzerland, with help. When there, we think he assumed the identity of a man called Dieter Scholler, who died in 1945. A lot of this is speculation, for now anyway."

151

"That was Albert Whiteman's name when he arrived here before he was naturalised," said Liam. "He took back his own name, almost? Was he really laughing at us when he did that?"

"It wouldn't surprise me. Anyway, now we have to somehow identify him, which won't be easy after all this time."

"By your clients? They must be elderly themselves."

"They are and maybe reluctant to put themselves through all of this trauma," Cydney said, "although I think they would want to know one way or another. They have no desire to keep the money they've been sent, but they are adamant they want to find out from where it came."

"Why would Whiteman expose himself at this stage? It must have been so easy for the bearer bonds to be traced."

"I don't know. Maybe he was having feelings of guilt, if that's possible. And yes, it was fairly easy to trace, almost as if he wanted to be found out. I have no idea why." Cydney didn't mention the fact she had a feeling her clients knew already the money was from Weissmuller.

"That man wouldn't recognise guilt if it came up and bit him on the face. So what is your plan now? How can we expose him and still preserve the integrity of the bank if what you say is true?"

"I'm still working that one out, to be honest."

"Should we tell what we know to Jackson? He's like a dog with a bone when he senses something and his hackles are up, I can tell you."

"Is that something you should do without me, Liam? I think it important we know Whiteman is Adolf Weissmuller before we do anything, although I don't have a doubt in my mind it is him. Can I suggest we wait until my associate speaks to my clients?"

"Yes, I agree. Let's get our facts straight first but, my God, I can't believe I'm so near to getting my revenge on this man who murdered my family."

Cydney placed her hand lightly over Liam's and her eyes never wavered from his, demanding him to believe how much he could trust her. "If it is really him, we will bring him to justice in one way or another. On that you have my word."

CHAPTER NINETEEN

"**D**O come in, gentlemen," said Richard. "Thank you so much for taking the time to join me, especially as Mrs Granger is in the States at the moment."

"We assume you have some news for us." Harold took a seat next to his old friend, Alfie. Richard gazed at them closely; although dressed in their usual dapper way, they seemed to have aged in the last couple of weeks, not surprisingly in view of the circumstances. However, one thing he noticed was that they gave the impression of being uncomfortable in his presence. Alfie was fidgeting about in his chair, fussing over the paper and pad in front of him and moving his hand around his shirt collar, as if to loosen his tie.

"Yes, I do have news, and some of it may come as a shock to you. Are you completely ready for this and anything I might tell you?"

"We have discussed this, Mr Barratt, and we are sure of it. However, you may like to hear what we have to say first. Alfie and I have made a decision. There are some things we have kept from you, not for any particular reason of wanting to lie, more to protect ourselves and our families." So that's why they wouldn't meet his eye. He recalled the conversation with Cydney, when she'd mentioned she thought they hadn't revealed everything they knew.

"I'm happy to listen, and I appreciate your candidness. Before you begin, I should say first we believe we've found Adolf Weissmuller." On hearing the name, Harold put his right hand to his heart and leant back as if he was about to pass out, and Alfie looked immediately frightened. His face had turned as pale as his friend's.

"That's what we were afraid of," Alfie said, without elaborating more.

"You believe he sent you the money?" Richard knew the answer already, judging by their expressions.

"Yes, Mr Barrett, and that's why we want to come clean with you." Harold turned to Alfie. "Shall I start?" His friend nodded, almost as if he was unable to utter a word. "I need to take you back to when I was in the Lodz Ghetto with my family, which was the first time I came across Adolf Weissmuller. It was 4th September 1942. My father and I were working in the factory making uniforms for the Germans when we heard so much screaming and shots being fired continuously, men shouting and whistles being blown. Nobody there had any idea what was going on. We were not able to leave our places for fear of being shot or whipped ourselves, but we were incapable of working or concentrating."

"A lot of German uniforms must have fallen apart in battle, thankfully," added Alfie.

"Good job we Jews retain a sense of humour. Anyway, we all wondered what was going on, but we soon found out. When we eventually left the factory we came home and found out my sisters had been taken."

"Taken?" Richard asked them, trying to understand the implication of what they were telling him.

"Yes. Along with twenty thousand other children. They were rounded up and marched out the gates."

"To go where?"

"We discovered later they were sent to the extermination camps at Chelmno, about fifty kilometres away. I never saw Gerthe or Mathilde again. My mother was in shock. Her hair turned grey overnight and she lay on the bed without moving.

We could get no words from her at all and only our neighbours were there to tell us. My mother never said one word again, never ate or got up from her bed. They moved her to the hospital so she could be tended properly. She slipped away over the next couple of weeks and never regained consciousness. So then it was just me and my father. We started out all of us together and then we were two."

"And Weissmuller?"

"On that same day when we came back from work, he was standing around with his troops, their guns at the ready in case anyone in the ghetto revolted against their orders. I asked someone who he was. They told me 'the devil himself'. We were forced to walk past him as if nothing had happened. I will never forget his face, though. He was smiling. Smiling! Pleased with what he had achieved. But, oh my God, he sent my beautiful, precious sisters to their deaths, and was responsible for killing my wonderful mama. If I live another hundred years, I will never be able to put him from my mind."

Tears he had tried so hard to contain were now flowing freely down Harold's face and his friend passed him a white, perfectly laundered handkerchief, patting him gently on the back to comfort him.

"I was reunited with Harold in late 1943," Alfie took over, "and purely by chance. My family and I had been there several months. Neither of us knew. I attended a secret meeting behind Molenzki's bakers and heard Harold speaking to the Committee. I would have known that voice anywhere."

"We have not been separated since," added Harold.

* * *

Lodz 1943

"How easy is it to escape?" These were the first words uttered by Hans.

"Virtually impossible. We have a committee in place, of course, but once in, that's basically it."

Hans nodded his understanding to one of the men. He didn't believe it though. He knew he couldn't leave his father now to fend for himself but he needed out; he could do more good working with the partisans than he could stuck in a factory helping the Nazi cause by sewing uniforms and manufacturing war supplies for the Third Reich, which was all anybody seemed to be doing. As he was about to enter into a further discussion on the possibilities of escape, he felt a tap on the shoulder.

In his frustration at the interruption, Hans swore and turned with a view to hitting someone, but found himself face to face with his best friend whom he hadn't seen for so long, and never expected to again. They looked at one another in silence; no words were necessary. Within seconds, Hans grabbed his friend in a hard embrace as if he would never let him go.

"I never thought ..."

"I would see you again ..." Ari finished the sentence.

"My brother!" He felt the fragile bones beneath the ragged clothes they were both wearing and for the first time Hans realised how much weight he must have lost also.

"My brother!" Unashamed tears fell down Ari's face.

"How on earth did you get here? I can't believe ..."

"The same way as you, no doubt."

"You've grown, Ari. You're the same height as me now. I have to know everything. Let's sneak out of here. We have to be careful. The bloody police will have us if they find us."

Later that night after the boys had caught up, Hans sneaked back into his building hoping his father had not heard his movements but if he had, thankfully, he had lain there and let him do what he wanted to do, helpless to stop him in any case. His boots in his hand, Hans nearly fell back down the stairs in the darkness, tripping over what was probably a rat that scurried past him. He managed to prevent any accident although he almost screamed out an expletive but then remembered where he was and stopped in case somebody heard it. The whole stairwell wreaked of that sickly sweet cloying smell of dead rats, which permeated the very walls. That, mixed with the odour of many unwashed bodies, damp, and human waste, was hard to ignore.

Hans recognised his papa had aged so much since his beloved wife and daughters had gone the year before but he was unable to help him anymore. He doubted his father would survive much longer, and it was important for Hans to get through this war and out the other side in one piece. It wasn't the fact of being selfish, because he certainly never supposed himself to be that. However, if he could survive, even just him, it would be one in the eye for Hitler and a chance for the future, for him, and Ari, and retribution for all the murdered Jews. The other reason was that he needed to tell the world, personally, just what was going on - because God knows anyone would be hard-pressed to believe the story.

A few nights later the boys met up again at the baker's shop, knocking at the door as advised. The door was opened a fraction and they were pulled in and taken through to the back where there were at least seventy others, men and women, crowded around the oven, grabbing as much heat as they could.

"Who told you to come here?" one of the older women asked. "We don't allow boys here."

"I invited them. They're my friends. We need young men to help us," someone replied, not giving Hans a chance to react, especially as he was chomping at the bit in his efforts to say something.

"Anyway, let's continue." One of the elder men brought everyone's attention to a new proclamation he was holding in his hand. "The Committee have been ordered to supply a few thousand of us for resettlement into the labour camps, starting from next week."

"What?" shouted out a Pole from the back of the crowd. "That's impossible."

"And it gets worse. It's per day. We are to have people ready each day, march them to the gates where they'll be taken off."

"How can we do this? How will we choose?" one asked.

"We can't do this," another shouted out. "We'll all be killed."

"I say we protest. For a change, say no!" someone else argued.

"Is this our way to escape, Ari?" Hans whispered, leaning in to his friend. "Let's volunteer. Once we're out, we can run away and join the partisans. I want to fight, not be holed up here."

"I agree, but I don't think it' going to be that easy. How can we possibly escape when we're always under guard? I think we should bide our time. There will be safety in numbers and if we are all together ..."

"Maybe. I don't know. That's what my papa told me and look where we are. Let's see. I think we should agree to go. Anything is better than being here. It has to be, doesn't it? I need to get out."

"I'll do whatever you want, but what about your papa, Hans?"

The boy next to him, all of sixteen by now, looked pensive. "I'll tell him we're leaving. I'll tell him to stay here and when all this is over, I'll come back and rescue him."

"I'll do the same. You make me brave. I don't know how my mama will react. Perhaps in a couple of months we can come back and see them again. This is for a short time, isn't it?"

The naivety of this statement from the friend he loved didn't fail to grab Hans' heart. Underneath, he knew there was no coming back and they were saying goodbye to what remained of their families.

"I'm not sure how long it will be. We may never see them again. We have to be prepared for this, Ari. Are you? We don't know what will happen to them, or to us."

"We have to do it. I'm with you, wherever you go. Let's do it." Their fates were sealed.

Present

"Of course you never made it to the partisans," Richard said.

"No, sir. Not then, anyway, not until after the war. We were marched out the gates the following week, a few thousand of us, under heavy guard, to the station and onto those same cattle trains again. We never even glanced back. We couldn't think of our families. We started off feeling so positive. Of course, there was no escape. It was impossible. We were packed in with all these other men and boys. We tried to break through the slats in the carriage but it would have meant certain death. We had to live; it was the only thought in our minds."

"And we never saw our families again," added Alfie. "We were so young, so positive, until we ended up in Auschwitz."

"When was that?" asked Richard.

"It must have been in early 1944. The uprising in Lodz was in August 1944. We were gone before that. I remember it was very cold when we arrived. The sky was obscured and there was this awful smell everywhere. We saw chimneys billowing out smoke and we didn't know why. They told us it was from the crematoriums. It was enough to send chills to our hearts. You see, Auschwitz was a holding camp, purely for selection as to who would live and who would die, and to provide labour to other camps. We had no idea. Nobody did. When we arrived, we were on a list. Everybody's names. We were sent to one side, to the left. Those to the right, well, we never saw them again."

"And you were how old?"

"We were almost seventeen, probably. I lost count of time. It meant nothing as every day was the same nightmare. When we left the train station, we had to go through selection still. We were classed as adults and we were all sent together to the showers. We thought this was it! We had heard about the gas chambers but …"

"I recall how scared I was," Alfie said, "and so cold. They stole everything we had, even our names, and destroyed us. We were nothing. Our clothes were taken and replaced with this uniform of striped pyjamas to wear, and we had wooden clogs for our feet. Nothing fitted. Our heads were shaved and numbers carved out in our skin. That's all we were - a number. We expected to die but we came out of the showers. Obviously, we were more useful alive because we could work. We were put in the barracks with a thousand others. You would not believe the smell. It was hardly bearable."

"And you worked?"

"No. There was no work. We were up at four-thirty in the morning. We had to share toilet facilities, which were wooden boards with holes. No privacy. No sanitation. Then there was roll-call. We were put into rows and had to listen to long lists of orders and instructions and made to stand for hours on end while we were counted, and counted again. Sometimes, if the guards were angry, they made us all squat with our hands on our heads for so long. Many passed out and were dragged away and shot or gassed."

"Mr Barratt, we had to keep going, for us and for our families."

"And you still have those numbers tattooed on your arms?"

"Yes." Both men lifted their sleeves. "Always there as a reminder," Harold said. "And, do you know what made us stay alive more than anything? When we saw Adolf Weissmuller again. I swore to all that was holy I would take my revenge on him one day and to do that I had to live."

"What was his role there?" Richard asked.

"When we were standing outside during all those hours, he would check out the guards, make sure they were doing what he told them. I watched him pull out his pistol and shoot so many people through the head if they moved, or looked at him, even. He strutted around like he was God, above everybody."

"And in some ways he was," added Alfie. "He had power over whether we would live or die."

"How long were you there?"

"Not too long. I think we stayed until January 1945. We never knew the exact date but I remember the snow and the freezing temperature. All we heard was that the Soviet army were advancing on Poland and they needed to get us out. The SS started removing all evidence of the killings that went on, destroying records and demolishing many of the buildings. Fifty-eight thousand of us were marched out by the SS under guard and they wanted to make sure not one single person would remain alive to tell their tales. We were put on freight trains once again, and marched to near the German border. Always on the march, the death marches they called them. Miles and miles, non-stop walking. No food, nothing to protect us from the severely cold temperatures, and practically everyone suffering with typhus or pneumonia. So many people died on those marches."

"How did you manage?"

"God only knows," Harold said. "It must have been His will. By nature we are neither of us very religious men but someone was looking out for us."

"And did you see Weissmuller again?"

"Yes. That man was sent to haunt me all my life. Even now, it would seem. When we eventually got to Dachau, he was there."

"Please, tell me," said Richard, as kindly as he could.

"We arrived exhausted, weak and very near death. Dachau was made up of nearly one hundred sub-camps, all work camps, located throughout southern Germany and Austria. We lived in constant fear. Our treatment was brutal, nothing like we had experienced before. It was beneath human dignity. We lived in overcrowded conditions and received hardly any food, yet were expected to work from dawn until dusk, heavy labour type of work. We learned that life expectancy was only two months; the work was intended to kill. It was as if they had this endless supply of people turning up to die."

"Let me continue," Alfie said. "We had some kind of breakthrough, which I think saved our lives, although at the time I thought we were going to our deaths. We were told to report to the administration block. Can you imagine our fear, though? We knew as well as everybody that was where the medical block was situated. You would not believe the screaming that came from there, every day. We heard everything yet had to try and ignore what was going on. There were all sorts of rumours about what went on. They did the ice experiments there, you know."

"Ice? What were they?"

"There was a special unit where they used to freeze men, women and children until they were nearly dead and then bring them slowly back to life, and start again. Yes, actually freeze them. Lowered their body temperatures to such an extent that their hearts would stop. The purpose was to carry out tests for soldiers in arctic conditions when they were on the Russian front, for naval and airmen and how they would survive in the sea. The pain must have been beyond anything we can imagine. We heard their screaming day and night."

"I never knew …"

"No. Normally people were sent there as a punishment. For a change we had done nothing wrong. The good thing was that we were taken away from the daily grind. We were so sure we would die, but we were wrong. We were sent to the kitchen, can you believe? All that food, staring at us, food we had not seen for so many years. It saved our lives, and those of our friends as we were able to smuggle bits out. Our job was to serve the officers, clear up. They only wanted young men."

"And Weissmuller?" enquired Richard.

"I saw him the first time I went to the officers' room," Harold said. "He was sitting with all his cohorts, smoking a large cigar, whisky in his hand, as if nothing wrong was happening in the world. My orders were to pass around trays of food, not to look at anyone, to stare at the ground beneath me. I wanted to stick a knife in his chest, you cannot imagine what went through my mind. I didn't, of course. All I could think of was what he had done to my family and all my friends. No. I would see it out, wait for my opportunity, and it came one day, out of the blue."

* * *

Dachau 1945

It was there, sneaking out from under one of the armchairs when he saw it. It stared at him -with a light of its own. In his heart he knew he should have totally ignored it and walked past before anyone noticed. He was drawn in like a magnet and there was no option but to pick it up.

Hans held the small and worn black leather notebook momentarily and then hurriedly hid it under his pyjama jacket inside his vest so it wouldn't slip out, looking around in case someone had noticed him. Music blared out from a five-piece band in the other room and the gravelly and raucous voices of drunken officers and their equally inebriated mistresses rose up around him. The sound made him sick to his stomach; that anyone could enjoy life against the abject misery of his every day existence. It was hard to suppress his anger but one day he would have his revenge; that was the one thought that kept him going.

He moved along the corridor and to the kitchen to collect more platters of food to serve to them, mouthing to his friend, Ari, that he needed to speak to him urgently. The chef turned on him, hearing him speak, and lashed out at him hard on his shoulder followed by a slap across his face, sending Hans sprawling into the side of the wooden table. He tasted the saltiness of the blood in his mouth and moved his tongue over the cut on his lip. The pain would have to come later.

"Jew boy, you lump of shit. Don't let me hear your voice ever again," the chef snarled. "Now pick up these platters and take them to the guests. Don't talk, don't look at anyone. Move! Now!"

Hans was pleased to receive support from Ari, who winked at him as he collected the food and ran out the kitchen. Later, when they had finished in the officer's club, well into the small hours of the morning, Hans withdrew the notebook, that by now was almost burning a hole in his vest, which he had managed to keep concealed.

"Look," he said, handing it over to his friend. "What should I do?" It was a simple enough question. "I haven't even dared open it but ..."

"Whose is it? How the hell ...?" Ari pondered for a few seconds. "Well, you can't give it back. You'll be shot without a minute's hesitation. We have to hide it somewhere, until all this is over."

"If we survive." Death hung over them like the sword of Damocles, entering every pore until it filled their lungs and blood. It was as certain as night becomes day, as the sun rising, as breathing.

"We have to, Hans. We have no choice. Where though? Someone will be searching for it. We may be questioned."

"Why? Anyone could have it. We need to look at it before we hide it. I want to know what's written inside. I'll have to put it somewhere."

"Where though? Are we ever going to get out of here?"

"We will be liberated. They told us the Allies are near. We'll come back and get it later."

"Please God," said Ari. "This is so dangerous. If you're caught ... you're risking your life."

"I know. This is so important. I can't let it go."

"Okay. Then I'm with you, but God help us."

* * *

Present
"So that's what it's all about."

"Yes, Mr Barrett. We have held onto this notebook, or rather

165

Harold has, all these years. It's been our insurance policy. Now it seems he has found us."

"He's given you money. Why? Why now?"

"Who knows? Perhaps he has a guilty conscience. I doubt it. He probably wants it back."

"What's in it?"

"Details of all the money he had stolen, deposits made, all the gold he had looted, diamonds, confiscated enterprises, everything written down in minute detail. More to the point, where it had gone." Harold looked straight at Richard. "We never thought he would find us. We thought we were safe. Every day we watched our backs, looking over our shoulders in case he was there. I have never lived in peace - not in over sixty years. The notebook taunted us."

"Do you have it with you?"

"Yes, sir, I have." Harold withdrew from the inside pocket of his suit a tattered leather notebook. Richard opened it tentatively, as if it were the Crown Jewels. The pages were thin from age and slightly torn at the edges. The writing on every page was small and neat, slightly italicised, with the right-hand margin indicating the amount against each entry, which went on for pages. It felt weighty between his fingers, more to do with the enormity of the meaning of what he was holding. Richard stared at the two men before him.

"All these years?"

"Now you understand. So, you have found him. Good. He is still a dangerous man, no matter his age. You must warn Mrs Granger. He will not think twice about harming anyone in his way now he's found us. I think he wanted us to know. He knew we would have no choice but to discover where the money came from and it really wasn't that difficult for you. He's a very clever man, Mr Barratt. Do not be fooled at all. I have seen him at work. Nobody who killed the way he did without compunction, without thought, for the fun of the kill, would change no matter how many decades had passed."

"Mrs Granger has discovered a lot about this Weissmuller. This is going to be difficult for you, but I have to ask. I have a photo of him here. Would you look?" He picked up a folder and taking the photograph out, held it towards them tentatively, not sure if he was doing the right thing or not. "It was sent to me by the Holocaust Survivors Centre. Is this Adolf Weissmuller?"

"I don't need to look. It is him. I can feel it," Harold said, his voice a mere whisper.

"I'll look. Pass it to me." Alfie took the folder and opened it. He stared at the black and white picture of a man in SS uniform and simply nodded to Richard, passing back the file. "I would recognise those eyes anywhere."

"There are no pictures of him as he is now, and no-one to identify him except you. Cydney wants you to go to America. Can you do this?"

The two gentlemen turned to each other and nodded simultaneously.

"Sir, we have lived for this day. Our answer is yes. We will go to America for you."

Alfie reached over and patted his friend's hand in confirmation. "I don't know how we managed to survive but we had each other. You kept us going, Harold. Now we will face our past together."

"And God willing, our future."

CHAPTER TWENTY

"HAROLD and Alfie have agreed to go."

"What did you tell them? Are they okay?"

"Yes. Shell shocked, if you pardon the expression. They want to see the end of this. You may have to stay out there a bit longer still, at least longer than you thought," Richard said.

"Christ. Lauren's going on holiday. I need to get home to Jake."

"I know that, but we have to see this through. I'll arrange their visas and travel plans. Hopefully for the day after tomorrow? I'll get Jenny to go to the American Embassy to sort this with them. It'll be quicker. I'll send you the flight details. I presume you can pick them up from the airport. I doubt they've been out of England for years."

"Richard, I suggest you get Jenny to bring them out. She'll be a good calming influence on them and, to be honest, I could do with her here."

"Yep, that makes sense. Leave it with me. By the way, did you speak to your psychologist friend?"

"Anthea? Yes I did. Interesting discussion actually."

"And …?"

"Well she has spent years studying psychopaths such as Weissmuller."

"Is that how she classes him?" asked Richard.

"Yes, and most of the Nazis."

"But Weissmuller must have been like this from a child. You can't just become psychopathic."

"You can appear normal. Nobody would know. Then something happens to trigger their actions. That's why they're able to kill without remorse. They have little or no conscience."

"So, no responsibility for their actions?"

"Exactly. They've done nothing wrong," Cydney said.

"Unbelievable. Weissmuller will do whatever he can to get away with his crimes. Is he dangerous - to our clients?"

"Possibly, or rather he was, but he's old now."

"Why did he send them money?"

"Fear. He can't stop his demise, so he's trying to save himself, trying to appear that he's sorry. Or, maybe, just letting them know he hasn't forgotten what they've got of his."

"Bloody hell, Cydney."

"I have to tell you - this is one of the worst cases I've ever worked on."

"You should hear what our two clients told me yesterday. Let's speak later and please take care. This Weissmuller, or Whiteman, whatever you want to call him, won't be rushing to shake your hand."

"We've been here before. It wasn't easy being run off the road last year by the friends of our dearly departed Benton, and look what happened to you."

"I survived. This entire story coming out, well, you know - you have a huge responsibility here."

"Yes. I realise that. Okay, later. Got to go, someone at the door. Probably Tom."

Cydney swung her legs off the bed and padded in her bare feet over to the door of her hotel room. It was obvious she wasn't going to get any rest today.

"Hi Tom ... George! What the hell! How come ...?"

"I couldn't live without you for another minute." He barged past her into the room, kicking the door behind him with his foot and enfolding her in a massive bear hug. Her arms remained by her side, she was far too shocked to move a muscle. "Haven't

169

you missed me?" His lips bore down on hers and she could feel herself responding. "I got the first plane out after my meetings and came straight here. Let me look at you. You seem tired," he remarked softly, his hands moving up and down her arms.

"I'm so surprised. I never expected you. You didn't call or anything."

"That was my intention, to surprise you. Rupert needed me to be in New York so I thought I might as well take a detour via West Virginia. Aren't you happy, my darling?"

"Yes, of course, but ..."

"I know, you're busy. I'll keep out of your way, eventually. Once I take care of a few of your, shall we say, requirements. And mine. God, I've missed you," he said with a groan. He kissed her again, this time with more passion, his intentions clear and not so honourable. She could not help herself, despite everything that was on her mind. She needed this release after what she had heard so allowed her body to take over her brain as she returned his desire in equal measures, with a desperation not felt before.

George manoeuvred her backwards to the bed, his tongue moving over her mouth, and pulled her top over her head and tossed it to the floor in his haste to get to her body. He unfastened her trousers and slid them off, leaving her almost bare and vulnerable, the way he liked her. His jacket was already off and discarded. He kicked off his shoes whilst she undid the buttons of his shirt, sliding it down his arms, and she bent to kiss his bare chest, nibbling all the while.

"Christ, Cydney," he said, his voice so low she could barely hear. "I want you. So much." Now he demanded her. He laid her on the bed, all the while his mouth covering hers until his body was ready to make its claim. "I never thought I would love anyone as much as I do you." His breath was slow as he removed the last of her clothes. "You are my life now, and forever."

Slowly, he entered her and their bodies moved cautiously at first. Cydney stared straight into George's eyes, searching for answers, and now believing what he'd said to her. Everything was clear as his body worshipped hers, tenderly and protectively. Thoughts of Steve were forgotten as the man with her, physically present, consumed her. His movements became quicker and more urgent, his breath shortened, and she knew he was almost there. She rose to meet him, her back arching under the sweet pain, and as they climaxed together, she cried out his name.

After a few moments George moved to the side and brought his arm around to encase Cydney in his embrace. His fingers trailed carelessly up and down her from her throat and over her breasts to her stomach, as if he couldn't bear not to touch her for one second. She loved the laziness of his caress and the feelings it evoked in her.

"Will you marry me?"

"What?"

"Will you marry me? I love you and can't bear to be without you for even a second. I want to be with you for the rest of my life, and I want to be a father to Lauren and Jake. Christ, I'll even adopt Sean."

Cydney sat up, the dream smashed into smithereens, the love-making brought to an abrupt end as she realised, with a resounding crash, that despite the fact she loved him, she couldn't marry him, not now. First she had to discover if Steve was alive or dead. Had a woman ever been faced with such an almighty dilemma before?

"Oh George. If only."

"Are you saying no? Don't you love me? Excuse me, have I totally misread this?"

"If only it were that simple. Yes, I do love you, but I don't think I'm free to marry you."

"What do you mean, not free? Your husband died five years ago. Of course you're free, unless you don't want to."

"And that's the problem. Oh George, I have to tell you and

171

I don't want to break your heart. I wish I could marry you, and maybe one day ..."

"One day? What does that mean?" His voice rose and she heard the pain in his voice as he tried to come to terms with what she was saying. "Explain to me, please. Now."

"I have reason to believe my husband may still be alive." There, she had spoken the words aloud.

"Alive? Are you insane?"

"No. Please let me speak."

"Is this Sean's doing? Tell me the truth."

"No, nothing to do with him, except he knows - something, anyway. Please don't be cross with me."

"Cross! Are you completely naïve? Cydney, this is not a joke."

"Please listen. Sean told me how he was ordered into the Special Forces HQ by his ex-commanding officer and they received a call from someone using Steve's codename. Apparently, he had been injured on a recce but presumed dead and his body was never recovered. He'd lost his memory and was nursed back to life and used in the field by his CO for another year. I know it sounds totally unbelievable."

"It sure as hell does. And you believe this rubbish? This tale that Sean spun you?"

"It's not a tale. I have to believe this, for my children's sake. If their dad is still alive ..."

"And where do I come into this sorry story, Cyd? What about me, exactly, or *us* to be more precise?"

"*We* have to be on hold. It's all I can say. I'm sending Sean out to search for Steve and to discover if he is alive, or in fact dead. Then I can move on. With you." She stroked his arm as she spoke.

"And if he's alive? My God. We've just made love. That was real, not some pie in the sky dream of bringing your husband back from the dead."

"I know." Cydney sat there, feelings of complete and utter

helplessness washing over her. "I am so very sorry. I never expected you to ask me to marry you."

"Well, what *did* you expect, exactly, Mrs Steve Granger?"

"Ouch."

"I think it better that I leave." He threw back the covers of the bed and stomped around the room, picking up his clothes, hurriedly dressing. "When you've cleared up this mystery of the missing husband, please feel free to call me in case you need another fuck."

"George! Please don't leave. Don't go like this!"

"I'm gone. I feel pity for your kids. Their mother forever chasing some dream. Bye Cydney." He marched to the door and left, slamming it behind him.

"Oh, what have I done?" She buried her face in the pillow and sobbed like she had never done before. "I need you, George. Please … Not like this …"

CHAPTER TWENTY ONE

THEODORE Gerald Whiteman, Governor of the State of West Virginia, and in his second term of office, stared out of the first-floor window across the beautifully manicured lawns of his residence, or rather his official executive mansion, watching his two teenage children playing with the family dogs. Jonathan and Estelle were eighteen and sixteen respectively, and his son was about to go off to Harvard to study law, as he had, what felt like so many years ago. The reflection of the man in the window bore little resemblance to the young man he still felt within. Now he saw himself as he was; slightly greying hair with a receding hairline and signs of weariness etched around his eyes.

What his father had told him was keeping him awake at night. To think all this, the life he had earned for him and his family, might disappear because of the deeds of his father - which he was still trying to get his head around without flying off the handle. He couldn't get past the anger, the knowledge of what his father had been in his past life and for so many years he had been lying to him, his brother, and what's more, their mother. This was not the man he recognised or with whom he had reached a reasonable sort of level in their somewhat chequered relationship, which admittedly, had all changed for the better when his brother, Philip, had died, as if his father had had an epiphany.

Alice strolled into the study and stood behind her husband, resting one hand lightly on his shoulder. He reached up to acknowledge her presence, without saying a word.

"You seem to be carrying the weight of the world. Something's wrong. I feel it. Is there something you want to tell me, perhaps?"

Ted turned to face his wife of twenty-two years. The love and passion he felt for her when they had first met as interns in the same law firm in Charleston remained unchanged. Brushing the fringe of her bobbed blonde hair out of the way, he bent forward to kiss the tip of her slightly upturned nose. Those smokey-grey smouldering eyes with the long black lashes closed momentarily and, when they opened, he witnessed the concern for him. If only she knew half the story.

"No, I'm fine, darlin'. Got a lot on my mind, what with the primaries coming up."

"We're all behind you, but this was never going to be a walk in the park. Are you sure it's really what you want to do? We have such a wonderful life together. This has been our home for the last seven years and I've no doubt you'd be re-elected again next year."

"I know, and to be honest I'm not sure either. It was something Daddy was pushing for me over the last few years."

"Well, he's more than retired. Perhaps he should be thinking of resigning as chairman at his age and making a quieter life for himself with your mom gone so long. Have you mentioned this to him at all?"

"No ... well, you know Daddy. He likes to keep his hand in, see what everyone's up to. Can't sit still. He believes they need him. Honestly, I think they would rather he was gone but they placate him. He enjoys the respect he receives, or should I say, demands from all of them, and I'm sure that's what's been keeping him going." If the Board of Whiteman Trust and Mutual found out what Ted now knew, well, he couldn't even imagine the consequences.

"No doubt. Anyway, where is he? Riley drove him off again this morning and he was supposed to be back for lunch and to help you with the arrangements for tonight. This is so inconsiderate of him. He knows how important this is to you. We have the entire Board coming, the Senator and his wife, the Cabinet Secretary and all the Cabinet, of course, all your senior staff, the Attorney General and his minions, Judge George Henry, the Mayor, Chairman of the United Mine Workers, Head of the farmer's union and steelworkers, the Labour Council members, all the Executive Board of Councillors, Chief of Police and his wife."

"Is there anybody in the state not coming?"

"No, darlin'. We have about three hundred and twenty people in total. The chef is going completely mad so I've left him to it. The last thing we need is him going AWOL."

"Honestly, Alice, perhaps it's better my daddy's not here. Sometimes he can say the wrong thing and Senator Jerome McCartney is not his best fan. They clash whenever they meet. Must be his upbringing. He says what he thinks but not always at the right time. I don't want anything to go wrong tonight."

"I know. I'm with you on this. However, the kids like him around for some reason. Anyway, tonight will seal your fate either way. We need to make sure everyone is behind you and we raise the monies you need for this. West Virginia is such a small state and you need to get the backing of both the farmers' and mining unions."

"That's not going to be easy. They hate the fact I'm a republican."

"They know you're an honest man and would do anything for the state."

"Sometimes, honesty, my darlin', is just not enough." Ted turned away, staring into the distance.

"Stop dreaming now, Mr President. Your first lady is off to get changed. I'll get Sorrell to call the kids in."

He kissed her affectionately on the mouth before watching her sashay away, swinging her hips in a slightly exaggerated manner, which he knew was solely for his benefit.

Smiling in spite of himself, he nevertheless felt the anger boiling up inside him again every time thoughts of his daddy and his past came into the forefront of his mind. This was a man he had looked up to, albeit reluctantly, all his life, despite everything. Theirs was not an easy relationship. His father was a hard man. Once he had made a decision he was incapable of changing his mind, sometimes to everyone's detriment. He and his brother, Philip, often hid away in their rooms listening to their parents fight. Their mom had been a typical southern lady with a mind of her own. She was beautiful, always well-dressed, though a little erratic in her treatment of her sons, and she was never one to hold back when she had a point to put across. Their daddy would also not back down on an argument. His word was law and their mom had no choice but to bow to her husband's will, resorting to angry and frustrated tears and locking herself away. Ted and Philip were cared for well enough, sent to the best schools and socialised with the top families in the state. What they really craved was a demonstration of their parents' love, a kiss, a hug, a kind word sometimes when they did well, instead of punishment when they didn't achieve what their parents, or rather their father, expected of them.

Ted recalled his brother's funeral. Philip was killed in Lebanon in early 1983 during the Reagan presidency when his unit was sent there to facilitate the restoration of the Lebanese government sovereignty. It was a quiet, sombre affair, a funeral befitting an officer in the U.S. Army, but there was no comfort there. His mother blamed everybody, especially her husband, and after venting her anger on him and all those around her within screaming distance, she removed herself, remaining isolated and alone. Ted tried to soothe her, console her in her grief, but she was incapable of receiving it from him. His daddy stood there without emotion, untouchable and remote. Grief was beyond him, it seemed.

Thinking back over the years of his growing up, going off to study law, returning to his roots and eventually entering the State District Attorney's Office, Ted realised he was, in fact, fairly ignorant of his father's past. As far as he knew and what he'd been told, his father had come over in 1946 from Switzerland, which explained his accent, invited by his cousins, the Ross family, who owned one of the oldest banks in the state and were worried about the situation in Europe after such a devastating war. His father had survived, as his domicile was neutral, and arrived in Richmond, allegedly an extremely wealthy man, and went on to marry his mother, Carolynn Ross, the chairman's one and only daughter. After some years he become the chairman of Prime which then merged into Whiteman Trust and Mutual, although it retained its original name in a few outbound localities, primarily to keep the farmers' mortgages in place; as a rule, such industry was not readily open to change. Most of the farmers had inherited their holdings and had been paying into the same banks for generations and were highly suspicious of any new one. It was intended for Ted to join the bank after college but he knew it was not for him. The law inspired him and made him want to fight for justice. It was an argument he and his father had many times. Ted stood his ground and refused point blank to go into the family business, no matter what.

Now, Ted knew he had to confront his daddy on so many levels and get to the truth before he died. His mother couldn't help now, and thankfully she didn't live to see the day. The one sentence his father had uttered when they had met the other week, almost in passing as if it had no importance, was not enough. It was sufficient to unbalance him completely and he desperately needed answers to all the questions running riot in his head. What was truth, and from where had all their wealth as a family accumulated? Tonight of all nights was not the time to dwell on this, at all.

William Templeton, his private secretary, knocked at the door and entered. William, never Bill or any other diminutive, marched into the library, dressed impeccably in his ubiquitous black suit, white shirt and dark blue striped tie and, like the soldier he used to be, stood to attention in front of the desk. Ted waited before speaking for the man to salute, which nearly occurred on every occasion, but he didn't of course, sometimes much to Alice's amusement.

"Good evening, sir," he greeted his boss.

"Good evening to you, too. I presume you're happy with the arrangements for tonight. Security? I don't want anything marring the evening."

"Yes, sir, everything is in place. We've taken on extra private security for this occasion and the police will be present in force."

"Good, because the Chief of Police is going to be here, and Senator McCartney. We don't want any of those troublemakers making a stand here like they did last time."

"They won't be allowed anywhere near the gates, sir, I can assure you of that."

"Perfect."

"The Senator will have his own security also, for him and his wife."

"Okay. Please make sure they all get to eat beforehand. We can't have these guys moaning about their empty stomachs. You know what they say about men marching."

"Absolutely. I've told Chef."

"Anything else? Have you seen my father, William?"

"No, sir. Wasn't he due back at four?"

"Yes. I'm beginning to get a bit worried." Ted moved away from the window, trying not to reveal his actual feelings, to sit at his desk. He picked up some papers, shuffled them, and set them down again.

"I've typed up your speech, sir, and made a few amendments, if you don't mind. I wanted to put some more information in about your goals and aspirations for the state and how you feel about the unions."

"Christ. Always those bloody unions."

"It's vital for your cause. And don't forget Jimmy Brown and Cale Tatum are attending tonight."

"Well, let's hope those sons of bitches behave for a change. They have no breeding whatsoever."

"We can't stop them. I've told the waiters to keep plying them with whisky."

"And that's going to help?" Ted asked, running his hand through what was left of his hair.

"It may keep them occupied."

"If we're lucky."

"Also, sir. We've had some calls now to reintroduce the death penalty. That case recently - the kidnapping by that lunatic of those poor little girls, raping and murdering them - have the hounds baying for blood."

"That's never going to happen, not whilst I'm Governor." The words were uttered with dismay and sadness. The entire case was dreadful and he had nothing but admiration for the courage of the parents as they were continually paraded on television and quoted in every newspaper in the land. "Although, personally, I would string the man up, I can't put my name behind condoning the needle. The death penalty was abolished here in 1965 and it isn't going to reappear. Is that what I'm going to be expected to answer tonight?" A sigh escaped.

"Maybe. Just warning you."

"And what do you think?"

"My opinions don't come into this, sir."

Ted viewed the man who had been with him for the last seven years, through every political and personal crisis, of which there had been many. An upright and principled man, fairly religious in his upbringing, married with four beautiful children. His wife was a senior cardiologist at the Thomas Memorial Hospital in South Charleston. However, the most important aspect was that William was a man on whom he could rely totally.

"Let's go through the speech then." He breathed out, resigned to the fact he had no choice, and took the papers from William. "Good evening and thank you for joining us for this year's state banquet. This is a particularly important year for me because, as you know, I'll be running in the primaries as my goal is to join the race for the White House."

"Wait for applause, standing ovation, sir."

"Sure." He continued to read. "I'm honoured to have served you and the state of West Virginia as your Governor for the last seven years and I will continue to do so with our common dreams to move this state forward and put it on the map. Everybody here is, I'm sure, dedicated and committed to this great state and it's been an absolute privilege to have worked with you." He looked up at William. "Then I go on to thank my wife and children, the senator and his wife, the various officials from everywhere for their continued support."

"Yes, sir, and try to act as if you mean it. You seem somewhat distracted."

"I'm tired, that's all. Okay," he looked at the speech, neatly typed in double spacing, finding it hard to concentrate on the words in front of him. "I say how great this state is, the generosity of West Virginians, their strength of character following the floods etcetera, the sorrow we feel at the deaths of those two children, how we pray for their families and reflect on everybody we've lost recently."

"Don't mention the death penalty, sir."

"I'm not stupid. Obviously, if I'm asked I'll say why I'm against it and what courses of action I do endorse as punishment. Can you put a few words together for me so I'm prepared, just in case?"

"Yes, of course. I've already thought of that as I do believe it will come up. I've included your hopes and aims for the state - labour, working together, getting people into work programmes, promoting local organisations, hardworking teachers and public employees, medical services and insurance cover for all. The usual," continued William. "Again, wait for applause. Smile. Grab hold of Mrs Whiteman's hand, put your arm around her. Show unity."

"That's the easy part. I like the bit about building new schools, availability of higher education. Our children are our future. We need to get the kids off the street and into employment. Off drugs. Create new centres for addiction. That should go down well. What about taxes? Did you mention that?"

"Oh yes, sir. Of course. A bit lower down. You want to reduce rates and put money back in the pockets of those hard-working Virginians. You recognise their contribution and you support them in return."

"What about businesses?"

"Cutting corporate taxes. I've included that."

"You've thought of everything, it would seem. I want to make the roads safer, the mines, also. I need the support of the Unions."

"You'll get it, I'm sure. They are as fed up of being taken to court as we are of hearing about it. One other big thing is the gun laws. We need to take appropriate measures. I want you to really bring this home. Your priority as you go towards the White House."

"Isn't everyone doing that?"

"Yes, sir. You've already started the conversation going here and you want to re-create it throughout the United States. You're prepared to back your words by putting millions of dollars behind this programme."

"It's never going to go through. There's too much money involved in the industry. Christ, even senators have shares in the gun manufacturing companies. It's part of the constitution; everyone's right to bear arms. We might as well forget it, and we don't have millions."

"I don't disagree. It's all about awareness. Families are fed up with what's going on here. Random shootings, young people involved."

"And you believe that's going to stop them? All they'll do is buy guns illegally and that'll mean even more on the streets. No, but I will talk about it if pressed. Next."

"As you wish. You go on to talk about the fact we have a strong economy. You want to protect and increase production of coal and other energy resources."

"Yes. The Unions will like that, too. We are all about economic growth in these troublesome times. I'm committed to West Virginia, positive about our future, which you have placed in my hands. I will continue to do this as we work together, and so on. Brighter future. How does that sound?"

"Perfect, sir. We seem to have covered everything. The big issue is to get people to dip their hands into their pockets. We need money to fight for the White House. Ten million, at least."

"We have some of the wealthiest men in the state coming tonight. That shouldn't be too difficult. If they believe in me and what I want to achieve, they will give me their backing."

"Yes, but only if it's in their best interests. You're going to have to offer them something more concrete than promises. We'll work on it. I'll adapt the end of the speech a bit and give it back for you to read through. However, is anything else troubling you? Is it about Mr Whiteman, sir?"

Ted paused for a brief second. "Oh yes, my daddy. It's all about him."

CHAPTER TWENTY TWO

THE smell of death was unmistakable. Albert Whiteman acknowledged this as he felt his life source ebbing away. He was barely aware of the rhythmic compressions against his chest, which was hurting with a pain so indescribable he begged to die there and then. The sound of people barking orders and running around him faded into the background. He wanted to die in pain; he deserved to die in pain for all he had done in his life. Closing his eyes, he remembered the absolution he had received from Father Goodheart. Absolution? As if. Would God still accept him into His embrace, despite the confession he had made to the Father whom he had left reeling from the knowledge of his crimes? That alone should lead him into Hell and he would not be kicking and screaming as the dark forces came to deliver him to the Devil. He deserved and expected nothing less. However, the fact he had confessed - could he be forgiven? Was there even a glimmer of hope? No. God was only playing with his mind now, and his soul.

"Daddy! Stay with me!" The voice of his son broke through the clouds of pain. Albert felt regret that he couldn't say how much he loved him, how Ted had been his redemption, along with his brother, of course, but the words wouldn't come out. He had never spoken those words to them and now it was too late to voice his thoughts anyway, and that was his punishment. He had never discovered how to love in a normal way. All his life had been about secrets and lies and even his wife had grown to hate him, deservedly so. He had sought absolution from the

Father in an attempt to salvage his conscience, if he had one. By sending those two Jews, whom he had encountered as boys, all that money, he was doing what was necessary, in his opinion. Or was it to warn them about the notebook? Now he wouldn't even get the chance to gauge their reaction. He knew no amount of money would ever give them back what they had lost in their young lives, for which he was accountable. However, they had held his secret for many years. Of course, they would not have told anyone about him. He had threatened them with their deaths and what was left of their families if they ever tried to find him. All back to him again. What a horrible and wicked life.

His eyes were closing. They felt so heavy and he had no strength remaining to keep them open. Images of Germany and all those thousands of people came rushing through as he recalled his confession with Father Goodheart.

"Bless me Father, for I have sinned. I have never been to confession before. I ... I don't know what to say to you. How do I begin?"

"You don't have to know. Just speak what is in your heart, my son."

"My heart? I'm not sure if I have one, if I ever did. My heart is heavy, but I shall try." Albert heard a rustling movement as the Father relaxed back into his chair to hear him.

"I have lied all my life. I was born in Germany, not Switzerland. I was a member of the Nazi party. Do I feel guilty, you ask me, for what I did? I have never thought about it until now. But, I was merely a solder, and yes, I know it's been said so many times before, we were just carrying out orders. For me it was different. I loved the life of a soldier. I loved the camaraderie of all my fellow officers. And, to be honest with you, I enjoyed the sense of purpose it gave to me. I never foresaw or contemplated the consequences of my actions. The people, so many people I was responsible for killing. They were enemies of the state, of our beloved Fuehrer."

Albert heard an intake of breath and another rustling as the priest sat up more, listening intently now he had his attention and, as the words tumbled out, ones he had held in for decades, he felt the most profound release.

"Please continue, my son."

"Do not judge me for what I am going to tell you. Recently, I have judged myself and found myself wanting in all respects. Being a soldier was a job for me and I joined as soon as I was old enough. My father was a general himself, my brothers had all joined the army and it was destined for me to follow them. I started off in Hitler's Youth and everything I was told, everything I learned, made so much sense to me. The Jews held all the money, taking it away from us Germans. They were responsible for the downward spiral of the economy before Hitler came along and for the failure of the First World War. He demonised them and we joined in. Every bank was owned by them, all the lending made at extortionate interest rates, the inability of Germany to halt the high inflation because they were in control. Every doctor, dentist, lawyer, university professor, musician - all Jews, giving no-one else a look-in. Taking our jobs, our homes. It was never-ending and it had to stop. Then Hitler came into power. Did we celebrate! At last, redemption from these people. He was our answer and suddenly we Germans were in control."

"They were Germans, too."

"Father, I know now, but that's what I was told and believed. We were indoctrinated into the Party and whatever Hitler told us was accepted as the truth."

"Please continue."

"We had a job to do, to rid our country of these vermin."

"Vermin? You use that term?"

"The Jews were like animals; de-humanised, de-personalised. So, we treated them as such. It was like killing rats. I can't apologise for what I did. It wasn't anything to do with me. I was young and I marched with everyone through the streets of Berlin in 1938, singing loudly. What a night we had. We smashed and threw lit torches through windows of shops, we kicked and punched our way along the road, pushing aside anyone who stopped us. I remember there was a Rabbi who begged me not to damage his beloved synagogue, where their scrolls were over a thousand years old. Do you know what I did? I grabbed hold of his neck and squeezed it until there was no life in him. I cut off his beard and threw it to the ground and stamped on it. I laughed, yes Father, out loud. The power was beyond anything I had experienced before and that was only the start." His voice rose as he spoke, as if he was reliving those feelings. "We pushed his family into the synagogue, locked the doors and burned it to the ground that night and danced around the flames in celebration, whilst listening to their cries for help, and afterwards I was awarded a special prize for bravery. There was no-one to stop us at all. Every action, murder, arson, theft, was applauded and never condemned.

"It was not long before I was recognised and promoted for my talents. My commanding officer liked the way I dealt with problems and put me in charge of interrogating enemies of the state."

"The Jewish people?"

"Not only them, anyone who talked out against our Party. I was fearless and I broke everyone who came before me. The power was intoxicating and I felt like the God I never worshipped. The more people screamed, the more I hurt them and got them to speak of their alleged crimes, the crimes which they may not have committed, but they would say anything to stop me. Sometimes they died from the torture we inflicted, many times they survived until the next round. I was merciless in my quest to get them to confess, simply for being who they were."

Albert became more excited as he thought back to his youth. What stopped him carrying on was the sound of weeping on the other side of the confessional box.

"This is too much. I should go. I'm sorry, Father."

"For what you did?"

"Maybe - more for what you've had to listen to. I will leave. I know this is unfair to you. I am salving my own conscience. Please, don't weep for me."

"I am not weeping for you: I am weeping for mankind. At what man can do to their fellow man. I am God's ears and I promised to hear you, no matter how I feel or how it affects me."

"If you are sure, I will continue, but my story does not get any better." He took a deep breath. "I was promoted quite quickly and took over command of a small unit whose task was to find Jews in hiding and either kill them, or send them to the work camps with the people who were aiding and abetting them. It was my choice as to what I did with them - life over death."

"How did you choose?"

"It was like tossing a coin. Some days I felt like killing everyone. I was angry these people were preventing us from achieving the final solution. How dare these Jews interfere with our ultimate goal? Other days I sent them away, knowing they would be dead soon anyway. I am not proud of this now, and lately, I have thought about everything I did. You need to understand the hatred we ... I felt against these people."

"I don't understand hatred."

"I wish I didn't but by then it was in my blood. Soon, my senior officers recognised my skills and in mid-1941, even though I was quite young at only twenty-six, again I was promoted and this time sent directly to Poland, to the ghetto in Lodz, to supervise the manufacturing of much needed war supplies for the army. However, Hitler's solution was to rid the world of Jews, our ultimate aim. Thousands of people went through my hands. Tens of thousands."

"To be killed?"

"Yes, Father. Eventually. It started in late 1941 when we began the deportations to the death camps of Chelmno, not far to the north. Twenty thousand at first followed by ten thousand per day from 1942 until I lost count. It was a major operation and I was in charge. I remember the dates so well. I was responsible for their deaths. Every one of them, over one hundred thousand people. You see, it was getting too crowded so we had no choice."

"And they never arrived?"

"No. They left by train. Of course, it was never the intention for them to survive for long. On arrival everyone was ordered to undress before they were taken to a cellar and across a ramp into the back of one of the waiting vans. We managed to load about fifty to seventy people in each one, or more if children. When the van was full, the doors were shut and the engine started. It didn't take long for the exhaust fumes from the carbon monoxide to work, probably no more than ten minutes. It was quite a clever construction. The vans were converted with sealed compartments installed on the chassis and metal pipes welded below into which the exhaust fumes were directed. Everything was tested beforehand to ensure the right amount of carbon monoxide was present. When the screaming stopped, the bodies were taken to excavated mass graves in the forest."

"And who were these people? Old, young?" the Father asked.

"Mostly the old and infirm, those who were of no use to us; children, people from the hospital who were ill or dying, everyone from the psychiatric unit. We knew the whole process would be difficult, so we decided the best way would be to tranquilise them and the night before they were injected with sedatives. In the morning, some of the children refused to move. I gave orders to throw them out the window. You must understand, our task was mammoth and we needed to make room for the younger and fitter men who would work in the factories making armaments. However, Lodz continued to grow despite our work. Then, one day, we rounded up twenty thousand children."

"Children? How could you …?"

"Yes, Father. Many families committed suicide rather than let their children leave. It made our work easier. I realise I say this in such a matter of fact way. Now I've had time to think about all I did; at the time it was my orders, and I do have so many regrets. I had no idea how one day it would come back to haunt me."

The quiet prayers of the priest sounded through the curtain of the confessional box. "Teach me, oh Lord. What am I supposed to learn from this kind of pain? What are you calling me to do? Open my battered heart and lead me to comfort and peace. Only you can give me the peace I need. Let me feel your presence in my life."

"Do you wish me to leave?"

"No, you must continue otherwise you'll never be granted peace. Or me," he said under his breath.

"We also needed people for our work camps in other areas, so it was decided to empty the ghetto of all males from the age of fourteen to fifty. We managed to get thousands out but …"

"But, what, my son?"

"At the time I couldn't work out why they were wailing, the sound of so much crying, how these women clung to their fathers, husbands and sons, trying to prevent us taking them. We had to kill so many of them to get the men out. At least we were clearing the area. I thought Jews had no feelings, I was impervious to their cries and sorrow, they were not even worthy of my consideration. I realise now how wrong I was.

"I stayed in Lodz until 1944. More Jews had arrived but again orders were received to reduce the size of the ghetto. You cannot imagine the impossible task we were given. You see, the Soviet troops were only sixty miles away and advancing rapidly. We decided to reinstate the operations at Chelmno and increased the deportation of up to twenty-five thousand people who were gassed and their bodies burned. It was in August when the transportations to Auschwitz-Birkenau began and that's where I was sent. It was my choice, once again, who was to die and who was to live. I was invincible. Answerable to no-one."

"Not even to God?" asked Father Goodheart.

"Never to God, whoever he is. Only to Adolf Hitler. It wasn't in my mind I was doing wrong. I was carrying out orders. I was a soldier, first and foremost."

"Oh, my son."

"The trains came in from all over German-occupied Europe. I sat on the station platform and sent the Jews to the left or right. I had no particular reasoning for my choice. In some cases it was merely the look in someone's eye, the colour of the coat they were wearing, the type of hat. We killed over a million in the four gas chambers that were continually operational. I didn't stay long there and left before the camp was evacuated in January 1945; everyone but a few who were sick and had to be left behind was sent on the marches to Bergen-Belsen.

"My final destination was to the work camps of Dachau in southern Germany, as second in command. I was glad to be back in my homeland again and not far from my family village, although I never saw my parents or sisters again, so assumed they were dead. In all honesty, I had no desire to see them. I was based in the administration building dealing with work quotas. I had no real involvement with the people there unless there was trouble or someone tried to escape. By that time I was bored of the killing. It held no real attraction for me. I was happy to deal with the everyday existence of the camp."

"And why was that?" The question came out so quietly, with a slight quiver to the voice, that Albert strained to hear.

"I had a feeling by then we were losing the war, or going to eventually. We heard so much news about the Americans and British making inroads into Germany and I knew if I was caught I would be imprisoned or hung. I needed a plan to get myself out of Germany."

"So you came to America?"

"Not immediately. First I escaped into Switzerland. It was not easy and took a while, as I was forever in hiding. I had money there, and a new identity already arranged by my cousins. Let me get to that part. There's more to be explained first. It was prior to 1939 when Hitler originally started closing Jewish owned businesses and appropriating their property, not only houses but art and jewellery. My cousins owned a bank in Bonn with a branch in Paris and they helped me to hide some of the assets."

"You stole these?"

"Theft was the least of my crimes, Father, as I've told you. Yes, as much as I could and it was done so simply. Nobody found out what I was doing. I made deposits into my cousin's branch and they sent the funds to Switzerland. Gold was the real currency and so many Jews bribed me with gold and diamonds and gave me access to their accounts in Switzerland to stop me killing them."

"And did you stop - killing them?"

"No, Father. I did not. I took their money and let them be taken to the camps anyway. I had no scruples, as I told you. I was not a trusting person even with my cousins. I kept details of every single deutschmark, every single piece of gold, every diamond deposited, every business or property I took and sold. At the end of the war, I knew it was all going to be mine. I didn't bother with artwork as it was far too cumbersome and difficult to hide. I had no doubt in my mind I would survive. I kept myself safe at all costs and out of harm's way. The camps were an easy assignment for me. Better than being in the artillery or at the front, where I was likely to be blown up or shot."

"And how did you keep these details?" the priest asked.

"In a small note book I kept with me at all times. I was confident nobody would find out, and as a senior officer of the SS I was untouchable and could not be searched. But I lost it. I searched everywhere possible, retraced my steps from my private rooms to the office, checked outside the area. No stone was unturned, but of course I couldn't tell anyone. After a week I realised it had gone for good. It had been stolen or someone had found it. I was distraught. How could I have allowed this to happen? I had no record of anything and I was now reliant on my cousins.

"The Allies arrived in April 1945 and I was arrested. All my long-term plans were now in jeopardy. I knew my fate was to be tried and hung. The Allies rounded us up like prisoners. Us, the elite soldiers of Germany. I will always remember that day. We were marched at gunpoint into an open area. Anyone who was still alive or left in Dachau stood around staring at us with hatred in their eyes. I was ashamed to be a prisoner but only because I had been caught. How dare they incarcerate me? Then something caught my attention in particular. I turned round and there were these two young men standing there. Their bodies were skeletal, like walking dead. Nevertheless, they glared straight at me as if they would murder me without a minute's hesitation. My thoughts were only to escape. I wanted to live, to see the fruits of my labours, all that money I had hidden away and might not get my hands on. Their eyes penetrated into my very soul. I stopped for a second and in that moment realisation hit me. One of the boys had the deepest blue eyes and the world seemed to stop as he held up his hand."

"He had your notebook?"

"Yes. He had everything. My life in his hands. I wanted to put *my* hands around his neck and wring it until he was dead."

"What could you do?"

"I shouted over to him. I swore I would kill him and every single one of his family. I vowed I would find him and his friend if I had to go to the ends of the earth."

"And?"

"He hid the book away, still staring at me, defiantly, taunting me, mocking me. I knew I had got to him. They turned from me and shuffled away."

"You escaped?"

"Yes I did, later that night, into the woods."

"And you never got it back?"

"No. But I did get my money."

"What about these boys?"

"I found them."

"How is that possible?" asked the priest, "after all this time? You didn't know their names."

"It's easy to check the records, who was in Dachau when the Allies arrived, who had survived. I investigated every single survivor and their photos. I would recognise that one boy anywhere; his eyes. It took me a very long time, and for many years I did nothing but sit on the information, until now."

"Why now, my son, after so long? What is the point?" The priest lowered his voice, his despair evident.

"I had to have my book. It was all I had to protect me. I couldn't allow the knowledge they had of me to get out. However, I considered everything and I decided I had to make amends for all my deeds. A last resort."

"Was that when you turned to God?"

"Yes, Father, and to you. I am grateful to you. I had no choice. I am scared and I need forgiveness."

"From them, as well as God?"

"Yes."

"How can that be? How can you seek forgiveness from these two men? Is it theirs to give?"

"I don't know."

"And what followed?"

"Nothing. Not immediately. But I sent them money. One million dollars each, to be exact"

"To what purpose? You must have realised they would seek you out and how easy it would be. Was that your intention? To find them? And do what?"

"I don't know that either. I wish I did. I am lost."

"Oh my son, I wish I could help you. I wish I could grant you peace and give you the answer to all your fears, but this is far beyond me."

"And me, Father. And me."

CHAPTER TWENTY THREE

"SIR, are you still going ahead with tonight?" William said, striding back into the governor's office.

"Yes, William. My daddy's in hospital now and I can't do anything more for him. I've left him in safe hands and the doctors will call if they need me. I'll go back after the banquet finishes. We can hardly put off three hundred people coming from all over the county. Christ, I could do with a drink."

"Shall I pour, sir?" William offered, already walking over to the cabinet.

"Only if you'll join me. It's so wrong for a man to drink on his own."

"Maybe a small one. On the rocks?"

"Yes. Thanks. William, I need you to sit down. No, no notes for you to take. You need to listen to what I have to tell you but you must promise me this stays within these four walls. If this gets out …"

"Surely it can't be that bad, sir?"

"Bad would be good. This puts bad into a totally different category altogether. Look, you've been with me during my entire term as governor. I trust you, with my life even. You know me better than my own wife, I'd hazard a guess, and you know my father. He's not been an easy man, by any stretch. He's a hard man to get close to, never gives anything away, and it's gotten worse over the years, especially after Philip died. I have no idea how my mother stood it for so long. Do you have any idea of his background? Anything?"

"No, sir, apart from what is generally known. Why are you asking?"

"A few weeks ago my daddy told me about his earlier life, before he came here."

"Back in 1946? Why are you asking me if I know something?"

"If this comes into the public domain, we're finished, I'm finished, and all our plans for the White House will have been for nothing. I always intended to take you with me, you know that. Your services have proved invaluable. When I tell you, you will have every reason to leave me. I'm hoping you won't and you'll help me get through this, some way or another. Anyway, I'm not quite sure how to even say this out loud."

"Sir, may I suggest you just tell me?"

"Jeez - that damned phone. Hold on William, it may be the hospital." Ted lifted the receiver and in the background could hear raised voices. "What the hell is going on out there? What's all the commotion? Who? Yes, let them in. Yes, it's fine. I'll see them." He turned back to his private secretary. "It's my Uncle Liam, and my cousin, Jackson. That's strange. Liam disappeared years ago. I didn't know they were in touch. Wonder what this could be about?"

"Should I stay? You were about to tell me something. Your daddy?"

Suddenly Ted realised the enormity of what he was about to impart and he couldn't do it. Thank God for the interruption. "You know, on second thoughts, it was nothing. Let's catch up after these guys have gone."

"Are you sure, sir? You seem kinda worried."

"It's okay. Give me an hour and then come back, please. We'll go through the speech again and the order for tonight. Please tell everyone I'm not to be disturbed, on any account."

"Sure. I'll be back later, but if there is anything, call me. I'll be in my office."

"Thanks, William. Much appreciated."

197

Ted fell wearily into his chair and waited for his uncle and Jackson to arrive. This could not be coincidental. They knew something and he could bet his bottom dollar this was about his daddy. It was almost as if the story he'd been told had been opened up into the universe for all to know, although that couldn't be true. Perhaps his daddy dying would be the best thing all round before his secret got out and ruined everybody's lives.

One of his security guards knocked at the door and came through into the office. "Governor, sir, I have two gentlemen to see you." He showed them in and left, closing the door on his way out.

"Well, this is a pleasant surprise, Uncle Liam. It's been years. Jackson," he said, acknowledging his cousin. He walked around his desk to shake hands with both men. "I hope this is a social visit, but I can see from your faces you have something to say. Let me get you some refreshments." He knew he was stalling them, prolonging the inevitable. However, why should they know anything at all? As far as he knew it was only between him and his daddy.

"No thanks, Ted. Unfortunately, this isn't a social call. You'd better sit down."

"Why do I get the impression this isn't going to be pleasant?"

"We have to tell you some things about your daddy and I doubt this is going to be easy."

So many thoughts swept through Ted's mind, whether he should come clean and say what he knew, or wait until they had told him so he could deny everything. Tell them they were wasting their time. Anything. He decided to hold out until he'd heard everything, not show his hand.

"I'm listening, but he had a massive heart attack earlier and he's now in intensive care."

"Will he live?" asked Liam, as if it was the last thing he wanted.

"I don't know. He's heavily sedated and we're waiting for news. Why? You don't seem too concerned."

"Why should I be? After what he did to me and my family. You have no idea, do you? You sit here in your mansion without a thought for anyone but yourself. Some governor. Anyway, let's not play games here. I'll get straight to the point. I've learnt in life, as I've got older, it's best to go straight for the bulls eye, so we're in no doubt at all. Ted, I've known you all your life and I sure am sorry for what your daddy has brought upon you, but he is a murderer, a thief and a fraudster."

"Now hold on a godamn minute. You can't come bursting in here and shouting the odds. Who the hell do you think you are?"

Jackson put a restraining hand on Liam's arm, willing him to remain calm. "This is not the way to do things, Liam. Let me tell him." Pushing his chair back in anger and frustration, Liam strode over to stand in front of the large windows overlooking the gardens, almost as if he felt claustrophobic and needed to see the outdoors.

"What exactly is it you have to tell me? I'm an extremely busy man. I have the state banquet tonight and I don't have time for this."

"I know that, I'm one of your guests," Jackson continued, "but this can't wait, and it certainly isn't a game. I don't know if you're familiar with your daddy's background. A few things have come to light over the last couple of days, things you should know about because it affects every single one of us, and probably many more people than I care to imagine. It could bring down the bank and the Federal Reserve, and that's something we have to prevent at all costs."

"Sounds serious. Go on," Ted replied, his mind trying to think clearly so he had his answers ready, but that was his difficulty. He knew whatever he was going to hear were going to be the indisputable facts. He had learned enough from his years as an attorney and prosecutor how to distinguish between truth and lies.

"It all started when we were contacted by this English woman,

Cydney Granger, on the pretext of wanting to undertake research on our dual banking system here in West Virginia."

"That's not abnormal though, is it? Why shouldn't you be interviewed?" Ted said.

"In the scheme of things, it was nothing unusual. However, the questions went further than that. She was asking about our activities back in 1939 and the investigations into our alleged activities of aiding Hitler by sending funds to Germany."

"There was no foundation for those allegations. I read about it. This was when your daddy was chairman," he said, directing himself to Liam, whose back was still turned and made no response. "Why bring this up after nearly seventy years? We had a branch somewhere in Germany, didn't we? So it would be normal to help capitalise it. I'm sure that was the findings of the investigation. What did you say to the woman?"

"Well, actually, I threw her out of my office. I lost my temper."

"Good move. And that's likely to help matters because …?"

"Yeah, I know, but I didn't like her tone, what she was insinuating. I had nothing to back this up with, so I lost it. I decided to go and see Liam. I thought he would know more than me." Both men gazed across at Liam who was still staring out, but at the mention of his name this time, he turned around.

"Your daddy," he said with a sneer, "is a murderer."

"Oh, come on, Uncle Liam, there's no need for that."

"There is every need, Ted." The older man trudged over and sat down again in front of the governor's desk. "You need to understand what kind of man he is. I went to see this Mrs Granger. I told her everything I knew. The truth, boy. No hiding this time, and she told me what she had discovered. That's why we're here."

"Damage limitation," Jackson added. "Hold on. You know something too, don't you? I can see it in your eyes. What the hell? This isn't much of a surprise to you."

Ted felt a relief to share, finally, the information his father had imparted to him and decided there was safety in small numbers, where everyone was aiming for the same goal: silence, and to lose the story before it came out and cost them sorely. "He told me a few weeks back about his past. That he was a member of the Nazi party in Germany, not Swiss as we were all led to believe. Just a soldier though, doing his job. He escaped via Switzerland when the Allies came and travelled here. I believe he was a distant cousin, anyway, so it was natural for him to want to be in West Virginia."

"And his name?"

"Dieter Scholler. He changed it when he was naturalised. All the records are here, before he married my mama."

"And he told you nothing else?" asked Liam.

"No, sir. Well, only that he wanted to make amends. He sent two survivors some money each as recompense. He wanted to send more but he told me it was difficult to trace people after so many years."

"What sort of money? How and from where?" Jackson said.

"From Prime. He didn't mention how much."

"And you believed him, this story, this bending of the truth?" Liam glanced up sharply.

"I had no reason not to."

"So that's what that two million dollars was all about," Jackson muttered under his breath. "I wondered why we couldn't reconcile the books. Now we have our subsidiary bank implicated in this mess. Christ, it gets worse. I am the president and CEO, Ted. I am responsible. I report to the Board."

"Two million dollars. You're kidding me, right? I thought it was a couple of thousand." He shook his head in disbelief.

"This is blood money, pure and simple," said Liam.

"You'd better tell me everything you know." Ted was resigned to hearing about his father, who clearly had lied to him in the gravest possible way. "I have time before I need to get ready for the banquet."

It didn't take long for Liam and Jackson to tell their tale. It was hard to comprehend though the facts spoke for themselves and it was too detailed for them to be lying. His father had been anything but honest with him and, moreover, had glossed over the facts, saying he had sent some money to a couple of German born English Jews by way of recompense for what his countrymen had done. Everything about Ted's life, his upbringing, was in question now. How could he face his father knowing what he had done, who he had been? A murderer! His father was a murderer and it hurt to even think the words. No, it was much worse; he was a Nazi officer, not a simple soldier, and responsible for the genocide of thousands upon thousands of innocent people; he was a fraudster and embezzler, taking millions from the bank to cover his tracks, and now he knew he was to blame for the lives of Uncle Liam's wife and children. And was his father repentant? He doubted it. He was probably just angry he had got caught out.

"What shall we do?" His question was simple because he had no answer.

"We have to hope your daddy dies," Jackson said.

"No. I want him alive. I want to challenge him and see what he has to say. If he dies, I won't ever get this chance." Liam stopped as his voice broke. "My wife and children - their deaths have to be for something, have to mean something, or what is the point?"

"We'll have to wait until he wakes up, if he does. I want answers, too, you know. He is my father, though God knows I wish now he wasn't. I have to get ready for my guests. Jackson, I'll see you later. Uncle Liam, you are welcome to stay."

"No, son. I'm going to stay with Joe and his family. They're all I've had for the last few years. We'll speak tomorrow."

"Okay. I understand and, Uncle, I truly am sorry. I …"

"You cannot apologise for your daddy. Only he can do that."

"One more thing. What about this Granger woman? What do you suggest, Ted?" Jackson asked.

"Do we know what she intends to do? If this comes out …

Go speak to her. Invite her here tomorrow morning. I'll see her with you. We need to understand her game plan. Christ, what an absolute mess."

"I don't think this is going to go away. She's like a tigress. She wants something from you," Jackson replied.

"Point taken. Let's hear first. Also, nobody is to know about this, at all. Not even Alice. We need to keep this within these four walls."

Ted finished the meeting knowing he would be haunted forevermore by the sins of his Nazi father. It was a heavy burden to carry and it was questionable whether he could distance himself from the responsibility he now bore.

* * *

Albert Whiteman was conscious of everything going on around him. He couldn't keep his eyes open and movement was impossible. He was aware of medical staff constantly checking him and from time to time he got a shock from the iced water being soothed on his dry, cracked lips. Annoyingly, they shone a light into his eyes on a regular basis. He wished they would talk to him and warn him what they were about to do. He was able to hear the discussion around him but couldn't understand the terminology being used, however, he sensed from the general tone that the outlook wasn't good. Thankfully, he no longer felt pain, only the muzzy feeling the morphine was giving him, but he didn't feel in control of his body.

The fact was - he was dying. He prayed to be given a sense of peace so he could pass over and face his Maker, though not yet. Now he needed to see Father Goodheart again and finish his confession, but he had to wake up. Perhaps, if he really tried to open his eyes, they might see he was alert, but it was as if someone had glued his lids together. Trying to move his fingers or toes wasn't working either.

Suddenly, his heart started to race and he began to drift off. There was a commotion around him and he was aware of people around his bed, noise, an alarm sounding, and everyone shouting orders. Would he not have time after all? Then there was silence, and darkness.

"Okay, everyone, he's back."

"Shall we call his son?"

Yes, he wanted Ted here; he wanted to explain more about his background but it seemed he was destined not to do so. Probably better in the long run. Perhaps his fate was to die alone.

"He's the governor. The state banquet's tonight. Let's not disturb him yet. See how the guy does. Check his vitals every fifteen, please." And with that, he was alone again, still unable to communicate.

CHAPTER TWENTY FOUR

THE governor's guests started arriving at seven o'clock in the evening and Ted and Alice were firmly established at the entrance to the mansion to meet and greet, with William hovering. Security was high and all members of the team were focused and on high alert. Police were guarding along the avenue to prevent any protestors gaining access, as William had fore-warned. It was hoped the public would stay behind the barriers and simply shout their declarations to bring back the death sentence and not cause too much trouble.

West Virginia society were out in force, the men dressed in their smart tuxedos with shoes polished to an incredible shine and their ladies dressed in glittering finery, diamonds ablaze, showing off to the rest of their competition. No-one was prepared to be out-done by their neighbour as this was the annual event nobody wanted to miss.

"You look amazing. Very sexy."

"Why, thank you, Governor," Alice simpered, adjusting her glamorous off-the-shoulder black gown, nipped at the waist with a flowing black silk train behind. "Good turn-out, I see. Let's hope Cale Tatum doesn't kick off."

"He won't. It's not appropriate tonight, not with my daddy ill. They've never got on."

"Your daddy doesn't get on with anyone," she whispered in return.

"Good evening, Senator, Mrs McCartney. So pleased you could make it."

"Wouldn't miss it for the world, Ted. I'd like a quiet word with you later, if I may."

"That would be my pleasure, sir."

"Wonder what that old curmudgeon wants?" Alice said, as the senator and his rather expansive wife, in a totally inappropriate tent-like, diamante-encrusted creation, moved off to greet other guests.

"It's probably some complaint. It normally is. Here's Cale. We need him on our side, Alice. Be nice."

"Always, my love."

"Cale. Good to have you here. Jenny-Lynn. Beautiful as always." He bent to kiss her cheek."

"Hope you've got plenty of whisky on tap tonight, Ted. We're gonna need it if what I hear about the Miners Union is anything to go by. How's your daddy? I heard he's not here tonight."

"No. Unfortunately. He had a heart attack earlier. He's being well tended."

"He gonna make it?"

"Not sure yet. We hope so," Ted said, though somewhere in the back of his mind he almost hoped he wouldn't.

"We never got on, you know that, but I rather enjoyed our spats. Wish him well for us. I need a few whiskeys inside me." Cale moved into the main reception with his wife in tow.

Half an hour later, Jackson Dwyer arrived with his wife. Neither of them appeared happy. Their body language was definitely not in tune tonight, as if they had been arguing.

"Glad you could make it. Shelley, how ya'll doing?"

"Just fine, Ted. Absolutely fine. Couldn't be better." She stormed off without her other half, ignoring Alice completely."

"Anything wrong?" Ted asked, taking his cousin to one side.

"What? The fact we are about to lose everything - the bank, your position, everything we've worked for? Oh no. Nothing's wrong, thanks to your daddy."

"You're drunk, goddamit. You need to keep a clear head. We discussed this earlier. What were you thinking?"

"Drunk? You ain't seen nothing yet."

"Jackson, I'm warning you. This is between us. Don't go making a complete ass of yourself in front of the whole of Charleston. We can sort this. Leave it with me."

"A fucking Nazi! How absolutely great. Just what the family needed."

"Keep it shut, I'm telling you now."

"Is everything alright here?" William approached, somewhat concerned. "Everyone's looking over."

"Could you take Mr Dwyer to my library? I'm sure he'd like to rest up for a while before we go into dinner. Maybe some coffee."

"Yes, of course, Governor." Sensing the situation, William took hold of Jackson's elbow and tried to escort him away from the crowds who were sensing a possible scandal about to take place.

"Take your hands off me," he ordered, trying to release the man's grasp, which was far too strong. "I can walk, dammit."

"I'm sure you can. I'll let go if you promise to come with me."

"What are you? The fucking gestapo? Okay, I'm coming, but I haven't finished yet with Mr Governor. Not by a long shot."

When the two men were out of sight, Ted started to breathe easier. He sensed everyone watching, including his wife who was totally ignorant of the previous day's revelations.

"What was all that about?" she asked, smiling at him, her voice low so nobody could realise her consternation. "Can we leave work out of this evening for once?"

"Sorry, darlin'. Let's go through. I'll explain later."

"This has to be about your daddy. You'd think laying in the hospital he wouldn't be able to do anything more but we'll never have any peace whilst he's still breathing."

"As I said, I'll tell you everything once the evening is over and when I come back from seeing him. Now, smile and hold my hand." Ted leaned over to kiss her gently and they paraded into the main ballroom as a loving couple to their guests' standing ovation and amid thunderous applause, some shouting out, 'Ted for President'. He knew this would not be the end of his conversation with his wife and Alice would be waiting expectantly for an explanation, which he was going to have to compile to her satisfaction.

* * *

Jackson was trying to sober himself up, albeit reluctantly, with the help of his cousin's private secretary, who was serving him with numerous cups of black coffee. His bow-tie was loosened and there was a real risk of him falling asleep. He knew his wife would be even more pissed with him for hiding out in a drunken stupor whilst she had to socialise on her own with people she hated. In fact, there weren't many people in her husband's world she did like. If only she could be a normal wife, loving, caring, considerate and supportive. She was certainly like that to their children but the looks she gave him were more of hatred than anything else. Oh well, it wouldn't be the first time there was a divorce in the family and it was probably on the cards, especially after his performance tonight. When the knowledge the bank was founded on looted gold was out in the public arena and there was a full FBI enquiry, well, that would just be the icing on the cake. As long as he had his children; that's all he wanted. He loved them with a passion and nobody, especially that damn woman of his, was going to take them off him. They might be all he had left.

"Can I get you anything else?"

"No, William, I'm fine now. Excuse me for putting you through that. Pressure of work."

"But did I hear correctly? Something about the governor's father?"

"No, that was me mouthing off. My fault. Argument with the wife and I had too much to drink."

"I heard the word Nazi."

"Just an expression."

"I don't think so, sir. If this has anything to do with the governor and his family, it affects me too. Do you want to tell me, or should I go and ask myself?"

"William, I realise you're protecting your boss. Really you should stay out of it, especially as the old bastard may die anyway, with any luck."

"Sir, I've known you for many years. You always keep a very firm head on your shoulders and I've never seen you act like this before."

"Jeez, man, leave it, will you? I need another drink." The thought of being sober after the day's events was unbearable; he simply wanted to disappear into drunken oblivion.

"I don't think that's going to accomplish anything, do you? I suggest you tell me everything. I heard what was said, and you were very clear. I have many contacts, if you know what I mean, and can help."

"Sure. So political, aren't we? Want to save your own arse, eh? That's what it's all about. You want to keep your job. I want mine and Ted sure as hell wants to be the next damn president of the good ole United States. Yippee."

William passed him some more coffee which Jackson took and downed in one.

"Christ, I feel sober and that's the last thing I wanted. Okay, you want to know so I'll spell it out. Albert Whiteman is a Nazi crook. German by birth, so it seems. He's a murderer, and all the bank's money is based on looted gold. Satisfied? Now you know it all and I'm going back to the banquet to lie through my teeth to all and sundry in the hope if the fucking Nazi dies, all this will go away. Ah, so now you look shocked. Never thought that in a million years, did you? Now say something to get us out of this damned mess with the 'contacts' you have."

"I'll speak to the governor tomorrow. May I suggest you don't drink any more tonight and that this is kept between us."

"Too fucking right, William. Yep, let's keep this under wraps for another sixty years."

"Come on, sir. I'll go back with you in case the governor wants anything." He glanced at his watch. "It's about time for his speech. I don't think we should miss that, do you?"

"Oh, definitely not. I can't wait. Another part of the comedy, no doubt. All a game, and we're all involved."

CHAPTER TWENTY FIVE

IT was later in the evening when Cydney woke up, and with a banging headache. Night had descended and the darkness was broken only by the glare of the street lamps, which were making shadows in her hotel room through the partially drawn curtains. Peering at her mobile phone to check the time, she realised she must have been sleeping for a few hours after George had left her as it was already almost eight o'clock. Then it hit her - George had left. Since the car accident last year she had been prone to periods of having quite horrendous headaches but this was an emotional pain that reached her heart and taking a couple of paracetamol tablets was not going to cure anything. It was the way he'd left, the words he'd shouted at her that pierced her heart and shook her. What else could she have expected when she'd told him there was a possibility her husband was alive after all and she wasn't free to have a relationship of any kind, never mind marry?

She picked up the receiver and dialled Tom's room but there was no reply. She noticed her red message light was signalling intermittently. When she dialled in to retrieve it, she heard Tom, advising her he'd tried to call and, as there was no answer, he'd decided to go out to eat and would see her in the morning. She must have slept through the ringing.

Getting out of bed was a chore. She made it to the bathroom and stepped into the shower cubicle, allowing the hot water to cascade over her, but it was never going to wash her feelings away. She leaned back against the cold tiles for several moments, her mind a whirl of emotions. This was not like her. She confronted problems head on and found solutions, never letting anything or anyone get the better of her. Now it was important for her to get a grip and concentrate on the job in hand, which was working for Harold and Alfie and finding out the truth. The situation with George, and in some respects Steve, would have to wait.

After she'd showered she decided to call Sean. Even though the UK was five hours ahead, she knew he never went to bed early. He'd probably be watching one of his favourite black and white detective movies after spending the day working in the house or pottering with her car, washing and shining it so he could see his face in the paintwork. It was something that relaxed him; he would spend hours singing at the top of his voice, his hands moving rhythmically over the car body, lost in a world of his own.

"You sound upset. Why are you calling so late? What's wrong?"

"You need to go. Now."

"What's happened to make you want to move on this quicker than we discussed?"

"I don't want to talk about it. Just … I have to know. I can't go forward with my life until then."

"This is about George, isn't it? He called me yesterday and explained he was coming out to surprise you. I presume he did."

"Yes. And you never thought to tell me?"

"None of my business, as you often tell me. And it didn't go quite to plan?"

"No. He asked me to marry him. How can I do that?"

"Ah, so that's what it was all about. Could have been worse. So you said no and now he's gone, I presume?"

"Yes. Gone for good this time. I told him I thought Steve could be alive and until I knew for certain …"

"Christ. Why on earth did you do that? It was supposed to be kept between us. What if he says something?"

"He won't. I'm sure he's gone back to Johannesburg. That's where he normally goes to lick his wounds."

"That's unkind. Not something I expect of you."

"Sorry. I can't go on like this for much longer. It's so unfair to everyone."

"I've summoned the troops and all arrangements are in place. We can leave in two days. When are you back exactly? And how's it going?" he asked.

"I really don't know, to both questions. I'll probably be another week, at least. My clients are arriving here in a few days. There's a problem with their passports and visas. Jenny's sorting it out."

"Are you sure you'd rather I wasn't with you? I can easily fly over." Sean was already up to date with Cydney's investigations, courtesy of his friend and colleague, Richard Barrett.

"No. I'm fine here with Tom. Thanks, though. It's much appreciated but I really have to find out about Steve. Please keep me informed. You have the money?"

"I have. Be careful, please. Though this Weissmuller man is old, you don't know who knows his secret. It could be dangerous and I doubt he will have any qualms about taking action to keep it well and truly hidden."

"Well, that's the strange part, because it appears he's doing everything in his power to be discovered. Call when you arrive, and please take care. I need you back in one piece."

"Ditto," Sean replied.

After a few hours of restless sleep, tossing and turning in an attempt to find a comfortable position, she dialled Rupert's private number in Johannesburg and it was answered immediately. Hearing his voice gave her an immediate sense of comfort. It was not anything she hid, this reliance on him for fatherly advice; he was always the first person she turned to in times of trouble because he never judged or criticised her but accepted who she was entirely.

"Hi Cyd, my darling. How are you? Still in the States, I presume? I heard George was on his way out to see you."

"Yes, I'm still here. So everybody knew but me, it would appear. Anyway, he's left. A few hours ago. He'll be back with you soon, I assume."

"Um. Not what I expected. What went wrong?"

She ignored his question. "Rupert, I have something to tell you which I should have done quite a few months ago."

"This sounds serious. The kids okay?"

"Yes. They're fine. No, it's not about them. It concerns Steve." As if on cue, Ray appeared next to her, his presence comforting. "I believe he might be alive."

There was silence on the end of the phone.

"Ah, come on now. How can that be? Cyd, you've been under a lot of strain recently, what with your mother …"

"No. Listen to me. I'm not making this up. Sean spoke to him, or at least he thinks he did. The MOD is hiding all of this, using Steve for their own good. You have to believe me."

"This sounds kind of desperate. He spoke to him? Really?"

"It sounds so ridiculous, even to me when I say it out loud. I know I'm right. I'm sending Sean out to Israel to find him."

"Israel? Why there?"

"Sean was supposed to go out there to pick him up some months ago. He didn't show. He must still be there and I need to find out."

"And does George know this?"

"Yes. He does now. I had to tell him. It wasn't fair, especially when he asked me to marry him."

"Marry you?"

"Will you stop asking me questions after every sentence?" she said, now her frustration coming out. "What should I do? I called you for advice."

"Seems like you have this rather under control without my interference."

214

"Well, I needed to tell you before George does. Sean is leaving tomorrow."

"Can I help in any way?"

"No, I'm fine. I must find him or know he's dead for certain. It's breaking me up inside."

"I can imagine. Keep me informed. I'll have a quick chat to Sean myself, if you don't mind."

"No, of course not. Please, but this must be kept confidential. If the kids find out …"

"If he is alive, don't you think Lauren and Jake would be overjoyed to have their dad back? I'm sure they would do anything for him to be back in their lives."

"Yes, but … Well, this is so difficult. Of course they would be happy, though after all this time, to have to explain everything to them, why he couldn't come home. And then the adjustment, for them, for me …"

"This is your life, Cyd. I only want you to be happy. And you would adjust, you know that. As for George… Actually, you don't have to say anything, I think I understand. So, on another matter, how's it going with my old friends, Harold and Alfie?"

"Good. We've found out why, or at least we think we've found out why they received the money and from whom. There's a lot going on here and it could all come to a climax in a few days, hopefully, when they arrive."

"They're going out to Charleston?"

"Yes. It's the only way. I'll brief you properly when I see you. When do you think that will be?"

"I'll stay here in Jo'burg until George arrives and afterwards travel to London."

"Can I ask, Rupert, how come you know Harold and Alfie? How did you meet?"

"That's a long story. I was with the partisans during the war. They made their way into Holland from Germany and I helped them get to the UK in 1946."

"Now I'm all curious. I never knew about what you did in the war. I didn't even know you were from Europe. Anyway, it can wait for a few more days. We'll have a lot to discuss. Speak soon, and thanks. I really appreciate it."

"My pleasure. You're like a daughter to me, the one I should have had."

Cydney replaced the receiver wondering what those last few words meant. She turned to Ray who had been quiet throughout. "That's unusual for you to remain silent."

"I wanted to listen."

"And…"

"I listened and waited. I'm not here for that. I'm here to tell you now is the time for you to help."

"Now? I'm not prepared."

"Yes, you are. I'll be with you but it is going to get rough. I need to warn you and this is very important. A lot is going to come to light and you will see things you've never seen before, worse than the last time, but I will be around. So will Sybill. She needs to be able to move on."

"I know that. Of course, and I understand. I'll do my best to help."

"That is your role, to link the two worlds. It's going to be hard for Harold and Alfie, confronting the man they never envisaged they would see again. However, Weissmuller is gravely ill. He had a heart attack earlier today."

"He did what? After all this they may not be able to see him?"

"He will hang on to life if he can and for as long as he's able because he's afraid of who and what is awaiting him in spirit."

"Cowards are always afraid and this man should be for all he did. Will he survive another couple of days?"

"It's not within my control. I know you're seeing his son. All will work out as it's meant to." Ray, once again, faded from her side.

* * *

Rupert sat on his veranda and gazed into the distance, wondering where all the years had gone. He was not a man for nostalgia or dwelling on what might have been, nor did he ever speak of his past and his work during the war but his discussions with Cydney and realising what she meant to him, brought everything back.

He was a teenager standing at the window of his parent's house and staring out in outrage and horror as the German army marched in full formation through the streets of Amsterdam, demonstrating their entire might. It was May 1940 and the Netherlands had eventually fallen to Germany after five days of fighting and despite valiant attempts by the Dutch military to hold back the invasion. It took the bombing of Rotterdam for the country to finally capitulate.

He vowed to do everything in his power to fight the invaders of his country and he persuaded his parents, somewhat unwillingly, to help him by hiding the Jewish family of his best friend in their attic until they could escape to England. It was a fearful period for everybody but it was important to him, and he refused downright to tolerate the way the Dutch Jewish people were rounded up in their tens of thousands and deported to the concentration camps.

That was the start of his involvement and although at the beginning his role was limited to the printing and distribution of leaflets and illegal newspapers, as time went on, he aided many people, especially children, to escape via established routes, providing them with false names and forged papers. The churches, both Catholic and Protestant, were important in these routes and by working together with the resistance, many were saved.

However, his work at the beginning was frustrated by the length it took to establish any form of resistance. The country was isolated and the Germans defended the Dutch coastline as well as the airspace, so it became extremely difficult for any covert operations to be put in place. Also, the geography didn't help. The lack of mountains and forests meant it was difficult to establish hiding places, and the flat terrain with many bodies of water only enabled movement to be made via railroads or road, which were controlled by the Germans and deemed highly dangerous. As time went on, however, he was enlightened by the many more Dutch who joined the resistance and recruited others.

In 1943 he joined a group known as the *Partisan Action Nederlands*, whose members consisted of about one hundred young men and women operating out of Eindhoven. Their task was to sabotage anything and everything under German control: vehicles, railroad tracks, bridges, using smuggled mining explosives. These aggressive operations were the tasks in which Rupert excelled and he became somewhat of a technical engineering expert, which was to hold him in good stead for the rest of his life. The counter-intelligence and network of people working against the Nazi occupation provided the key support that was so important to the Allied Forces, which led to the liberation of the Netherlands on 5th May 1945.

After the German surrender, Rupert was somewhat at a loss as to what to do with himself. He realised the extent of the problems facing Europe with all the displaced people, so he and a few of his colleagues from the partisans actively sought out young men and women who had survived the camps and assisted their passage to England. That was where he first encountered the young Hans Frankelman and Ahron Gotlieb, extremely weakened by their ordeal and years in captivity.

Cydney was the person who most reminded him of his wife and his daughter. Adela was a Jewish Austrian refugee and it was a mutual love at first sight when they met at one of the displacement centres. There was something about her that drew him towards her, despite the fact she was bone-thin and suffering from malnutrition after leaving Bergen-Belsen, an inner beauty that nothing could disguise. She was alone in the world and his determination was such that he was going to be the one to save her. They were married as soon as she was able to travel and, for both of them, leaving Europe was not a hardship.

They settled easily into life in Johannesburg and after less than a year their daughter was born. To say Rupert idolised this beautiful bundle settled in his arms was an under-statement. Katarina and Adela were his world and, as he started to build up his engineering company and invested into gold and diamond mining projects, he was able to give them all the material things they deserved. Their life was idyllic until that fateful day, 1st May 1950. Adela was in the township of Alexandra, situated close to the centre of town. It was one of the poorest districts and she and a few of her friends would visit and help as much as they could with the prevailing health and insanitary conditions by providing medicine and clothing, despite opposition from many of their peers. This particular day, Adela was on her own with only Katarina, unbeknown to Rupert, and afterwards had journeyed into Johannesburg. There had been unrest recently in the town and a general strike had been called against the discriminatory apartheid laws. Many of the protestors had organised a rally but the police had opened fire against them. It was being in the wrong place at the wrong time that resulted in Adela and Katarina being caught up in the middle of the rally and crossfire.

Rupert was told of their deaths by his friend, the police superintendent, who was full of apologies and sorrow at his loss. That was the day Rupert stopped believing in God and vowed he would never remarry or have children again as, firstly, he could never replace his wife and daughter and, secondly, he would never want to go through the same misery and guilt that haunted him to this very day, that he wasn't there to protect them. Instead he concentrated on his various enterprises, building them up into the global conglomerate it was today. Now he had thousands of employees, offices throughout the world and not much time to reflect on his past.

He was looking forward to seeing Cydney who was as feisty as Adela; they had both carried on in the face of adversity, Adela at the hands of the Nazis and Cydney through losing her father at an early age, her mother a few months ago, and coping with the loss of Steve for the last five years.

He took a sip of the whisky he had poured earlier which normally helped to calm his palpitations. His heart was not in the best of condition and after some eighty years it was beginning to display signs of wear and tear. The fluttering he experienced occasionally had caused him some concern, enough to take him off to see a renowned cardiologist, who warned him to slow down. Rupert understood the implications and had been to see his lawyer to make suitable provisions upon his death. Most of his estate would be going to Cydney, some to staff and employees and the rest to charity, as he had nobody else. He couldn't make up his mind whether to tell her or not about his Will. If he did, he had a feeling she might resist but he could think of no-one else who could continue with what he had started after the war. She would protect his corporation and ensure her children in turn would do the same. Well, maybe not Jake who wanted to be a pop star. He smiled at the memory of seeing Jake perform last year at the competition he had won. Afterwards, Jake had run up to him and given him a huge hug. That was really when he decided what he wanted to do for this family, whom he considered his own.

CHAPTER TWENTY SIX

T HE banquet went on interminably and Ted thought he would never be able to escape the clutches of the West Virginia elite. Everyone wanted to have a 'quiet word' with him, shake his hand, congratulate him, raise a toast to his campaign, and more importantly ensure they ingratiated themselves into his possible presidential camp. Thankfully, there had been no hitches, at least that he knew about, especially after the drunken behaviour of his cousin, Jackson, and even Cale Tatum had managed to keep his mouth fairly shut. The best thing was that he'd received firm promises of support of nearly twelve million dollars from a consortium of the biggest industrialists in the state because it was thought to be about time 'our state was put on the map'. Well, judging by his father's actions, putting West Virginia on the world map was going to be a foregone conclusion, albeit for the wrong reasons.

Alice was reluctant to let him go off when the last guest left at just before midnight but Ted was insistent. There was no way he was waiting for the new day to dawn before going to the hospital. It was his fervent wish his father would somehow regain consciousness to speak to him, explain at least, and give his side of the story, if he had one.

His chauffeur was waiting outside the mansion and they arrived at Thomas Memorial Hospital a little after one o'clock. Ted was escorted to the lift by the night porter, who took him to the intensive care unit on the second floor where they were caring for his father. There was an eerie silence as he moved down the corridor towards the nurses' station, the only noise coming from the trainers he now wore. He could smell death in the air and it reminded him of when his mother had died many years ago when he was a boy. Now he had no choice but to go through it all again. As he arrived, the night staff were sitting and drinking coffee, talking in whispers so as not to disturb the patients, the only sound coming from monitors bleeping in the background. They stood up when they saw him.

The wife of his private secretary was the senior cardiologist on duty when his father had arrived and she had explained the entire situation to Ted. The ambulance paramedics had given him initial treatment to stabilise him and he was now attached to a heart monitor. He was extremely weak and not very responsive so he had been admitted. A little later, once his father had been assessed and diagnosed, Ted was asked if he wanted to sign a 'do not resuscitate' order but he had not finished with his daddy yet and it was imperative he survived long enough to tell him the truth.

"Good morning, Governor," the senior nurse greeted, her face solemn.

"How is he?"

"I'm sorry but your daddy is old and his heart has been damaged. He is weak still. The doctors are concerned that any treatments they carry out may not help him, only make him worse."

"Has he said anything … at all?"

"He's been drifting in and out of consciousness. Mumbling and mostly incoherent. To be honest, in my experience, I doubt if he will be fully awake again. I'm sorry, sir. Let me take you through. You can sit and talk to him as he may well be able to hear you."

Ted accompanied the nurse and followed her into the room where his father was laying, his skin almost translucent, barely alive. The steady beat of the electrocardiogram monitoring his heart and blood pressure was the only indication of life as Ted attempted to analyse the abnormal wavy lines between the short peaks shown on the screen. Despite everything, this was his father, the man who was responsible for bringing him into the world, who had supported him, or at least drove him on, and loved him, maybe, in his own heavy-handed way. It was difficult to imagine what the man really was and all he had done in the past.

"I'll leave you, sir. Call me if you need anything or press this red buzzer." She indicated the button to the left of the bed. "In the meantime, I'll bring you some coffee. I think you may need it."

"Christ," he said, taking the chair to the side of the bed. "Only you had to be this dramatic. Why couldn't you goddamn well wait until we'd finished our conversation? Instead I had to hear everything from Liam and Jackson. All these years you lied to me, Philip and Mom and now I have to sit hear listening to that god awful monitor and watch you die, and you can't even deny what you did or explain yourself."

Ted scrutinised the man whose visage hadn't changed at all in the last few decades. His features were unquestionably hard, haughty even, which didn't exactly encourage people to like him, and not many did. He and Philip had been brought up with a rod of iron and there was little leeway to getting their father to change his mind once a decision had been made, so Ted had given up even trying once he'd realised that. His mother had been scared of her husband and when he was angry or frustrated with her she simply took to her bed. Most of the time Ted and his brother were raised by the domestic staff who oversaw their time-table and organised the chauffeur to drive them around, to and from school and soccer practice, plus the various extra-curricular activities.

"Why couldn't you be like other fathers?" Ted asked. "I so wanted to be close to you but you were never there for us. All I wanted was for you to put your hand on my shoulder and say how proud of me you were. Forget the fact I never heard you say 'I love you' to us or to Mom. How hard would that have been? Were you really incapable of showing any emotion? Now I'm all alone and you're being kept alive by a fucking machine and I'll never get to know the truth. That's what's so painful. I need to hear your side of the story. Are you really the murderer they say you are? Did you defraud the bank for so many years to fund our lifestyle?"

Ted breathed a long sigh and sat back in the chair. His hand hovered over his father's; he so wanted to touch him but he couldn't bring himself to do it. They didn't have that sort of relationship. Suddenly, the noise of the monitor changed, signalling his father's heartbeat was racing and Ted physically jumped. The numbers were rising. Supposing it was true his daddy could hear him?

"It's okay. I'm here with you." The heartbeat went slowly back to normal. "Ah, so you can hear me. Well that's good. I wish you could talk back to me. There's a woman here from London, a Cydney Granger. She's investigating you. She knows about the money you sent to those two men in England. Was it a bribe, hush money, even? I wish I knew."

There was a slight movement, barely imperceptible, a finger grazing against the sheet.

"Are you awake? Daddy? I need to speak to you. Christ almighty."

"Good ..." His voice was a thin whisper, a struggle.

"What? Good what? What did you say? For God's sake, wake up."

"Ask R-Riley."

"Ask him what? I don't know what you're saying."

When it was obvious his daddy was going to say nothing more, he got to his feet. "Okay, I'm going to speak to him now. I'll be back. Don't you go and die on me yet."

Ted ran from the room, ignoring the stares from the nurses, along the corridor, foregoing the lift for the stairs in his rush, and stopped outside the main entrance where the driver was waiting in the car.

"I need you to tell me - to ask you. Good something. What does that mean?"

"I assume he means Father Goodheart. A priest. I've been taking your father to his church for the past few months. That's all I know, sir."

"You've been doing what? Church? Well that says it all."

"Excuse me, sir. He did request me not to tell you."

"Not your fault. He's asking for this priest. I want you to go and get him and bring him here as soon as you can."

"Now, Governor? It's a few hours' round trip."

"Yes, now. Get going before it's too late. I'll be here waiting still. It's going to be a long night. And, not a word to anyone, is that clear?"

Back in the room, the monitor was beating steadily again as Ted made himself as comfortable as possible in the chair beside the bed. "Father Goodheart will be here soon. Whatever it is you need to do, you'll be able to do it. I can't deny you your final absolution, if that's what you're wanting. Not up to me anyway. Someone higher than all of us will take care of that."

Ted settled himself down for the wait. The fact he had summoned this priest defied everything he knew about his father. He had, for as long as he remembered, fought against any type of religion and certainly never encouraged him and his brother to go to church, which they had only done with their mom.

The hospital chair was not meant for lengthy stints and his long legs, no matter which way he moved, prevented him from finding any kind of restful position. He knew his neck and back would suffer. Nevertheless, the next thing he awoke to a light tap on his shoulder.

"Mr Whiteman, I'm Father Goodheart."

Ted sprung to attention immediately, as if he had always been awake. The priest was dressed in the usual black attire with a purple stole around his neck. Ted was surprised to see how young he appeared.

"Oh, you're the Governor. I recognise you. Your father never told me."

"There's a lot of things, apparently, my daddy never said. He asked for you."

"Yes, I expected him to."

"You know him quite well then, Father?"

"Yes, he's been coming to my church for the past six months now. He's had a lot to talk about."

"Not with me, he hasn't. Anyway, I'll leave you here with him. I have to get back. After my meeting I'll return. I don't think he's going anywhere just yet. I believe he has unfinished business."

"Yes, Governor. I believe he has."

* * *

As Ted strode into his bedroom to change, Alice, as expected, was sitting up in bed waiting for him.

"I had some coffee brought for you. I had a feeling you would need it. You look completely done in. How's your daddy?"

"I left him with a priest hearing his confession, or at least giving him the last rites or whatever they do."

"He was what? He's awake?"

"Hard to believe, eh? My daddy and a priest." Ted took the proffered cup of coffee and sat wearily down on the end of the bed. What he wouldn't do to climb in between the sheets and sleep for twenty-four hours, but it was never going to happen, and the day ahead was destined not to get any better for him.

"Impossible, I would say. What on earth is that all about? He hates the church and everything about it. What did he always say?"

"He vowed never to take one step inside it, could never understand God's pull to people and if he died he wanted to be buried with no ceremony and in a cardboard box. He's changed his mind, it would seem."

"Maybe the thought of dying …"

"I think it's more than that, my darlin'."

"He's scared?"

"Apparently. He's been seeing this priest for many months. They've built up some sort of rapport, I'm told."

"Ted, I realise you're tired but you're not telling me everything."

"It's nothing, darlin'. Honestly. Been sitting up all night long, and after the banquet, I'm plain exhausted."

"Go get a shower and I'll have some breakfast brought up here."

"Thanks. Good idea." He shed his clothes carelessly on the floor on the way to the bathroom. He didn't have the strength to pick them up and fold them away like he normally did.

"Want some company?" Alice called after him, which stopped Ted in his tracks. "I know a way to take your mind off things."

"Christ, you sure do pick your time right." He turned to face his wife and suddenly the thought of making love to her was one of the best ideas of the last twenty-four hours. "Get your pretty little ass in here before I change my mind."

CHAPTER TWENTY SEVEN

IT was a joint decision not taken lightly for Harold and Alfie to gather their children together and explain the reason for their summons. At their age they were about to embark on a journey across the Atlantic to confront the man they never thought they would see again in their lifetime, and they were frightened to the extent they believed in their hearts they would not return. Everything they had gone through when so very young was coming back to haunt them and now it was important their children knew the truth. It was going to be the hardest thing in the world to tell them. Like so many survivors of the holocaust, they would never talk about their lives in Germany, their time in the Lodz Ghetto, the transporting, the death marches between all those camps, nor what they had seen, all the despair, the murders, the sights before their eyes. It was not even something they shared together as it was enough they understood and recognised their past and that of their families during those catastrophic years - until now, when they were forced to face their demons, or rather one of them.

Their children, now grown up with families of their own, and cousins all but in blood, sat expectantly, waiting.

"I'll start," Harold offered. "We have something to tell you. Your dad and I," he began hesitantly, looking directly at Matt and Sarah, "are going to America tomorrow."

"You're what? Sorry, I'm not sure I heard this right," Mikey said.

"Oh no, you're not." Matt stood up and searched for support.

"There's no way, at your ages, we're letting you go off on your own on some jaunt. What on earth are you thinking about? Dad?"

"Listen to him. We have to go. There's no choice in the matter." A small tear appeared in Alfie's eye and slowly slid down his face.

"Hold on a minute, everyone. This sounds serious. What's it all about?" Sarah asked.

As one, Harold and Alfie lifted their left arms to display the numbers indelibly imprinted into their skin.

"We know about that. What has that got to do with this trip?" Matt asked, his voice still raised.

"Listen, *meine Kinder*. Your uncle and I love you beyond words. Believe us when we tell you we have tried to avoid this. Now we have no choice. We have never talked of our lives before coming to England."

"I know. We never raised it with you. We knew how painful it would be," Sarah said. "We read the books and learned what we could and we would never force you to tell us."

"And we appreciate this, your uncle and I. However, the man whom we hold responsible for the deaths of your grandparents and my sisters, and so many others, has found us."

"What on earth are you talking about? This makes no sense," said Mikey, still not comprehending what he'd heard.

"A Nazi officer, Adolf Weissmuller. He escaped after the Allies liberated us from Dachau and it seems he has been found in West Virginia. We've been asked to go and identify him."

"It can't be as simple as that. You're not telling us everything. A Nazi! After so many years. God, he must be in his nineties if a day. I can tell by your faces you're holding something back. Pops? Uncle Alfie?"

Harold scrutinised his oldest friend's face, and the difficulties he was encountering relaying this tale were echoed there.

"Alfie, you tell them now. Everything. It's best and it's time, in case we don't come back."

With tears in his eyes and sorrow in his heart, Alfie told them the entire painful story of their youth, omitting nothing. "We nearly didn't make it, after everything. The Nazis knew the war was ending and they accelerated the pace of their killings. We were in Dachau. Two days before the Allies arrived in April 1945, they rounded us up again. There was so much activity. Everyone was being sent away on trucks, or marched out. There were huge bonfires of papers burning, but most of all, there were dead bodies everywhere, stacked up by the side of the square."

"Where were they sending you?" asked Sarah.

"Who knows? Just away, clearing us out, anywhere to hide evidence of what they had done. Later, we learned they were sending us to the Swiss border in exchange for German prisoners. Himmler had agreed privately and without authorisation to hand over some of us in Dachau in order to protect himself. They started marching us towards the border and many were shot on route. I think we managed to reach about thirty odd miles south of the camp but there was no food and certainly no shelter. We could hardly stand, never mind walk. Slowly, the guards disappeared and we were left to our own devices and we had no idea what was going to happen to us. Those of us who were still alive, barely alive, well, we didn't know what to do. Luckily some advance scouts of American soldiers found us laying at the side of the road. They gave us some food and water, which was the first we'd had for so long, but still we had to wait two days before the medical team arrived and then, of all things, we were transported back to Dachau. By that time all the Germans who remained had been imprisoned and the camp had been liberated."

"When we got there," Harold continued, "we were given clothes to wear, though nothing fitted, and for the first time in so many years, we had a clean bed to lie in. The first morning we woke up, the bed was covered in lice from us. Can you imagine? Anyway, it took us a while to recover. They kept us hospitalised for many months there. The camp was turned into a centre for some of the liberated prisoners. We both had dysentery and were so malnourished, and we watched people dying around us. After a while, when we were better, we were sent to another camp for displaced persons near Hamburg. That's what we were, displaced, along with thousands of others from all different nations that had been invaded or occupied by German forces, and neither the British, the Americans nor the Russians knew what to do with us. There were too many people and conditions were bad. We were still behind barbed wire, imprisoned. Ach, our parents and families were dead.

"The military wanted all of us to go back to our original homes. You know, we could never remain in Germany after what those people had done to us. We were fearful because we had no home, no country and no family left. Nobody wanted to go back, although a lot were repatriated. God knows what they found when they got there. We refused. The Allied Forces wanted to set up temporary Jewish camps or assembly centres for those displaced persons who wouldn't return. We were German and we were considered as enemies in some ways, despite all we had gone through. Everybody was wary of us, though we got some help because we were still so young."

"How old were you?" said Matt.

"I was seventeen and Uncle Harold was eighteen," Alfie said, taking up the story again. "Our future was so uncertain. We were broken physically, psychologically and spiritually and the atmosphere was hostile, still. We were liberated but not yet free. Everyone thought as the war had ended we would leave so what were we supposed to do? We were incapable of making decisions as they had been made for us over the last six years. Also, we had nowhere to go.

"We had heard about Palestine from the Zionist groups and all about living in a kibbutz and it seemed to be everything we had dreamed about, so that was where our destiny lay. You see, we needed to have a Jewish identity, a Jewish pride and dignity that had been taken away from us, and we wanted to be Palestinian soldiers and have a sense of belonging. They all wore a yellow star like we were forced to wear, though now it was not worn with shame. There was no future for us in Europe anymore and we were promised so much, but going to a kibbutz was not to be. The Americans and British did not recognise Palestine and refused to send us, or anybody. I became ill again so we were forced to stay where we were. We waited and waited for a ship to take us but nobody wanted to send us to Palestine so we literally walked out and made our way into Holland. We were rescued by some ex-Dutch and Belgian partisans who helped us out of Europe and got us to England in late 1947."

"The war ended two years before. Why did it take so long?"

"Governments had no desire to help us, Sarah. They were not sympathetic as every country had their own problems and were trying to deal with them. The task of reconstruction after the war was monumental and there was no room for compassion. Despite everything we had been through, there was a refugee crisis and nobody would deal with it. Anyway, when we arrived eventually in England we were still so young. We had the appearance of old men, and that's exactly how we felt. We could hardly speak English. The authorities placed us in a hostel where we had to learn the language and we were given some simple work to do. We met up with many others from Germany at this centre in Finchley Road. The Association of Jewish Refugees looked after us, finding us jobs and lodgings and helped us with our naturalisation. We chose English names as a new start. We met your mothers at one of the meetings at the centre. They were best friends."

"This Adolf Weissmuller ... I don't get it. How did this man find you after so many years? And more importantly, why?" asked Mikey.

"We had something he wanted," Harold said. "His notebook.

I found it by accident and hid it away, and then retrieved it, luckily, when we were returned to Dachau. It contained every single detail of all the money he had taken, the gold and where it had been sent, the businesses he had plundered. Everything. I was in possession of that and still am, well, I was until I gave it to someone here who has been helping us."

"Pops, this is too incredible. Explain."

"He knew I had the book. I flaunted him with it when he was captured, before he escaped."

"How could he possibly have found you both?"

"Well, obviously he did or we wouldn't be sitting here now discussing going to America. He sent us some money. A million dollars each."

"What on earth! What did you do with the money?" Mikey got to his feet and started pacing around the floor.

"We don't have it, but it's safe."

"Does he want it back?" Matt asked.

"Why did he send the money?" Mikey probed further. "What's he trying to do? Bribe you?"

"So many questions. I don't know why. Through one of our old friends, we were introduced to a lovely lady called Cydney Granger. She's in Charleston, West Virginia, waiting for us and she's the one who found Weissmuller. He calls himself Albert Whiteman now. We're going out there at her request to see if it really is him."

"You can't go, not with your angina. Neither of you is in a fit state to travel to the other side of the world. I'm going with you."

"We should all go," added Matt.

"No. We are going alone, together. This is for us to do. After all these years. We have to do this. Please understand, all of you. We have no choice. It is written. Our destiny. We need this closure and it's our one chance, for us, our parents and all our people."

Nobody said a word. Their children studied each other and

233

slowly something dawned. They now knew the truth, and if their fathers had to do this, they would support them in the hope they would return with peace in their hearts.

"Then you go with our blessings but on one condition - come back to us."

"You have our promise. Now, give your papas a hug."

CHAPTER TWENTY EIGHT

C YDNEY woke up with a heavy heart and a feeling of unease.
This was the day of the meeting with the governor, Liam
Ross and Jackson Dwyer III. In her mind it was time to lay all
the cards on the table, especially if Albert Whiteman was dying;
they had nothing to lose now. She had called Jenny previously
to make sure she, Harold and Alfie were on the flight out and
to confirm that Tom would pick them up at the airport later that
day. She would take them to the hospital tomorrow to see the
man they had hated all their lives, to identify him in his last hours
so they could find some peace, she hoped. This was, of course,
reliant on obtaining permission from the governor but she was
sure that with exactly the right kind of persuasion there would
be no issue. The man had no choice due to what was at stake.

To be honest, Cydney had no preconceived ideas as to how
to play the meeting. She was convinced the governor, at least,
would do everything in his power to prevent stories about his
father leaking out to the press. Liam would be on her side and
that of her clients. Regarding the murder of his wife and two
sons, on that she was unsure, especially with the perpetrator near
to death. If he died there would be no case to answer. About
Jackson, she had no clue. Again, he would not want to see the
bank fold, as certainly that was what would occur if the story got
out about the provenance of the funds, the fraud and the
embezzlement over the years. However, this was one case the
FBI would be all over. Bank fraud and embezzlement was
classified in 1924 to cover investigations into fraud perpetrated

against financial institutions and the FBI had complete jurisdiction over this type of crime. It would only take one phone call to set the whole thing in motion and watch the playing field open up.

Jackson had called Cydney at the hotel earlier that morning, full of apologies for being on the defensive, and explaining he had met with Liam and now recognised the issues they were facing. That would be the under-statement of the century but phones have ears, so perhaps he was being cautious, which would be more than understandable.

The car collected Cydney and Tom shortly after breakfast and took them the short distance to the mansion. As guests of the governor, they were driven directly through security and to the front of the glorious white building where they were met by the governor's private secretary, William Templeton, and taken across the black and white chequered marble foyer and up the right-hand side of the stairs directly to the governor's office. The chandelier was as spectacular as Tom had described and the whole building emanated a sense of space and history. Either side of the hallway were two flags - the stars and stripes along with the official flag of West Virginia, consisting of a pure white field bordered on four sides by a blue stripe. They could just about make out the centre of the state flag emblazoned with the Coat of Arms: two men, a farmer and a miner standing either side of a boulder, representing agriculture and industry, with the lower half wreathed by two swags of rhododendron maximum, the state flower. The bases of the small mahogany tables next to the flags were carved eagles.

On entering, they found Liam and Jackson already present. Both men stood up to greet them, the older man seemingly happy to see them, the younger one not quite so, gauging by the haggard look on his face, despite his earlier call.

"I hear Albert Whiteman had a heart attack," Cydney said. "Is he still alive?"

"At the moment, so I've been told, more's the pity," Liam answered, "but I doubt for much longer."

"It would be better for him to go. All *this* hanging over us. Christ, I need a drink," Jackson added.

"Don't you think you've had enough already?" said Ted as he entered the room, "especially after your performance last night." With an engaging smile that didn't fool Cydney, he strode forward to shake her hand. "I'm pleased you could come to clear up all this nonsense about my father. Please excuse my being late. I've been up all night at the hospital. You heard about the heart attack?"

"We did." She watched the governor's face carefully. He seemed to be waiting for her to offer her commiserations at the news, what someone would say in normal circumstances. There was no chance, bearing in mind the reason for the meeting, which the governor obviously didn't want to acknowledge. However, he was obviously worried or why would he have agreed to the meeting in the first place? No, in Cydney's view, he knew exactly what was at stake and was not going to give it up easily. "And why would it be nonsense, in your opinion?"

"You have nothing to substantiate your claim."

"My claim? Perhaps you could tell me exactly what it is you know."

"Only what my uncle and cousin have told me. I don't readily accept this."

"May I show you something, Governor?" Cydney pulled out from her briefcase a picture that had been faxed over to her by Richard Barrett the evening before, after his conversation with Harold and Alfie. She handed it over and he took it hesitantly. "It's not a good photo, unfortunately. It was taken from Nazi war criminal records. You can see the man is wearing SS insignia. This man is Adolf Weissmuller." She waited for the words to sink in. "He escaped from Dachau after it was liberated in April 1945. Killed an American soldier in the process. We believe he reached Switzerland and took the identity of Dieter Scholler. Here's a picture of him also. He's been hunted ever since but managed to evade capture."

"What has this to do with me?"

"Stop mucking around, Ted. You know this Weissmuller is your father. We discussed it all. Even I can tell after all these years. He didn't look much different when he arrived here and married my sister," Liam snapped. "He killed this Scholler person and came here on his passport."

Governor Theodore Gerald Whiteman obviously knew the game was up. "Yes, I can see this could well be my father."

"It is your daddy! For God's sake, man. An idiot could see this." Cydney caught Liam's eye. His tone quietened as if he realised showing his anger and frustration would accomplish nothing at all. She realised he wanted justice for the murder of his wife and children and he would get it, but slowly, slowly. "Everything points to him."

"Even I can see it and I was too young at the time," added Jackson, silent until then.

"How much do you know, Mrs Granger?" Ted said with a sigh, clearly resigned now.

"Everything."

"Ah, everything. Such a global word. What do you want to do? Are you intending to get all of this out into the open?"

"It would mean closing," Jackson said. "All those people losing their jobs. And you, Ted, everything you wanted, gone! The scandal would be unlike anything witnessed before in West Virginia. Christ, in the whole of the United States. The press would love this."

"Governor, my intention, primarily, is to seek retribution for my clients," answered Cydney. "These are two old men who survived through so much. They have evidence of all your father did. They witnessed everything and they received money from him. My question is why? To shut them up? To make recompense? Or maybe to get them to come here, to face him once again?"

"I know about the money." Ted paused and searched everyone's faces. "Okay, yes, I admit it's him. He only told me recently and I had no knowledge of any of this before. Please believe me. The money - I've no idea why. Recompense, yes, probably. All I know now is that my daddy is dying."

"Have you even thought about the extent of his crimes after our discussion?" Liam said.

"It's all I've thought about."

"Governor, my two clients are arriving here this afternoon."

"They're doing what? Who gave you permission? This is not the right thing to do."

"They want to see your father before it's too late."

"That's impossible. There is no way I'm letting them go to the hospital where my daddy is dying. No. I can't allow this."

"Ted," Liam said, his voice now quiet and calm. "You have no choice."

"My clients are not vindictive men. Their sole wish is to seek an answer, and closure before they die. They need closure - to confirm your father is Adolf Weissmuller …"

"And walk away? Really? Do you honestly believe that?"

"They have something that belongs to your father. A notebook. He lost it not long before he fled Dachau. It contains a list of everything he stole. It's in my safe-keeping now and I intend to keep it that way."

"And you're telling me they want no other recompense?"

"No. Just an acknowledgment of the truth. They believe your father's crimes will be dealt with by someone other than them."

"And Uncle Liam, what about you?"

"I lost everything due to your daddy. Nothing can bring back my Margaret or my two beautiful sons."

"What can I do? If I could bring them back …" Ted sighed in defeat.

"To hear him repent might be enough for me but, of course, he won't. I am too old for retribution." Cydney could see Liam was on the verge of breaking down.

"I can't believe how everybody is so accommodating," shouted Jackson. "This is absolute shit. You're telling me everybody's gonna shake hands and say goodbye?"

"What good is it going back over the past?" Liam said sadly. "I've learned you can't change what's gone before, only deal with the present. It's taken me a long time to reach that conclusion, at some cost to me. Cydney has told us what these two men want to do. I think you should let them, Ted. It is their right."

The silence was palpable as every man in the room tried to read Ted's reaction, and they waited whilst he pondered their suggestion. "Okay, yes. With so many reservations, I will allow it. It puts into question my very existence. I will let them go to the hospital. I insist on being there, too. What do you intend after that?"

"Well, Governor, that depends on the FBI, I would think," Cydney said, and watched the faces of the men around her. Nobody spoke.

CHAPTER TWENTY NINE

"I SEE you have your own little army going on."

Sean and Mo Hemmings marched out purposefully into the glorious sunshine of Tel Aviv after their flight into Ben Gurion airport to be met by their colleagues, Baz and Sparks, who had entered Israel via Jordan the day before, and Dixie who had flown into Jerusalem, only to be stopped immediately in their tracks by an all too familiar face.

"What the fuck?" Mo said out loud, not even trying to disguise his surprise.

"Corporal Hemmings, good to see you, too. And you, Sergeant O'Connell. I presume you're in charge of this group of merry little men."

"Sir?" Sean stood in front of General Bowles-Smith. It was no surprise to be greeted by the CO on his arrival; in fact, exactly as expected, especially after he had cottoned on to that couple in the pub. "I can explain."

"Yes, please do, but perhaps we should do this somewhere a little less conspicuous. Can I suggest you all come with me?"

"Do we have a choice, sir?" One glance directly into the man's face was sufficient. "That would be a no. Come on lads, let's see what the CO has to say to us."

An hour and a half later they reached Nevatim Air Base, situated in the south of Israel on the edge of the Negev desert. The area was vast and the burned yellow terrain where nothing green stood a chance of surviving was flat and bland. Once through the high security at the main gates, it took a while to drive through to the main administration blocks, passing alongside the two runways. As a strategic air command post, the place was teaming with activity. Everyone had a job to do and nobody took notice of the new arrivals.

Whilst the rest of his guys were taken to the mess, Sean was accompanied to an office, which clearly the general had been occupying for some time judging by the huge quantity of papers strewn around.

"I can guess what this is all about, Sergeant. A certain Captain Steve Granger." He walked around his desk and sat down, leaving his subordinate standing facing him.

These were the sort of games Sean loved playing. "Well, we're here on holiday. Thought we'd take in a bit of sunshine."

"Stop fucking around with me." The general slammed his fist down hard on his desk. "I've had enough of this."

"Well maybe you can be straight with me, for a change."

The CO sat back and paused whilst he seemed to consider the situation. "I knew you didn't buy my story and, in some ways, I would have been surprised if you had. That would not be the Sean O'Connell I knew. If there's something I've learnt over the years, it's never to under-estimate my men."

"I don't know what you mean, sir."

"I would have done the same in your shoes, so I don't blame you. We've had this conversation before, as I recall. Captain Granger was never going to be allowed back into normal life with his family. We all know that and don't look as if this is the first time you've considered it. The Israelis don't take kindly to anyone encroaching on their territory. Thankfully, we are working with them rather than against, which is why they haven't monitored your arrival but left it to us." General Bowles-Smith smoothed the seam in his trousers.

"So, you're admitting he's here and now you're working out how to deal with us," Sean said. "It goes against the grain."

"I can't have you all running amok here. It's not what the

Israelis would like and we have to keep them happy, considering we're using all their resources."

"We're on holiday, sir."

"If only that were true." General Bowles-Smith stood up, using the top of his desk to steady himself. "Back playing me up today. I could do without all this from you. It doesn't make my life easier but it seems I have no choice but to deal with you. I suggest you barrack down for the night and we sort this out in the morning."

"Will we though? I know this is all about the Official Secrets Act. You can't hide someone, keep them against their will. There is a protocol here and Mrs Granger deserves to know."

"I can do whatever I want, is that clear? She's treated like a widow. She gets her pension and everything else to which she's entitled."

"That's not the point, if you forgive me saying so, sir. She needs her husband and she has more than an inkling he's alive and will do everything to get him back to her and their children. I doubt the national papers will be too impressed, either."

"Are you threatening me?"

"No, sir. Telling you like it is."

"I intend to discuss this further tomorrow. Good night, Sergeant O'Connell." The CO exited, leaving Sean alone in the room and wondering what on earth had gone on.

* * *

It was only a short while later that Sean met up with Mo.

"I think the captain's here. The question is where."

"Is this a double-bluff, though? The CO knew we were on our way out so maybe he's brought us here to think that. I'm not sure."

"There's a definite game being played out but I don't know why. He told me the captain was never coming home so obviously they have something lined up for him."

243

"He said that?"

"Yes, and that's a sure indication he's alive."

"The phone call you had. What did that American girl say, exactly?"

"That 'my son' is well and misses me and can't wait to come home. That he especially wanted to see the walnut tree that must be in bloom by now."

"Anything else? Any clue as to where he is?"

"No. Nothing."

"The CO will realise we're going to look around and the entire base is protected by armed soldiers every which way. You think they're going to let us wander around indiscriminately?"

"No, which is why we're going to do just that."

"What about getting out of Israel once we do have him?"

"No idea."

"There must be a difficult part here," said Mo.

"Well yes. We have to find Captain Granger."

"Let's go get a beer. I feel like some female company tonight."

"What a pleasant idea."

A couple of hours later, Sean and Mo were in the arms of two not unattractive ladies from the catering corps who had taken a shine to the British army twosome, who by now were on their way to becoming exceedingly drunk, and Baz, Dixie and Sparks were not too far behind them. Sean was singing 'Danny Boy' at the top of his voice and the others were hanging on to him and attempting to join in with their own version.

"I need some air, lads. Come on everyone, let's take this party outside." The men followed their sergeant dutifully, leaving the rest of the soldiers in the mess breathing a sigh of relief to finally get rid of this noisy bunch of Brits. "Show us around, ladies. I want to see where the planes take off." He pushed the two of them forward, and they followed behind, holding on to each other to keep from falling over. Every so often, Sean shouted out "shush," which caused even more mirth, and their peals of laughter rang out. A couple of Israelis passed them by and gave a look of disdain, which made them laugh and fall about even more.

They moved across the camp and towards the airfield and hangers where the usual maintenance work was being undertaken on several F-16 fighter jets, despite the hour.

"I want to fly," shouted Sparks at the top of his voice, starting to run around, his arms out-flung as he made swooping noises. One of the engineers glanced over and laughed. "Go to bed," he called, and a few of the others stopped what they were doing to stare at this group of drunken louts, this farcical comedy of British soldiers fooling around.

"I think that's enough," Sean whispered. "We're going," he called out. "I need another drink anyway. Let's take these lovely ladies back to their beds." The ladies in question had graduated towards a semi-comatose state and had sidled next to Sparks and promptly collapsed either side of his broad shoulders. He was holding them up to prevent them slipping to the ground. He nodded to Sean and moved away, dragging them with him, whilst the others followed, still singing.

Out of sight of the engineers, they immediately sobered up and slipped silently around the back of the end hanger. To their advantage, the moon was on the wane and the illuminated areas were progressively diminishing. They found themselves on the ramp overlooking the runways.

"Now what?"

"If I knew that, Mo …" Sean said. "I suggest we move off separately. It's dark so we won't be seen, but we need to be careful. Look for anything unusual. Everything is centred around the hangers and admin blocks. There's nothing much else here from what I noticed when we arrived."

"Suppose there is an underground facility," Baz said. "We'd never find him."

"I did hear rumours there was one, though it was just that. This base is too well-known and look where it is, right on the bloody edge of the desert. It's going to be monitored by every Arab state surrounding it and everyone would know if there was a facility, especially now more squadrons have been relocated here. It wouldn't be secret for long."

"Well whatever it is, it's not going to be right next to the runway. Too noisy, for a start, and also too dangerous and noticeable," Mo said. "If it was me, I'd find somewhere away from everybody, but near enough that if I wanted to exit, I could."

"Agreed," replied Sean. "Let's move further out towards the south. Maybe a look-out building, for example."

"Christ, it's hot. These fucking mosquitoes are biting the crap out of me." Mo began waving his arms around in a frenzy. "Let's go. I'm a sitting target here."

"It's the red hair," Baz piped up. "They're honing in on you."

"Enough, lads. Move out. If you find anything, call out."

Sean knew exactly where he was going and he wanted to do this part alone. He had noticed a building beyond the supply store, in front of which stood two armed guards. It jarred on his senses as it was so out of character with the rest of the site. He lit a cigarette and sauntered in the main direction. His objective was simply to view and walk around, as if he was meant to be there, not under cover of darkness. If stopped, he would be out for a night-time stroll.

"You can't leave things alone, can you?" a familiar voice said.

"Ah, of all the towns, in all the world …"

"And where are your band of men?"

"Out having a few bevvies and a night stroll, like me. Sir."

"Come with me, Sergeant. I've had enough of this now," General Ian Bowles-Smith ordered, and he escorted him away from the supply store and back towards the main block. "You think I have him under house arrest? Follow me." The general led him into a large recreational room. There was a man lounging in the corner, reading a newspaper, one of his legs resting on a stool in front of him.

"Well, I'll be damned if it isn't Captain Steve Granger himself."

"I'd recognise that voice anywhere," Steve said, carefully moving his leg off its rest and rising to his feet. He turned to face his old colleague and grabbed hold of his hand in a firm handshake. "Good to see you Sean, you old reprobate. It's been a while."

Sean tried not to appear too shocked at the appearance of the man after all this time. The ravages of all he had been through were apparent. He was considerably thinner, there was a scar running across his temple and down the side of his face and the hair he still possessed was certainly showing signs of greying. "You don't seem too surprised to see me."

"Why should I be? I knew you'd come. Eventually." He turned to his CO. "Good evening, sir. Pleased you saw your way to bringing O'Connell to me."

"I didn't have much of a choice as he decided to take matters into his own hands."

"All the gang here then, eh?"

"Indeed," Sean said, with a slight grin across his face. "As if I could've left them behind."

"I'm going to leave you to catch up. I'll try and round up your lads, who are no doubt scaring the locals, and I'll see you both at zero eight hundred hours tomorrow in my office. We have a lot to discuss."

Steve waited until his CO had departed. "Let me get you a drink. Whisky?"

"Guinness, if you have one. Nice and cold."

"Nothing changes. Come on, sit down." He nodded to a pair of comfortable chairs near the window. Sean watched him wander over to the area, noticing a slight limp on his left leg. "Leg's bad, I'm afraid. I got rather injured on that recce and it never quite healed properly. Didn't help nearly dying in the desert trying to reach our reconnaissance point, either."

"We need to get you out of here. I'm not yet sure how to do that."

"I doubt that's on the agenda. Here, take this. I think we could both do with it. Anyway, before all that, I have to know about Cydney and the kids. How are they? Are they managing without me? It's been five long years and not a day goes by I don't miss them. They are everywhere - in my thoughts, in my dreams." He put a hand to his temple and rubbed his finger along the scar, scratching at it. "Bloody thing. Always irritates in the heat."

"I can't say it's been easy for her, or Lauren and Jake," Sean said. He was not going to mention the Benton and Crossley case she had been working on where she was nearly killed, or the fact they nearly lost Jake when he was kidnapped by those two desperate fraudsters. "I think they're coming to terms with your not being around." Nor was he about to mention Cydney's relationship with George. Some things were better left unspoken. "Look, I've brought some photos." Sean removed from his inside breast pocket a few pictures which he had carefully chosen to show the twins growing up, and a recent one of Cydney.

"Christ, what I've missed, and for what?" He flicked the pictures over and over again, checking every single detail so that it bored into his memory.

"You know, it's because of Cydney we're here at all. She didn't quite believe you'd been killed. I have to say I found it hard to take in, too, after what the general told me about finding your body and burying you in Israel."

"Ah, that's the story, eh? I wondered what he'd been telling you."

"She was bombarding the MOD with calls but got nowhere. She sensed something not quite right and we had a wee chat." Again, no mention of the fact that she cornered him and gave him little choice.

"That sixth sense of hers? Comes in useful sometimes."

"Sure it does. Sometimes not to my advantage, let me tell you."

"Ah, she got you. She has a knack of that, if I remember. And how's my little girl? What's she doing now?"

"Growing up into a fine young woman. Beautiful, just like her mother. And Jake, he's the image of you. Big into his music." His voice changed to one not so buoyant. "Cydney lost her mother a few months ago. Took it hard."

"I'm sorry about that. She was a good woman. We always got on." There passed a few moments of silence, whilst Steve assimilated everything he'd been told. "I'm not sure you're going to be able to get me out of here. They have me scheduled to go to Iran. Military attaché to the British Embassy in Tehran. Under a new name. I'm now Captain Alan Campbell MC, for fuck's sake."

"MC? Congratulations."

"Well, you know what that means. It's partly a desk job, not that I'm much use anywhere else with this leg." He slapped the side of his thigh.

"Why there?"

"They've had the presidential elections and with Mahmoud Ahmadinejad elected, everyone is worried. He was a hardliner as Mayor of Tehran and they want me out there to represent the government, meet with our counterparts from the host country and oversee all the military and civilian personnel assigned to my new office. I'll be travelling around, too, observing Iranian facilities and activities and reporting back to the MOD and Israelis."

"And what they're up to?"

"Exactly. They want me to get a complete and detailed knowledge of their capabilities, operations, training and readiness to go to war, plus check they're complying with the EU and US proposals not to develop nuclear weapons. The problem is, trying to stop Russia from supplying them with nuclear fuel."

"Surely they have to comply."

"You would think. Anyway, I also have to ingratiate myself into working with the new regime. They want me to recruit someone there to assist our government, give out a few secrets with a promise of asylum."

"You're going to be running an agent? Is this MI6?"

"I've been told I'm still Special Forces, but who knows? I'm grappling in the dark here."

"Sure you are, but where in the dark?"

Steve shrugged his shoulders. "Obviously someone is running this whole bloody mess. Basically, that's my new role, plus as primary advisor to the ambassador on any significant changes in the country's military leadership or strategies, particularly where it affects us. There's no way I'm going to be able to escape from that."

"You're doing what? What if anyone recognises you? And the Ambassador will be aware? By the way, I've been told the Syrians know about your activities."

"I've no doubt they do, but do they know it's me? They're aware someone was reporting information on their activities. To be honest, I'll probably be safe in the Embassy. Anyone important coming over will be briefed and anyone not will simply be introduced to me under my new name. Steve Granger is dead and buried, long ago. I'm just the balding grey-haired guy with a bloody scar and gammy leg but with an important job to do."

"And you're happy about this? I can get you out. Me and the lads."

"No, you can't. Forget about it. How can I go home? To what? I'm not missing in action. They declared me dead. How will Cydney react, no matter what she says to you, and feels? I can't be the husband she wants now, or the father to my kids. God knows, I want to be. My fate is sealed now by that bloody man and the powers that be. I've been re-assigned, and when that job's done, they'll send me out to the middle of South America to be lost. I'm a commodity and always will be, until the day I die. Really die."

Sean sat opposite Steve and took a long draft of his drink. In his heart he knew what he was being told was true. The MOD had the man by the balls, for sure.

"I'll send the lads home. They shouldn't get involved. I'll tell them I've sorted everything but it's top security. They'll understand. I'll stay and see if they'll take me on as your liaison back in the UK. I'll be able to move around without getting noticed and at least I'll be there if you need me."

"Need? Never a truer word has been said. And you'll keep me up to date with Cydney and the kids? If I can't be there, I can't think of anyone I'd rather have looking after them."

"You can count on me, though what I'm going to say to that wife of yours is anybody's guess. She'll see through me like a glass of water. Perhaps I should stay here."

"Don't be scared of Cydney. She's a pussycat really."

"It's that sixth sense of hers. She'll know, and blame me."

"Well, we'll have to get our story straight, to protect her."

"And what is our story exactly?"

"How long have we got?"

"I can't go back empty handed. You do realise that. She's expecting some answers. I suggest we tell her the truth. That you're alive but have been moved to another assignment and nobody knows where. She'll be able to accept the truth more than my lies. I can't face her when she gives me that look of hers."

"I know that look well enough, Sean. I used to get it all the time." Some memories far away in the distance passed across his face. "If only ..."

"Let's sleep on it. Reconvene tomorrow. My priority now is getting the lads home. They aren't going to like it, leaving me behind. We're like the musketeers, 'All for one' and all that."

"I know, and I wish it were different. I'd do anything to go home."

"What are the chances we could swap you over? Just an idea. One of the guys can take your place. Sparks and you are fairly alike. The CO won't find out until we're out of Israel if we plan it right, but we won't have much time."

"Where would I go, though? They'll be after me from the get go. No, I can't risk you doing this for me. Let it be."

"Well, forgive me for trying."

"Don't get annoyed. It's not possible, not thought out. It would accomplish nothing whatsoever, as I still couldn't go to Cydney. No, I'll go to Iran as planned. It's the best all round."

CHAPTER THIRTY

T HE priest organised his makeshift altar by placing a crucifix and two small wax candles on the table at the foot of Albert's bed, together with a wine glass containing a small amount of water for purifying his hands, a vase containing holy water and a small cloth. He genuflected at the altar, took the holy water and, moving around to the side of the bed, sprinkled it over Albert in the form of a cross, in front of himself, and then to his left and right.

"Through this holy anointing may the Lord in his love and mercy help you with the grace of the Holy Spirit, May the Lord who frees you from sin save you and raise you up." Father Goodheart began making the sign of the cross above the supine body of Albert Whiteman, anointing him with the blessed oil he'd removed from his bag. "Through this Holy Unction and through the great goodness of His mercy, may God pardon thee whatever sins or faults thou hast committed."

"I know you're here." The voice was weak and barely discernible. "Thank you."

"You don't need to thank me. I am here on the Lord's work. I will hear your final confession."

"I'm … dying."

"Yes, my son."

Those final words of confirmation. Albert lay there in silence, knowing now there was no escape. He had neither the strength nor the ability to voice what was in his mind. All he was capable of was thought, back to those days when he managed to get out of Dachau and escape the Americans. His aim was to get over the Swiss border and head for Zurich, to lay his hands on all the money he had been hiding. Many of his comrades would be going to South America but that wasn't for him. His sight was very much set on the United States of America, to go to his 'family' as their long-lost cousin escaping war-torn Europe.

There were so many people wandering around aimlessly that he managed to divest himself of his identification and get lost into the 'ratlines', a network spread throughout Europe that had been secretly organised beforehand in readiness for senior Nazi criminals to escape prosecution and then imprisonment or, worse, hanging, as war criminals. Some of these ratlines were operated by the Catholic Church for their own political and spiritual interests. They wanted to bring former sinners back into the Church rather than turn them in to the Allies.

However, the decision to go it alone, and still use the network, was on the basis it would be safer for him. Help was at hand along the route from sympathisers who provided shelter and papers for him under the guise of a prisoner of war and he looked the part by now, his clothes dirty and torn, his beard fully grown and his body thin from lack of nourishment. He could have been any one of the people he had imprisoned and not recognisable, even by his own mother. Ironically, at one stage, he was helped by one of the Catholic priests who gave him false papers issued by the Vatican as a displaced person, not a passport in itself but enough to pass through Red Cross scrutiny and obtain a visa, should he want. The authorities were overwhelmed and had few means to identify escaping Nazis.

He was clever and made sure he was never manhandled or questioned if stopped, feigning deafness or suffering with an infectious disease. Once they realised he could not understand, he was left alone; everyone had enough to do and was focused on their own lives.

The journey took him several weeks. He took the best and

shortest route into Switzerland across Lake Constance, travelling only in the dead of night, bribing an old boatman he'd found. The fact he had to kill and rob him left him with no regret; it was a means to a very successful end and he performed the task professionally, throwing the man overboard once he had served his purpose.

Immediately over the border, he headed towards Zurich where the son of a family he knew worked for the Swiss National Bank, a man similar in age and appearance to him, called Dieter Scholler. The man had been primed in advance with flattery and the promise of riches beyond his imagination. He was a simple clerk with no imagination and little intelligence but, nevertheless, a loyal Nazi sympathiser, and Albert used that to his own advantage. There were more than a few pro-Nazis in Switzerland with their own agendas, hedging their bets, with money their prime motivator. It was true, money was the root of all evil.

Dieter was easy to manipulate. For the last couple of years everything Weissmuller had been stealing was transferred to the SNB via his cousin's bank. The process was easy. They received the gold and jewellery, which he had hidden away in a secret location, loaded it onto numerous lorries and transported it into Switzerland. There was a lot of traffic into the so-called neutral country and nobody checked as it was done under the insignia of the Nazi flag. However, once there, instead of it going into Hitler's coffers, Scholler credited it to the account Weissmuller had established long before. He wasn't the only one doing this, which was probably why he managed to get away with it, that and assistance on the inside. Now there was more than a considerable pile accumulated which he was anxious to get his hands on. Trust was not normally in his thinking but he'd had no choice in the matter and he relied on the clerk. Switzerland, being neutral, was easy as it still maintained relationships with the U.S Federal Bank, albeit in secret as the path was closed to their doing business.

Once the money that had been transferred to SNB was clearly identified and the war was at its end, there was no further need for Scholler and it was not the hardest thing in the world to organise a little accident to keep his silence, and what better way than death? With the man's Swiss passport to hand, it was easy for him to travel over to Ireland and after by ship to New York and onwards to West Virginia. He could have gone to any state but it was easier to hide out in a place with one of the smallest populations in America.

He was greeted by the Ross family with open arms. They knew all about his German roots and had assisted in the transfer of his assets to the bank in New York. Edward Ross was especially keen to gain a hold of all that money and encouraged the coming together of the two families by marriage to his daughter, Carolynn. She was attractive but rather stupid and silly with no education, and furthermore spoiled beyond imagination. However, Weissmuller saw his life beyond that and could only think of the power he would gain by marrying into the immediate family. He envisaged himself within a few years as chairman, subject to removing any obstacles in his way, of course, and there were many as he was not easy to like. If he had to marry, something that abhorred him as he was a loner and always had been, then he would have to do it no matter what, so he smiled at Carolynn, treated her with little presents and sweet things to tempt her, and promised her a life of love and luxury such as she had never experienced. It was no surprise the girl fell for it, fell for him, and once married he knew he could do what he wanted with her and she would be loath to report back his mistreatment to her family.

Their wedding night was more than predictable. After the wedding, which was attended by everyone in the county and more, and once they were alone in the hotel suite, she changed from her wedding dress and came out of the bathroom dressed in her frilly concoction of white satin and lace, her lips coloured ruby red, her virginal eyes ready for him to take her, expecting the love she felt for him to be returned. In fact he detested her coquettish behaviour, acting like a slut, like the women that were brought to him in the camps for him to fuck and throw away like the rubbish they were. This was his wife now and he felt nothing for her at all. She interrupted his thoughts and his plans to become as rich as Croesus. Sex was something he never enjoyed as it was giving in to certain feelings for which he had no time nor inclination, and he hated the loss of control.

The horror on Carolynn's face as he ripped her disgusting costume from her, exposing her licentious body yet to be touched by any man, was enough to give him an erection, and he threw her down against the bed and took her painfully from behind so he wouldn't have to look at her face, ignoring her screams and cries for help as he battered and rammed into her soft and unyielding body until he found the relief he sought. Afterwards, he left her bloodied and bruised and went out to a nearby bar and got exceedingly drunk. Now she was his to command, completely broken, and he took her whenever he felt the need, which, in all honesty, was not often.

The turning point came when, after one of these episodes, and after many years of less than marital bliss, she announced she was pregnant and begged him to leave her alone in case he harmed her child. The thought of him bringing a son or daughter into the world gave him a few qualms. Love was not in his psyche but maybe having a son, someone he could mould to his own image, to hand over the not-so clean reins to when he became chairman of the Board, might be a bonus he had never thought of before. Even Hitler wanted to procreate so why not him?

The day Ted was born was one he would never forget because something rose up in him that he never thought possible. He saw this little miniature of himself and his heart skipped a beat that surprised him, even though his conception came from an act of hatred, not love. It sealed the deal in his mind. He would never admit to this feeling and he decided it was an interest he would nurture selfishly for himself and see where it would take him. He hadn't felt it when his first son, Philip George, had been born three years earlier; all he had felt was indifference to the screaming child presented to him.

His relationship with Carolynn had deteriorated to such an extent that in order to avoid his presence at home, she spent most of her waking and sleeping moments in her room when she wasn't with her boys, whom he acknowledged she loved to distraction in equal measures. This annoyed him, as he wanted total possession. However, as he was at work most of the time it was not feasible to keep a twenty-four hour watch on them, but he ensured that someone did so on his behalf. He also saw to their education, as without that they wouldn't be able to accomplish what he had in mind for them. Carolynn fought with him constantly. As a married couple they now had no physical contact and the door to her own bedroom was firmly locked each and every night. He had no desire anyway, as his efforts were concentrated on Philip and Ted.

Work was a bonus for him and he enjoyed going to the bank every day with all the wheeling and dealing. He needed to learn his craft so he put in a lot of hours to do that, as all he had known previously was being a soldier. If he didn't comprehend the ways of the banking system, he couldn't hope to manipulate it to his advantage. The other important factor was to learn to speak English as if he were a native, and he spent hours with a tutor to try to lose his German accent, which eventually he did, except for the odd word that escaped him.

When old Edward died in 1963 and Liam Ross as heir apparent took over, Albert realised his plans were almost at fruition, and it was about time after preparing his moves for so long. He was becoming frustrated with the fact the old man had taken so long to die but still he had Liam to deal with before he could reach his final goal and the chair he had been coveting for so long. For years, he had been defrauding the bank, skimming off a little from customers' accounts so nobody would notice. With no internal audit procedures it was easy and virtually undetectable, especially when he was promoted and the only person to whom he reported was Liam, who was next to useless as chairman. Money was always his incentive. It felt good to him to build up a stockpile and to fund his lavish lifestyle with the proceeds. After such a long period, taking money became part of his daily routine and he was constantly finding new methods until, one day, he was accosted by Liam following a clerk's discovery, who threatened to expose his little game.

This was to his advantage, of course. The Board were already on his side, they knew Liam didn't have his heart in banking and, as Edward's son-in-law, Albert was next in line to the throne. He didn't have long to wait before he made his move. He didn't deny nor confirm his actions but instead turned the tables around and carefully explained, in no uncertain terms, how he intended for Liam to take all responsibility for the fraud and how he would go about this. How the man didn't kill him he had no idea, as he would have done so in the reverse situation. Liam thereupon resigned and stormed out of the building never to return, leaving the way clear for him.

However, he needed to ensure the man disappeared for good and he sent a warning message to him he was not to be played with. He considered many options before landing on a sure fire solution, a small matter of playing around with the brakes of his wife's car, not that he undertook the task himself. His intention was to scare rather than kill her and it was very unfortunate Liam's twin sons were in the car with her. He heard that the explosion and ensuing fireball when the car went over the cliff and landed several hundred feet below could be heard and seen from miles around. He did feel pity for the man as he had two boys himself but that emotion was momentary, and the outcome accomplished more than he could possibly have wished for when

Liam disappeared from society and skulked off to the mountains to lick his wounds. Of course, it all came resounding back at him with a vengeance when his own son, Philip, was killed in action in Libya. Then he knew loss like he had never known before. He queried his own capacity for grief and that was the first time he ever questioned his own past, the effect it had on people and families, and wondered about what kind of game God was playing, whoever this God was.

* * *

"You're ... still ... here."

"Yes, my son. I wanted to stay with you. You've been sleeping. I was wondering when you were going to wake up."

"Was ... awake."

"Can I do anything for you?" Father Goodheart asked. "Have you made your peace with God?"

Albert flickered his eyelids. Uttering a few words had exhausted him.

"I am pleased." Silence ensued and the priest began to pray. "Our Father who art in heaven, hallow'd be thy name ..."

Albert wanted to go to sleep for eternity. However, at the back of his mind he knew there was something else he needed to do and he had to hang on to life as long as it was heavenly possible. With all the strength he could muster he had to get these words of instruction out. "Promise ..." he took a few seconds to catch his breath. "Tell Ted." He paused. "Everything."

"Your confession is sacred. It is between you and God."

"Pro-mise," he begged, the syllables coming out in gasps.

The priest had no choice. "I will. I give you my word before Jesus Christ."

Albert knew he was drifting in and out of consciousness and there was little time left. He considered why he wanted his crimes known to his family, after all, what good would it do for them to know what he was? A murderer, a fraudster, an embezzler, to say the least. Was he not as remorseful deep down as he'd thought? He had told Ted a few things about his past after sending the money to those two Jews. The idea had come to him a few months back when he'd started visiting the priest and it had festered for a while before he made it happen. They had been easy to find. A private detective, who from time to time over the years kept him appraised of their lives. When he sent the bonds, he knew they would guess from where they had come and why. The only question in his mind was whether they still had the notebook and whether sending the money was a waste. However, he needed to know, especially as he doubted he would live much longer, and he couldn't allow the uncertainty. Yes, he wanted to be found out. He wanted them to find him so he could claim back what was his, or have confirmation it had been destroyed. After so many years it was probably time.

* * *

Father Goodheart had never doubted his calling before. Since a child he accepted without question that God and Jesus Christ were around him and guiding him in the only direction he wanted to go, which was to be a priest and serve them throughout his days. The church he had now been given by the Bishop had a large congregation. He was still young, in his early thirties, and learning, but he loved the people around him and gave everything he possibly could to helping people in their times of need, whether it be a young couple about to embark on marriage, a young girl vowing to die of unrequited love, attending to the sick or administering the final sacrament.

Now he wasn't sure and he questioned himself, and God. Why did this man choose to come into his church amongst the thousands in the United States? Was God testing him now and wanting more from him? Was he able to give more? After hearing the man's confession, he felt mesmerised, as if he had been hypnotised by the man - or had he just been manipulated? Despite that, Father Goodheart knew his duty was to forgive. He was a servant of God. He recalled Matthew Six: Verses fourteen to fifteen, when Jesus said so clearly, "For if you forgive others when they sin against you, your heavenly Father will also forgive you. If you do not forgive others their sins, your Father will not forgive your sins."

He felt burdened with shame because he was finding it beyond hard to forgive Albert. It was a process he had to go through, to find a way through this mire, and find his direction. He often preached to his congregation that as Christians they should forgive their neighbours and if they don't they will find themselves on the way to hellfire and damnation. Jesus' last words as he was dying were, "Father forgive them, for they know not what they do."

Now he was faced with the same problems he was often asked to absolve. The decision to go to his Bishop was easy in a lot of ways. He knew he was not capable of this level of work and finding himself wanting and in doubt, he begged his mentor for help to see him through. The Bishop recalled the story of Rudolph Hess, who was commandant of the Nazi camp at Auschwitz and Albert's superior, and was responsible for the deaths of over three million people. Before he was due to be hung he'd pleaded to return to the Catholic Church and Father Wladyslaw Lohn was brought to hear the man's final confession, which the Father did because he believed in the power of God and knew his love and forgiveness knew no limits. As a man this must have been difficult for him, but as a servant of God, it was easy because he trusted Him.

With this uppermost in his mind, Father Goodheart knew he was now being called to walk the same path as Father Lohn, which immediately gave him the inner strength to continue. Therefore, in his humility and with his love of God and Jesus Christ, he would do what was asked of him without doubting any more. That was his fervent prayer.

CHAPTER THIRTY ONE

"ARE you sure you don't need anything? A drink, something to eat?"

"No, my dear, we're fine. Thank you," Harold told Jenny when they were a couple of hours into the flight. "I may take a little nap. These business class seats are very comfortable."

"Maybe I could have a little orange juice, and if there's a cake or biscuit going, that would be good."

"Alfie, you've just eaten. You'll make yourself ill. Isn't it enough we're taking ourselves half way around the world? You'll end up with indigestion, or worse. Sleep, rest. We've got hours to go. Watch a film."

"I have no idea how to work this new-fangled thing." He picked up the screen control, turning it every which way. "How do you switch it on? There are too many buttons and I don't have my glasses."

"Here, let me help," offered Jenny. "It's very easy, really. Now, what would you like to watch? A comedy maybe?"

"Oh yes," answered Harold with a slight touch of sarcasm. "Just what we need. How about a war film?"

"I need to take my mind off something. You sleep, I'll watch."

"Hello Pops. Uncle Alfie."

"What? What the hell are you doing here, Mikey?" Harold couldn't believe his son was standing in the aisle right next to him, after all they had agreed.

"Did you really think we were going to let you travel completely alone? The two of you? I was persuaded by Matt and

Sarah, and don't look at me like that. I managed to get a flight at the last minute. I'm sat a few rows back but I nearly got caught out at the airport. It's not easy trying to hide from you two."

"We're not children, but I suppose you can't go back now. We told you we were going to do this alone."

"Yes, I know. I promise I won't interfere. We thought it best for someone to look after you, just in case. I'll follow behind and won't even speak." Mikey smiled and there was no doubt he had worked his magic with his father.

"As if. Anyway, my son, the lawyer, and single," he said to Jenny. "Mikey - this lovely lady works for Cydney Granger."

"Pleased to meet you. I hope they're behaving. The two of them together can be quite incorrigible," he said. "I'll go back to my seat, then." He turned to walk away.

"You're here now so yes, you can stay." In a lot of ways, Harold was pleased his son had taken the initiative. He was still experiencing pain from the recent angina attack and he would hate for something to happen and for Alfie to be left on his own in America.

"I thought you'd say that, Pops." He leant to kiss his father on the top of his forehead. "I love you very much."

"Yes, and I do, too. Your mama would be very proud." He turned to Jenny. "Did I tell you he was a lawyer? Such a good one, too."

"Enough already with the lawyer," Alfie protested. "We all love him. Go sit down. We're watching a film."

Mikey signalled to Jenny and she followed him to the bar area where they found two vacant stools.

"Can you catch me up on what this is all about, do you think? I've been told some of the background but I'm sure there's more they're not telling me."

"Your lawyer brain working overtime?"

"So it would seem. I heard their story for the first time a couple of days ago. We're very worried about what the shock could do to them both after so many years. Can you fill me in at all?"

"In all honesty, Cydney's the one to do that. My job was to get your dad and uncle to Charleston in one piece. Look, this is difficult, and I was instructed not to tell them. Albert Whiteman suffered a serious heart attack. He's in hospital."

Mikey put his hand to his head in utter disbelief and took a long gulp of the vodka and tonic handed to him by one of the cabin crew. "Alive?" Jenny nodded. "You mean this may all be in vain? I think that could be worse for them, being so close to the man they have hated for so many years and not being able to identify him in person."

"Do you think they'll be able to recognise Weissmuller? Age plays strange tricks. They have all changed so much."

"Imagine somebody killed your parents, your sisters, and then you learn the murderer is responsible for many more deaths. You know the face of this person, this monster you've lived and dreamed about with his face haunting you. What's more, he's evaded capture for all that time. I would want to bring him to justice. I would want to be responsible for bringing him down. Yes, years have passed but I doubt they have forgotten anything, especially what he looks like. My dad told me of the man's eyes as he shot men, women and children, how they remained cold and unfeeling throughout, how he smiled with satisfaction, laughed even. Those are eyes that would never change and my dad and uncle would recognise them anywhere."

Jenny didn't respond. "How are they now, knowing what lies ahead?"

"They're scared and nervous, no matter what they say or how they appear. They've known each other since they were boys. They're like brothers, no, they are brothers. Nobody would believe all they've gone through in their lives."

"I honestly can't imagine."

"I hear your boss has got Weissmuller's notebook."

"It's in our office safe. We thought it better in the circumstances."

"I agree. Have you seen it?"

"Yes, briefly."

"And it's everything they say? All the details?"

"And more. There are lists of not only that, but factories commandeered, property, all neatly hand-written, in columns with exact dates."

"As if having it in front of him, totting up his ill-gotten gains gave him a sense of power, made him feel wealthier than anybody else. How on earth did he think he would be able to get to everything after the war? Where would he have hidden everything?"

"That's where our investigations come in. We believe the money was transferred to the States, some maybe long before the war ended, as if he realised Hitler was going to lose. Weissmuller was a distant cousin, through his grandmother allegedly, of the Ross family, who originally owned Prime Corporation in West Virginia. They also had branches in Germany and France, which were established well before the war."

"And this Prime was the bank which issued the bearer bonds that my dad and Uncle Alfie received?"

"Exactly."

"So, it's possible it is more than implicated, in fact it may have been founded on looted assets?"

"That's what we're looking at now and why Cydney went to the States."

"This is absolutely incredible. And they have got away with this for, well, how many years?"

"Since before the war."

"Who knows about this? What if it gets out? I'm not a banking lawyer. My area is corporate but I do know about these matters. It doesn't take a lot to bring down a bank. Remember Barings back in 1995 and the collapse caused by the fraudulent activities of one person? I don't think my dad would want all this out in the public domain, his name bandied about. He's not like that at all. He's a quiet and unassuming man."

"Like a lot of survivors of the holocaust."

"Exactly. He wants justice. Very simple, and to live his life with his family around him. Not even the money would mean a lot to him."

"And how will he get that?"

"With Weissmuller dying, perhaps. I don't know, except I hope we make it in time. It would be too awful to think they got this far and ..."

"And they didn't get to see him?"

"Yes," he said. "Beyond that, I've no idea. I wish my dad was younger, and with his angina, who knows?"

"He didn't mention that, Mikey."

"He never does. It's always, 'Yes I'm fine. Stop worrying'. It's been the same since Mum passed away many years ago."

"I'm sorry. It's not been easy, has it?"

"No." He looked up and smiled. "You're very sweet, Jenny. Has anyone ever told you that?"

"Oh, millions of times. Shall we order another drink?"

CHAPTER THIRTY TWO

"ALF. I've been thinking."
"Me too. You know ..."

"Yes, I know. Good. We've come to the same conclusion," Harold said, who after so many years could read his friend's mind without hesitation.

"That's good. I think it would be wrong to see this man now. What good would it do? I don't think I can face him. I don't want to. He wouldn't look the same. I remember him as the monster in an SS uniform and now he wants us to feel pity for him as he's old and dying. To give him the satisfaction. No. Absolutely not!" Alf shook his head as if to ward off the unwanted vision of Weissmuller that had sprung into his mind.

"I won't give him that pleasure. He wanted us to come here, I'm sure, and again we are doing his bidding. That's all it is, Alf. Let him die alone, knowing we give him no absolution. It's enough." Harold banged his hand down on the armrest between them.

"We mustn't get angry no matter how much this hurts us. And the money?"

"We'll give it back. We've managed very nicely without it all this time, so what's the point of being rich? We have our families. That is richness itself." Harold patted his friend's hand. "And each other."

"Yes. And we tell Cydney that? She's such a lovely lady. Will she be cross?"

"Why? No, she'll understand, I'm sure."

"Well, it's nice to have an adventure at our time of life. Very comfortable here. Maybe we should go on holiday more often," Alfie said, relaxing back in his seat.

"Israel. I always wanted to go back. We should do that."

"You're so predictable. What about California? All that sun and the sea air. We can go in business class again. I like the seats."

"And plenty to eat."

"You and your stomach. Anyway, we're coming in to land now. Make sure your seatbelt's tightened. Shall I tell Cydney, or will you?"

"We both will."

* * *

"There are many people waiting for you," Ray said, as he joined Cydney in her hotel room.

"Is this what you warned me about?"

"It is, and now I have to tell you again. This will be the hardest thing you have ever done in your life. It goes beyond this family you're helping."

"And you? What is your role here?"

"To facilitate."

"Who?"

"Those people who didn't survive. Those Weismuller murdered, or the ones whose deaths he was responsible for."

"What do they intend to do? You need to explain to me."

"Challenge him. You see, they have not moved on and are unable to do so."

"You mean they're still here, on the earth plain?"

"Exactly. They are stuck here. You will see and hear things, but remember you are merely a conduit between the two worlds. It is important you take none of their sorrow or hurt into your own body. The pain is not yours, so protect yourself as much as you can. I will be by your side, to guide you, as always."

"I'll do whatever I need to do."

The curtains were closed in Cydney's hotel room and the only light came from a lamp in the corner of the room sitting on a small side table. With her eyes tightly shut, she allowed herself to drift, freeing her thoughts and opening her mind to prepare for whatever or whomever was going to come through. All her strength was focused on protecting herself and placing a complete and impenetrable shield of light equally around her and Ray.

The next time she opened her eyes she found herself transported and looking into the hospital room that held the dying Adolf Weissmuller. It was evident to her he was on the point of leaving for the spirit world as his ethereal body was hovering above him, and she was aware of dark forces surrounding him, waiting for the exact moment of his demise before taking him away to whatever fate awaited him.

Before long, she felt the presence of Sybill and Mordecai next to her. Cydney was hardly aware of the tingling all over her body, the hairs on her arms standing up from the cold, as she was in a cocoon of her own making, her mind concentrating on the task she had been given.

"Thank you." Sybill was the first to speak as always. The role of her husband, constantly by her side, was solely to protect. She was the appointed spokesperson.

"You never have to say that. I am doing this for you and I want nothing in return."

"But I do, because now we can confront him. Finally, he will hear our voices. This is our moment. We have been screaming inside for so long. So many years."

In her mind's eye, Cydney realised the extent of her task as so many others drew near to the foot of the bed, glaring directly at the man they had been waiting to challenge, the man they detested for what he had done, seeking the justice they deserved.

"I accuse you! I accuse you of crimes against humanity. I accuse you of

270

orchestrating mass murder, of brutality, of atrocities so fundamentally evil *they go beyond condemnation. I wish I could have caused you more pain in your life. Now you are old and death is upon you. I have kept this hatred within me for so long. You are the devil."* Sybill screamed at him, unleashing a torrent of held in emotions. *"You are incapable of understanding the suffering you have caused."* Cydney saw the woman before her break down and turn towards her husband for support, her anger palpable, even after so much time had elapsed. *"I hope God has no mercy on you for all you have done."*

"You killed my mama and papa." A small child of maybe five years of age took her place next to Sybill, her eyes doleful. She carried a doll with the same blonde curly hair as herself, cradling it in her arms. *"I watched you shoot my brother and I was left alone."*

"You hanged my husband and made me watch," a woman accused him next. *"I had nothing to live for and my unborn child and I died from a broken heart."*

"You burned my family alive in our synagogue," a Rabbi said. *"I heard their cries as you strangled me and left me to die."*

"You took our house and all our possessions. You sent us to Lodz where we perished in a raid on your orders," an older man added. *"My wife and three children. We had no chance to escape."*

"All our school class were marched out of the ghetto and put onto trucks. We couldn't breathe when the gas came in." Cydney watched so many children of varying ages as they paraded past Weissmuller, all holding hands, their faces drawn in anguish and so much sorrow.

"My sister and I were thrown out the window," a small girl said, crying out in torment.

"Why did you kill my mother? Why did you look on and do nothing as one after another of your soldiers raped and abused her?" a teenage boy asked. *"You could have stopped this. You made me watch."*

"You forced me to strip and writhe over the dead bodies of the men you had gassed. Did it really give you so much pleasure?" a beautiful woman in her twenties said as she approached.

"You tore the gold fillings from the mouths of so many of us. Do you

have any idea of the pain you inflicted? Then you sent us to be gassed."

"My brother and I had to dig the mass graves for all our friends and family and throw in the bodies. Our hands were bleeding, and our hearts. You threw us in alive after them and buried us beneath piles of rocks and earth."

"You stole everything from us to keep it for yourself."

"You killed mercilessly."

"You abused and tortured."

"We watched you as you laughed at your actions and seemed so proud of yourself."

"You were responsible for all this, Weissmuller," Sybill accused, pointing a finger at him. "We were humans. You treated us like dirt. I want to see you suffer now. I want to see you rot in hell for ever for all you have done."

"Enough! Please," he begged. "I can't bear this anymore."

"Oh no, this has not even started. You will listen to everyone." And he had no choice, as many others came forward, accusing him of all the many sickening and atrocious crimes he had committed.

"Are you okay, Cydney?" Ray said. "This is too much, I can tell."

"I have never, and will never, hear anything like this again, but it has to be done. I know that."

"I want you to realise all you have done," Sybill said. "The pain you have caused. The sorrow."

"I do. I am sorry. Please forgive me for all my crimes," Weissmuller cried out.

"We will never forgive. We cannot forgive you. The reason we are here is to make you understand. The agony you feel now is nothing in comparison to what we felt so many years ago. We are unable to move on; do you comprehend at all?"

"Oh God, yes. I do repent. May God forgive me. I will take whatever awaits me. I have made my peace with God."

"You think giving money is enough? A life for a life," Sybill said. "Your life in eternal purgatory for all our lives. You are shortly to leave this world but your journey is not with us. There is another fate awaiting you."

272

She stared at him, searching his face for signs of contrition. *"Hah, not such a brave man now, I see. Not so proud and haughty."*

At that moment, the spirit of Adolf Weissmuller was lifted up and whisked away amongst a cloud of dark shadows. Cydney and everyone she was helping watched the pathetic sight of the monster as he was taken towards his destiny.

"I hope you've got what you wanted now, I really do."

"The dead won't get their lives back. There is still blood on his hands. They wanted his apology such a long time ago. He could have done that but he chose to wait until he was about to die."

"Yes, I know. Perhaps in the end he will receive his punishment. It's all we can hope for."

"We are leaving now. We can all move forward. You have brought this about. Look after my son and his friend. They need you." Sybill and her husband, and everyone she had brought forward, melted away into the brightest light that rose up to the heavens.

Cydney came out of her trance-like state to find herself back in the hotel room, as if everything had been a dream. She saw Ray was still with her and looking visibly moved.

"You did it. You got retribution for his crimes."

"I hope so. Can they really move on?"

"Yes. You saw it yourself."

"I need to lie down, Ray. My head is banging."

"Sleep well, then. Our next step is to help Harold and Alfie come to terms with everything. They now have no chance to get to see him."

CHAPTER THIRTY THREE

"Is the plane on time? Have a look at the board."

"Yes. It's just landed. You seem anxious."

"I feel it." She truly did after all she had gone through. Her mind was all over the place and her entire body was still feeling the effects. Even though aware that Albert Whiteman had died, she had to hold up the pretence in front of Tom that she knew nothing; he was unaware of her gift and she had no desire to explain. It wasn't a lie for she only shared the information about herself with certain people. "Liam called me at the hotel before we left to come here. Ted told him his father's death is imminent."

"It's going to be too late. After all this. What are you going to do? You need to sit them down for a few minutes and explain, don't you think? They're elderly and may not be able to take all this in."

"Let's go to the arrival gate. Gives me something to do, at least."

"They may not be out for ages yet. You know what passport control is like."

"Jenny ordered one of those electric buggies to save all the walking. Come on. I can't bear looking at this screen any longer."

It was another hour before Jenny emerged with their two clients, accompanied by a tall, dark-haired man who was acting quite solicitously around them.

"At last. I can't believe the queues to get our luggage and get out here," Jenny told her boss.

"Hello, Harold, Alfie," Cydney greeted them.

"This is my son, Mikey. The lawyer," Harold said. "He takes after me. Never listens to instructions. He took it upon himself to follow us."

"Again with the lawyer," Alfie said, grumbling under his breath.

"Hi, Mrs Granger. I didn't think it was right for them to come by themselves. Who knows what could happen."

Cydney carefully assessed the man in front of her. Although dressed casually in jeans and a New York Yankees sweatshirt, his friendly manner and easy air of confidence caused her to thank her lucky stars he had chosen to come on the trip.

"It's the best news I've had today, so far. I wonder if I may speak to you quietly before we leave the airport. Jenny and Tom will accompany your dad and uncle to the limo outside. I need a few minutes with you first."

"Something wrong? Okay, look, there's some seats over there. Shall we?"

"Tom, we'll be out in a moment." He nodded in return. "Brief Jenny, please."

"I'm afraid it's not good news and I'm sorry to break it to you like this ..."

"He died?"

"No. It's imminent, and I think they've lost their chance." Cydney couldn't believe the words coming out of her mouth to keep what she knew silent.

"Christ. Jenny told me he'd had a heart attack but I never thought ... I hoped they would have time to get over the flight."

"If only it were different. Will you tell them or should I?"

"I think you should. It may be better coming from you."

"I'm so glad you're here with them, Mikey, isn't it?"

"Yes. My dad and uncle are very special people. I would do anything for them."

"So I've discovered. I have so much respect for them and all they've been through. It can't have been easy for you growing up, knowing about their past lives."

"I only just found out about it. You probably know more than I do, and have known for much longer than I have."

"Really?"

"Yes." He stood up, and although Cydney was tall herself, she had to raise her head to him. "Let's go. This isn't going to be easy but we'll deal with it. They're strong men, despite their appearance."

"They would have to be," she said.

* * *

"Alice! Where are you?" Ted called up the stairs to his wife, his voice anxious. "It's the hospital. We've got to get there. Daddy's heart's fading fast."

"Now? What about the kids?"

"We'll call ahead and pick them up on the way. They're at a friend's house. The car's ready. Come on, let's go," he said, grabbing his jacket and calling for his chauffeur.

Despite everything, he wanted and needed to say his goodbyes properly. His daddy had not been a particularly brilliant grandfather to Jonathan and Estelle though he had a place in their lives and he knew they would want to see him, too. With regard to Alice, she was a warm and loving wife but she and Albert were never going to see things the same way; they got along with a degree of tolerance, which is the best he could have hoped for. He had changed considerably over the years, especially after Philip was killed, and Ted had reached a point of understanding of his daddy's actions and way of life, and accepted them. After all it was because of him he was now Governor of West Virginia, and furthermore, was pushing him towards the presidency of the United States. What he had learned earlier from Liam and Jackson, however, had undeniably changed his outlook on the life he wanted going forward, which would possibly not be one in the spotlight, especially if the news got out, and he certainly wouldn't be able to keep his office, or aim for the ultimate goal of all. Now it was about saying his goodbyes and nothing else.

It wasn't long before they reached the hospital entrance. There were already lots of press hanging around, waiting for some news; somehow the story of his daddy dying must have been leaked. Hopefully, that was all it was. Getting out of their car was difficult with everybody clambering for information, and the lights from the many cameras flashed before Ted. He gave them short shrift, requesting their patience at this very sad time and asking for his family to be left alone. Some chance, he thought, considering all the circumstances, and notwithstanding his office.

Ted, Alice and their two children were escorted to the private room and stood outside the door, hesitant to enter. The sounds of prayers being said held them back. They didn't want to disturb that but the door was opened by the same priest whom Ted had met the night before.

"You're still here, Father?"

"Yes. I couldn't leave."

"Can we go in now?"

"Of course. I've given your father the sacraments. He has declared his faith in the Church and God, and I believe he's at peace."

"Will you wait still? I think we'll all need you very soon."

"Yes. I'll do that. Your daddy has requested me to tell you everything about his past, leaving nothing out. It is not something I would do normally. Every word said in a confession is only for my ears and that of God, but he has insisted."

"I thought he might. I do know ..."

"About what?" asked Alice. "I knew there was something you weren't telling me."

"Not now, darlin'. It's not the right time. Come on, kids. Come and give your granddaddy one last kiss."

They all filed into the small room where Albert was laying. All

Ted could see was his father's head, pale as death, his skin almost translucent, with a bluish tinge around his lips. The monitors next to him were still bleeping, though so quietly, as if to silently indulge the last signs of life ebbing away. The body beneath the covers was tiny now, the last vestiges of life almost disappearing, despite the man's height of over six feet, and there was no discernible rise and fall of his chest.

Jonathan was the first to approach and, as he did, he scanned his father's face for encouragement.

"It's okay. You can touch him."

Estelle could no longer hold back her tears and as she started to cry, she was pulled into her mother's protective embrace. "You don't have to stay. Neither of you do." She gave a warning glance at her husband, who took the point she was making.

"Why don't you two wait outside? Mom and I will be out soon."

Left alone, Ted and Alice brought up two chairs to sit beside Albert.

"Are you going to tell me?" she whispered.

"Yes, I will. Later."

"Did the doctor say how long?"

"Any time. God, I hate this. I remember sitting with Mom when she was dying."

"On your own?"

"Yes."

"And where was your daddy?" Alice asked.

"At work. He came for the last hour, before she slipped away. He had no choice; all about appearances. Poor Mom. She didn't have it easy with him. I don't think there was any love lost there."

"Why did she marry him?"

"Rather, I would ask, why did he marry her? For the money, the bank, the prestige, the power."

"He had money, you told me. When he came to the States. He put money into the bank."

"Yes, he did, but coming from Europe, he was an outsider."

"Your daddy was many things, but he never let anyone treat him as an outsider."

"True."

"Now, with him gone, you inherit all his shares, and become chairman. What are you going to do? Can you still run for the presidency?"

"I've decided not to after all. I'm happy with the life we have, and the position. I think I should sell my shares to Jackson."

"What about holding them in trust for Jonathan, for when he finishes Harvard?"

"No, darlin'. I'll explain later. I want nothing to do with the bank, either now or in the future. At this present time, I want to take the money and run."

"So, it's about the bank. I might have known. What's your daddy been doing?"

"Alice," he reiterated, "I told you; not now and I mean not now."

"Okay, sweetheart. I realise this is hard for you." She rested her hand on his and leaned over to kiss his cheek. "Should I be worried?"

"Christ knows."

CHAPTER THIRTY FOUR

"Do you think a father doesn't know when his son is hiding something from him? Tell me - what's the big secret?"

"I'm sorry Pops, Uncle Alfie. Weissmuller has little time left. I didn't know how to tell you."

"So the man is dying. Hah. I thank God we're too late," said Alfie.

"What?"

"Oh, did we forget to tell you? We don't want to see him. No. We've made up our minds. We want to go to the hotel and rest now."

Cydney and Mikey could hardly contain their surprise but Cydney was silently giving thanks.

"Can you repeat that? You don't want to go? After travelling here? Do you not want your moment? To confront him?"

"No, Mikey. We made up our minds, didn't we Alf? We've decided not to do what he wants. Let him die and nobody will be more delighted than us. Good riddance. He has lived longer than any of our family and friends from so long ago. Why should we give him the satisfaction of knowing we are beside his bed? No."

"We're tired now. Can we go to our hotel, please?" asked Alfie.

"Um, well, yes, of course you can," said a rather confused Cydney. "I thought the whole point of coming here was to see him. That's what we discussed." Then she realised how brash that seemed. "Sorry, that came out wrong. I didn't mean to sound cross."

"Mrs Granger, Alfie and I have all we need in this world but it took something like this to make us realise the past is the past and we cannot change it nor do anything about it. We have lived with our story for so long and now Weissmuller is dying, well, we have nothing more to fear. He can no longer hurt us."

"Are you sure, Pops? It's not too late to change your mind."

"We are absolutely positive."

"Okay, then to the hotel it is."

"I do respect your wishes entirely," added Cydney. "I do understand. You won't mind if I go? I'd like to see it for myself." That was one part that was entirely true; she needed to obtain confirmation.

"I'll accompany you," Mikey offered.

"You do whatever you want. We have to sleep, don't we Alf?"

Cydney knew that was their final word and it was easy to acquiesce. Maybe they were right after all. She had done what she had been engaged to do by them, discovered the provenance of the bearer bonds, so what else was there to do? By taking the action on which they had equally decided, they had taken control of the situation, and why should this man still have power over them? No, she agreed entirely.

The limo dropped Jenny, Tom, Harold and Alfie at the hotel and she and Mikey continued on their way to the hospital. On arrival they found the entrance blocked by gangs of press and cameramen, causing them to have to park further away and around the corner, near the ambulance bays.

"Is this all for Weissmuller?" Mikey said as they entered the hospital and made their way towards the lifts and up to the ICU.

"His son is the governor. I doubt they know about the background but it's news when it affects his son."

"If they only knew. This is never going to come out, is it? With this monster dead and buried, everything will be lost. Is that fair?"

"No, Mikey, it isn't fair. At all, and in all probability, it will be brushed under the carpet. The trouble is, the Board will not want this leaked. It will bring about their collapse and possibly even the Federal Bank itself. Can you imagine the consequences?"

"Yes, and that's the trouble. In my mind I would report everything to the FBI and let them deal with it. I wouldn't want anyone to get away with anything. It angers me so much. Whiteman Trust's assets are based on money stolen from my people, my ancestors, and it should never have happened. The whole world watched and did nothing to prevent what was going on in Germany, and that was before the war even started. No, I won't allow it."

"I agree, especially after what I've learned. We need to discuss this properly as it will involve your dad and uncle. I take it they're going to return the money?"

"You've heard them. They are men of principle. They wouldn't want tainted money, which is basically what this is."

"Supposing it was given to charity, something of their choosing?"

"You mean like Yad Vashem in Israel, or to help families of survivors somehow? Um, I could possibly persuade them to do that."

"Let's suggest this," Cydney said. "We're nearly there."

As they neared the nurses' station, Ted Whiteman and an attractive blonde lady were standing in deep conversation with a young priest. Cydney watched as the priest put his hand reassuringly on the governor's shoulder and patted it. She guessed by the looks on all their faces they knew now what she'd been shown before.

"He died. You missed him," Ted said, with no regret in his voice at the last phrase, as if he was pleased she no longer had the opportunity to confront his father and maybe thus prove her case. Dead, he was no longer a threat.

"This is the son of one of my clients, Governor, Mikey Franks."

Ted held out his hand, but withdrew it when the other man made no attempt to reciprocate.

"I thought your clients were coming here."

"They had no desire to see your father," Mikey interrupted before Cydney had a chance to respond. "We all know him for what he is. They were not willing to do his bidding any more. I can't say I'm sorry as who knows what it would have done to them."

"What does that mean?" asked Alice. "Could someone please tell me what this is all about? Ted?"

"Leave it, please hon," he ordered her.

Father Goodheart stepped forward and put his arm between the two men to diffuse the situation. "I have strict instructions, as his dying wish, to tell you Albert's story, from beginning to end, no holds barred. He was adamant in this."

"Will it help my dad and uncle?"

"That I can't tell you. I can only give you what he has given me. May I suggest we resume in a couple of days?"

"Make it tomorrow. We have no desire to stay here in Charleston one moment longer than necessary," Mikey said. Cydney gauged he was struggling to keep his temper in check.

"That's okay by me. At my office," confirmed Ted.

"Are you please going to tell me what's going on?" Alice asked once again.

"No darlin', I'm not. You can come with me and hear it all, though. I think we should leave now." He turned to address Cydney. "My private secretary is waiting outside and we need to issue a statement to the press. We will see you all in the morning, at eleven. I apologise for my father and what he did. I wish I could change history, but ..."

"You can't apologise for the deeds of your father," Father Goodheart said. "Let's wait until tomorrow."

"I need to go," Mikey said. "I've had enough here for one day."

"Can I meet you outside, please? I won't be long. Just going to the ladies' room."

"Sure, I'll be waiting for you."

Ensuring nobody was watching, Cydney sneaked along the corridor and into Albert Whiteman's hospital room. It was important to her to see his physical body, to obtain confirmation for herself and not what she had been shown by Ray. When she entered, it was exactly as she had seen previously. There was a body but nothing else, no discernible spirit. He had gone and all that remained was a visible corpse. The man's face was at peace in death, his skin a waxen yellow. She half expected him, nevertheless, to sit up and condemn her for watching him so closely. He was not unlike the photo she had been sent by Richard of the young Nazi soldier, except his eyes were closed and that cold darkness she had seen was hidden. Thankfully, now her clients could spend their lives going forward in the knowledge the man would never be able to harm them again.

Time passed as she sat there. Nobody came in to disturb her and her thoughts wandered. There had been no news from Sean. What the hell was he up to over there? Surely they must have discovered something by now? With her eyes closed, she tried to reach out to her husband in the hope he was still alive and would feel her. Five minutes passed. Another ten minutes. Nothing at all; no images, no prickling feeling along her arm, only blank dark space.

When she opened her eyes, it startled her to see a body laying before her, the place where she was sitting having been momentarily forgotten. She glanced at her watch and realised how much time had elapsed. Now she had to leave him and go out to Mikey, who must be wondering how long a visit to the toilet must take. She stood and turned to leave when the door to the room opened. The noise made her jump; the last thing she wanted was to be found sitting beside someone who the hospital staff would deem to be a stranger to her. She tried to think of a million excuses but then realised who was there.

"I couldn't stop them," Mikey said. "I was waiting outside for you when they turned up in a cab. I had a feeling you'd be here."

"We changed our minds. We're old men. We're entitled."

Cydney made no comment to Harold's remark. She moved out of the way as the two elderly men trudged slowly, step by small step, hesitantly towards the dead body of the man they had equally loathed and feared all their lives. She had no idea what they were going to do. The man couldn't touch them now but still their faces appeared like frightened little boys, as if they had been cast back sixty years, their whole past flashing before them. They held on to each other, their hands clasped together, clinging on for support. Tears rolled down their faces. The distance could not have been more than twelve feet to the bed though it might as well have been one hundred miles for the time it took them, as after every couple of steps they stopped, as if questioning their ability to continue. One of the candles lit by the priest beforehand chose that moment to flicker and die, which cast the room in late afternoon shadows.

"Pops," Mikey spoke soothingly to his father. "You don't have to do this."

"We do," answered Alfie for his childhood friend. "We do."

"Das ist er," Harold said. "It's him."

"Ich würde ihn überall erkennen.*"*

Cydney glanced across at Mikey, who mouthed back, "He said, I would recognise him anywhere."

They had reached the side of the body and it was as if time stood still. Nobody moved, nobody spoke. The silence in the room was intense as Cydney and Mikey watched the two men from the side, and rushed forward together to catch Harold as his legs buckled beneath him.

"I'm fine," he said as he steadied himself. "I'm fine. Please," he begged.

"He was a monster," Alfie said, his voice even and calm despite the circumstances. "He deserves nothing from us. Look at him. An old man. Pah. Everyone is equal in death but they shouldn't be."

"This despicable excuse for a human - he claimed our youth, him and all his henchmen."

"I will never understand why. Why us? We are simple people who only want to live in peace." Alfie shook his head in dismay. "I want to be angry, to spit in his face, attack him, but I am past all of that. I shouldn't even be asking why. Nobody can answer that question."

"Pops, Uncle, let's go. It's enough now. Why put yourselves through this?" He tenderly took his father's arm with the intention of leading him away.

"I know," he answered, and patted his son's hand. "Let's go, Alf. We have seen what we wanted to see. We have had our moment, as you called it. We confronted him."

Alfie, still holding his friend's arm, leant over the body of Albert Weissmuller and screamed directly into his face, the words spitting out. *"Auf dass Du ewig in der Hölle verrottest, Du Drecksack!"*

"May you rot forever in hell, you bastard," Harold repeated in a thin whisper.

CHAPTER THIRTY FIVE

"**Y**OU'VE got to be fucking joking."

"I wish I was, Mo. The truth is, I can't tell you the truth. Official secrets," Sean said.

"So this has been a wild goose chase. I don't bloody believe it."

"Not entirely. We forced the CO's hand and he knows we're out here and watching what he's doing."

"So the captain's still alive?"

"I can't say."

"You don't have to, your face tells it all. I'm glad he's got you on his side. When are you coming home?"

"Not sure yet. I'm trying to organise a plan for me."

"You know we'll always back you," Mo said, "and I realise I'm not going to get any further information from you so I might as well give up. I'll get the guys together and we'll be on our way. You only have to ask ..."

"Sure. I know that. I'll call you when I'm home. I owe you big time."

"Indeed you do. Say hello to the captain for us."

Sean didn't respond. He had the measure of Mo and all the guys who used to be under his command. They would take it as a 'given' to keep their mouths shut, and anytime he wanted them he only had to shout. He would now remain in Israel for as long as he was required and do all he could to facilitate his boss's transition from Steve Granger to Alan Campbell, act out any orders from General Ian Bowles-Smith, and then get the hell back home to Cydney and the kids, and most of all to his beloved daughter, Sophie. The story of his ailing Irish aunt was going to have to remain alive for a little while longer.

However, there was not a cat in hell's chance Cydney would buy his story of finding nothing at all, no information whatsoever, about her husband in Israel. She would draw it out of him, every last bit of the story that even now he was trying to concoct in his head. The more he thought about what he would say, the more incongruent it sounded, even to him. He was really in for a sticky time with her and knew he'd better come up with something that would sound and feel right. What on earth could that be? She already didn't quite believe her husband was dead, which was why she had sponsored his mission to Israel after calling the MOD repeatedly and unsuccessfully. The fact was, he was seriously conflicted. He had been living with her and the twins for the last five years since Steve's alleged death, protecting her, catering to her every need, working in her consultancy, putting himself in danger, even. There were no two ways about it, they were his world, along with Sophie. He would do anything for them, and he had, and he needed to ensure whatever he said would protect Cydney going forward.

Supposing he told her the truth? Sometimes that was the better option and there was nothing so strange in life as the truth. She was an army wife and she should realise her husband had no option and had a special job to do. He was so highly trained because he had to be; a pilot, highly intelligent, a fully functioning field operative, a medic when he needed to be, and the powers that be would never waste that honed talent. All Sean had to do was explain that. However, and this was the big question - how could she carry on her life knowing her husband was out there somewhere? Would she accept this? It would be impossible to function, have any type of relationship, and the most important factor of all, she would have to lie to her kids. No, he decided, the truth was never going to come out. So what about a partial lie? He realised it was going to take him a while to put together a plan of action but he had a rendezvous with Steve and a certain officer to deal with first.

This time they met up in the CO's temporary office. Sean was anxious to understand exactly what was in store for him and how he could be of service, because he wasn't going home without an answer.

"I see your lads have left," the general opened the conversation.

"They had no choice, sir. I presume no action is to be taken against them."

"Why would it? No, in actual fact I applaud you - and them. As I mentioned before, I would have done the same. But this has to stop now. I'm allowing you to become involved because you seem to have discovered the army's little secret."

"That would be me," Steve said.

"Indeed." He coughed to clear his throat. "The question is, what am I to do?" He turned to Sean. "I'm sure Captain Granger has told you of our plans for him. He is to be seconded to the British Embassy in Tehran."

"So I hear. Under an assumed name."

"Precisely."

"I would like to go with him, sir. I can be of use to you. The captain can't readily do everything you require in case by chance he's recognised. The Middle East is not that big a place and Iran is now in the headlines following the election."

"I'm not sure about that, Sergeant. You're a bit of a loose cannon."

"I think it would be helpful, sir," Steve said. "I need someone I can rely on, to be my eyes and ears. I'm hoping you've received correct intelligence that the Syrians know someone was reporting back to the governments of their activities, not that it was me."

"Yes, that's correct. They're aware we had someone out there in the field."

"So, they believe I'm dead."

"Yes. What are you getting at?"

"If it were to get out this Captain Alan Campbell was really me, it would not look too good on us."

"Get to the point," ordered the general, his impatience beginning to show. "Are you threatening me in some way because I certainly don't take kindly to that?"

"No, sir. Not my intent."

"Well, carry on."

"If someone were to come to the Embassy and recognise me that would compromise our efforts," said Steve.

"We believe you'll be safe there, safer than anywhere else, in fact."

"You don't know that. Nobody does. After all, the intention is for me to check out the Iranians and their fighting and weaponry capabilities and they aren't going to like it any bit more than the Syrians."

"I'm sure the Iranian Government is fully cognizant of the fact we have an Embassy there for a reason and not just to invite people for afternoon tea."

"Do they trust us?"

"Doubtful, Captain. We're trying to build relationships. We want to work with them in mutual trust and confidence, build up trade, and we are hopeful with this new government."

"There have always been political tensions between our two countries."

"Which is why we want you there. Nobody is better equipped than you are. You speak the language like a native, you're fully aware of security protocols, and nobody would guess you were working for Special Forces with your injury."

Steve inspected his leg and subconsciously rubbed his hand along his thigh, banging it twice on the side to remind himself it was damaged. "Not MI6?"

"Well, I can't say they didn't have a hand in this, for obvious reasons, but no, you are still under our auspices. So how would having Sergeant O'Connell with you help?"

"It's obvious. I need someone who isn't necessarily known or recognised like I might be. My leg could be my downfall."

"I have to think about it."

"Also, sir, I would like to think he would be looking after my wife and kids still."

"You want him in two places at one time?"

"No, that's not what I said. Let's compromise. He remains my direct contact and he comes out on a, shall we say, trade visit, once a month on the pretext of finding ways we can continue to trade with Iran."

"So he's now a trade delegation of one."

"I quite like that idea, sir. I've always thought of myself as a man of industry," Sean said.

"I don't believe this is a time for frivolity, do you? Let's keep to the matter in hand."

"Sir."

"Well, yes, that might work. Let me sort out the mechanics. Once a month, yes, I could agree to that. We would need to set you up properly, Sergeant, and no running things on your own, is that very clear? With your shenanigans, you could jeopardise the whole plan."

"As if."

"I'm off now and will leave you two to catch up before the captain and I take the flight to Gibraltar in a couple of days."

"Where?"

"Your captain is about to receive the MC. I want you back in the UK though."

"Thanks, Sean," Steve said, once the CO had left. "I really appreciate your help on this one."

"As if I would leave you to him and his devious plans. Anyway, I prefer a sunnier climate to London."

"Well, you'll certainly get that in Tehran."

"The MC - who's presenting that to you?"

"I don't know. One of the royals, no doubt. Probably the Duke of Edinburgh. He likes to get involved with MI6, and us."

"So I've heard. Anyway, now we're sorted, but it still doesn't help with Cydney. Any thoughts on that yet?"

"Not one."

"I suggest we sleep on it. We have time over the next couple of days. She's in the States now investigating a case for some new clients."

"On her own?"

"No. She has an assistant with her. Tom Patterson. He used to work with Richard."

"Ah, must be good."

"Yes. I've met him quite a few times."

"When is she back home?"

"Not for a few more days still."

"I just don't know what's going to happen with all this. Christ," he said, running his hands through his hair. "It's a fucking nightmare."

"It could be worse. You could actually be dead."

"That may have been the better and easier option all round."

CHAPTER THIRTY SIX

"IT'S been a tough few days for everyone," Ted said the following day when they were all assembled in his private rooms at the mansion. They were quite a large gathering this time, including his wife, Harold, Alfie and Mikey, Liam and Jackson and, of course, Father Goodheart. "Not least because I lost my father yesterday. May I begin by thanking you all for coming here. My daddy seems to have left a legacy, but not the one I was expecting."

"You can say that again," Liam said with a sneer.

"It's not that easy, now I know everything. I am here, I am ready to answer any questions you may have and I want to help, especially Mr Franks and Mr Goodman."

Cydney studied her clients. The two elderly gentlemen were clearly exhausted, whether from the recent events or the jetlag, or probably both. Their eyes were red-rimmed against their slightly pallid skin, and Harold, particularly, showed signs of breathing problems as he was continually taking extra breaths of air.

"Carry on, please," Alfie said. "We're waiting to hear what you have to say."

Ted took out a brown quarto sized envelope from a file in front of him and removed the contents. Standing up for his voice to carry to all the people seated around him, he continued. "My daddy left a letter to be opened upon his death, which I have right here. It was written about six months ago when he started to visit Father Goodheart, as I've learnt. I have only just read the contents for the first time and his words don't concern you as they are addressed to me as his son." Cydney watched as he hesitated, seemingly to gather his thoughts, or perhaps because he was the governor and, like all politicians, wanted to create more drama. Perhaps she was being unfair, but the thought crossed her mind as to whether he had cried at all at his father's death or had any regrets. "With the letter was this video." He held up another package to everyone. "He wants us all to watch it. I hope it will explain a lot."

"Cut the crap, Ted," Liam interrupted. "He was a murderer. Don't make excuses."

"What was that? Ted?" Alice called out. "Are you now going to tell me what's going on here?"

"Yes," he turned to her. "Of course I am. That's why we're all here. Please listen." He addressed everyone. "The best I can do is set up the recording. I think this is what Father Goodheart knows about already but it's important everything is out in the open." Everyone turned to the priest who nodded wearily, the same clear signs of exhaustion showing on his young face.

"Pops, are you sure?" Mikey turned to the governor. "I don't think this is a good idea."

"No, it's okay. I want to see what this man has become," Harold said. "I need to know."

"So I'll start." The governor pointed the remote at the television screen on the wall and waited for the video to begin.

If you are watching this, it's because I am now dead and I have confronted my fears, which were to face my Maker and to know my fate. I have carried a burden. I imagined I was feeling a guilt that took over my very existence. However … I believe the thought of death, and the fact I was probably acting out of cowardice, added to this. I cannot take away what I've done and neither will I apologise for what I carried out so many years ago. I intend to stay true to myself because in that way I can give a meaning to my life and all I have done, no matter how hard and uncaring that sounds.

The shudders moving through the bodies of Harold and Alfie

294

were discernible to all those in the room and Cydney felt completely powerless to help them. This was their journey and they had to work their way through the horror of facing Adolf Weissmuller.

"Those eyes!" Harold leant forward to get closer to the screen. "Still."

"The way he terrorised us so many years ago. So cold and menacing," his friend agreed.

First, there is one apology I can give. Not for my deeds, because I was following orders as a professional soldier and got caught up in the whole furore of Nazi Germany, and because I doubt there's any point as you wouldn't believe me and it would accomplish nothing whatsoever. No, I wish to make amends for what I did to you all personally, as that is the only way I can ask for forgiveness. I am not trying to justify my actions, merely to explain.

"Nazi Germany," shouted out Alice. "What on earth?" Ted ignored the interruption of his wife's outburst and let the video roll.

I believe I know who's present watching this video, so I will start first with Liam. You did nothing wrong, except discover my deeds. I wronged you on so many levels. I took you for a fool, which you are not, and I thought I had my trail covered. Yes, for many years I was defrauding the bank, in what amounted to millions of dollars. Money was my aim. It was all I ever wanted. Call it greed if you will but there was something magical about accumulating wealth and the more I had, the more I wanted. I had no real use for more. It was more like a sickness in me, this desire to build and build as much as I was able. Perhaps that was how you found me out as I was not being as vigilant as I should have been.

I coveted your position above all else, and you made it easy for me as you never really wanted to be there. To get the Board on my side was not difficult at all. They saw your faults and your unwillingness to lead in the direction I wanted to go. They were also money-led and they saw the future as I did. You have to agree with me, whether you like it or not. However, and this was my downfall, you discovered everything I had done so I had no

295

opportunity to cover my tracks, and more importantly, you threatened me. Yes, me! You made me so angry and I was not going to be put in a situation where I could lose everything. So I took the only action I could, which was to send you a warning. I never meant for your wife and children to be killed. It really was to warn you off doing anything against me. I know what it is to lose a son. Until my Philip was killed I never thought I would feel pain or realise what love for another person could feel like and, for what you lost, I apologise. There, I doubt you ever thought you would hear that from me. I know you hate me and I don't blame you for one second.

"I sure do. You took my life away," Liam whispered.

Once I was in control, I took the bank to the heights it deserved. I made it what it is today, the largest private enterprise in the State of West Virginia. I stopped all those stupid and unnecessary loans to farmers and miners who had no money to pay us. What was the purpose? Now we have funds under investment in the multi-millions and we are a force to be reckoned with. No matter what I did to get there, you know I'm right.

"My God. The arrogance of the man is never ending," muttered Jackson. "As if the ends justify the means. He might still have been chairman but he wasn't involved for years, and had no idea of anything we did."

Yes, I am arrogant, I can hear you say it, and rightly so. I made sure you're all sitting pretty and have no financial worries at all. Yes, you Jackson, as I'm sure you are present at the little gathering. You can now take my place as chairman and that's where you should be, as I doubt my son wants it. You are young and you are almost as ruthless as me. That's not a criticism. I applaud you. The difference between us is that you are emotional. That was not something I suffered from. Continue to be what and who you are, but do it within the law. I took a lot of chances, made a few errors, which I managed to turn in my favour, and got away with so much. I will come back to you, however, as you will be wondering about my past and how to go forward now you realise what I did.

Next I turn to Hans Frankelman, alias Harold Franks, and his partner, Ahron Gotlieb, or Alfie Goodman, as he is known now. Am I now able to apologise for all I did to your people, you will be asking

296

yourselves? As I told you, I was a soldier. I think you took what I did personally and it was not personal to either of you. Yes, I did you wrong in so many ways and I knew you would find me. Naturally, you would when you got all that money from me and the amount was enough to make you question it. However, you knew all the time it was me that sent it to you.

"He knew you would be here!" Mikey said. "Unbelievable."

"Don't you understand, that was his power and he always intended to wield it to this day. This man could never change," Harold said.

I found you fairly easily, although I did nothing for so many years. I had no doubt how scared you were when I threatened you in Dachau and those chilling words would have stayed with you. You had something of mine, my notebook, the details of all I did and all I stole, yes I admit that, and I would never allow anyone to have that control over me. However, you remained silent, for whatever reason. That was your choice. I would not have done if the roles were reversed. Now you are rejoicing at my death but you have no idea what to do going forward - should you keep the million dollars? A moral dilemma, I'm sure. Money you and your family have never seen before. If I were you I would keep it, but then I had no morals.

"We will never touch that money," Harold said, his voice firm so nobody was in any doubt as to his thoughts. "Never as long as I live. It's tainted by the lives of all those who died simply for being born into a religion that goes back centuries to the beginning of civilisation. No, no, *no!*"

"Pops, please keep calm." Mikey turned to Ted. "Can we have some water, please? This is proving far too much for them."

Alfie shook his head. "Let's continue. I want to hear what else he has to say."

"He confessed to me," Father Goodheart said, his voice low. He looked around at everyone in the room. "Why would he do that? I gave him absolution for his crimes. I will never be able to live with myself."

"He's a coward, Father," said Mikey. "He was scared and always wanted to save his own skin. There was no remorse. Men like him who've committed so many crimes against humanity, they are basically wicked, born that way. Something in their make-up. You can't blame yourself."

"I can."

"So why now, all of a sudden? I'll tell you why, because he's dying. Do you think he felt anything over the last sixty years when he could have repented at any time? He told you what you wanted to hear because he wanted, needed absolution. You didn't know you were being exploited by him. He was using God as a means to project his fears. He couldn't stop himself." Mikey quietened his tone. "You should not be upset, Father. You did this in good faith."

"Shall we continue?" Ted pressed the button to let the video run again, ignoring Mikey's outburst.

I believe hate is a very powerful emotion and the Nazi party was based on hatred for anyone who did not follow their ideology. Hitler wanted to create a world where all were equal, provided they fitted his criteria, and to do that he had to annihilate all those who got in his way. He did a lot for the world when you consider things, initially. He wanted Germany to be all-prevailing and when he came to power he brought the country out of the economic devastation which had followed the loss of the First World War. His strategy was to make Germany a world leader in the financial markets, to build and to create, but he did this with brute force which was never going to work and be accepted by other countries. He was a tyrannical megalomaniac and, although I followed his doctrines, I knew it would never last. He was never going to win the war and so I ensured my future after the fall of the Third Reich, which was surely going to happen, was secure in every way.

The money was so easy for me - almost laughable - to attain. Yes, I can hear you hating me even more for those words. Ask yourselves how an entire civilisation can be led to their deaths without doing something about it? Why did nobody fight us back? Hitler thought we were invincible but he was a man like any other, not the God he assumed he was. The Jews were like lambs to the slaughter. Anyway, I digress. I moved millions in gold to Switzerland and then to New York where the Chairman of Ross Bank,

Edward Ross, yes Liam, your father, assisted me to move the monies to Prime. It was all planned, even down to my marrying your sister, Carolynn. Edward was a Nazi sympathiser, probably because his grandmother, Elise, was a big influence in his life. Of course, you and the family never knew that and yes, they did aid Hitler in his build up to the war by shipping gold and bonds to Germany via their branch there. Thankfully, despite investigations into this, nothing further was pursued and once again we got away with it.

"This just gets better and better," muttered Jackson.

"My father was involved? No, I knew him. He wasn't like that. I would have known," said Liam, his face one of utter disbelief. "I would have known," he repeated.

Again, nobody expected this and so it was well hidden and, don't forget, a lot of industries here were making loads of money before, during and after the war. Why put a nail in the coffin to their endeavours? Everybody benefitted and none of you in the family would be sitting as pretty as you are now, enjoying the fruits of my labours. You all live very nice lives, apart from Liam, apparently. That was his choice and I apologise if I sound so deprecating to your situation, which was my doing after all.

Ted, my son. I never gave you much love growing up but I never learned how and had no role model. I was probably devoid of emotion but I think we came to an understanding when Philip died and that was a huge lesson for me. I took your mother and brother for granted and that they would always be there, and then they weren't. Your mother was a spoilt child when we married and although she loved me at first, I was unable to reciprocate. I treated her badly, I know that, and she deserved better. Maybe it was her father's fault. She was a commodity to him, to be sold to the highest bidder, which was me because of what I could bring to the bank. It was all organised, you see, even before the war started, when I first met your German cousins and we compiled a plan for our future.

Liam looked over at Harold and Alfie. "I'm so sorry. I had no idea. About any of this, all we've heard. This has caught me totally unawares. How can I make this good, put this right?"

His question was left unanswered. Cydney waited for any reaction from the governor and his wife. The shock was apparent on their faces and it was as if Ted had aged in the last half hour listening to what his father was spouting. The words addressed were meant to be an apology, she assumed, but it sounded simply an excuse. The man clearly was not going to make any act of contrition. Father Goodheart was also silent, occasionally shaking his head as the speech unfolded, and that's exactly what it was; a speech to a captive audience.

Ted, you are a great man and can be even greater. I wanted so much for you. You are an impressive and skilful governor, your judgment impresses those around you and I know you would have made a remarkable and distinguished president. What a thought! The President of the United States, the son of a Nazi. Of course, you will never run for that office now. You're probably thinking you should resign as governor. I hope you don't do that. The people of West Virginia deserve a man such as you. I have never said this before - I am proud of you. Love? Maybe, but that's not a word that readily slips off my tongue. I wouldn't know how to define love except that I probably got near to that feeling when we lost Philip. Discuss this with Alice. She's a wonderful wife and she will guide you in the right manner.

So, now to Jackson. You will want to hide everything about this away, slip it under the carpet as if it never happened, and why do I say that? Because you are a proud man and you enjoy the power being head of the bank gives you. I would say continue. Forget about how the money got into the vaults and think only of what you can do with it now, without me around. Nobody needs to know about the past, so many years ago. Other banks were complicit in hiding gold looted from the Jews of Europe. Not just us. The difference is you know about it now and the others probably don't as the heads of their enterprises are long dead. You should think long and hard. That's my advice to you. If this comes out, think of how many people it will affect and the catastrophic waves it will cause, which will reverberate throughout the financial world.

Jackson sat upright in his chair. Cydney observed his expression carefully, trying to gauge his reaction to what he'd heard from Albert Whiteman, his voice coming to everybody from beyond the grave. "The fact is, the man is totally right. Our hands are tied in many respects, but how can we let this disappear? I don't know …"

I assume none of you have any idea what to do for the best. Somewhere in the back of your mind are these huge morals waiting to get out. You are torn now between doing the right thing and carrying on as if nothing has changed. My advice? Seek Liam's guidance. I have no doubt I underestimated his talents. However, be warned that sometimes it's better to let sleeping dogs lie.

I will let you all go now. I've kept you long enough. What I did in the past should never be allowed to happen again. It's been said many times. Atrocities are going on everywhere in the world. Use the bank's resources to help those in need. Assuage your guilt by giving to others, something I never did. My life has been long, undeservedly so. I have made my confession to Father Goodheart and I thank him for listening and again apologise for what he had to hear. I don't think he was expecting this. I was hoping for some sort of redemption. However, there are too many events in the past for which I cannot hope to seek God's forgiveness. Although sacrosanct, the Father has my permission to tell you about my past in all its awful detail. I ask for nothing now, although if by making my confession God will look down on me kindly, then I thank Him - but I doubt it.

The video faded to black and silence ensued as everyone tried to make sense of what they had heard, of what was relevant to them. It seemed nobody wanted to be the first to speak and break the quiet that had descended on the room until Ted rose to his feet.

"It's been quite a revelation. For all of us," he said, glancing at his wife. "Mr Franks, Mr Goodman, I apologise that you had to bear witness to all of this. You should never have had to go through this at your time of life, especially after what all you and your families went through so long ago."

"We thank you for your time and appreciate your words. Nothing will change for us. We will tear up the bonds. We do not want this money and never did. It's not about that," Alfie said.

301

"No. I thought you would say that. What are you going to do with this knowledge?"

"You worried you're going to lose your place as governor, or all your money?"

"No Liam. It's just ..."

"What? Do you in all seriousness think we can carry on, after all you've heard? Really? He admitted killing my family, admitted stealing all that money from those poor people. He was evil, Ted." Liam's despair was evident for all to see. "Your daddy was nothing but pure evil."

"Now hold on. Do you really want to bring this out into the open? Think what we could all lose. Our reputations, jobs for all our employees. Think about this," said Ted.

"I don't give a toss for that. It needs to come out. The FBI need to be informed. Jackson?" Liam turned to his cousin.

"He's right, Ted, but on the other hand, think of what could happen. If it closes its doors, all the mortgages and guarantees we have written and underwritten will be called in. The whole of the state could be in jeopardy."

"You're saying that to preserve your position."

"No, Ted. That's only partly true. I think we need to think this through carefully. However, can you really carry on as governor?"

"If the bank remains as it is, yes, why not? I'm now the majority shareholder. My view is not to rush into anything and maybe some good will come out of this. We will reconvene. One question though, Mr Franks, Mr Goodman - what are you going to do with the notebook?"

"Ah yes. I was wondering when you'd ask about that. I presume you want us to hand it over to you?" Harold said. "No. I don't think so. We've had it this long and we will keep it. This is our children's legacy. A reminder."

"I understand but ..."

"No buts, Governor. My word is final on this." He turned to Alf for confirmation, who nodded his agreement.

302

"I think we should head out to the airport now. Our flight is in a few hours," Cydney said to everyone, in an attempt to break the atmosphere and bring things to a conclusion.

"Let me arrange a car for you all. It's the least …"

"No, Governor, thank you. We have transport already," said Harold. "It's tragic you had to learn all of this. A son should be equally proud of his father."

"And I have nothing to feel proud about. No legacy. At least let me shake your hands."

"I don't mean to be rude to you, but that's not something we can do." Alfie stood, ready to leave. "The sins of the father extend downwards, unfortunately. It was enough we had to sit through this last bit of self-gratifying entertainment, which served only to enforce what we already know. And no, we will still never forgive, nor forget. We will live the rest of our lives in the secure knowledge he can never get to us again."

"I still … I mean, I want to apologise for him. It's all I have." Ted pulled his hand back and let it linger uselessly by his side. "I wish I could do more."

"Your wishes are not our problem or concern."

Cydney escorted her clients outside to the waiting cars.

"It's nice to feel the sun on our faces. I thank God we're still alive," Harold said, looking up to the heavens. "We can now carry on our lives with our families. I doubt the governor and anybody else there will ever be able to find peace, knowing what that man has done. We found our peace long ago."

"Sirs!" Harold and Alfie turned around to see Liam walking swiftly over to them from the governor's mansion, closely followed by Jackson. "It's been a pleasure to meet you both, albeit in these circumstances." Liam extended his hand to each man in turn. They took it, accepting a kinship based on mutual suffering received at the hands of Albert Whiteman. "If I could change the past, I would. You're very lucky to have this lady on your side. We should all be thankful to her."

"We are indeed. Without her, God knows," he said, and holding hands, supporting each other, they trundled to the car where the driver was waiting to help them in. The sight brought tears to Cydney's eyes.

"What will you do now, Liam?" asked Cydney.

"I really don't know. These revelations have knocked me sideways. I'm going to stay living in the mountains, although I shall venture down now and again. I believe I might like a bit of civilisation occasionally. Jackson may need me now we know about the bank's history."

"That's true enough. I do need him," Jackson agreed. "We have work to do."

"So my job here is done," said Cydney.

"Indeed it is. Thank you," added Liam. "I'll know who to come to if I'm ever in trouble again."

"Well I hope that never happens, though you know where to find me." Cydney smiled at the man she had come to admire for his resilience. "And you, Jackson? What are you going to do?"

"Carry on, I believe, is in all our best interests. I can't speak for Ted, though. We have to deal with the possible fall-out of this huge and devastating news."

Cydney nodded. "I wish you luck."

"I take it this remains private now?" Jackson said. "Purely between us?"

"My clients' interests have always been at the heart of this but I can't say. Now Whiteman is dead, the case is closed from my side and I can't believe taking this further would help them or anybody at all. I want them to lead a normal life for what they have remaining, without having to look over their shoulders all the time thinking he's going to come after them."

"That's what it's been like I presume, since they last saw him."

"We've all learnt a lot over the last few days, Jackson." Cydney decided no further comment was necessary.

"I agree."

"Liam needs some looking after. I take it …"

"Yes, I'll ensure he's okay," he said, putting his arm around Liam's shoulders. "It's been a very traumatic time for him especially now the truth surrounding his wife and children is out in the open, well at least within the family."

Cydney climbed into the car beside Mikey and stared at the mansion as they drove out and onto the main route towards the airport. At the last minute she glanced up at the window of the governor's office where he and his wife were standing, observing everyone leaving, their faces impassive. She doubted their lives would ever be the same again. As the mansion faded into the distance, she was rewarded with a final dwindling image of Sybill and Mordecai.

* * *

"Are you going to let them get away with that? After all your father built up. With what they all know now, are you sure they'll keep their mouths shut about this blasted notebook?"

"No, darlin', I certainly am not. I want it back, and I will get it."

"And your father's legacy?"

"He was a bastard to us all our lives. I hated the way he treated our mom and walked over everybody without a goddam care in the world."

"So what are you going to do, Ted? The bank's yours now."

"One thing I am not going to do is resign as governor. I can do more in this position than anything else."

"The primaries? I don't think you should let that go."

"Nor me, Alice. I know I mentioned before that I wasn't going to run. I don't take kindly to pressure and I refuse to be pushed into a corner by anyone, especially now. No. We have the backing and I'm not going to lose that at any cost."

"What if this gets out, about your daddy? Are you willing to chance that?"

"There are only a few people in the world who know about this. Jackson, I think I can buy off, or at least persuade, unless that woman goes to the FBI and that's always the big risk. She did threaten me and I don't take threats from anyone. Jackson knows where his bread's buttered, and he loves power. Liam is old and his time is nearly up. However, William heard about everything from Jackson and he's someone I have to deal with. He's such an upright citizen."

"William! That's the last thing we need. But, he's been loyal so far so why would he go to the authorities? He's got too much to lose. No. But this Cydney woman …"

"Well, maybe she and her crew won't be around too long either. Anyway, revenge is a dish best served cold. I suppose my daddy taught me something after all. I can wait like he did and I will deal with them in my own way and in the fullness of time. Watch me."

* * *

"Mikey, I don't think this is going to disappear, no matter how much we want it to," Cydney said.

"What do you suggest?"

"You're a lawyer. You tell me. Do you honestly think the governor will resign and give everything up? Because I don't, especially as we're holding that notebook. He will want that more than anything now. Did you see the look on his face?"

"I did."

"I'm thinking he may have inherited some of his father's traits."

"What do you mean?"

"Some psychopathic tendencies. Well, from what we heard, the governor's role model was his father. He had a detached childhood and now look what's happened."

"You're saying that it's genetic?"

"Maybe."

"What an awful thought. Do you think Weissmuller was telling us the entire truth or just the parts he wanted us to hear?"

"I don't know. There's no-one left now who can verify his story. Anyway, I think this is far from over."

CHAPTER THIRTY SEVEN

"I'M still Stateside."

"Morning George. I was expecting you here," answered a rather sleepy and disgruntled Rupert Van der Hausen. At his age, although he was still jetting around the world and working hard, he insisted, as far as his staff were concerned, that the mornings were sacrosanct when he was at his home in Johannesburg. He hated being woken. Occasionally, he vowed to slow down but with so much expansion going on within his organisation, now was certainly not the time.

"Ah, so you've spoken to Cydney already."

"Yes, I have. You knew she would call me. Hold on a moment." He clambered out of bed and grabbed his silk dressing gown. "Let me make myself more comfortable." He opened the doors to his veranda and took a seat on one of the rattan chairs overlooking the fifth fairway and green to his golf club where he still maintained his handicap of five.

"Excuse me, I know it's early for you. You would be her first port of call," George said, "and that's the problem. She tells everyone everything except me."

"We're old friends and colleagues. I've known her for many years and we're close."

"Yes, like a father and daughter."

"Come on, sarcasm is not usually in your vocabulary, George. I presume you don't believe what she told you."

"No, I do not. Do you honestly think there is any credence to her husband, and I can just about say these words, being alive?

308

Christ, Rupert, what on earth is it all about?" His voice rose in anger and Rupert could tell he really was almost at the end of his tether.

"The British Army Special Forces are a law unto themselves, and especially if the Secret Intelligence Service, or MI6, is involved, which may well be the case. Their powers in foreign intelligence stretch beyond anything we can imagine. Nothing would surprise me at all and I'm sure they'd like another political triumph."

"So you believe it's true?"

"I'm not saying that. Listen to me," Rupert said, trying to calm the situation. He lent forward in his chair at the sound below him to see one of his staff watering the many colourful flowers and bushes that made up his garden, necessary before the sun was at its highest. "I'm telling you nothing is impossible and Cydney would not even say those words if she had any doubts. She's an amazing woman, as you've discovered, and she is not one to fantasise. I was hoping she had moved on - and with you."

"I asked her to marry me."

"I know that, too, and nothing would have made me happier than to see you two together as a family with the twins."

"So what should we do?"

"I believe there may be some merit to this and I'm leaving for London soon. I was going to travel there in a few days anyway. I want to see how our new project is going."

"This is my future. I love this woman, more than life itself."

"Are you prepared for the truth? Because if her husband is alive, that's the end of your relationship."

"I realise that, Rupert. God, I know, and it's eating me up inside. Her happiness means everything to me and if he is, although I realise it's the end for us, well …"

"You're a good man, but if the army is using him, he can never come back to the UK and his family. She will be on her own forever, without you, and without Steve. I understand about the secrecy of the army. That's not a life, at least not one I would want for her, and I doubt she would want it for herself."

"We need to find out the truth and then she makes her choice. She mentioned about Sean, that he was out in Israel looking for him."

"If anyone can find him, Sean can."

"What a hero." He paused, immediately regretting his words. "Sorry, I didn't mean that."

"I know. You're upset. He's a highly-qualified army man with many means at his disposal. Yes, he is extremely protective of Cydney but he promised Steve he would look after her and, until you came along, that's exactly what he'd been doing."

"Came into her life in my cack-handed way."

"I didn't say that. You are good for her, and have been. Don't give up just yet. Let's get to the bottom of this. I'm not without contacts and resources myself."

"Okay. Thanks Rupert. I know you're only doing this for her. It means a lot to me, too."

"Let's discuss this further when I know more. I'm not sure what time my flight gets in but I should be there by the evening."

"Will you tell Cydney? What I've said?"

"Yes. Maybe. Well, I have no reason to lie to her and have always been straight. We need a plan of action and I'll be as honest as I can, as long as it doesn't destroy her."

"I can't believe this. I'm actually encouraging you to find her dead husband."

"I suggest you sort yourself out and get a flight back to Jo'burg."

CHAPTER THIRTY EIGHT

"SPILL."

The kitchen had always been their usual sparring area and this time the early morning confrontation between Cydney and Sean was no different. Sean was studying her as she paced like a predatory panther across the floor.

"Can't a man walk through the door, even?"

"You've walked. Now I want to know the truth."

"Sure. An' you're taking no prisoners."

"Exactly, and no hiding things from me."

"What's gone on? Why are you so agitated?"

"I'm tired, jetlagged after returning home last night. Why do you think? You do remember George left me and my husband might be alive." Her voice was steadily rising.

"Yes, of course. Why don't you take a seat?" he said, trying to placate her which, in her current state, was not going to be easy. He had only left Steve in Israel the day before and he was becoming slightly panicked as he still hadn't got his story together. He needed to play for time, try to forestall her and make it up as he went along, especially after his chat with Rupert. He sat at the kitchen table, examining her expression carefully. "I'm still not sure telling George was the best idea. The more people who know about this, the worse it will be."

"Worse for whom exactly? I doubt this can get any worse if it tried. So tell me. Is my husband alive?"

"This will hurt, but if you want the truth and no stories ..."

"Well, I'm in the mood for a story. In fact, I relish it and see,

311

I'm taking a seat as you've asked me so I can get comfortable while you spin your yarn." Cydney made a noisy demonstration of pulling out the kitchen chair, and slamming it on the floor so it made the cups on the table rattle and the milk tumble out of its jug. "I'm ready."

"It's not a yarn, believe me, though I don't know where to start."

"You can start by not trying to delay matters. Something significant happened, so, as I said, spill. I'm waiting. Tell me everything. I mean it."

Sean took a breath. "Okay. Well, me and some of the lads met up in Tel Aviv. I had two of them come in via Jordan, as planned. However, when we arrived we had a welcome committee awaiting us."

"Let me guess, the one and only General Ian Bowles-Smith."

"The very man. He took us to one of the airbases but made sure I sent the lads home so it was the two of us. He wasn't best pleased about 'our little army', as he called it."

"How did he know?"

"It seems he had me followed. Your phoning every day seemed to alert him to the fact something was going on and he wanted to know exactly what, so he arranged for one of his team to check us out. I knew he had. I ignored it, as I was waiting for him to show his hand."

"So he obviously didn't take me for a complete raving lunatic?"

"He probably did." Sean laughed at her remark. "You're quite convincing and it worried him, especially as you were so near to finding out the truth."

"Worried I would go to the papers?"

"Maybe, or something. Anyway." He placed his hand over hers tenderly. "What I have to tell you is not good news, I'm afraid. Yes, until a few months ago, Steve was alive."

"You're telling me he's dead. Answer me. Please. He's dead? Really?"

Sean scrutinised the woman in front of him, noting she was doing her utmost not to fall apart, and was failing miserably. "I'm sorry, but you wanted the truth." It killed him inside to have imparted the biggest lie of his life, though what choice did he have? "And telling you gives me no pleasure, you know that."

"I thought … He came to me."

"Oh, Cydney. Come on, let me get you a tissue."

"What happened?" she asked.

"He was in Syria and …"

"Not Afghanistan?"

"No. He was found but it seemed he had lost his memory and had no recollection of his previous life."

"Not me or the kids?"

"Nothing at all. Slowly he remembered things and, although he wanted to come home, apparently begged, the general had other plans and made him stay out there for another year collecting information." Sean decided it was better to tell her some half-truths than nothing at all. When she'd accosted him before, saying she knew Steve was alive, he hadn't gone into too many details about how much he knew, and he wasn't prepared to do it now.

"The general told you this?"

"Yes, he did, when we first found out. He admitted what a difficult choice he had to make but that the government's interests were foremost."

"I can believe that. And then what?"

"Please don't cry. I hate to see you like this." It was breaking his heart in two. His loyalties were torn between the captain and the grieving woman before him, not only to protect her but also to protect the situation. If the truth came out, anything they would be doing in the future could be made even more dangerous and possibly compromise both their situations, Steve, as the military attaché in Iran, and Sean as his liaison officer. "After the year, arrangements were put in place to get him out of the country across the Golan Heights."

"That's when you were there? The first time when I thought you'd gone out to Ireland. You told me this."

"Exactly."

"You never found him."

"He never arrived at his rendezvous point. I was ordered home. I never believed he was dead. You know that. I wanted to believe he was alive and I would have done everything in my power to find him and bring him home to you. I'm sorry, I really am." There, he had lied to her, although maybe he hadn't exactly spoken the word 'dead' so there was some retribution, and God, it hurt him to the very core. He questioned everything in which he had ever believed, crossed the fingers on both hands and prayed to every saint that had ever lived to forgive him. He may even have to go to confession, something he had not done since a child, when he concluded it was a pointless exercise for him, accomplished nothing, and took up his valuable football and boxing time. Once in the army, he didn't have a place for religion.

"You going there was a waste of time. Are you sure? Really sure?"

"Yes," he said, "and it hurts me so much to tell you this."

"Ray!"

Sean turned around as Cydney called out, searching the room, expecting someone to be there, but it was still just the two of them.

"I've been told you're still lying to me."

"What?" He had no idea how she knew but her face was very clear.

"Right." She stood up. A look of alarm passed across Sean's face momentarily. "It's been staring at me all along. It's always the army that comes first in everything. Official Secrets Act be damned. It hurts you? Do you know what? It hurts me too. I have to say, you're a great actor."

"I don't know what you're talking about." Sean tried to avert his gaze.

"I'll say it again - you're lying to me. I'm not sure why though. Something's going on. Are you going to tell me or do I have to find out for myself this time? I thought I could rely on you."

"You can. For God's sake, why would I lie to you about something like this, something so important as finding Steve?"

"Because the army got to you yet again. As always." Sean was feeling more and more uncomfortable by the second, especially as Cydney was once again pacing the kitchen, all the while her gaze never moving from him. "Sean, this is me. Look at me. What do you think I'm going to do? Pass out when I hear the truth, like some weak woman? I can take the truth and I want to know. Now!"

"Let it go. Concentrate on Lauren and Jake."

She marched round and stood right next to him, leaning forward and speaking directly into his face so quietly he hardly heard the words. "He's alive, isn't he? Tell me. I won't do anything rash but I have to know before I can go forward. Just to know, that's all. I beg of you."

Before he could utter a word, Lauren raced in and flung herself at Cydney, nearly knocking them both over. "Oh, Mum, I'm so pleased you're home. I've missed you so much. Did you buy me anything?"

"Of course I did, my darling. Wow, let me look at you. I swear you've grown."

"It's all that sun and sea air. Hi Sean. I'm pleased you're back, too. Oh, by the way, I wanted to ask you, who's Alan Campbell?"

"I haven't finished with you yet," Cydney warned Sean.

CHAPTER THIRTY NINE

THE plane started to lose altitude and Rupert could see below him the wonderful landmarks of London as it descended into Heathrow Airport. It felt like a second home to him and he had numerous investments here he intended to view during this trip, which he may have to extend now. It didn't matter where he was in the world as home was always where he had buried Adela and Katarina. However, he was prepared to compromise a bit now as his life was lonely. That was a hard fact to admit to himself. An age thing, he mused. He finished his whisky and handed the empty glass to the stewardess who rewarded him with a beautiful smile. Money was responsible for so many things, good and bad, but travelling on a private jet in comfort and avoiding all the crowds of people at airports was a bonus to him and well worth the cost and upkeep.

Now he faced the problem of trying to determine whether Steve was alive or not. He sincerely hoped that Cydney was imagining all of this as he could not comprehend the implications after all this time. It was the sort of thing governments would do, using men for their own purposes, and it was certainly not beyond the realms of possibility. His plan was to talk to Sean in the first instance and gauge his reaction as an army man. That would give him an indication of what to do. George was of course the other issue. The man was clearly in love with Cydney and he felt for him.

After passing through Immigration, his private chauffeur drove him to his club in Piccadilly where Sean was waiting for him, as pre-arranged. "I think you'd better come up to my suite so we can chat in private. I doubt this is going to be an easy conversation and I want to hear everything, right from the very beginning with no omissions."

Rupert believed he had now made himself very clear on the subject and he was not one to let anything pass him by, especially where Cydney was concerned. The thought of the utter heartbreak she and the twins had been going through over the last few years, until George had come into their lives, made his own heart ache, and thoughts of Adela and Katarina flooded back to him. He knew they would be waiting for him in the future but he wasn't ready to go just yet; he still had so much more to do. Now he was going to get to the bottom of this business about Steve, a man he had met on several occasions and respected as the officer and gentleman he was, and nobody, not even anyone from the British Army, was going to stop him.

"I need to share the enormous weight I've been carrying for so long," Sean said, as they made their way up in the lift. Rupert made no comment and the two remained in silence until they reached the suite and the bellhop had set down the suitcases.

"I'll call for some refreshments. I think this is going to take a while."

A little over an hour later, Sean finished reciting all that had happened up to the time he'd left Steve in Israel the day before.

"What are the plans now? My concern is for Cydney and the kids, you know that," Rupert stated, standing up and walking over to grab his jacket. "Want to join me?" he asked, pulling out an ornate antique silver case and removing a rather large Churchill cigar.

"No thank you. I'm a cigarette man. Down to ten a day now. With regard to Cydney, she's also my concern and if the truth be told, I have no idea what to do. The army and, I'm sure, MI6 are intent on sending Captain Granger on this new mission and under a pseudonym. Christ, I shouldn't even be telling you this."

"I never cared for all that 'Official Secrets' crap. All that does is maintain some sort of club for those in the know and damn everyone else." Rupert made a cut above the cap line of the cigar using a single bladed cutter and commenced the age-old ritual of lighting it. First he held the cigar above the flame of the lighter, patiently twisting it around to evenly char all parts of the end, placed it to his lips, alternately gently blowing and puffing and all the while rotating it until the flames jumped up. "Like kissing an angel," he said with a smile, and returned to sit next to Sean.

"Of course. Always on a need to know basis. That's the army for you."

"Do you have any suggestions? You've met him. How's he feeling?"

"Like he wished he was dead, sir. The thing is, I don't think he feels he can come home anyway."

"I can understand that. With the army on his back, it will be impossible. They have him where they want him, and for as long as they want him to do their dirty work for them."

"He's a commodity."

"No doubt, and they aren't going to let him go, so now the question is Cydney. She believes he's alive."

"Yes, I know. She grilled me as soon as I stepped through the door."

"My view is she can take whatever we tell her. She's a very strong woman. Had to be to go through everything she has so far in her life. Is there a chance we can get her to Steve, maybe in Gibraltar, where he's going to get his MC?"

"You reckon if she sees him, she'll be fine and will live with that without telling Lauren and Jake their father is alive? That she'll go off into the sunset in the hope they can meet up once a year? Not a cat's chance in hell. Lauren is just like her mother and you can't keep secrets from her for very long, either."

"No, I know. Christ. The only solution is to lie to Cydney or …"

"I've tried that and it didn't work."

"As I was saying - or get him out for good. We have a huge bargaining tool once we have him safely in our hands. There's no reason for Steve to give up his career, although he may well want to. What if he works for the army in a slightly different manner?"

Sean raised his eyebrows. "You have something in mind?"

"Possibly. It may help that I know the governor there quite well. Sir Robert Alstom. Ex Royal Marines, well in fact the Commander General. Met him when he was the High Commissioner in Namibia until his appointment in Gibraltar in 2002."

"Namibia?"

"Yes, I was working with the government there. Diamonds and copper mainly. We became quite friendly."

"And how is he going to help us exactly?"

"Not sure. I'll call him. He hates injustices, never mind who's involved. And in my mind this is a huge injustice. How closely is Steve going to be monitored?"

"Like a hawk. However, I've agreed to be his liaison officer in Iran so the CO won't be expecting me to get him away now."

"He believes you'll keep to your word?"

"Yes, sir, I think he does. Basically, he's getting what he wants; two of us for the price of one."

"So, on that basis we go ahead."

"Just the finer points to work out. No problem at all. All in a day's work."

"I wish that were true. All I have to do now is keep George at bay."

"George? How does he come into this?"

"He wants to help. But I think that would be wrong."

"He could be useful, don't you think, sir? And he's not known to the general, unlike my crew."

Rupert paused. "Let me think about it. Either way, I want your guys out in Spain in the next week and across the border into Gibraltar. We may not need them all but better to be safe than sorry."

"I agree. Immigration is easy for those coming in by car from Spain and they don't keep tabs on visitors. I'll get them to stay around for a few days and check flights coming in and out. The runway literally crosses the road as you go in to the Rock and it's used for both military and commercial flights."

"How will they be flying him in and when?"

"I'll find out from the CO. Probably RAF Hercules. I'm his friend, until he discovers what I'm doing, but that's for another day. We have a bit of time I'm sure, unless plans are changed."

"We have to keep this quiet. It could all go horribly wrong."

"Don't I know it. What about Cydney? That's the big question."

"I have to work that out."

"The CO is going to have me locked up. He'll know I'm involved and all his plans for glory are going to go up in flames."

"Then you can't be involved. At all, you realise that. I want you out of the country somewhere, but the general has to know where. Maybe a trip to Tehran in advance. I'm sure you can organise that."

"True. My first foray into the world of a trade delegate. The CO will like that. Feel I'm taking an interest and getting things ready at the Embassy for Steve, or rather Alan Campbell, to arrive."

"One question. Something occurred to me. Do the police act separately to the military? What rights do they have on Gibraltar?"

"Why do you ask?"

"Thinking aloud really. What if we set something up? Would the police intervene, do you think?"

"As far as I'm aware, the police have jurisdiction over the military but, as normal, the military do what they want when they want and anything they do is kept quiet. The police come under the British sovereignty and report to the governor, who is the Queen's representative. There have been occasions when the police have tried to intervene in a situation. However, whether it's the army, navy or air force, somehow the MOD staff come out on top. I heard it really pisses off the locals."

"I've no idea how the British managed to retain that stronghold," Rupert said, puffing again on his cigar and taking a moment to allow the smoke and smell to encircle the already nicotene-permeated walls. "Do you know the layout of the airport? Are the terminals separated?"

"Yes. The civilian one is on the left as you come through the border control and the military terminal is across the airstrip."

"And what about when the army want to board? Do they simply walk from the terminal to the plane?"

"Usually, from the hangers. What's your thinking here? You want to create a diversion?"

"Yes, that's the general idea. After the ceremony, when Steve is back on the plane and about to take off, we tip off the police with some story or other."

"Who arrive with all sirens blazing ..."

"And when they do, I assume everyone has to disembark and that's when your guys come in."

"The general will recognise everyone."

"Is that going to matter by the time the hoo-ha has died down?" Rupert said, relaxing back in his chair.

"I like the idea. I have a pal in the police over there, ex-army. He may come in useful."

"Is there anybody in the world you don't know?"

Sean laughed. "And?"

"Once we have Steve safe and sound, we negotiate with your CO. All he wants is to have Steve under his control in Iran, it would seem. Well maybe that can still go as planned but in his own name and with the blessing of his wife and children."

"It sounds perfect, what could go wrong?" Sean said with some scepticism.

"We need to get Cydney out to Gibraltar. She needs to see her husband is alive and well. I'll fly out once we know the arrival details. You need to get out to Tehran."

"Yes, though what a shame to miss the fireworks."

CHAPTER FORTY

J ENNY popped her head around the door of Cydney's office. "You remember Ted Whiteman's personal assistant? William Templeton."

"Yes. I met him briefly when I was at the governor's mansion. He showed us in if I recall. Why?"

"He's here."

"On the phone?"

"No. Here in person. He's outside in reception. He wants to see you."

"Why on earth would he have travelled to London to see me? It must be something urgent to bring him all the way here. You'd better show him in."

Cydney stood up and moved around her desk to welcome the man, her mind working overtime and speculating as to the reason he was here. "Mr Templeton. This is totally unexpected. Please come and have a seat. How can I help you?"

"I apologise for just turning up here. It's important and I didn't want to talk about it on the phone."

The man appeared totally in control of himself but the feelings he evoked in her were more distressing. Images floated in front of her eyes of sights she thought she had cleared from her mind following her return from West Virginia a week ago. She surveyed him up and down. He was seated completely upright, his back like a board, his hands firmly placed on his knees as if he was appearing before his commanding officer. Definitely an army man, she surmised, clearly recognising all the signs.

"You took a chance hoping I'd be available."

"Yes. I'm sorry, again, and I would have waited if you hadn't been. I realise I should have telephoned in advance but there wasn't a lot of time. I felt I owed it to you and your clients. I'm afraid I've been instrumental in having the governor arrested."

"Arrested? That's a bit of a shock after the last meeting I had with him. For what?"

"Fraud and intent to commit murder."

"Murder?"

"Let me start from the beginning, if you wouldn't mind. A while ago, before Albert Whiteman died, the governor tried to tell me something. We were interrupted and he never got a chance. At the reception, I overheard a conversation between him and Jackson Dwyer, who was considerably drunk. I was requested to take him away from the crowd and get him sobered up and it was then he told me about Albert being an escaped Nazi war criminal."

"Ah, so much for keeping this quiet and within the family."

"I'm sure that was the intention and I realise you're party to all this information and it was due to you that your two clients were able to see their tormentor, albeit after his death."

"You know everything?"

"Well, I didn't, but I used a few of my contacts and carried out my own research. Obviously, when you hear something like this, so extraordinary and so tumultuous, you can't let it go."

"Yes. I agree. And what did you do, Mr Templeton?"

"I am a man of principles. First, you should understand that. I am also a man of God. Having served my years in the army and having escaped death more than a few times, my belief is what strengthens my life, that and my family. I discovered Albert Whiteman was Adolf Weissmuller. I searched his profile which is easily obtained, and read all the abhorrent detail about everything he'd done for the sake of Germany, all about the torture and murder of those poor men, women and children. I couldn't believe what I found out. That man, whom I had sat beside at dinner so many times, driven in the car with, talked to about baseball and everyday things, and what's more introduced to my wife and children, was no more than a cold-blooded mass murderer. My wife even tried to save him at the hospital - she was his cardiologist. I was beside myself, as you can imagine. I let him into my family, although I never liked the man, but I did so for the governor."

"The whole matter has hit us all."

"I can imagine." He hesitated for a second. "You see, I was so confused about what action to take. So conflicted. Then the man died and I knew all his crimes would die with him. I couldn't let it go. I went to see Liam Ross."

"A lovely man."

"Indeed. He told me everything. About his wife and children. About the fraud and the looted gold on which the bank's capital was based."

"And …"

"I had to do something. I went to the FBI, in Washington. Told them all I knew. At first, they didn't believe me. Thought it was an astonishing tale. I showed them a picture of Albert, and one from the wanted list of escaped Nazis, and they could see it was one and the same man."

"And they went into overdrive I presume."

"Yes. There was no stopping them. They turned up in force with all guns blazing to Charleston and arrested the governor, plus Jackson, and closed the doors, stopping all trading. The staff were assembled in the dining room and each one was questioned in detail as to their role, how long they'd worked there, what they knew of the Board of Directors. You can imagine the uproar this caused as nobody knew why they were being interrogated. The press got wind something was up, obviously, but so far it's all been contained in West Virginia."

"Even though Whiteman's is one of the biggest banks in the state?"

"Yes, and the consequences are huge. The FBI are investigating every single bank Whiteman's worked with or had any dealings with. And all their customers. I doubt many are going to get out of this with their reputations intact."

"Has Jackson been charged with anything?"

"Good question. He remained in custody for a couple of days and was released without charge."

"You appreciate he was not complicit in any of this," Cydney said.

"Yes. I do believe that. Who else would you go to but the president and CEO?"

"His only crime was to know about Albert and that only came out when I was there. And what about Liam?"

"He was also questioned and he told them his entire story. I believe it was a complete and utter relief to him, Mrs Granger. After all these years."

"I would agree with that. Such a good man and such a sad life."

"I can't imagine how it felt to lose his family in one go, and at the hands of a man he knew was culpable but couldn't point the finger at."

"So now everything's out in the open. This was not a route my clients would have chosen. They preferred to let it go once Whiteman was dead. Personally, I would have gone to the FBI, so I applaud you. One thing though. The governor only just found out about his father and his crimes and he had no involvement whatsoever. I don't understand. He was arrested for fraud and, what? Attempted murder?"

"Yes. As I have learnt. I was watching him closely. A couple of very strange individuals met with him in the gardens of the mansion. I was curious. Why there? But then he can't go out to just anywhere without being recognised. Anyway, I ran through the CCTV and took some pictures of the so-called visitors to show to a friend of mine in the police. They are well known criminals, part of a gang involved in all kinds, and not just petty crime; money-laundering, drugs, you name it. He'd been after them for years and could never pin a thing on them. The question was why they were meeting with the governor of West Virginia? It all seemed extremely odd. So, my friend had a tail put on them and caught them at Liam Ross' place in the mountains, laying some sort of explosive device. They wanted it to look like an accident."

"They intended to kill him! To shut him up."

"Precisely. The governor couldn't even do his own dirty work. Anyway, once arrested, they sang their hearts out all about the governor, hoping to get immunity from prosecution."

"So why are you here? I could have read all about it, once the news filtered through to the U.K., as I imagine it would have done. You can't keep something like this quiet when all the world would want to know about the deeds of an escaped Nazi such as Weissmuller."

"Yes I know. Let me continue. The thing is, the FBI then raided the mansion and seized all the governor's papers."

"And …?"

"That's where the fraud comes in. Ted had located all the funds his father had accumulated over the many decades, millions in fact, all deposited in a bank in the Grand Cayman. Apparently, Albert had left access and coding details in a private letter."

"So he was going to use these funds? Why does that not surprise me? What will happen to all the monies?"

"I'm not sure. That's up to the authorities. There is something else you should know and I'm not quite sure how to tell you this. It seems, and do forgive me here, that you and your family were next on his hit list."

Cydney couldn't quite register what William Templeton had

reported to her and the shock shook her to the core. She attempted to remain calm although inside she was shaking. "Us? I don't believe it. Why?"

"Something about a notebook he was after. But I should add, you are perfectly safe - now. Nothing to worry about."

"Thank goodness for that. And yes, I have that in my safe custody. What could he hope to achieve though?"

"He probably only thought of the hold you had over him and he wasn't prepared to let that carry on. In my opinion, he wanted the whole sorry matter to disappear when his father died and he couldn't make that happen while you knew all about his background."

"But what did he think I was going to do?"

"Exactly what I did."

"But he never asked you about this?"

"No, Mrs Granger. I assume he imagined he had my loyalty."

"You know what the notebook contains and its significance?"

"Yes, I've been told. I needed to come here. The FBI want to question you and I'm sure they'll need to see your clients also."

"I presume they'll want it now. What next?"

"Basically, the bank is closed."

"You know, rightly or wrongly depending on how you view this, it was the correct thing to do, in my opinion. How can a bank continue when its entire capital is based on tainted gold and money from those poor people? It should reverberate throughout the whole of the commercial world. It is right and proper."

"And it will, I can assure you of that, Mrs Granger. The scandal will be like nothing ever witnessed before."

"Extending to the Federal Bank, no doubt. Good. Weissmuller should be made accountable for the crimes he committed, for his involvement with Nazi Germany. And what about Ted Whiteman?"

"He'll probably go to jail for a good many years, although I suspect he's going to have them running around in circles for a long time to come. According to my sources, he's denying everything, and not taking any responsibility for what he's done. He'll probably set someone else up."

"Just like his father. There's truth in the adage about the sins of the father."

"Yes, it finally became evident. You know, the worst thing is that I never knew. My fault maybe. I worked with him for so many years and I never realised. I thought he was a good man."

"How could you have known, Mr Templeton? Nobody knew. He probably was but it's amazing what money and greed can do to a person. You shouldn't feel responsible, there's nothing you could have done. You've taken the right action."

"You're right. Thank you for those words. Will you report everything to your clients?"

"Of course."

"Right then."

"Will you stay in office with the new governor?"

"That's something I have to think about with my family. Who knows?" William stood up to go and Cydney came from around her desk to shake his hand.

"I do appreciate your coming to see me in person. I'll let you know what happens with the FBI. It was a brave thing that you did. I admire you for it."

* * *

Cydney was greeted at the door of Harold's house by Mikey and shown into the living room where his father and Alfie were waiting for her. They rose on seeing her and came forward to kiss her on each cheek.

"We're very pleased you're here. Come in, sit down."

"I won't keep you long, but I have some news."

"Good news, I hope," said Alfie.

"That depends on how you look at it." She proceeded to recount everything that William Templeton had told her a few hours previously.

"And now what do we do, Cydney?" asked Harold. "With the notebook, the money?"

"The notebook we have to give to the FBI."

"The right thing, eh Alfie?"

"Yes. What good would it do us now? He's dead. He can't touch us. Let it go to them - with our blessing."

"I assume the bearer bonds are now worthless?" Mikey asked.

"Unfortunately, the FBI will want them back. The bank has closed you see, so all trading has stopped and the assets have been frozen," Cydney replied. "There is no money."

"Ach. Who needs it," Harold shrugged. "And what now? What about you, Cydney?"

"Me? Oh, I just carry on," she said, but the question made her think about everything going on in her life and the uncertainty. As she left the two men and Mikey, she felt no further forward, and the thought of that gave her an almighty sinking feeling in the pit of her stomach.

CHAPTER FORTY ONE

"LAUREN, what's that name you mentioned before to Sean? Alan Campbell? I've never heard it before."

"Nor me, Mum."

"Why did you ask Sean?"

"I was thinking about Daddy and when he and Sean were in the army together and suddenly that name popped into my head."

"Bit strange isn't it? And what else popped into that gorgeous little head of yours?" Cydney grabbed hold of her daughter's long pony-tail and swished it around.

"Hey, I've just done my hair. Anyway, nothing else much. I saw a picture of a large mountain in my head and an aeroplane and that name. It's probably nothing. By the way, Mellie's picking me up soon. We're going to the cinema. That's okay, isn't it? You can spend the evening with Jake. That'll be fun. Not!"

"What did the mountain look like?"

"A tall thing with a point at the top. For goodness sake, Mum - it's a mountain!"

"Was there snow?"

"No. I saw a lot of blue sky and sea though."

"Helpful! Thanks sweetheart."

"You mentioned some monkeys, stupid," Jake said as he strode into the kitchen and dived straight into the fridge. "What's for dinner tonight? I'm starving."

"You two spoke about it? For goodness sake. You're always

starving. I'm making spag bol, your favourite, so stop eating and close the fridge door. Dinner's not for a couple of hours yet. Monkeys?" Cydney repeated.

"Oh yeah, I forgot about that. Was that the doorbell? Must be Mellie. I'm going. Bye, Mum." She fled off down the hallway with Cydney following in her wake.

"What time will you be home?"

"Late, about eleven. Love you."

Cydney realised that now the twins were fifteen, they would be off to university soon enough and only coming home the odd weekend, if she was lucky, and away in the holidays with friends. What did she have to look forward to? Possibly a lifetime of loneliness without Steve, and George out of the picture, too.

"Don't worry, Mum, you've still got me." Jake put his arm around his mum and pulled her into his embrace as if he could read her thoughts. "As long as there's food in the house." He sniggered as he strolled out of the kitchen, a bowl of crisps in one hand and a can of coke in the other.

"Great. Just great," she called after him.

Alone, she thought through what Lauren had told her. Her daughter had such a good sixth sense and her instincts were always right on point. Everything she'd said must have been for a reason and it had to do with Steve; she knew it. Mountain, aeroplanes, sea, monkeys - what the hell did that mean when all put together? And that name, Alan Campbell. Who the hell was he? Questions for Sean for certain because she had absolutely no idea if it even meant anything.

Meanwhile, it gave her a sense of peace and optimism knowing Rupert was now in London. She needed him to insert some clarity into everything that was going on around her. Thoughts were running riot in her head and it was hard to concentrate on anything, never mind what Lauren had told her, which could mean nothing at all. Monkeys? What on earth would her daughter come up with next?

331

As she was thinking of Lauren, the phone rang.

"Sorry, Mum. In a rush but - Gibraltar. That's the place I thought of before. Aren't monkeys famous there? Gotta go. Love you." Before Cydney had even a chance to throw a question back, the phone was put down and she was left staring at the receiver. Then, as if on cue, Sean sauntered in.

"Gibraltar," she said. "And who is Alan Campbell?"

"Christ alive, woman."

"Not me this time."

"Ah, your daughter."

"So you're not denying anything. Just come clean, once and for all. You're hiding something and it's doing my head in."

"I've met up with Rupert."

"And? That's your answer? I know he's here."

"Can you get the kids to stay with Claire do you think? We're going on a journey."

"What the hell are you talking about? I've just come back from the States and I'm certainly not going anywhere, thank you very much."

"Cydney, you're about to get what you want, though the CO's going to string me up and I'll be hung, drawn and quartered as sure as night follows day. He's expecting me in Tehran."

She remained quiet for a few seconds whilst she let the words Sean had spoken filter through into her mind. What she wants? Well, all she ever wanted was Steve. Was he about to be delivered up to her, after all this time? Was what she had been dreaming about on the point of being realised? It was impossible to take in. Those few words held so much meaning to her and her brain became a scrambled mess as she attempted to make sense of them. The room moved out of focus momentarily and she was lost in another world where there was hope and everything was conceivable, where tragedy and loss was in the past, where all she had to do was walk along the path to attain true happiness. A single tear fell down her face. Despite her pounding heart, she felt the presence of Ray as he came to stand by her side. Not a word was said but she understood enough to know he would be with her, no matter what the circumstances. She wiped the tear from her cheek and took a deep breath, ready to face her future.

* * *

"We're going on a slight detour."

"I have no idea why you're telling me this. I'm hardly in a position to object. Sir."

"Come now, Captain. I thought we'd got over our little difference of opinion. We need to pick up essential supplies from RAF Lyneham before heading off."

"I haven't been there for a good few years. I thought the Hercules were moving to Brize Norton."

"Not yet. Lyneham's still the primary airfield. You know, no matter what's gone before, I only wish the best for you, Granger," said General Ian Bowles-Smith.

"Is that right? So, the best for me is heading off to Tehran under a new identity and not ever able to see my wife or kids. There's one thing that puzzles me. Why are you spending so much time on me? What have you got to gain?"

"You're my success story."

"Who else knows about me?"

"The MOD likes what I'm doing. It's down to me you're getting the MC in the first place."

"I didn't ask for it, sir, I told you that. What I do get though is that this is all for you and you care nothing for me in this whole bloody scenario. You're retiring soon. What do you hope to gain? A knighthood? You must like the sound of that."

"It does have a certain ring about it. Why don't you relax? You've got a busy few days ahead of you."

"Have you ever tried relaxing in a Hercules?" he responded, stating the obvious. He knew he was in for a most uncomfortable journey with his leg already giving him pain. He'd been in a Hercules many times in his career and, more to the point, had jumped out of the back at high altitude with only night vision goggles to aid him. In fact, the bloody pilot had been flying them with only night visions; it had been complete and utter madness as they had no idea what awaited them on the ground as they parachuted. Now he knew where he was headed but in many ways he was still flying blind. At least when he jumped off a plane he knew he had to hit the ground; now he didn't know what he was about to hit.

The plane hadn't changed much inside and he recalled every detail as they entered from the rear and moved forward and to the starboard side. Although he remembered the earlier C-130 model, he was told this one gave an increased tactical airlift capability with greater range and power. As they took off from the Israeli airbase it was impossibly noisy still, that certainly remained the same, and they were strapped in most uncomfortably, adjacent to each other in red nylon webbing seats. The seats folded down so there were two lines facing each other. It wasn't first class travel, that was for sure, and there were no niceties, although Steve was being treated somewhat like a VIP as they were the only passengers. It must be costing the MOD an absolute fortune to ship him out, he thought, as normally the aircraft could carry up to ninety-two troops, less for paratroops.

"Try these headphones. We have a very short stop-over and we'll be in Gibraltar overnight before you fly out to Tehran."

Steve removed the headphones from the mass cabling above him and, with them suitably positioned, he closed his eyes and tried to drift off. The thundering of the turbo-prop engines momentarily lapsed and gave way to the realisation he was about to set foot on British soil, right back where he started. However, there was not a chance he was going to be left alone for even a nano-second; the CO would be sticking to him like the proverbial glue.

Some hours later as the sun was rising, the plane taxied to a standstill in Lyneham and Steve waited patiently for the supplies to be loaded on board. Within a few hours they were off again to their penultimate destination. The airport at Gibraltar was deemed to be one of the most extreme in the world and quite unique as the relatively short runway juts out into the sea. Entering the approach path to come into land, he peered out at the famous Rock, which was so close now, and waited for the quite unusual wind patterns to hit the aircraft when they came around the bay. The barriers blocking the road either side of the runway were down so the pilot could ascertain it was safe to land, and three hundred feet onto the runway he planted the wheels and the props were thrown into full reverse as he stood on the brakes. As the weight was put onto the landing gear, the anti-lock brake system came into play to prevent the craft skidding out of control.

Safely in situ, General Bowles-Smith escorted Steve off the plane and they were taken to a car waiting on the runway and driven off towards the governor's offices. Obviously, they had received military clearance in advance, as they bypassed the terminal building and any customs formalities, which was unusual in itself. Steve felt completely out-manoeuvred, and not for the first time, as he sat back in his seat and waited for the day to play out. The barriers either side of the runway were lifted and the car passed through allowing access to the people and vehicles patiently waiting to cross.

There was nothing different in the scene around him, except - who was that? Standing to the side was a tall, heavily-built man in civvies but what drew Steve's interest was his unmistakeable mop of red hair which he'd recognise anywhere. Well, if it wasn't Corporal Mo Hemmings himself. The man turned as the car approached and walked off and away from the runway. His aim had clearly been to be seen. With his head buried in The Times, he hoped and prayed the general had not noticed one of his former troops. Thankfully, it appeared not as he carried on reading without looking up. So, Sean was organising something, but he had no idea what. The message, though, was he had to be ready and alert for any eventuality at any time, and it was received loud and clear.

The car made its way towards the south of Main Street in the city centre and after a ten minute drive, arrived at the official residence and offices of the governor, aptly named The Convent as it was formerly a convent built in 1531. It had been requisitioned in 1728, some seventeen years after Gibraltar had become a British possession, for the purposes of housing the head of state and safeguarding the interests of the British Crown.

Alighting, they passed by the one guard from the Royal Gibraltar Regiment standing to attention in front of the stone portico and entered via the security entrance to the right, and were led straight into the main entrance and up the wooden staircase to the upper cloister. On any other occasion, Steve would have taken the opportunity to admire the interior and take in the history of the building. Now he was too on edge. His eyes were searching every face of the people and soldiers he passed, in case he recognised someone from his old unit. Nothing would have surprised him about Sean and his capabilities, especially after spotting Hemmings.

Rather than going directly to the governor's office, they were paraded along the red- carpeted landing to a room located in the new wing where the security guard left them to enter alone. They were confronted by the sight of two men clearly engrossed in the final shots of their snooker game. Neither Steve nor the general wanted to interrupt them so they waited a short time until the final black was cleanly potted. Both men shook hands and, amid hearty congratulations, turned to face their guests.

It was with the greatest effort that Steve registered no surprise or any type of expression on his face as he was confronted with someone he knew extremely well.

"Oh, you've arrived," Sir Robert said. "Bowles-Smith, allow me to introduce my very old friend, Rupert Van der Hausen. We knew each other when I was out in Namibia. So good of him to drop in like this. I was due a rematch but the bloody man always beats me. And this would be Captain Alan Campbell I presume." The general nodded at Steve as if to remind him of his new name and he stepped forward to shake each man's hand.

"Yes, sir."

"I've heard all about you," the governor continued. "Congratulations on what you've been doing for us. Not easy I know. Been there myself, of course, and now you're to get the MC."

"So it would seem, sir."

"You don't sound very convinced, Captain."

"We're very proud of him, sir," interrupted the general. "And then he's bound for pastures new. A posting as our military attaché in Tehran."

"Good for you," commented Rupert. "I've been there several times myself, although it was back in the days before the Shah was ousted. How long are you likely to be there?"

"That depends, sir."

"Ah, non-committal. And your family? I'm sure your wife will be joining you soon."

Christ almighty. How on earth was he going to get through the next couple of hours in the company of Sir Robert Alstom and Rupert, and with all this innuendo? Acting was not one of his strong points. He knew he was going to have to pull everything out of the bag to allay any suspicions his CO might have about all this banter. He was a strong man who had been through hell and back. Suddenly, at the thought of Cydney, he was in danger of losing his strength completely and he could just about get his words out.

"Well that would be great, sir, but it's doubtful."

"Shall we go to the dining room?" suggested Sir Robert.

"Talking of wives, mine has laid on a splendid spread and I always find losing at snooker gives me an appetite."

Rupert laughed and slapped his friend on the back, and all four men piled out of the room and headed to the small private dining room. Steve followed behind his CO with Rupert at the rear. "Good man," Rupert whispered. "Not long now."

CHAPTER FORTY TWO

L ITTLE did Cydney realise that she and Sean were following in her husband's footsteps less than a few hours after he had landed in Gibraltar. Sean had spoken little on the commercial flight they had taken from Luton Airport. She had literally put her faith in his hands; surely he was never going to take her on a wild goose chase? However, nothing was guaranteed, she had been warned of that in no uncertain terms, and was told to be completely cognizant to the fact that anything could go wrong, that Steve may not turn up. If General Bowles-Smith had any inkling of what was going on, the manoeuvre would be relocated or entirely called off, her husband would disappear into the ether once again and it would not be easy to trace him the next time, especially as Sean would no longer be the trusted sidekick as far as the CO was concerned.

Before travelling she had called Rupert but he'd been quite reticent about his own plans, simply telling her he would be staying in London for another week and would be around for her, offering his undivided services and attention should she require them. She felt slightly uncomfortable at having to involve her client and now close family friend, however, his words pacified her. If he didn't want to be involved, presumably he would have distanced himself and not have travelled to her in the first place.

Restlessness and impatience made the journey an absolute ordeal for Cydney, almost to the extent of being complete purgatory. She didn't dare to hope. At one stage Sean reached across, covering her hands with his if only to prevent her wringing them and clicking at her nails. Her thoughts were running riot and her heart could barely cope with the strain; after five years was she really going to see her husband, the man declared dead and buried? The entire scenario playing out was unreal, the stuff of dreams. And what about Lauren and Jake? How would they cope with their dad returning? Obviously absolute joy on the one hand, but what about their anger at the fact he hadn't come home immediately? Well, that wasn't his fault. However, it could scar them for life.

It was all about trust and Cydney had been unfaithful to their dad with another man whom she had introduced into their lives and they had welcomed him into their family. That would not be easy to cope with for anybody and the twins had really had to cope with such a lot in their young lives. Their joy would surely be overshadowed by her actions. She was proud of her kids, what they had achieved and who they had become, so maybe they would understand and forgive her. Telling Steve would be the other issue and for that the army would be to blame as, without a doubt, she would have to own up about her relationship with George. She had simply been getting on with her life in the best way she could and couldn't be held culpable for that. In fact, Sean had been complicit, at least to a fashion, and so had Rupert. What about George? No, she would not even think about him now. He knew everything, she had told him, tried to be honest with him. She only wished happiness for him. He deserved that from her at least.

Cydney had no idea where she was headed once they arrived at the airport. She and Sean were met by Mo Hemmings who had a car waiting. Again, they followed Steve's journey direct to the governor's residence and were taken through security. It seemed they were expected. This was happening too quickly now. She had no time to put her thoughts in order; they were a jumbled mess of cascading emotions and her legs were going to give way.

"Just remember - this is all you ever wanted," said Sean,

340

supporting her arm and guiding her up the staircase into a small office. "I want you to wait in here. I'll be back."

"What? You're going to leave me?"

"Not for long. There's something we have to do first. Don't worry."

* * *

"Let's go to the drawing room, shall we? I have some wonderful port," offered Sir Robert, "and I'd like you to tell me more about your time in Syria, Captain."

"Of course, sir. As much as I'm able."

Steve noticed how quiet his CO had been throughout the meal and worried he had picked up some vibes that something was about to take place. The man had not reached his position in the army, and particularly the special forces, without having a particular intuition for the unexpected. However, he was probably exhausted and as he took the offered glass of port, he sank back in his chair and crossed his legs, as always smoothing the seam of his well-pressed trousers.

At that moment, there was a knock at the door and everyone turned to see who was interrupting their meeting.

"What the hell!" yelled General Ian Bowles-Smith, rising to his feet and knocking his glass over in the process. His face turned a blazing red of fury as he stared daggers at everyone around him.

"Oh yes, did we forget to mention to you we had other guests arriving?" Sir Robert said.

"This is the man I told you about, Robert - Sean O'Connell, and I see he has Corporal Mark Hemmings with him," said Rupert.

"Good evening, sir."

"This is outrageous. You can't come barging in here like this."

The governor smiled. "Well actually, Bowles-Smith, they can, because I invited them."

341

"Hi Sean, Mo. Good to see you. I was wondering when you would turn up." Steve surprised himself with how calm he felt. Sean nodded his greeting, saying nothing.

"What do you mean you invited them? You can't do that. They're under orders."

"The thing is," continued Sir Robert, "I know what you're up to here. My friend, Rupert, has told me everything."

"What's he got to do with this?"

"A lot, as it happens," Rupert said. "Steve and his lovely wife and kids are like my family. I didn't like what was going on at all so I'm afraid I intervened."

"You what? You know them?" The general began to pace the floor. "Do you have any idea what you've done? You don't have the right to get involved in government matters. My God, man."

"I do, and I have. I've also called the MOD." The governor spoke calmly but with authority so no-one could be in any doubt.

"But ..."

"Captain Granger," Sir Robert said, ignoring the general. "This is very simple. Do you want to go to Tehran or would you rather be reunited with your family?"

"That's a question I don't think I need to answer. I was under orders."

"Yes he bloody well was, sir," the general said, "and not just from me."

"The thing is, Bowles-Smith, there are orders and there are orders. It seems to me you were taking matters into your own hands somewhat, for your own reasons which we don't necessarily have to go into. You do recall you have an obligation to report a man who is no longer missing in action, believed dead, and I do believe Steve Granger is remarkably alive at this moment?"

"Yes, sir. Indeed I am," answered Steve, rather enjoying his CO's discomfort.

"And furthermore, he has a right to return to his family. I

don't know where these orders of yours came from and frankly it's of no interest to me. However, what is of interest is the fact you are using him for your own means. This Alan Campbell matter is of your making entirely and I hate injustices, always have done. This has come from the very top, if you get my meaning. Captain Granger is no longer to be considered MIA. He is still a member of the British armed forces, until he resigns. You happy with that, Granger?"

"Oh yes, sir, extremely."

"And as for your posting as military attaché in Iran, well they still want you there and I think it would probably be a good career move, especially if you want to transfer into the diplomatic realms. Of course, under your own name."

Sir Robert's speech certainly had everybody enthralled and Steve recognised the fact that he was indeed a force to be reckoned with, which probably explained why he held his current position.

"But that's impossible," the general said, his voice a growl and his rage evident. "I can't allow this."

"Actually, sir, I don't think it is and I don't think you have a choice," Sean said. "You see, we've had a little word or two with the police here should you want to leave with the captain in tow. They don't like their authority being usurped, and especially when the military want to fly an alleged 'drugs dealer' from their island and out of their jurisdiction. They were quite pleased to receive the little tip-off we imparted to them. So you see, if you try to take the captain out of here, they're going to be surrounding your aircraft before I can say 'mine's a Guinness', if you know what I mean."

"Bowles-Smith, I think it's your turn to be out-manoeuvred, wouldn't you say? I don't think you have a choice so if I were you I would give in gracefully and head back home."

"I will not succumb to blackmail or threats."

"These are not threats, sir. I'd say they were more promises." Sean smiled, knowing they'd won.

"You haven't heard the last of this." The CO stormed out the room, slamming the door behind him.

"So Granger, apart from awarding you your MC, there seems to be one more little thing for us to do."

CHAPTER FORTY THREE

THE door opened quietly. There was no rushing in and he didn't grab her immediately in a passionate embrace. Instead, Cydney and Steve stared at each other, drinking in the sight they never expected to see, taking in the devastation of his war and her hurt and all it had cost them over the last five years. It was as if time stood still and they were the only two people left in the world. Cydney wanted to speak but there were no words she could find sufficient to express how she was feeling. She waited instead, willing her husband to be the first to move, to prove to her she wasn't dreaming and he wasn't a figment of her imagination. She needed to feel his touch, to feel the blood circulating around his body, to feel his warmth, his life source, and more importantly, his love.

"I never thought I would ever see you again," he said, his voice quiet, moving one step closer to her.

Those few words encircled her and broke the barrier. She was no longer hesitant and as they embraced for the first time, she knew without a doubt that at last she was home and everything that had gone before melted away into a distant past. Everything she ever wanted was hers now.

"Please don't cry my darling," he whispered, his eyes penetrating into her soul. He wiped her tears away with his hand. "I'm here now."

"To stay?"

"Always and forever."

"I ... it's been so difficult."

345

"Yes, I know. I'm so sorry. This was never meant to happen."

"I can't believe you're here. I dreamt so many nights of your coming back. In the back of my mind I never believed you were dead." She buried her head into his shoulder.

"This wasn't my fault. You need to know that. I wanted to come home, back to you and the twins." His voice was urgent now and it was clear he was willing her to believe him with every ounce of his being. "I never thought I would hold you again."

"Me neither."

Cydney pulled back from Steve. She needed to really look at him. His eyes were the same colour but deep within she could see immense sorrow. His face was still the one she remembered and loved, handsome and strong, though now there were lines. She passed her hand lightly around his face, caressing the ravages of time, stroking the scar across his temple and down his face, touching his greying hair as if for the first time.

"This is me now, Cyd." How she loved hearing him speak her name out loud. "I'm not the same. Inside. Things have gone on, things I can never tell you. I may never be the person I was before."

"You are to me. I'm never going to let you go."

"Just as well then." His mouth closed on hers for the first time and it was as if they had never been apart.

They were interrupted by someone opening the door and before anyone could be announced, Steve and Cydney were almost mowed down by their daughter hurtling in and jumping at them. Cydney stepped back to allow Lauren to be with her dad. She saw Jake standing slightly back and in the doorframe, hesitant.

"It's okay, darling. Yes. It's your dad," Cydney said, her voice quiet as if to beckon a frightened animal.

Steve opened his arms wide and waited for Jake to come forward. "Son," he said, and all Jake's bravado melted. All Cydney could do was watch as her husband embraced their two children as if he never wanted to let them go.

"See, Mum, I told you so," Lauren said, still hanging on to her dad, the tears still in her eyes.

Cydney and her children were about to enter a new phase of life, complete now with the man they had always loved. Nothing else mattered. She knew together they would conquer anything that was thrown at them.

As she watched her husband and children being reunited, her body shivered and a prickle swept along her right arm as Ray entered her vision.

"I need to say thank you," she said.

"You don't at all. I wished I could have brought this about sooner but it was not up to me."

"I know that."

"It's all turned out for the best. Anyway, that's not why I'm here."

Cydney took a breath and held it. She could sense what was coming. Of all the times he could have chosen …

"I have someone with me who needs your help."

AUTHOR'S NOTE

THIS book was an extremely difficult one for me to write as it concerns a subject that is so close to home. My research took me on a harrowing journey, during which I interviewed two holocaust survivors, and read letters and documents from those who were in the concentration camps. Their stories will stay with me forever.

I also researched extensively into what happened to all the money, gold, diamonds and other assets looted by the Nazis before and during the Second World War. A lot of what I read was pure speculation and never proven (although the foundations of these accounts were plausible), but some of the events contained are founded on truth.

The idea for the book came to me because I wanted to explore the reactions of two survivors when given the opportunity to confront one of their persecutors, a Nazi in the SS. I gave them a voice and an opportunity to demand answers. Perhaps, in doing so, I have also given their persecutor a platform, but it was crucial for me to force him to question his horrific deeds and the consequences. I wanted to explore how that Nazi felt about the horrors he had inflicted on a race purely for the religion they followed. Would he feel remorse? Would he want to seek forgiveness for his crimes against humanity? Could he ever be redeemed in the eyes of God? Or, was what he did locked down so deep in his psyche that he would never give it a passing thought?

The criminal mind, especially one of a psychopath, is difficult to understand for the majority of us, but when the scale of the crime reaches mass proportions, it is virtually impossible to comprehend. How could anyone murder and inflict such pain with no compunction, and there be no consequences, no qualms?

I looked at all these aspects, as far as I was able, and put together my own theories; drew my own conclusions. It is for you, the reader, to look into your own heart and mind and make your own judgement.

Karen Millie-James
London, September 2017

Questions and Answers with Karen Millie-James

When and why did you start writing?

I don't believe there was a specific time or point but it's something I always wanted to do. I started my first book, The Shadows Behind Her Smile, in April 2013 so to me that felt right. Now writing has become my passion and it's something I do every day and, when not doing so, I am always thinking of plot lines and how my characters would react to different situation. Suddenly I will think of a great sentence and have to scribble it down before I forget it.

I have always been surrounded by books and started my reading journey from a very young age, especially the classics; I must have read Black Beauty umpteen times when I was young. I liked the idea of being lost in another world where anything could happen, allowing my imagination to roam to far off destinations and to become involved in characters and situations that were beyond my life experiences. That's probably why I studied English literature and languages.

What do you love about being a writer?

The alternative world that I create, where anything is possible. My mind is constantly working and sometimes it's difficult to get my thoughts down on paper before the next idea springs to mind. I find that time just disappears but thankfully I can type fast and I've never experienced writer's block.

I also love hearing from my readers, meeting them at book-signings and everyone is so receptive and pleased to find out about you and your experiences.

What made you write a thriller?

I have always loved thrillers and, because of my business background, I would say that the genre decided itself so I didn't have to think too hard. I really enjoy creating a fast-moving story where everything comes to life and there is suspense, action, danger and possible high stakes. I want my readers to be excited and concerned about my characters and their lives and want to find out what happens to them at the end. In that way I've achieved everything I set out to do.

Now I'm able to combine writing with my corporate background which proves the old saying that you write about what you know.

What is the background to Where In The Dark?

My dad came from Germany and escaped in 1939 with the kindertransport. He was an amazing man who died so young before he had a chance to fulfil his potential. I never knew about his background until after his death when I discovered all his papers and letters and reading those stayed with me for a long time.

When I began writing, I had no intention of visiting his story, but an idea came to me which led me to explore the possible connection between two men who survived the holocaust and that of an escaped Nazi. What a deadly combination?

How did you characterise Cydney? Do you see herself in you?

I liked the idea of having a strong businesswoman like Cydney Granger so I do see myself in her, but a novel gives you literary licence to expand wherever you want to go, which is an ideal scenario. I put her into situations that are sometimes dangerous and she comes up against so many obstacles but succumbs them despite the odds.

I like how feisty she is, that she takes no nonsense from anybody, the way she is vulnerable sometimes and strong others. She is loving and caring with her family and others in her life and her determination means she always strives to do the best she can. Does she have faults? Of course, or she wouldn't be human, one of these being impatience, of which I am slightly guilty also.

What about your other characters?

I have lived with them now for nearly five years and they are all very important to me. I know how they would think and behave, like having close friends. I am very protective of them and only want the best outcome for them. Obviously there are some people you wouldn't want as friends and with those I try to examine their actions and reactions to situations. It's important to make these characters realistic though and if they are evil, it has to be within certain parameters. It's a fine line.

What books or authors do you like?

I love the classics, adventure stories and thrillers and I read every day as a way to relax and maybe as a form of escapism. Wilbur Smith is one my favourite modern authors because he entices the reader into his stories through his descriptions. I also love John Grisham and the legal world he writes about.

One of my favourite genres is historical novels, anything from which I can learn, whether that be going back hundreds of years to the days of Henry VIII, or to events in the last century.

My favourite novel of all time is Pride and Prejudice having studied it in great detail for A levels many years ago.

What is your writing structure?

I'm not sure I have one. I usually write in the evenings and weekends. I keep a notebook by the side of the bed in case I get an idea in the middle of the night, which I do regularly. I love writing in Spain where my house there has magnificent views of the mountains which I find so relaxing and inspirational.

I don't write too many notes, I don't keep character cards and I don't work out plots in advance as that would stop the writing flow and not allow me to give full rein to my characters. It is too structured for me. I normally write a few chapters then have a read through, write a few more and as time goes on I do tend to move everything about so that the pace of the book is maintained.

Has writing changed the way read books?

Yes, incredibly. I look at structure and how important this is, and I appreciate descriptions. I can now understand how much effort goes behind a writer's work to portray scenes. You have to enter the mind of the reader and help them see, through your words, what you are trying to depict - the colours, the smells, the sounds. This is what makes a good book, for me anyway, especially if you as a writer get it right.

What is the most challenging aspect?

Continuity - it's a bit like a putting a jigsaw puzzle together where everything has to fit exactly and you can't leave a piece missing, especially in a thriller. It is a continuous process to go back and review your characters' actions.

To whom do you owe your success?

This is not easy to answer as I think you have to have this in yourself to start with – the ability to want to be successful.

However, losing my dad at such an early age gave me the instinct to survive and do well as I had to support my family. I am hard on myself and expect a lot from myself.

What advice would you give to anyone writing?

Be true to yourself. Write for yourself and do so with honesty and integrity. That is really what I have tried to do. At the moment I am still working in my corporate consultancy business so haven't given up my day job. Maybe that is my ultimate aim at some stage but for the moment they co-exist. So my advice is probably never to give up and to enjoy what you're doing.

One other point is to be disciplined because, even when you finish writing, the process afterwards takes a lot of time and energy, especially editing which is long and laborious but worth it in the long run. The day you finish and send everything off to print is one of the most satisfying. Then you wait for your book to arrive and that is beyond anything you can imagine - to hold something you have created in your hands.

Then it is the best feeling in the world to have people tell you how much they have enjoyed reading your book, something you have created from an initial idea. Amazing.

What are your personal and professional goals?

Writing my novels and having them published is a great personal achievement for me and something I have wanted for a very long time. I would like to be recognised for that. I also hope people read and enjoy what I have written.

If you weren't a writer, what would you do?

In all honesty I love what I currently do - mixing my business world with writing my novels - so I probably wouldn't change that. However, I have a passion for music and would love to play the piano properly; after several years of taking lessons, I have come to the conclusion that my passion exceeds my ability.

What's next?

I intend to commence the third in the Cydney Granger series, but also I've come up with an idea for a stand-alone thriller, which I have started working on, called A Thousand Silent Cries.